Fish Kill

a novel

Dennis Mitch Maley

copyright © 2026 Punk Rock Publishing

For my father, whose sense of humor and love of this particular genre of fiction led me on a literary adventure that greatly influenced this book. His pride in my work was fuel for the many late nights spent writing it.

To my publisher, Joe McClash, who provided me with a much-needed opportunity at a pivotal point in my career and life. Together, we have spoken truth to power, comforted the afflicted and afflicted the comfortable, all the while making the little slice of paradise we share better for it.

For you, the readers, those who have been here since the beginning, the casuals, the occasionals, the strays I've picked up a long the way... pass it on.

The radical, he rants and rage
Singing someone got to turn the page
And the rich man in his summer home
Singing just leave well enough alone
But his pants are down, his cover's blown

And the politicians throwing stones
So the kids, they dance, they shake their bones
'Cause it's all too clear we're on our own
Singing ashes, ashes, all fall down
Ashes, ashes, all fall down

— John Perry Barlow/The Grateful Dead

Chapter 1: Banana Republicans

"Order in the chambers," yelled Mullet County Commission Chair Dick Myers, a puffy, pinkish, 60-year-old man with a graying beard, as he repeatedly banged the gavel against the dais. "Order in the chambers!"

The raucous crowd that had convened in the commission chambers of the county administration building that morning had just heard a bought-and-paid-for "environmental expert" give testimony as to why the county ordinance requiring a buffer between wetland marshes and land development was "unnecessary and duplicative."

County Commissioner Connor Welsh, a short and portly man who looked much older than his 35 years, was visibly sweating despite having removed his jacket and loosened his tie during the presentation. He dabbed his brow with a handkerchief and tried to compose himself.

"So, what I'm hearing is, despite the pleas of the radical leftist environmentalists who are trying so hard to hijack today's proceedings for their own liberal agenda, the current ordinance offers no discernible benefit to this community," said Welsh, again dabbing his moist brow. "Is that correct?"

"I haven't personally *seen* any evidence of such a benefit, and I have been in this business for nearly two decades," the bespectacled consultant continued in a slow, measured, and disciplined tone.

"The business of spewing bullshit for Hernandez?" yelled a liver-spotted octogenarian in cargo shorts and a Jimmy Buffett's Margaritaville t-shirt seated two rows behind the lectern.

The old man was quickly and aggressively ejected by a sheriff's deputy with bulbous, tattooed arms and a 19-inch neck that sat beneath a shaved head.

Ignacio Hernandez, a 65-year-old Cuban-American development mogul in a white Tom Wolfe suit, flashed a luminescent shit-eating grin at the old man as he was frog-marched past him.

"The State of Florida has excellent environmental protections for wetlands at the state level and makes no specific requirement for such a buffer," the consultant said nervously. He jumped at the loud sound of the chamber doors closing in the deputy's wake.

On cue, the Reverend Billy Sunday hit his button.

"Commissioner Sunday," said Dick Myers.

"My fellow commissioners, we are in a housing crisis," said Sunday, a tall and rotund man in his forties who always spoke in his pulpit cadence and had a predilection for rubbing his tummy while he waved the other arm about. "We have brave police officers and other first responders who cannot afford a home because there's so much demand to move into a good, conservative Christian community like ours and precious little supply. Every time I go to my children's schools, I hear from teachers who just don't know if they can stay in Mullet County if they have to keep throwing their money away on skyrocketing rents that we all know are a result of *Bidenomics*. I don't know about y'all, but the idea of fewer houses for the sake of wasteful over-regulation just seems, well, liberal at best and downright un-American, even communist at worst."

"Show me a teacher who can afford one of Hernandez's half-million dollar McMansions, and I'll show you a skunk ape and the Bigfoot," screamed a retiree in loudly colored Guy Harvey gear.

"Order in the chambers," screamed Myers, banging the gavel as the hulking deputy escorted the second senior citizen out of the chambers just as roughly as the first.

"Commissioner Hagerty, you're next on the board," said Myers.

Candice Hagerty was the county's only female commissioner. A third-generation Mullet County native, her late father, a cattle rancher, had spent nearly 30 years on the commission before passing away five years earlier. While Thomas "Ace" Hagerty had been a run-of-the-mill, chamber of commerce Republican, his daughter had exuberantly ridden the MAGA wave to a landslide victory in her first election following a gubernatorial appointment to fill her late father's seat after he keeled over from a massive stroke. A tall and buxom blonde with stunningly large breasts and a penchant for push-up bras and low-cut shirts beneath her sport jackets, you could practically hear the erections snapping to attention under the dais whenever she spoke—excepting Welsh, whose tastes were said to lie elsewhere on the sexual spectrum.

"I couldn't agree more with the good reverend," said Hagerty in an affected drawl. "We cannot worry more about whether some silly bird species has a home than we do about homes for the hard-working folks of Mullet County, who are the backbone of our economy—especially law enforcement. I know for a fact that our brave officers are feeling the pain on this issue. I back the blue on this one."

"You back it up for the blue is more like it," yelled a middle-aged lesbian standing against the back wall of the overflowing chamber. "What cost more, Hagerty, your seat or those tits?"

"These are real!" shouted Hagerty from the dais.

While the commissioner was not above some Botox, lip injections, a little filler, or the occasional liposuction session, she despised the presumption that she'd had breast augmentation. In fact, Candice even kept an album of photos from various stages of her youth in a file on her phone as evidence of her early development and steady progression from junior high through college, should she have to disprove the accusation in social settings.

"Deputy White," said the chair with a nod.

The deputy, who'd been admiring the sleeve of tattoos on his big and veiny left arm, snapped to and quickly moved toward the woman with the spiked mullet and leather biker jacket. Meanwhile, Commissioner Hagerty feigned additional indignation while puffing out her chest and readjusting her sports coat.

"Order in the chambers," screamed Myers.

"Go ahead, you fucking fascist. Try it," the woman said as the deputy approached.

Having caught hell the last time he physically removed a female protester from the lobby in front of news cameras just a few months back, Deputy White cocked his head and jerked his thumb toward the exit. Standing with her back against the double doors, the woman put both middle fingers in the air, then crashed her elbows into the latch bar and backed out as she mouthed the words, *fuck you*. Even the deputy was impressed by her exit.

"I have Commissioner Blanton next on the board," said the chair.

Jeffrey Blanton was a middle-aged Afghan War vet who had either been born stupid or had his brains scrambled after finding himself in close proximity to too many IEDs.

"So, like, what I'm thinking is, like, that from an economic standpoint, you get more, um, like... property tax money from a house than from a pile of mangroves, am I right?" said Blanton with an exaggerated shrug. "I mean, you don't get *any* from mangroves, am I right?" the commissioner asked, scanning a gaggle of genuinely confused members of the county's staff with arched eyebrows and an even more exaggerated shrug.

When they incorrectly assumed the question had been rhetorical and failed to answer, Blanton gave another exaggerated shrug, this time toward his colleagues, who were also confused into silence.

"Seeing no one else on the board, I'm going to open it up to *public comment*," said Myers, his contempt for the legal requirement dripping from the words. "When I call you, come

4

to the lectern, state your name and town of residence for the record, and you'll have three minutes to speak."

Myers looked at a sheet of paper and seemed to smile.

"Emily Bartleston," he said in his most congenial voice.

Dr. Emily Bartleston, PhD, was the "Chief Science Officer" for the eco-non-profit Tampa Bay Environmental Watch. With wholesome girl-next-door looks, she had a presence that caught men off guard regarding what they expected under the circumstances in which scientists are front and center. In actuality, she had the sort of beauty that could have easily been played up to stand out among any crowd. However, as a leading expert in a male-dominated field, Emily's experiences had inspired her to go to great lengths to play down her looks. Unfortunately, with minimal makeup, a ponytail, and nerdy glasses, she unwittingly but routinely evoked the so-called librarian fantasy in perverts like Dicky Myers.

"I'm glad you could join us today, Dr. Bartleston," said Myers in a pathetic attempt at sounding suave. "Please state your name for the record, and you'll have ten minutes to speak, as I see you are representing a group and have the appropriate signatures."

Dr. Bartleston did as instructed, although Commissioner Myers had already begun undressing her with his eyes and didn't regain his composure until she had completed her detailed presentation and delivered the closing line.

"For all of these reasons, it is undeniable that eliminating our local wetland protection policies not only fails in the requirement to demonstrate an overwhelming public benefit but would clearly damage the public's interest by destroying critical environmental resources, the downstream effects of which would be calamitous not only to our community but also to those surrounding us. The item you are considering today, if passed, would not only violate your duties to protect your own constituents' best interests, it would be an affront to every resident of the Gulf Coast."

While the chairman hadn't broken eye contact with Dr. Bartleston once during her presentation, he nevertheless had not heard more than a few words and certainly hadn't seen any of the nearly two dozen informative slides she'd offered. To be fair, Commissioner Welsh had been busy texting with Ignacio, while Commissioner Sunday texted with his wife, Commissioner Hagerty eye-fucked Deputy White, and Commissioner Blanton fantasized about his days manning an M2 Browning .50 caliber machine gun in the Army.

"Thank you for that informative presentation," said Myers. "It really was quite impressive, doctor. You may know that I'm a civil engineer by trade, and while I've expressed some disagreement with your positions, I'd be eager to discuss them with you sometime, perhaps over—"

Despite his stumpy legs, Welsh delivered an impressive kick to the chairman's shin, and Myers did his best not to shriek in pain as he bit down on his lower lip, nearly to the point of drawing blood. Dr. Bartleston gave the chairman, who was five years older than her own father, a look of contempt as she packed her laptop and slides.

Commissioner Myers cleared his throat and looked at his list. His face lost any trace of enthusiasm once he realized who was next in line to speak.

"Micky Pesch," he said wryly with a slight but perceptible eye roll.

Audible groans from the other commissioners were picked up by their microphones as a slender pony-tailed man in his sixties wearing faded jeans, a buckskin shirt, moccasins, and turquoise beaded bracelets approached the microphone.

"Micky Pesch, Mullet County, for the record."

"Go ahead, Mr. Pesch. You have three minutes," said Myers as he opened an older gentleman/younger lady dating app on his phone to surf for potential hookups.

Better known as Micky Fish, Pesch was a contrarian's contrarian. He had inherited a considerable amount of money from his mother, but only after being cut out of the will by his father, Arturo Pesch, the son of Italian immigrants who had owned McPesch Potato & Tomato Inc., a farming and cannery empire that, as per his will, was sold and divested upon his death.

This was primarily to prevent Micky from instituting "sustainable farming practices," a cause for which his son had always displayed tremendous passion. A pessimist by nature, Micky was among the first to identify an emerging Florida real estate bubble in 2004, ultimately making a fortune on credit default swaps. He used a good deal of that money to finance his spectacularly unprofitable media investments, in an unfaltering effort to call the community's attention to all of the environmental woes that were destroying his hometown and the state at large. Micky owned the DeSoto Gazette, a hyper-local independent newspaper that featured a weekly print edition and strong online presence; WMLT, a low-power FM community radio station with mostly talk news; and he directed self-produced, low-budget documentaries about the ravaging of local environmental resources. To put it mildly, he was a pain in many powerful asses.

"Commissioners, county administrator," said Micky as he addressed the board, mentally noting that Administrator Wayne Beaufort, who looked like he was coming off a three-day bender and had slept in his car, had nodded off.

Commissioner Hagerty, who was sitting next to Beaufort, also noticed. She gave the administrator a sharp elbow to the side of his belly, and he came to, expelling a gin burp that caused her to scrunch her nose.

"Most of you know that I have a degree in environmental science, and I can tell you that the presentation you all just received was pure poppycock," said Pesch.

"You tell 'em, Fish!" yelled a tall, thin man in a Grateful Dead Europe '72 shirt.

"Order," warned Myers, not bothering to bang the gavel or even look up, as he swiped right on a Russian immigrant who had successfully ended her mail-order bride marriage right after she received her citizenship and was now in the market for a sugar daddy.

"I know that at least two of you sitting up there have places out on the island," said Micky. "You've seen all the fish kills from the red tide this year. Heck, I was out there on my boat yesterday, and the smell alone could have choked a horse. There's so much Lyngbya floating around, it looks like someone emptied a fleet of port-o-potties. Wetlands are nature's filtration system. I don't need to tell you that. The bigger the buffer between the structure and the wetlands, the more effective they are. You develop the land, do your elevation, and harden half the permeable green space. Where does the new runoff go? Down the slope toward the waterline. The more effective those wetlands are, the better the filtering, and the less nitrogen winds up in the water to charge up all these algal blooms we're having. This isn't hard to grasp, folks. Now your bought-and-paid-for *consultant* over here tells you he's never seen any evidence that bigger buffers mean more effective wetlands—"

Commissioner Welsh glared at the chairman—who was now focused on a busty red-headed dental hygiene student at the local junior college—grabbed the gavel and banged it himself.

"We will not tolerate personal attacks in this chamber, sir!" Welsh screamed.

Chairman Myers added a "yeah" before shrugging apologetically at Welsh for being asleep at the wheel.

"Well, I emailed every one of you five different studies," said Micky, "each of which clearly demonstrates that bigger buffers benefit wetland quality, so if *he* hasn't seen any of them, it's only because he's got his damned eyes closed, and his real boss won't let him open 'em up," blared Pesch as he shot a look of contempt at Ignacio, who returned a wink and another shit-eating grin.

Sitting next to Myers, Welsh reached over and hit a button that had been installed so that the chairman could cut the microphone at the lectern anytime he felt someone was out of order. Myers picked up the queue.

"You're out of order, sir," he said, feigning anger. "That's more than enough."

"I have a right to speak," said Pesch. "You all are always blathering on about the Constitution. Have you read it'?" said Pesch, barely audible over the vulgar protests of the crowd.

The deputy moved toward him but remembered he was under strict orders not to lay a finger on Micky, who had successfully sued the Mullet County Sheriff's Office on more than one occasion.

"Let's go, Fish," said Deputy White, hands on his oversized leather belt as he flicked his chin toward the door.

"You realize that you don't need to follow an order if it's unlawful, deputy?" said Micky. "They still teach that at the academy, right?"

"They say you're tossed, you're tossed," said White.

"Even if I'm legally afforded the right to speak for three full minutes?" asked Micky. "That personal attack bullshit, it's made up. You know that, right?"

The deputy cocked his head and folded his arms.

"You'd have made a good Nazi, brother," said Micky, grabbing his faded corduroy satchel and heading toward the door.

The members of the public who had not yet been thrown out of the meeting gave him a standing ovation as he exited, whooping and hollering words of encouragement.

Give 'em hell, Micky — Get 'em, Fish! — Atta'boy, Mick!

The board had deliberately scheduled the item for the last meeting before the July recess, when the snowbirds would be back north, enjoying cooler climates, so they would have to endure fewer citizens exercising their right to give three minutes of public comment before the vote. Still, the angry opposition went on for over three hours. Only one citizen—an owner of a construction company that did a lot of subcontracting for Hernandez—spoke in favor of the gutting of the policy.

Nevertheless, the board voted 5-0 to neuter the wetland buffer protections. When the vote was announced, the chamber roared in disapproval. Micky had been listening from a nearby conference room where the overflow audience had been seated, already plotting his legal challenge.

****

Commissioner Connor Welsh felt on top of the world despite having made enemies with nearly everyone in his hometown who followed matters of local government. Welsh was the sort of person who felt perpetually wronged by the world around him. He fancied himself smarter, more talented, and better looking than people saw him and grew up longing to stuff others into lockers rather than getting stuffed into them himself. All it took was someone to tell him, *Hey, kid. I think you're much smarter and more talented than you get credit for,* and he was keen to believe it, regardless of the mountain of evidence to the contrary.

Ignacio told Welsh just that, right before making sure he was elected to the seat four years earlier. It was the first taste of power Welsh had ever known, and he found it intoxicating. The low six-figure salary of a county commissioner was nearly triple what he'd been making as a "parent/student liaison" with the school district, and he eagerly resigned.

In truth, Welsh was on the verge of being let go after two internal investigations and a transfer to a different school in the district. It was all very vague, but there had been *parental concerns* regarding what they deemed to be *inappropriate behavior.* Nothing concrete came of it, and Ignacio was able to have his stooges on the school board see to it that Welsh's personnel file remained sealed.

Rumors of deviant behavior proved little more than an inconvenience during a campaign in which the developer carpet-bombed Welsh's opponent, a local shrimp fisherman, with hundreds of thousands of dollars in attack ads accusing him of being everything from a Russian plant to Barack Obama's secret lover. Welsh won in a landslide and immediately leaned into a villain role in which he'd impose his newfound power on just the sort of people he had longed to sit at the lunch table with while growing up.

Following the meeting, Commissioner Welsh adjourned to his 7th-floor office in the large tower that housed the commission chambers and dozens of other county departments to enjoy some respite. He'd been seated for a minute or two only to be accosted by an elderly constituent who had somehow managed to make it past the receptionist.

Sitting at the big desk in his recently renovated digs, the commissioner fidgeted in the seat of his leather chair. Based on his facial contortions and body movements, the old woman sitting across from him assumed he'd been suffering from gastrointestinal discomfort. In reality, Welsh had stuffed a butt plug in his rectum just before his elderly constituent had shown herself into his office. The commissioner's assistant, Enrique, controlled the speed and direction of its vibration from another room via an app on his county-issued cell phone.

Unlike Welsh, Enrique was not a pervert. However, given the immense pleasure the young Peruvian man often felt when going full throttle on "circle mode," it may have been fair to call him a sadist. He hated that his boss made him do such things and fantasized that Welsh might ultimately suffer his comeuppance via a rectal tear, or even a prolapse, at the hand of one of his less compact toys.

Unfortunately, Commissioner Welsh mistook the aggressive play-calling for romantic interest, which only led him to ramp up the water-cooler leering and less-than-subtle elevator gropes.

"I want to know why someone can't do something about it," the woman crowed. "I've called code enforcement ten times! They still haven't done a damned thing!"

"Mrs. Fiddlebaum, your neighbor is not violating any code or ordinance by revving his motorcycle in his driveway after starting it up," said Welsh, imagining a shirtless, muscular, mustachioed man in a black cowboy hat kick-starting a Harley while wearing black leather chaps with only a matching thong beneath.

"It's loud enough to wake the dead!" she yelled.

With circle mode now in high gear, Welsh's eyes rolled toward the back of his head as he orgasmed into the pair of women's underwear he was wearing under his suit pants. He let out a low moan as drool pooled in the corner of his lip.

"Stroke!" the woman screamed. "Call an ambulance!"

Commissioner Welsh was in a fit of post-coital glee and did not register what was happening until the geriatric woman demonstrated impressive physical dexterity by jumping onto his desk.

"Don't worry, sailor," she told him, pulling him from the chair and into a prone position on the desk. "I was a nurse during the war!"

The woman had just begun mouth-to-mouth when the commissioner started flailing his arms wildly at her.

"Easy, fella," she said. "We're almost home."

Enrique and a receptionist named Jan heard the commotion and ran into the office. The blue-haired woman was still atop the desk, straddling the commissioner while locked at the lips. Enrique and Jan froze in confusion. The woman looked up at them.

"CPR," she said. "I think it was a stroke. His pants are wet. Emptying of the bladder is common during a cerebral infarction."

With her mouth otherwise engaged, Commissioner Welsh finally got the upper hand, grabbing both of her arms and toppling her off the desk before uprighting himself.

"Ouch!" the woman yelled. "My hip!"

Welsh wiped his sleeve across his mouth in disgust and glared at the two employees still frozen in the doorway, realizing they were looking toward his crotch. He looked down and saw a small, dark, wet spot.

"Get this lunatic out of here!" he yelled.

Jan and Enrique helped the old woman to her feet and led her into the lobby, assuring her that someone from code enforcement would contact her.

The commissioner's phone rang, and Welsh sat back down.

"Commissioner Welsh," he said into the receiver.

"Buenos dias, commissioner," said the voice on the other end of the line.

"Ignacio," Welsh said with excitement. "Congratulations, I take it you're a very happy man right now."

"No, not yet, my friend," said Hernandez. "There will still be lawsuits and other pains in my ass. This thing is far from over."

"Well, I wouldn't worry about that," said Welsh. "Our attorneys tell me we're on very solid legal ground."

"Your attorneys tell you what my attorneys tell them," said the Cuban, subtly reminding the commissioner that he never called with questions, only instructions.

"It's time to move forward with the other elements, commissioner. I want to catch my opponents off guard. Turn on the fire hose and see how much they can drink."

"Right away, sir. I'll have Dick add impact fees to the next agenda."

"Good boy," said Ignacio. "Now, why don't you come down to the Ritz Carlton and enjoy some good rum with me after a productive day's work?"

"Sounds good," said Welsh. "I just have to, uh, change clothes real quick."

****

Several people were waiting to get the attention of Mullet County Administrator Wayne Beaufort when the meeting adjourned, but he used crude miming to explain that he needed to make use of the men's room. Just past the private restrooms behind the chambers was also a private elevator that the board had installed at significant taxpayer expense. Beaufort was glad to find that he was the first to access it, but beads of sweat formed on his brow when the digital readout showed the car was on its way back down from the 7th floor.

Beaufort was already getting the shakes and did not want company in the elevator car. He heard voices approaching and foot traffic heading towards the restrooms when the bell finally rang. Once inside, he slouched in the front left corner where the control panel was located and hurriedly pressed the "close doors" button, breathing a sigh of relief as they came together.

Once the doors had closed, Beaufort quickly removed a flask from the inside breast pocket of his sports coat and took a long pull of vodka to hold him over until he could get to his desk. Vodka was the administrator's liquor of choice for his flask owing to its odorless nature and ability to play nice with nearly every mixer. Each workday, the small container would contribute a splash to his coffee, another to his orange juice or afternoon diet soda, and a few emergency swigs straight up when he had to be away from his office.

14

However, to his terror, the doors reopened as soon as they closed, with Commissioner Candice Hagerty standing before him while adjusting the bustier under her sports jacket.

"Christ, Wayne," she said, shaking her head at the sight of the flask as she entered the elevator car. "You're the only public employee I know who still gets away with keeping a bar in your office, and you can't even white-knuckle it through an elevator ride?"

Beaufort hung his head in shame as he popped a menthol cough drop, of which he kept plenty on hand as further insurance against booze breath.

"It was a rough night," said Beaufort.

"A rough night?" the commissioner asked with arched eyebrows that were almost noticeable, her penchant for Botox notwithstanding. "When was the last time you had a night that *wasn't* rough, or a day, or even an hour in the middle of the afternoon, for fuck's sake?"

She shook her head and began shuffling through a folder of papers she had pulled from an oversized Louis Vuitton handbag.

"Bonnie flipped out, started going on about—"

Hagerty extended her arm with a flat hand inches from Beaufort's face.

"No, uh uh, I don't want to hear it, Wayne," she said with an exaggerated wave of her head. "I hear enough about the drama between you two on Facebook. And not for nothing, but that woman could use a talking to on the subject of oversharing."

Wayne nodded in agreement as he took another pull from the flask, noticing that even a Halls menthol paired nicely with the cheap vodka.

"I know it," he said, shaking his head. "Do you think maybe you can talk to her about that?"

The commissioner looked at him as if he had grown another head.

"Hell no, I'm not talking to that crazy girlfriend of yours!"

"Fiancée," Beaufort said, shrugging his shoulders.

"What? You're even dumber than you look, Wayne. Anyway, I ain't got time for that silliness. Here are two lists. This one contains constituents of mine—good patriotic Americans—who are being unfairly harassed by your code enforcement department, which apparently does not respect the concept of individual property rights. I want you to call off the dogs on these folks immediately. It's an election year, and they are donors. Do you understand?"

Beaufort held out the sheet at arm's length, hoping that his blurred vision would fade with the distance. It did not. He nodded, nevertheless.

"Will do, commissioner."

"And this sheet contains a list of individuals and businesses who are being a pain in my big ass by putting campaign signs up for that cunt who's running against me," she said as she handed him another sheet of paper.

Beaufort's attention momentarily fell toward the commissioner's buxom hips. Hagerty put one finger under his chin, redirecting his gaze toward her eyes. She was not gentle about it.

"These sons of bitches could actually benefit from a bit of code enforcement harassment, a subtle message to get with the goddamned program. Do you understand me, Wayne?"

Wayne shrugged.

"I can send them over, but I mean, if the signs aren't on a public right of way, we can't really do anything about it, Candice."

"God damn it, Wayne," she said, hitting the emergency stop button on the elevator.

The commissioner dropped her purse, unbuttoned her jacket, and pulled down the bustier. Two enormous breasts with areolas the size and shade of silver dollar pancakes lurched forward as if they were separate entities escaping of their own

16

volition. Candice Hagerty had used this trick on Wayne Beaufort several times over the years, but its effectiveness never seemed to dissipate. Apparently, there is no such thing as a diminishing rate of return when it comes to a perfect set of natural boobs.

In almost slow motion, Beaufort raised the hand not engaged by his flask. It was as if his booze-soaked, strip-club-hardened brain assumed copping a feel was part of the exchange. The commissioner slapped him across the face hard enough for his quickly created drool to hit the elevator wall behind him. She re-affixed the bustier just as quickly as it had been jettisoned and hit the stop button again to deactivate it.

Seconds later, the bell rang, and the doors opened on the seventh floor, steps from Beaufort's office.

"Don't fuck this up, Wayne," Candice said in a harsh whisper as she departed.

Beaufort felt the twitch of what he suspected to be his first Viagra-free semi-erection in years.

"You got it, commissioner," he said, wiping menthol-infused drool from his lower lip and cheek.

By the time he entered his office, Beaufort was beginning to feel close to normal, his bloodshot eyes clearing and his clammy skin drying as the hooch worked its magic—although any trace of increased lower body blood flow had dissipated as quickly as it appeared. Upon entering his well-appointed confines, he filled a tumbler with two ice cubes and two fingers of high-end bourbon from the wet bar he'd had installed after Ignacio directed the board to shit can his predecessor and install the woefully under-qualified "Director of Development Services" as her replacement.

It was Ignacio's boldest move yet: have the board fire the county's first female county administrator and, rather than conduct a national search for a qualified replacement, promote from within an employee who had been the subject of three unflattering internal investigations, failed two of the four audits since taking over the department and been convicted of Driving Under the Influence on two occasions, not to mention the Boating Under the Influence charge he was slapped with after captaining his Sun Tracker pontoon while three sheets to the wind. Two *deweys* and a *buoy*—pretty impressive, even by Florida standards.

While it was typical for a county administrator's contract to include either the use of an automobile from the county motor pool or an allowance for using their personal vehicle, Beaufort had instead been assigned a county-employed, taxpayer-funded driver to minimize the potential for any further vehicular embarrassments. He was there for one reason and one reason only: to get whatever Ignacio wanted done, and to do so without the inconvenience of moral scruples that might slow down the process.

If Beaufort and his pickled liver could hold on for just three more years, a fat government pension awaited. He could move to a beach in Mexico and drink himself to death on fruity libations garnished with tiny umbrellas—accompanied by his aforementioned fiancée if that held, perhaps a mail-order Colombian bride if it did not.

****

Ignacio was sitting in a booth on the hotel's veranda when Commissioner Welsh arrived, looking a bit disheveled, sweat stains marring his Oxford, which didn't quite match the fresh pants he'd changed into. Although a Mullet County native, Connor Welsh didn't have the right sort of blood for the sub-tropics. He was one of those pinkishly-pale, hopelessly Anglo-European types common to South Florida who glistened with a sheen of sweat at least six months a year and didn't quite know how to adjust their wardrobes accordingly.

Conversely, with his Cuban blood and Miami sense of style, Ignacio looked cool and collected in his lightweight linen suit. His brow breathed easily through his straw Tommy

Bahama hat, and his demeanor instantly made the commissioner feel vastly inferior.

Welsh dabbed his own brow with an already-saturated handkerchief as he sat.

"What's the matter, my friend?" asked Ignacio with a chuckle. "Too much humidity? You're a native Floridian, no?"

"Yes, well, further back, my people came from Scotland," said Welsh, letting loose his own nervous laugh. "We're not built for this."

"Thank god for air conditioning, then," laughed Ignacio, toasting his small espresso cup.

Good god, he's drinking coffee in this heat, thought Welsh.

"Would you like a cafecito, my friend?"

"Uh, no, no, thank you," said Welsh. "Perhaps a sweet tea?"

"Bah!" said the developer. "Let us drink like men."

He put a finger in the air without glancing away from his guest, and a waiter appeared almost magically.

"Dos Máximo Extra Anejo, por favor," Ignacio told the waiter, "y dos cervezas también. Red Stripe."

"Si, senor," said the waiter, bowing his head. "De inmediato."

"I am very pleased that you got things done today," Ignacio told Welsh. "It was very important to me that we secure a unanimous vote. Any dissent at all only breeds more opposition. Clearly, we had enough of that already. A good general rallies his troops, and you did so. Bien hecho!"

The commissioner blushed.

"Thanks, it wasn't easy," said Welsh. "Dicky and Candice were no problem, of course, but you know how Sunday can be. He's always thinking about the nine NIMBYs who are gonna show up in his office the next day or what one of his rural yokels is gonna say after Sunday service at that strip mall church of his."

"How did you get him to come around?" inquired Ignacio.

"I promised him I would put that stupid right-to-life proclamation on the next agenda," said Welsh, who wasn't the board's chair, but told Dicky what was to be on the agenda, nevertheless.

"A fantastic bargain," said Ignacio. "An important vote in exchange for a toothless gesture that only costs a bit of political theater. He could have played his hand smarter and gotten much more. Thank goodness that one is so dimwitted. What about Rambo?" he asked, referring to Commissioner Blanton.

Welsh, more comfortable now that he'd gotten the proverbial pat on the head, chuckled.

"That one was even easier," he said with a twinkle in his eye. "He couldn't even come up with something he wanted, so last week, I told him I didn't think the county was doing enough to show our support for the veterans. I suggested we erect a small statue commemorating locals who'd served in the Global War on Terror, but felt he should run point on it, being one himself.

"I take it he was pleased?" asked Ignacio.

"Ecstatic," said Welsh. "I told him we just need to get this wetland policy vote across the finish line, and then I'd hit you up for donations. Even that illiterate moron was able to read between the lines."

"Very nice," said Ignacio. "That one scares me a bit. Loose cannons are unpredictable, and, as you know, I prize predictability above all else."

"I hope you don't mind that I, well, that I implied you would be willing to put up some money for the memorial without conferring with you first," said Welsh, only now realizing he may have cooked his own goose.

Ignacio laughed.

"A statue is a pittance," he said. "We'll make tens of millions off of this policy in just the first few years. Besides, it won't cost me a dime. I'll find a few subcontractors who owe me favors, and they will gladly cough up the donations. It will be settled by the next time I play a round of golf."

The waiter arrived with their drinks. Ignacio toasted his shot of expensive rum at the commissioner and laughed to himself as he saw Welsh wince while taking it, hurriedly reaching for the Red Strip to chase it down.

"Slow down, my friend," Ignacio said with a chuckle as he lit a cigar. "Your people aren't built for this."

Ignacio winked, and Welsh attempted to smile, but it quickly morphed into a frown despite his best efforts.

"What about the Fish?" asked the commissioner, referring to Micky Pesch.

"What about him?" asked Ignacio, his mood having seemed to turn.

"Well, I mean, as you said, he's almost certainly going to file a legal challenge."

"He'll shit if he eats right," said Ignacio, puffing smoke not precisely in the commissioner's face but making no effort to spare him discomfort.

Welsh had assumed Ignacio had been referring to Micky when they were on the phone, but had forgotten how much the Cuban hated being forced to take a long-haired hippie such as Pesch seriously.

"Yes, sir, I'm just trying to get ahead of—"

Ignacio put down his beer bottle hard enough to make a sound.

"I'm the big picture guy, chico, si? I have placed you in a position where you can handle some details requiring official action. Be a good boy, get done what I ask of you, and don't waste time worrying about things above your pay grade, *entiendes*?

Commissioner Welsh spoke almost no Spanish, but he could tell from the inflection that the last word was something akin to what Italians meant when they said *capisce* in the mob films he enjoyed.

"Yes, sir," he said, nervously knocking back a long pull of his Red Stripe.

"Now, I've got another meeting lined up, and I'm sure you've got a lot of official responsibilities to attend to," said Ignacio with a subtle but dismissive wave.

Commissioner Welsh's eyes darted to his watch, an unconvincing counterfeit Rolex Daytona he bought online after Ignacio had made a snide remark about the digital Timex Ironman he had been wearing during the campaign.

"Yes, I hadn't realized it was so late," said the commissioner nervously. "I've got a thing tonight, and traffic will be hell."

Welsh rose and returned Ignacio's handshake, although he was self-conscious about how clammy his palm had suddenly become. He dodged another puff of smoke from the Cuban's Churchill maduro as he hurried away. In the lobby, a well-tanned woman with raven hair and what could only be described as radical augmentations was at the maître d podium.

"I'm meeting Mr. Hernandez for dinner," she told him in what sounded like a Spanish accent.

She wasn't quite Welsh's *type*, but he had to admit he was impressed.

"Right this way," the man told her.

She made eye contact with Welsh as they passed, but looked at him in the manner in which a princess might regard a bug.

Chapter 2: Star Spangled Fucktards

Shelton Hamner's favorite part of living on the Gulf Coast of Florida was enjoying the serene beaches, even during the savagely humid months of July and August, when the air became so thick it challenged even the cleanest, most smoke-free lungs. He usually managed to get out to one of the nearby barrier islands at least two or three times a week. However, having recently found himself unemployed, he'd enjoyed even more opportunity, which he took advantage of despite the lingering red tide the beaches had been experiencing.

Red tide is a harmful algal bloom increasingly common to coastal waters off the Florida Gulf Coast. It's caused by the Karenia brevis organism, which produces brevetoxins that can kill fish and other marine life, while causing respiratory irritation in humans. It can even be passed on if one consumes affected shellfish, causing severe illness.

It's a naturally occurring phenomenon that was already made worse by agricultural runoff, although the nitrogen-rich runoff from phosphate fertilizers and a lack of adequate stormwater retention, as Mullet County had been overdeveloped in recent decades, coincided with their worst blooms on record.

Persistent blooms can last several weeks, even months, fouling the powdery sand beaches with the stinky, bloated corpses of fish and other aquatic life, discolored water, and the chronic coughing of beachgoers eager enough to soak up some sun to brave the whole affair. As most coastal communities rely on tourism as the lifeblood of the local economy, one particularly bad season can all but decimate small, local businesses.

Shelton hated going to the beach on a holiday, especially the 4th of July, and even more so if it fell on a weekend. But the red tide report that morning had been the least daunting in weeks, and he also knew that the county's beach maintenance department would double its efforts to remove the bloated fish carcasses that washed onto the sand after a bloom had robbed the water of oxygen, so he decided to risk it.

Shelton had come to hate the celebration of Independence Day ever since a pre-college stint in the U.S. Coast Guard brought him to the Sunshine State. That was nearly two decades ago, and his hatred for the holiday had grown steadily with each passing celebration of what he had come to think of as *redneck Christmas.*

Shelton had grown up in rural Pennsylvania, where, despite its ample population of hillbillies, the firework festivities were mainly confined to the 4th. In Florida, however, the bourgeoisie would typically begin with modest explosions by the 2nd or 3rd, while the dregs of society might start as early as the last week of June, before celebrating in earnest by the 1st and using classes of ordnance that approached military-grade as it got closer to the big day. By the time the 4th rolled around, even the upper classes would get in on the festivities, and, combined with the official spectacle put on by the various municipalities, the noise would render anything other than submission futile.

Each year, Shelton would vow to leave town for the holiday. He had managed to do so a few times, although, as a modestly paid journalist, he usually got roped into a holiday assignment that he couldn't afford to pass up. Being presently out of work—aside from occasional gigs shooting photos of residential real estate listings—meant there were no assignments to pass on. However, it also meant that his bank account had grown anemic. Given the inflated cost of travel associated with federal holidays, even the most modest getaway had been out of the question.

To make matters worse, Shelton was dog-sitting his roommate Ringo's oversized boxer, whose fireworks-induced anxiety fell on the extreme end of the spectrum. Anytime a loud crack would ripple through the neighborhood, Rufus, whose best trick seemed to be impersonating a thoroughbred racehorse while urinating, would reliably part ways with a thick stream of urine, the volume of which seemed to vary in direct correlation to the decibel level of the explosion.

Despite being even more severely unemployed, Ringo had managed to get out of town by hoarding the generous allowance of medical marijuana his dubious prescription allowed him to purchase so that he could sell it in Texas, where no such healthcare provision existed, and the sale or even possession of reefer could still earn you a state prison sentence. The rush of growers entering Florida's marketplace had resulted in a ganja glut, and holiday fire sale pricing on everything from flower to vape cartridges to gummies meant the perennially broke freelance photographer would return flush, at least for a month or so.

Ringo had invited him to come along, but Shelton found the notion of spending hard time in a Texas prison dissuasive. He also found it difficult to imagine that Texans were any more subdued on the 4th than Floridians. He would have usually insisted that Ringo make other arrangements for Rufus, especially on a fireworks holiday—which, in Florida, included just about everything besides perhaps Valentine's Day—but they were already losing the small bungalow they rented, as their landlord had given notice of his intent to sell.

Sarasota's real estate market was soaring, and even a hundred-year-old, 2-bedroom, 1-bath California-style bungalow in need of *serious* TLC would fetch half a million bucks from a flipper or short-term rental specialist. Rents were rising even faster than sale prices, which meant, absent a miracle of sorts, they faced the prospect of being homeless in less than a month's time.

Under such circumstances, preserving the security deposit might seem crucial, but the various damages Rufus had already inflicted on the property and the fact that they had absolutely no intention of paying the final month's rent rendered the matter moot. In truth, putting aside the idea that he had to clean up the piss puddles, Shelton found himself taking a certain level of comfort in the notion that their greedy landlord, who'd proven himself to be a proper prick on all fronts, would be tasked with removing the distinctly foul odor of dog piss from the home's ancient hardwood.

The house was across the causeway from Siesta Key, a white-sanded paradise of a barrier island just off Sarasota's coast. Because of rampant overdevelopment, however, the drive could take as long as 45 minutes if you left later than 9:30 a.m. on a weekend, let alone a holiday. So, Shelton roused himself out of bed at 8:20 to ensure he'd have enough time to walk and feed Rufus before departing. He wasn't typically an early riser, but he had also considered that the eventual descent into drunken chaos that typically set in by late afternoon on a holiday had seemed to be occurring earlier and earlier in recent years.

Shelton arrived early enough to secure one of the back-row spots in the free parking lot adjacent to the public beach. Still, he could tell by the large assembly of low-brow, lite-beer-drinking natives with expensively modified pickup trucks emblazoned with fishing, NASCAR, and/or "Salt Life" regalia that serious shenanigans would soon be afoot.

"Your girlfriend called. She needs you to return her car," a man with mullet hair and bad teeth snarled as Shelton removed his Tommy Bahama beach chair from the tiny backseat of his Mini Cooper convertible.

Shelton ignored the barb but decided he had better raise the top once he determined that the man was tall enough to relieve himself into the small car should the urge strike him.

"You mean boyfriend," an obese man in a sleeveless shirt walking with the same group chimed in.

Shelton wasn't much of a fighter and was also outnumbered by a group that contained four men, all of whom looked like they were no strangers to fisticuffs or the county jail. He desperately searched his mind for a course of action that wouldn't see him competing for ER space with the victims of drunken firework injuries, and could feel the men growing bolder in his silence.

"What's the story, compadre?" asked a wiry gent with a roofer's tan and a tattered, straw cowboy hat carrying a can of Bush Light. "You pussy whipped, or are you dick whipped?"

The others cackled.

In a panic, Shelton did his best impersonation of a deaf man trying to talk while his hands issued an incoherent stream of American Sign Language consisting of all the signals he could recall from a class he'd taken in college in order to avoid having to complete a foreign language course in order to graduate.

"Oh shit," said the only man who had yet to speak, a fat, bald man with an eagle tattooed across his chest. "He's deaf, man. Leave him alone."

The one in the cowboy hat cocked his head.

"That don't mean he can't be a queer," he said, jerking the empty can toward the ground to expel its foam while seeming to lose interest.

Shelton had successfully avoided an ass-whooping, but such conflict right out of the gate seemed foreboding.

He set up his chair as far from other humans as possible, put in his earbuds, and cued Miles Davis' Flamenco Sketches on his phone before opening his small cooler and grabbing some cold-press coffee he had prepared the night before. It wasn't even 9:30 a.m., and the sound of cans of light beer and hard seltzers being opened rang through the air.

Despite the coffee, the jazz and sun had managed to put Shelton to sleep within half an hour, and it was nearly noon when he finally awoke, thankful that he'd applied 50 SPF sunscreen when he arrived. The vibe had definitely descended. The crowds had swelled, and the alcohol was being imbibed much more liberally.

It was already a menacingly hot 94 degrees, topped with staggering humidity. The "feels like" on his weather app registered 106. Most beachgoers had long since run out of bottled water and were now drinking their hooch more for the sake of hydration than relaxation—never a good recipe at this devil's latitude of just 27 degrees north of the Equator.

It's hard to adequately describe a day like the one Shelton was experiencing to anyone who has never been a problem drinker in a subtropical environment. The southwest Florida heat in July and August is nothing short of evil, a relentless blanket of bad vibes that fouls the air with the scents of dying musk and vegetative detritus. Even those who have no problem exercising a healthy degree of restraint under normal circumstances seem to have no choice but to drink cold, heavily alcoholic beverages that, while refreshing, have the effect of pulverizing good sense and obliterating sound judgment. For those in this region who begin their cooler, air-conditioned, non-alcoholic mornings with much less common sense and sound judgment than the average high-school dropout, the results range from disappointing to felonious.

By 2 p.m., the scene had turned ugly. A few feet from Shelton's now-crowded spot on the beach, a pot-bellied man who one could only guess sustained himself with a bogus disability claim had begun yelling at a fat lady in a confederate flag bikini whose daughter insisted on feeding Cheez Doodles to the seagulls.

"They're gonna bite her fucking finger off!" the man screamed. "What'cha gonna do then, you dumb broad? DCF will take her ass off you for sure."

"I *told* her not to do it," the woman slurred back. "What the hell do you want from me? She don't listen! If I beat her, they'll take her from me just the same. I suppose you think she'd be better off in foster care?" she added as a stream of tears began to flow. "I fuckin' hate you, Randall!"

It took a couple of moments for Shelton to assemble enough of the conversation to surmise they were, in fact, a couple, and though they had recovered enough of their anger to be kissing sloppily by the time he had finished packing up his gear, it seemed like an ominous foreshadowing of things to come.

As he crossed the parking lot at just past 2:30 p.m., cars were now hovering for open spots like vultures looking to descend on fresh carrion. An available space had apparently emerged, and two rednecks with aggressive trucks began fighting over their entitlement to it from their respective cabs, each revving their engine and inching toward the other's chrome bumper.

The one whose bumper stickers ran the gamut from *INFORWARS.COM* to *Vaginatarian* and *Your Girlfriend On Board* seemed to be winning the pissing match thus far. However, the beefy-armed gent with the *Louder Than Your Girlfriend Was Last Night* sticker over his suspiciously large exhaust pipe seemed to be making inroads.

"I'll be pulling out of my spot in the next row, gentlemen," said Shelton. "No need to scratch the paint on such fine trucks."

The groups turned their collective gaze to Shelton, looking only half-happy to receive such news, as it meant the redneck mating ritual would come to an end without bloodshed or gunplay. As he left the lot and headed toward the mainland, Shelton noticed the clouds forming and prayed that the thunderstorms might be downright torrential, soaking the evening's festivities. However, while the skies did open around 4 p.m., they had cleared by early evening.

The mood for the night was set in stone around dusk, while Shelton was walking Rufus up and down their street, hoping the beast would vacate as much of his bladder and bowels as possible before the real noise set in. A large woman with red and blue curlers in her hair and too much of herself

spilling from a tank top emerged from a neighbor's pool party
with the kind of rubbery-legged sway that suggested
inebriation of the highest order.

"Fuck you and the horse you rode in on!" she screamed at
the much skinnier man who was only halfheartedly giving
chase. Her words came through the sort of slur that is generally
only facilitated by a full day of drinking hard liquor in the
Florida sun—that or a liberal dose of prescription opioids.
"FAAWWWK youuuuuuu," she said again to punctuate her
statement, using a slurred-out oral elongation that would have
impressed Michael Buffer.

Just then, another woman emerged to successfully cajole
her distraught friend back into the party, which, by 9 p.m., had
become a full-on cacophony of high-powered munitions that
left the neighborhood sounding like the war-torn streets of the
Gaza Strip. Rufus had already begun pissing on the floor when
Shelton decided to open a $55 bottle of estate Pinot Noir from
the Willamette Valley he'd been hoarding. It was the last good
bottle of wine he was likely to enjoy until he sorted out his
employment situation.

Shelton had hoped that the joy he would receive courtesy
of a near-perfect Oregon red would offset the misery. It did not.
By 10 p.m., the neighbors had severely upped the ante, and
Rufus had muddied the hardwood floors with a particularly
loose bowel movement. As Shelton cleaned the rancid mess, he
found himself thinking about the term hardwood. Was it not
redundant, he wondered. Was there such a thing as softwood
floors?

Having had about all he could take of this absurd carousel
of hillbilly horrors, Shelton finally stormed across the street to
the tiny, dilapidated Spanish mission-style house and fought
through the overgrowth of landscaping toward the yard. When
he reached the back patio, he saw a small party in and around a
decades-old, four-foot-deep, above-ground swimming pool. It
had a tiny cylindrical filter, and Shelton immediately thought it

could not possibly be managing all the dirty urine these exceptions to Darwinism were spilling into the chlorinated (he hoped) water—at least judging by the sizable pile of semi-crushed Natty Ice cans littering the yard.

"Excuse me, my friends," he said in the voice of an angry pacifist. "Might we have adequately awoken the dead?"

"What?" said a tall, thin peckerwood with tattooed arms, one of which held a beer, the other a vape pen.

Shelton recognized him as the man who had been lazily chasing the woman with the curlers down the street earlier in the day.

"The fireworks," he explained. "Any chance we can call it a night?"

"It's the 4th of July," the man answered.

"This is true," Shelton conceded, "but while I can't be entirely certain, I'd be willing to bet that we've met whatever quota on explosives might be required to prove that we're good patriotic Americans."

"You don't sound American," said a red-headed gent with freckles and bottomless eyes, who was standing in the above-ground pool while lighting firecrackers.

"What do I sound like?" asked Shelton in genuine curiosity.

"Like a fuckin' Canadian," the ginger responded, tossing a small firecracker about five feet to Shelton's left, where it exploded, causing him to jump, much to their amusement.

"Actually, there is a little Canadian on my mother's side," Shelton said, now wondering if anything about his voice actually did make him *sound* Canadian.

"So you're an immigrant?" asked the tall one.

"No," said Shelton. "My mother was born here. My father was born here. I was born here. When you're born here, you're automatically American, particularly when you're born here to other people who were born here. I mean, not more so, but it should be *clearer*, I would think. What I'm trying to say is that my citizenship is not in question. I am, as they say, a *native*."

They looked at him as if he were speaking Portuguese.

"You pray to Allah?" asked the ginger.

"What? No, I'm an atheist, though I did consider praying to Buddha, L. Ron Hubbard, and Jesus Fucking Christ Almighty that the explosions would cease, but I thought that instead, I might come over here as a good and decent human being, appeal to your humanity, and ask you to cool it on the fireworks so that my dog, Rufus—well, he's my roommate's dog—will stop pissing on the hardwood floors."

"What do you want us to do, light fuckin' sparklers like a bunch of fuckin' pansies?" the tall one asked. "Maybe throw some snaps and light them little snake things while we're at it?" He laughed. "That shit's for kids!"

Shelton was losing his patience.

"Look, Ace," he said, "I hate to point this out, but it's *all* for kids, and I feel that it's worth mentioning that I don't see any of them around (thank God), just a bunch of grown men getting their rocks off by way of loud explosions. I'm unsure what that's all about, although I know Freud had some interesting theories."

"You sayin' we're queers?" asked the redhead, who had clearly not worn sunscreen for the afternoon leg of the party.

"No, and neither was Freud," said Shelton. "He was suggesting impotence, or at least fears of inadequacy in terms of, shall we say, boudoir skills."

Both men cocked their heads sideways and looked at Shelton as though they knew they *should* be offended, but couldn't quite put their finger on *why*.

"He's sayin' your dicks don't work, you fuckin' retards!" shouted the large woman who'd suggested leaving town on a horse earlier in the day. "And I know he's right in at least one of y'all's case."

Apparently, there is such a thing as *soft* wood, and this house had some.

"Look, buddy," said the tall fellow. "I didn't serve ten years in the Navy to come home and be told that—as a veteran no less—I don't have the right to celebrate our country's birthday."

Finally, some commonality thought Shelton.

"Look, I served too—Coast Guard—but I—"

"Fuckin' Coast Guard?" the man managed to say through his hysterical laughter. "Are you shittin' me? What the fuck kind of pussy are you?"

At this, they all enjoyed a jolly good laugh.

"Listen here, pal," said Red. "You can call the cops, or you can come over here and try to stop us from settin' off these here fireworks, *or* you can go fuck yourself, for all I care. But that's about the long and short of it. So, why don't you just take your pansy Coast Guard ass back home and clean up the dog piss?"

Once again outnumbered, Shelton put his palms in the air and walked off, shaking his head as he lost a bit more faith in humanity.

"Yeah, go on now," shouted the large woman who had caught the Freudian reference. "And one more thing, FAWK you and the horse you rode in on, AND your damned dog Rufus!" she cackled as they all broke out into side-splitting laughter.

"It's my roommate's dog," Shelton muttered in dejection without looking back toward the laughing crowd.

Thoroughly defeated, Shelton headed back to the house, cleaned up the newest puddle of piss, and decided to make the best of a bad situation. He pulled out the last of the California edibles he'd managed to hide from Ringo in a shoe box under the bed and devoured them, though not before tossing Rufus two of the sweet gummies to help with his anxiety. Wanting to get as close to comatose as possible, he opened a second bottle of wine, this time a cheap but drinkable Malbec from Costco, and put the extended director's cut of *Apocalypse Now* in the DVD player.

Somewhere around the time Captain Willard and the boys had made it halfway up the river toward the camp of Col. Kurtz, the THC began to take hold. By the USO scene, the collective fireworks were blending into sync with Coppola's masterpiece. Soon, Shelton couldn't tell the firecrackers in the street from the bombs on the TV.

The gummies also had the desired effect on a now-sleeping Rufus, and somewhere around the point when Robert Duvall issues his famous *Charlie don't surf!* line, Shelton dozed off into a peaceful sleep, where he remained until Rufus jumped on the couch and began licking his face, signaling that he was ready to resume the routine of waiting until the morning walk to relieve himself.

When he awoke, there was nothing but that smell, that distinctive sulfur scent of expended fireworks. It smelled like … well, not quite like victory, but something close to a draw.

Chapter 3: Flotsam and Jetsam

"No, Mr. Chalmers!" Millie's voice rang out, a mix of concern and exasperation, as she tugged on the leash, pulling the dog away from the bloated fish carcass he was so enthusiastically sniffing. "That's yuck-yuck. It'll make you sick."

The smell from the most recent red tide bloom had receded in recent days, and Millie had thought, or at least hoped, it would be safe to brave the narrow shell-laden beach along the bay front for the dawn ritual. There was no sidewalk on the road leading out of their cul-de-sac, so she hated rounding the blind corner with her 14-year-old Shih Tzu, as she had been forced to do for the previous ten days when it was noxious enough to burn her throat and cause her eyes to water, surely doing far worse to her beloved little Mr. Chalmers. But the dog liked to splash in the surf, and she found the view of the sun rising rather tranquil, so she decided to give it a shot.

The blooms had grown increasingly persistent in recent years, and Millie should have known that just because she couldn't pick up the foul smell from their nearby home, the fish kill would have been intense enough to leave some straggler corpses, the beach patrol's intense efforts to remove the tourist-repelling objects notwithstanding.

"You stay away from those nasty things," she further admonished the dog, who dropped his head, seeming embarrassed.

However, no sooner had she regained control of Mr. Chalmers than the little scamp darted off once more. This time, the dog's tiny legs put an impressive stretch of sand between them before she could push the button to lock the expandable leash.

It was too late. The dog had already made it to the object of its attention, which looked to be a giant piece of driftwood in the early light. Before Millie had even closed the distance, however, she became distressingly aware of the fact that it was *not* a piece of driftwood. It was a person—one that she hoped had just passed out in the sand after a few margaritas too many.

"Mr. Chalmers, get over here!" she scolded the dog. "Now!"

The dog paid her no mind.

"You will not get any bacon treats, mister. I mean it this time."

As she arrived at the body, which was slumped in a near fetal position, Millie gained a sort of preternatural knowledge that this was not some beleaguered sot on the back end of a three-day bender. The figure seemed far too wet and still and had not responded to the dog's pesky sniffing. This was a corpse, she decided, and she was correct.

Millie jerked the leash one more time and cautiously used her Croc-covered foot to peel back the shoulder and expose the front of what appeared to be an older male.

"Holy shit," she whispered as Mr. Chalmers let out a knowing whimper. Millie instinctively looked toward the bay and noticed what appeared to be floating metal boxes moving in and out with the tide. In the distance, she saw a large sailboat that seemed to be anchored about a kilometer out.

The sudden shift in tone caused the dog to pull in the opposite direction and fall into a barking frenzy. Millie pulled out her phone and dialed 9-1-1 while shushing the now manic dog.

"9-1-1, what's your emergency?" asked a female dispatcher.

"I just found a dead body on the north shore of Mullet Bay, near Sea Grape Cove."

"Are you sure the person is deceased?" the dispatcher asked.

"Am I sure?" Millie asked indignantly. "He's got a bullet hole in him, his face is blue, and his eyes are wide open. I doubt he's taking a nap!"

36

The dog's barking grew louder.

"Okay, stay calm, ma'am," said the dispatcher. "Can you tell me anything else?"

"Yeah," Millie said softly. "I think it's Micky fucking Fish."

****

Dicky Myers cursed his club as his drive continued to slice down the fairway, eventually landing out of bounds.

"Goddamned fucking $400 piece of shit graphite mother fummmmmphinnnn!"

The commissioner regained his composure, remembering what his cardiac specialist had told him about having to choose between nitrates and erectile dysfunction medications.

"So, I told him straight up," said Commissioner Jeffrey Blanton, "I don't think that's constitutional, and I took an oath to uphold the Constitution."

"Do commissioners actually take an oath regarding the U.S. Constitution?" asked Howie Plaveth, the parks and rec director whom Dicky had invited, so as not to have to endure Blanton's bloviating solo.

"Well, no, but I have some thoughts on that, too," said Blanton. "I took one as a soldier, though, and I take my oaths *very* seriously. Take Promise Keepers, for example."

"Promise Keepers?" asked Howie.

"For the love of Christ, man, do not get him started on this tangent," whined Myers. "I beg you, Howie, not today!"

Commissioner Welsh had cajoled Myers into spending some recreational time with Blanton, hoping it might make him easier to sway on important votes. The fact that Blanton, who was married and a deacon at his church, did not drink or attend strip clubs meant that most of Myers' favorite pastimes would be off-limits. He wrongly assumed, however, that no man could screw up a free round of golf at one of Ignacio's top-tier, private courses.

"Do you look at porn, Howie?" asked Blanton stoically.

Howie blushed as he fished in his bag for a ball and a tee.

"For fuck's sake, Jeffrey," screamed Dicky. "Everyone but you watches porn! It's free on the internet. Hell, even women watch it now!"

Blanton was unfazed.

"And that's what's ruining this great nation," said Blanton, calmly returning his gaze to Howie Plaveth.

"Did you know that fertility rates among American males have been steadily dropping for years?" asked Blanton.

Howie didn't answer. He and his wife had, in fact, been trying to conceive for some time, but it never took. Lately, if he were to be honest, their sex life had slowed to a crawl.

"It's the porn, Howie," said a deadpan Blanton. "It creates unrealistic expectations. It teaches men that women should act like whores of Babylon in the bedroom—spitting, choking, hair pulling." He shook his head in disgust. "At our last Promise Keepers meeting, our chapter president brought in a list of the category menu from one of those flesh peddling websites. Softcore, hardcore, threesomes, gang bangs, lesbian, gay, bisexual, oiled, shaved, pregnant, you name it, Howie, it's there. There's even a category for grandmas, for God's sake. Grandmas, Howie. Is nothing sacred in our republic anymore? There are women having sex with vegetables. There's fisting, bestiality, and even something called ass-to-mouth. But do you know what the most popular category is, Howie? Do you?"

"Midgets?" guessed Dicky with a chuckle as he lined up his next shot.

"No," said a stone-faced Blanton, still looking at Howie intensely. "Stepmom porn. That's right. Two generations of sullying the sanctity of marriage through a 60 percent divorce rate and allowing same-sex… (he couldn't bring himself to add the word marriage or even unions). It's led to *this*, Howie. A generation of young men who can't even get it up unless they think they're gonna have some revenge on their absentee father by stuffing that boner of theirs in his new wifey."

Dicky feigned wiping his hands with the towel on his golf bag, removed it, and tucked it into the front of his waistband, hoping it would hide the tent he had begun to pitch.

"Stepmom porn," Blanton repeated, tilting his head and arching his brow for effect. "Number one with a bullet."

Howie Plaveth began to sweat.

"But what if not all men who watch stepmom porn are interested in that, well, aspect of it?" Howie stammered. "Has anyone considered that if a middle-aged man prefers to fantasize over age-appropriate women, he has very little choice? The only role they give women in their 40s is that of a stepmom. I … I mean—*they* would probably rather see two people in their 40s, but middle-aged men are only cast as stepfathers. It's completely screwing up the algorithm!"

"That's not all it's screwing up, Howie," said Commissioner Blanton.

"You know, when I was a kid, you had to jerk off using your imagination," said Dicky Myers. "Maybe the bra section of the Sears catalog, if you were lucky. Tell me, Jeffrey, what do you wax your carrot to? I'm dying to know."

"I *don't* masturbate," said Blanton, turning his dead eyes on Dicky. "Ever!"

"Never?" asked Howie, clearly impressed.

"Nope," said Blanton, shaking his head solemnly. "I save it all for the misses, and what she don't need, I push way down into the depths of my soul, and I turn that lust into passion for our Lord and Savior Jesus Christ. And you know what?"

"What?" asked a suddenly captivated Howie.

"I got the sperm count of a teenager," Blanton told him, again tilting his head and arching his eyebrows for effect.

"Take this," said Blanton, handing Howie a card with information on the Promise Keepers' local chapter.

"Thanks," said Howie, tucking it carefully into the front pocket of his fanny pack.

"Goddammit," yelled Myers, looking down range to where a sandhill crane was ambling along the green, preventing him from proceeding.

Before Howie or Dicky knew what happened, Commissioner Blanton removed a Desert Eagle .50 caliber pistol from a holster under his baggy polo and obliterated the bird into a whirlwind of goo and feathers from an impressive distance.

"What the fuck are you doing, you lunatic?" screamed Commissioner Myers.

"The right to hunt and fish was recently legally enshrined into the Florida Constitution," said Blanton, referencing a statewide ballot referendum that had passed in the last election. "And I told you. I'm a constitutionalist."

****

Amber Pesch was pouring her second cup of coffee from a French press on her riverfront pool deck when she heard a car pulling up the shell driveway out front. Amber hated the nails-on-chalkboard sound she would have to endure as she pulled up in her Mercedes, even more so when the convertible top was down. She also hated the errant scraps of fragmented fossils that she would invariably find on the house's ceramic floor tiles. Still, she liked the aesthetics and the early warning it gave when someone had arrived unexpectedly.

When she reached the window of her front door, Amber immediately noticed it was a police squad car, and panic set in. However, she soon saw that it was not from the Mullet County Sheriff's Office, whose vehicles were green and white, or even one from the City of DeSoto PD, which had transitioned exclusively to Ford Explorer SUVs. It was an unmarked Crown Vic, nearly extinct among police patrol cars, which suggested it was Chief Lawrence Washington of the LeGrotto Police Department.

The dark giant opened the driver's door and erected himself to his full six-foot-four-inch frame, and any doubt regarding the squad car's provenance disappeared.

"Good morning, Chief. A little out of our jurisdiction this morning, aren't we? It can't possibly be about Micky's unpaid parking tickets north of the river," she said with a laugh.

LeGrotto, referred to by its many detractors as *LeGhetto*, was a small city of around 15,000 on the north side of the DeSoto River. It evolved organically into a small business hub for agricultural interests, which were primarily concentrated on the north side of the county. Because the fruit pickers had traditionally been Black and LeGrotto had the county's only Black high school during segregation, it remained home to most of the Black population in Mullet County. As Hispanics replaced Blacks in the fields, the demographics shifted, although it continued to be the most blighted and poverty-stricken area in an otherwise prosperous county.

A standout defensive lineman for the legendary Thurgood Marshall Spartans, Lawrence "Big Cat" Washington became an All-American at Florida A&M before being signed by the Tampa Bay Bucs as a free agent, where he was a backup tackle for two seasons. However, another player's injury saw him starting for the Bucs in their first Super Bowl victory in 2003, logging two tackles and a key fumble recovery. He was on his way to winning the starting position the following season when he tore his ACL in a pre-season game.

Following his injury, Washington was released, playing one season in the CFL and another with an arena league team out of Tampa before entering the police academy. He eventually earned the rank of chief for the small department. Washington's sister had a son named Cornell, also a standout athlete, who was later elected Mayor of LeGrotto, putting him in the young man's employ as the Mayor was the city's de facto police commissioner. While he supported Cornell's campaign, the chief did not enjoy having him as his boss, even though his nephew knew better than to treat the man as anything other than a respected colleague.

"Good morning, Mrs. Pesch," the large man responded. "No, Micky's square on all his LeGrotto infractions, to my knowledge," he laughed. But his tone turned more serious when he added, "You think we might go out on the back deck for a moment? There is something I need to talk to you about."

Amber's pulse quickened. Micky and Chief Washington got along quite well, and the chief had visited their home on a few previous occasions, but not since Micky had moved onto the boat. A house call surely meant that something was up. At best, he was here to warn her about the dangers of whatever her husband was sticking his big nose into at the moment. At worst, well, she didn't want to think about that.

"Sure, Chief. Come on back. I was just having some coffee. I'll get you a cup. Do you take cream or sugar?"

"Thanks, ma'am. Cream, no sugar if it's not too much trouble."

"None at all."

The chief rose as she passed through the kitchen sliders and onto the deck, but she waved him back to his seat with a sigh. At 62, Amber appreciated good manners, particularly when expressed by those more youthful than the target. However, given the history of racial politics in Mullet County, she was never quite comfortable accepting even the slightest deference from someone like the chief, who, as a Mullet County native born in the late '70s, she was sure held more than a few good reasons not to extend such courtesy to an old Southern white woman.

"Here you go, Chief," she said, handing him a cup. "It's from that lovely little coffee roaster on your side of the river. Micky picks it up every week."

"Speaking of which," he said, "may I ask when the last time you spoke to your husband was?"

Amber's heart sank, and her pulse quickened.

"Well, let me think," she said, shifting her hands nervously. "The last time I saw Micky in the flesh was Monday. He stopped by to get some papers or something, and I made him lunch. But he phoned yesterday to tell me he would have to cancel our plan to meet at the Rusty Rudder for dinner today."

"Did he say why that might be?" asked Chief Washington.

"No," Amber said, her face growing tenser by the moment. "He doesn't tell me what he's involved in, and, in truth, I will cut him off if he even tries to. I know my husband likes to stick his snout into places where it's not safe to be stuck. Hell, that's why he's been living on the sailboat. I told him that if he weren't afraid of the goons he'd been picking fights with, that wouldn't interfere with me being petrified. Sure, it starts with slashed tires, keyed cars, and even a rock through the bay window, all of which we've had, but if you don't get the message …"

"Can you tell me who he might have been picking fights with as of late?" the chief asked, realizing he was straddling a line ethically by waiting this long to deliver the news, and also because Micky's murder was not in his jurisdiction.

However, he also realized that Amber would be in hysterics shortly and that no one from the sheriff's office, who had asked his nephew to have the chief give the notification as a "professional courtesy," would likely be very enthusiastic in their investigation.

"Chief, what's this about?" Amber asked, her voice cracking slightly.

"Please, Mrs. Pesch, can you think of anyone that might have it in for Micky?"

"Have it in for Micky?" she said, her voice quivering. "Is that a friggin' joke?" she asked, failing in her attempt to punctuate it with a laugh. "Take your pick: the phosphate companies, those fellas trying to put a gambling resort on the island, our crooked sheriff, or any of the minions on that county commission. Then there's Ignacio," she added. "I'm surprised he hasn't had one of his goons give Micky a Cuban necktie years ago."

Ignacio Hernandez was exceptionally rich and had half the county in his pocket. The half that weren't in his pocket were scared shitless by the half that were, which was all he had needed to gut the county's land development code of any regulation that stood in the way of more units on each bland, characterless development he was littering the community with.

"Micky didn't say anything specific recently regarding what he'd been working on?"

Amber Pesch stood from her chair and turned whiter than any human Lawrence Washington had ever laid eyes on. The chief rose but softened his posture by putting his hands behind his back.

"Oh, dear," she stammered. "My Micky's not in any trouble, is he, Chief? He's not in trouble because he's already gone."

Tears had already begun falling down her wrinkled, sun-kissed cheeks before the chief could answer.

"I'm so sorry," Chief Washington said.

"Jesus Christ," Amber shrieked. "They sent you because they couldn't even face me, could they? Sheriff Brock isn't gonna lift a finger, and they know I know that!"

"Mrs. Pesch ..."

She wagged a finger in his face.

"Or am I being naive?" she asked. "Did they send you to find out if I knew who did it? If I'd be a *problem*, someone who needed to be dealt with?"

She backed away from the massive police chief and glanced over his shoulder toward the mighty river. Lawrence

Washington couldn't be sure if she was wondering if he was going to deposit her body into it, or had been contemplating a running jump from the boat dock as an escape.

"Mrs. Pesch, please," the chief implored, putting up his palms defensively and lowering into a squat to diminish his size. "Micky was a friend, and the basis of that friendship was mainly owed to our shared contempt for the same people. I mean you know harm, ma'am. Yes, the sheriff asked my nephew to send me out to notify the next of kin as a professional courtesy because I was friends with Micky, and probably because he didn't want to face you, but I have no idea who killed your husband. It's only because I don't trust them sons of bitches to do a proper investigation that I tried to see if you knew anything that might suggest a suspect before you were overcome by grief. I apologize if that seemed disrespectful, deceptive, or opportunistic, ma'am. I really am."

Amber softened her posture.

"How did he die?" she asked.

"He was found early this morning, washed up on the sand near where his boat's been anchored. He was shot in the chest."

"Did he suffer?" she asked softly.

"I don't believe he did," said the chief. "It was a shotgun. He probably died before he hit the water."

"Micky would have preferred it if the sharks had gotten to him," she said with a punch-drunk chuckle. "Give a little something back to the sea on the way out. Circle of life and all that Native American business he was into."

The chief managed a muted chuckle and patted her on the shoulder.

"You probably shouldn't be alone right now," he told her. "Can I give you a ride? Maybe to your sister's house or something."

The woman looked dazed and took what seemed like forever to answer.

"Yes, that would be very kind. Let me freshen up."

Chapter 4: Down and out in paradise

"Goddammit," Shelton shouted, realizing that he had either lost the light or would have to wait a considerable amount of time for it to arrive. He was not entirely sure how the shadows would be affected by the sun's movement because he was not a photojournalist, even by the broadest definition. Ringo had mostly handled that part of the job.

Shelton had always hated the photography aspect of his journalism work, so a side gig shooting real estate listing photos had about as much appeal as gas station wine. The fact that the Realtor employing him for this work was his ex-wife made it more like a bottle of grocery-store Chianti that had long turned, after being open for months in some rube's liquor cabinet.

"Fuck it," he said aloud as he started snapping the pics with his low-end SLR, gambling that she would want to get the listing on the MLS badly enough not to be her normal pain-in-the-ass self when she received them.

They all look the same, anyway, he thought, more closely assessing the monstrosity of a recently erected home following the demolition of what was likely a charming, early 20th-century Spanish mission revival style cottage or maybe even a craftsman bungalow. How many quartz countertops, stainless steel appliances, and engineered hardwood floors could a prospective buyer suffer through looking at?

When his phone rang, Shelton was surprised to see "Lars" as the caller ID on his screen. Lars Olson was the editor of The DeSoto Gazette. It was a small independent alt-weekly in a neighboring county that had been started only two decades prior as a counterbalance to the overtly pro-business bias of the City of DeSoto's main daily, The Mullet County Monitor. Over the years, they had occasionally bumped into each other, usually at press events. Lars had even given Shelton some occasional freelance work, but it had been two, maybe even three years since they last spoke.

"Lars, what's good?" he asked.

"Not a whole lot, my friend. How you holding up?"

"About as well as a single-wide trailer in a Midwest tornado, to be honest," Shelton replied.

"I haven't seen any bylines recently," said Lars. "You go civilian?"

Shelton had recently been fired from a very cushy job at an alt-weekly in Sarasota, which Lars would undoubtedly have known in such a small regional media ecosphere. And, no, he had not been inundated with freelance offers when he hit the free agent market.

"It's been slow coming since the whole thing with the Planet," he told him. "Truth be told, I've been shooting real estate listings to pay the bills lately. I'm on a job right now, as a matter of fact."

"Christ almighty, man, don't tell me you're working for Darian?"

Shelton rubbed the bridge of his nose as a headache began to form at the base of his neck, threatening to climb toward the small but growing bald spot on the crown of his skull where they usually liked to settle.

"It's occasional freelance work, Lars," he snapped. "It's not like I'm punching a clock for her."

"Jeez, Shelton, relax. I'm just busting your balls a little. As a matter of fact, I have some work I want to offer you. Not just a freelance piece, but a temporary full-time position. There's a chance it could even lead to a permanent gig."

Shelton took a long look at the home's homogeneous, corporate-hotel-like interior decor and immediately regretted his tone.

"For real?" he asked. "I guess the old man is finally thinking his money is better spent on cheap journalism, which a few people actually read, than expensive documentaries that no one watches."

"Not exactly," replied Lars in a tone that made Shelton apprehensive.

"What's up then?"

"Shit, Shelton, you really are out of the loop, aren't you? Do you even watch the news or pick up a paper?"

"Not if I can avoid it."

"Micky Fish is dead," Lars said flatly. "Double barrel shotgun to the chest. He washed up on the shore of the bay yesterday, about half a mile from where his sailboat had been anchored."

"No shit?" said Shelton.

"No shit," confirmed Lars.

"What do you know?"

"Not much," said Lars. "Look, I'd really rather have this conversation in person. Can you meet me for some food and a few drinks around four, maybe at the Rudder?"

"Look at you; the boss is barely cold, and you're already knocking them back before five?" laughed Shelton.

"Fuck you," said Lars. "I'm thinking about what kind of traffic you'd hit if I made it any later."

Lars had made a good point. The overdevelopment of the area occurred rapidly and with little planning in terms of securing right-of-ways and undertaking the necessary studies for long-term transportation projects. The roads were a mess, and only the fact that schools were on summer recess made 4 p.m. a manageable time to rendezvous.

"Yeah, I can do that," said Shelton. "So long as you're buying or expensing it. I'm flat broke, my friend."

"Of course. Hell, give me the address, and I'll order you an Uber in case we tie one on. It's all on the company card, the ride back, too."

When the call ended, Shelton immediately searched Micky Pesch on his phone's internet browser. The search returned the local ABC affiliate's account as the top result. It was a brief and concise report that told little more than Lars had. The same went for the next two links. Micky Pesch, an independent media mogul also known as Micky Fish, 63, had been found dead from a gunshot wound to his chest. Police had no further information at this time.

****

Micky Pesch had been better known by the English translation of his Italian surname. He'd gotten the nickname as a derogatory moniker, but leaned into it once he realized it wasn't going away. He was a life-gives-you-lemons, you-make-lemonade type of fellow. Shelton always admired that about him. Micky's father had been a prominent farmer in Mullet County, vastly expanding an operation he'd inherited from his own dad, an Italian immigrant who'd come over with nothing. However, it was enough of a start for Arturo to become one of the county's early agricultural barons and an influential man about town.

Arturo Pesch married a woman who worked in a cannery the Pesch family had engaged to process its potatoes, which the family added after years of specializing in tomatoes. They named their firstborn son after her late father. When Arturo and his wife eventually built their own canning operation, they nodded to the irony of the union of Irish and Italian staples by rebranding their enterprise, McPesch's Potatoes & Tomatoes, Inc.

Micky was a sharp kid who developed a love of the environment at a young age. He had spent summers working for the family business and weekends trolling the gorgeous waterways in his canoe or fishing for grouper and mullet on a pram his father had given him one Christmas. Coming of age during the 1970s, Micky developed a radical streak by his early teens. He was soon protesting all manners of environmental degradation, of which there was an endless supply to choose from at the time. Perhaps that's why his father could never understand why a son he had treated so well seemed so intent on focusing on matters like the dangers of pesticides and monoculture crops when there were much sexier options like nukes and acid rain that wouldn't see him pissing on the ankles of Arturo and his mates.

Micky would go on and on about the need for the family to lead a return to regenerative farming techniques that employed an "integrated, symbiotic, and holistic system." His father dismissed him outright and happily sent him off to the University of Florida, where he graduated with high honors and a degree in Environmental Science. Worried that he would be twice the pain in the ass once he'd received his degree, Arturo excitedly supported his son's desire to study jurisprudence while simultaneously getting an MBA at nearby Stetson Law.

Of course, this only worsened the situation. Micky began doing pro bono environmental work that often targeted some of the old man's closest friends, particularly those in the phosphate mining industry. When his son eventually filed suit against his own father, seeking an injunction on a plan to expand operations on a portion of the farm that was already fouling the beleaguered DeSoto River, the two entered an estrangement that persisted all the way to Arturo's death.

Micky's father had arranged to sell most of his farmland to development interests and the rest of the business to a multi-national food conglomerate upon his passing, which arrived following a bout of stomach cancer. Micky was convinced that the illness had been associated with the pesticides his old man had regularly employed. While Micky had been cut out of the will, his mother, whose relationship with her treasured son had been deeply strained by her husband's refusal to be in the same room, quickly rekindled their connection and enlisted Micky, the most financially astute of her three children, to manage the considerable fortune Arturo had left her.

A pessimist by nature, Micky was among the first in the state to spot signs of a real estate bubble in the early aughts. Everyone he knew had been building spec houses and expanding their rental portfolios at prices that didn't make sense, given the community's modest wages and the low rents they supported.

"You're crazy," he told his wife, Amber, when she suggested they take advantage of the interest-only bubble loans that had become fashionable and scoop up a few for themselves. "This can't last. How can prices go up if no one is actually buying the houses being built?"

She looked at him like he had two heads.

"Look around, Micky. Everyone is buying them," she said, confused by his logic.

"No, everyone is speculating on them," he explained. "The rents wouldn't cover a traditional mortgage, which is why they're mostly secured by interest-only loans. You securitize the debt and loosen the money supply, and sure, it'll stay afloat for a while. But it's musical chairs, darling. People are buying high with the inflated equity of their previous sale and counting on the next one to inflate just as much. That's just not sustainable. And these debt instruments are vaporware. Once the principal payments come due, bonds will fail, the music will stop, and no one will be able to roll over their debt because the banks won't be able to lend. Just like that, the homes won't be worth half of what's owed on their notes. Mark my words, it's gonna be a bloodbath."

Amber had never been certain just how smart or dumb her husband might be. He knew a lot of stuff, that was for sure. But his opinion always seemed to contradict the other intelligent people she knew, nearly all of whom had much more money than they did. And for all of Micky's railing against his father, the elder Pesch had amassed a fortune, while Micky was a broke lawyer whose small organic farming operation was lucky to break even in a good year.

That all changed, however, when the music did indeed stop. The once-wealthy speculators were suddenly flat broke, trying to sell off houses, boats, Hummers, Corvettes, and other toys, ranging from luxury RVs to tricked-out Harley-Davidsons, in an economy where nothing was moving. The bottom fell out of the housing market, and tens of thousands of homes across the county soon became vacant and were in foreclosure.

"Will we be alright?" she asked Micky one night as they lay in the bed of their modest yet charming mid-century tract home a few blocks from the bay that Micky's mother had purchased for the couple after his father died.

"We are going to be more than alright, my dear," Micky told her.

He was being truthful. As his frustration and conviction grew with every tale of someone flipping a home for twice what they had paid for it six months earlier, Micky began investigating ways to bet against the continued rise in real estate prices. He found it in an instrument called a credit default swap, a sort of insurance against default, in which the purchaser makes a series of payments to the seller in exchange for the promise of a payout should the loan default, typically the face value of the loan.

Micky had invested an unthinkable amount of his mother's fortune into these then-obscure instruments and stood to take a bath on the spread payments until the bottom finally fell out. When the music stopped, Micky Fish found his bony ass sitting in a chair that was big and comfortable. He managed to improve his mother's low eight-figure fortune tenfold, and when she died a few years later, Micky was worth eight figures himself.

Micky wasn't much on materialism but had no qualms about spoiling Amber. He bought her an expensive car and a historic brick colonial on the DeSoto River—at dimes on the dollar in a post-crash "short sale," of course. Amber quickly settled into the life of a wealthy society wife, taking in daily lunches at the country club with the girlfriends she quickly made there, and augmenting her activities with bridge club and pickleball.

No longer under any pressure to make money, Micky hired someone to manage the organic farm and began working on documentary films. His first effort, *Dirty Needle*, was an exposé of Florida's phosphate mining industry, the connection between its toxic discharges and the algae-ridden waters, and alleged cancer clusters near mining sites. He sent free copies to environmental groups all over the state and to anyone willing to host a watch party. It got in front of plenty of eyes, but Micky remained frustrated that no larger call to action emerged.

His next film was called *Breaking Point*. It focused on the overdevelopment of southwest Florida, particularly in Mullet County. While it was a modest success among the no-more-growth crowd, it was poo-pooed by the many folks whose wealth or employment was somehow tied to the development industry and mainly played to small audiences in HOA rec centers and local libraries. His most successful film was called *Poison Pill*, which detailed the state's pill mill crisis. It was shown at three independent film festivals and was credited with helping to create the pressure that ultimately led the state to finally implement a digital registry to curb doctor shopping among oxycodone addicts and dealers.

Micky also sought to revitalize local media in Mullet County. The paper of record, the Mullet County Monitor, had been bought by a large media conglomerate narrowly focused on the bottom line. Its publisher knew that Emblem Homes and Montage Phosphate paid for a lot of space in the Sunday circular, and he made sure the editor in chief handled matters of criticism accordingly. At some point, it became clear that Micky had been blacklisted from having letters to the editor published. Mostly out of spite, he founded the DeSoto Gazette, a small operation focused mainly on issues the Monitor wouldn't touch. He also bought a bankrupt local AM radio station, converting it into WMLT, a non-profit, low-power community FM operation to complement the paper.

****

Local reporter Ally Mason had asked to meet Lars at the newspaper's offices that afternoon. Ally had been a stay-at-home mom and true crime aficionado when she finally decided to try to do something about the blatant corruption that was allowing her hometown to be raped and pillaged by outsiders. She diligently researched how local government worked and started several social media groups, successfully rallying other mothers to the cause.

After writing a few very well-researched letters to the editor that Lars happily published, he convinced her to join the staff as an investigative reporter. At first, Ally, whose upbringing hadn't allowed her to build much in the way of self-confidence, resisted, citing her lack of experience or even a college degree.

However, Lars explained that he didn't have a degree in journalism and hadn't received any formal education in the field beyond his on-the-job training in the military. He noted that, historically, reporters had risen from the working class and that it was only Watergate and the film *All the President's Men* that had led to an influx of Ivy League-trained journalists. In Lars' estimation, this is where things began to go pear-shaped.

"Look, I don't want to unteach some coddled brat who thinks Columbia taught them more than I can," he told her back then. "Most of these kids were born with silver spoons, yet manage to find injustice everywhere they look. In the end, however, they've benefited from the status quo and have been taught to defend it. It's pretty difficult to speak truth to power when all you've ever experienced is being on the side of the institutions and benefiting from them. I want reporters to have known their share of struggle and lived their share of injustice. I want them choc full of piss and vinegar, eager to pick fights with those who hold the real power anytime they abuse it. You fit the bill, young lady. I see it in your work."

Ally came on board and proved to be the missing ingredient. She had a genuine knack for digging, and not only didn't mind the tedium of researching public records and fishing for clues, she rather enjoyed it. Ally also had a motherly quality that put people who would normally clam up at remarkable ease when talking with her. As a result, she developed an impressive array of well-placed, diverse sources within the community. With her on staff, Lars finally started to believe they might pull on just the right threads that would unravel the whole ball of corruption in Mullet County Government.

Although Ally hadn't told Lars why she wanted to stop by the office to see him, he had a pretty good guess. She was married and had two teenage daughters at home. Ally was the nervous type to start with, and Micky's death would have undoubtedly spooked her. Lars was perusing a fishing boat magazine when she arrived.

"Hey, rock star, what's crackin'?" he asked.

"Lars, I'm freaked the fuck out," she said, dropping an oversized canvas bag and placing her keys and a water bottle on his desk.

"Talk to me," he said, gesturing toward the chair across from the desk.

Before taking a seat, Ally grabbed a tumbler and poured two fingers of Rhum Barbancourt, an aged Haitian rum that Lars always kept on hand in a liquor cabinet next to his desk.

Rustic would be a generous assessment of the DeSoto Gazette offices. A more accurate description would be ramshackle. Micky had never been one to spend money frivolously unless it was on Amber. The building was industrial in nature, with mostly aluminum siding and very few windows. He had split off the back two-thirds and rented one space to a marine upholstery shop and the other to an industrious young Mexican man who did an impressive trade selling and repairing new and used tires for the Spanish-only speaking residents of the neighborhood, of which there were plenty.

The front third was split into two floors, with the bottom floor housing the Gazette. The top was home to WMLT, his low-power FM station, which featured daily local news gleaned from the Gazette, as well as some art and cultural programming centered around jazz music and local theater—Micky's two greatest interests outside of politics and the environment.

These days, the offices of the Gazette consisted of a small front lobby that was neither manned nor used; an open office space where multiple workstations once used by reporters now served as a sort of museum, housing decommissioned tech artifacts like old bulky desktop computers with CRT monitors and dot matrix printers, multi-line telephones, and even an old Xerox machine that, in days of yore, had gotten a few employees in trouble during office Christmas parties.

Post-COVID, however, everyone but Lars worked remotely. So, of the two individual offices in the back, one was his, and the other served as storage space for the many useless trinkets that Micky refused to get rid of and Amber would no longer allow at the house.

Lars' office was the only space approaching respectability for a legitimate news publication. It was small but contained a beautiful, antique burlwood desk that some twenty-something stoner had sold him for $200 while cleaning out the house he'd inherited from his recently deceased grandmother. Lawyer lamps illuminated the room, and he had installed a coffee bar complete with a professional-grade espresso machine.

"Sorry, I need a drink. You want one?" said Ally.

"Sure, I'll have what you're having," said Lars.

Ally handed him a tumbler, sat down, and took nearly half her glass in a single pull.

"I was talking to Mike this morning, and we're just really scared that whoever got to Micky might be looking to get to the rest of us, especially since the paper hasn't shut down. My pieces have been the most damaging to just about everyone who would have it out for Micky. If I keep kicking up dirt, who's to say I won't be next, or even my girls?"

Lars sipped his drink and exhaled.

"Look, I'm not gonna sit here and tell someone's wife, let alone the mother of two, that there's no danger in this. I have no idea who killed Micky or why, but we can both make some pretty educated guesses. You're right; we keep pissing on the same trees, and we could be putting a target on our own backs."

"You don't seem nearly as freaked out," she said. "I know you were a SEAL or something, but fuck, I never thought someone would kill people over this sort of stuff."

Lars was a Navy veteran who had relocated to Mullet County from the panhandle after completing his 20 years of service. He'd begun as a Seabee—a stint that included two tours in Afghanistan. An avid newspaper reader, he enjoyed the base papers, even if the journalism was often lackluster.

While stationed in his native Pensacola, Lars frequently contributed to the base publication and immediately wowed his superiors. He enjoyed it so much that he completed the improbable MOS switch to Navy Communications Specialist so he could spend the rest of his career in journalism, eventually becoming the publication's editor while a Chief Petty Officer.

"I was not a SEAL, just a Seabee," Lars chuckled, "but I did make it through wartime deployments without incident, and I am genuinely looking forward to retiring early, spending my days on my fishing boat and my nights trolling the beach bars for wealthy divorcees. I do *not* want to get my ass killed. *That* I can assure you."

Ally finished her drink in one gulp and stuck the piece of nicotine gum she'd removed back in her mouth. With her elbows on her knees, her face fell into her hands and she sighed as she rubbed it.

"I don't think I've got the nerve for this," she finally said. "My girls are scared. They can't believe I haven't quit yet. Mike's the breadwinner. We can get by without my paycheck. Plus, you know that I've been wanting to spend more time with the girls before they get their driver's licenses and boyfriends and have no time left for Mom."

Lars rose, grabbed the rum, and gave each of their glasses a splash.

"How about this?" he said, taking a seat. "You announce your resignation on social media, and then I make note of it in the paper. You stay on the payroll part-time and do some legwork, plus you'll get more time with the girls. You don't have to call anyone yourself, and when your sources call you, you confirm that you're no longer working for us but assure them they can confidentially speak with me or the new guy."

"The new guy?" she asked.

"Micky's wife boosted the budget a bit. She wants to find out who killed her husband and knows that no one at the Sheriff's office is going to be all too interested in closing this case. I know an ex-investigative reporter who's pretty good with this sort of stuff. He all but solved the Zoey Patterson case. I'm meeting with him later this afternoon. I'm also gonna see if we can get a professional investigator on the job, an ex-cop I know."

"I need it to really look like I'm a civilian, Lars. I mean it."

"Christ, I'll pay you in cash if it'll make you feel better," he told her with a smile. "No paper trail. Not even a bank teller can rat you out."

"I don't hate the sound of that," she told him. "Let's try it, but if things get any more hairy …"

"Say no more," said Lars. "One whiff of danger, and I'll shut the paper down myself."

"I die, and I'll haunt your ass," said Ally.

"Deal," he told her and toasted his glass.

For the first time, Lars wondered whether he actually might be in danger as he caught a glimpse of a framed picture of him and Micky, each holding up impressive gulf groupers on the dock of the Pesch's riverfront home. He suddenly missed his friend as the permanence of his departure settled in.

When he retired from the Navy, Lars moved to Mullet County for its leisurely pace, serene natural beauty, and legendary fishing. He'd hoped to get on as a reporter somewhere, but few places seemed interested in a middle-aged beat reporter who they didn't think would be motivated much by the poor pay and crappy hours. But he had built up an impressive nest egg while serving and had his military pension to supplement whatever salary he'd earned, so he was more than willing to prove his worth.

Lars was just about to give up and try his hand as a charter fishing guide when he met Micky at a screening of one of his documentaries. Once Micky found out that Lars had editorial experience, he immediately hired him to run the Gazette, which had been without an editor for nearly two months after the last one died of a massive heart attack. That had been nearly 20 years ago, and there had not been one day since that Lars found himself regretting taking the job.

Lars was smart as a whip but a genuine Florida cracker, a juxtaposition that often caused him to be underestimated, which he routinely used to his advantage. Unless he had to attend a formal event, which was rare, his daily uniform consisted of flip-flops, cut-off and frayed denim shorts, a T-shirt (usually bearing the logo of some dive bar he'd frequented), a gas-station cowboy hat, and a pair of dollar-store aviator sunglasses. If he did have to attend a formal event, he'd don a pair of Levis, his cowboy boots, one of three western shirts he owned, a proper Stetson, and—if it wasn't too damned hot—an old camel hair sport jacket he'd picked up at the Salvation Army store years back.

Wardrobe aside, he was something of a throwback to the golden days of journalism and always felt as if he had been born too late to match his true calling. His office reflected this fact. A matching burlwood credenza that came with the desk had been converted into a dry bar, with the bottom storage space filled with top-shelf scotch, rum, and brandy. A crystal decanter full of Laphroaig 10 was placed on top, accompanied by four matching tumblers. There was even a box of Cuban cigars on his desk. Black and white photos, concert billings, and framed copies of his favorite front pages of the Gazette littered the walls.

Lars enjoyed spending time here as much as at home, especially on the occasions when he could play host to someone, which had somewhat blunted his misgivings about Ally asking him to meet up. Now that he'd talked to her, he was glad she wasn't set on leaving, although he felt a lot more weight on his shoulders.

"Buck up, cowboy," he said to himself, affixing his hat as he began to lock up so that he could head to his next meeting of the day.

****

"Shelton?" the man driving the dark gray Kia asked in a vaguely Eastern European accent.

"Yes," he responded, grabbing the door and quickly putting in some earbuds to discourage conversation.

"Rusty Rudder in DeSoto Village, yes?" the man identified on the app as Igor asked.

Shelton wasn't actually listening to anything, so he reacted to the voice with his eyes and knew he'd have to respond, even though he was hoping to catch some sleep on what would likely be a 40-50-minute ride.

"That's right."

"I've eaten there once," said Igor. "Good grouper sandwich, I recall, yes?"

"For sure," Shelton told him. "The fried mullet's pretty good as well."

"You live down here in Sarasota?"

"Yeah, what about you?" asked Shelton, giving up on the idea of some shut-eye.

"Tampa," said Igor. "I took someone to St. Armand's Circle and was headed back north when I caught this fare, thank goodness. Otherwise, it would have been a bust. I thought they would be a good tipper, but not so much."

St. Armand's Circle was a bougie shopping district on Lido Key, another one of Sarasota's barrier islands.

"Ain't that always the case?" said Shelton.

"What do you do, my guy, if you don't mind that I ask?"

"I'm a journalist," said Shelton.

"Ah, a journalist," marveled Igor. "That's good. Exciting work, no?"

"Sometimes," said Shelton, reminding himself that he was not presently employed in the trade.

"What kind of stuff do you write about?"

"You name it," he said. "I've covered sports, travel, food and wine, music, some investigative stuff. I had a column for the Weekly Planet for a while. It's one of those free papers you see in those dispensers downtown."

Shelton found talking about his work distressing now that he was unemployed. He'd once been proud of his occupation and the small amount of notoriety it had afforded him. Occasionally, an Uber driver or a patron on the bar stool next to him would recognize his face and tell him they liked his work. It was more than enough for him to feel validated.

"I've seen that one," said Igor. "It has ads for gentleman's clubs and massage parlors in the back. It's useful."

Yes, now that the Dr. Feelgood "pain management" ads had dried up, it was mostly the flesh trade and medical marijuana dispensaries that paid the freight for the few free alternative weeklies that managed to stay afloat in the digital age.

"You don't work there no more?" asked Igor.

Seriously? Shelton thought to himself. Either this guy knows the embarrassing story and wants to hear it firsthand, or he has a gift for poking for wounds.

"No, I've moved on."

"Good for you, my friend," said Igor. "I can't imagine they pay good money if the paper is free."

In actuality, it had been the most enjoyable job Shelton had ever held. The money hadn't been great, but it wasn't terrible either, and when you compared it to other comparable gigs, he had been doing far better than most.

He'd been hired as a staff writer, making just $500 a week. But it was his first real writing job, and he dove in with gusto. Within his first year, he had stumbled onto a lead in a local child abduction case that had drawn international attention. True, it was only because he'd begun sleeping with a woman who happened to live in the same trailer park as the young girl's mother, but it put him smack in the middle of the story. The woman convinced the mother she could trust Shelton, and the details she provided in her interviews proved invaluable as he stumbled his way into solving the case—or at least assisting the local police in doing so.

Overnight, he became a credentialed journalist, appearing via satellite on several prime-time cable network shows and writing a feature for Rolling Stone. He even received a small advance to write a true-crime book on the matter, but the publisher went belly up following the downturn after the subprime crisis, before Shelton had even finished his manuscript. He'd hoped Rolling Stone would be interested in bringing him aboard or at least giving him some freelance work, but no such luck.

However, the publisher of the Weekly Planet had been thrilled to have been referenced by so many prominent news outlets and was delighted to have Shelton stay on, even if they didn't really do that kind of journalism, which was fine by Shelton. In truth, he was much happier interviewing local musicians, chefs, and theater directors than doing the deep dives into investigative pieces.

Even after they gave him a prominently-featured weekly column and a significant raise, he would still accept the invites to cover big music festivals, spend a weekend in some nearby beach town on the chamber of commerce's dime for his "staycation" series, or attend the "soft opening" of a trendy new restaurant where there would be heavy pours and samplings from the menu, all gratis.

Shelton had always wanted to be a writer. He studied English literature in college and was involved with theater, where he met Darian, a theater major whose apartment was in the same building as Shelton's. They had both come down from up north to study at Eckerd, a small liberal arts college in St. Petersburg, although Shelton's matriculation followed his stint as a Coast Guardsman.

After college, the couple's plan was for Darian to try to break into the surprisingly robust southwest Florida theater scene while Shelton worked on his first novel and supplemented his income with journalism or bartending work. As the real estate market rapidly expanded following the Great Recession, however, Darian got her Realtor license to take advantage of the profession's flexible schedule, which would make it easier to audition for roles.

Before long, Darian became a real estate broker. She soon had three agents under her and was making money hand over fist. Darian convinced Shelton to become a mortgage broker so that she could refer clients to him and they could keep more of the money under their roof. Shelton hated the idea of working anywhere near the real estate industry, but she argued he could earn more money in far fewer hours, giving him additional time to work on his novel.

By the time they married, it felt like Darian already had one foot out the door. She spent far more time chasing leads and socializing with other people in the industry than going to concerts, plays, and dive bars, the way they had always done. When they met in their sophomore year, she had a pink stripe dyed into her blond hair and a nose stud. She wore a black leather jacket with a white Misfits logo stenciled on the back. That woman drove him wild. By the time she told him she was unhappy with his lack of growth and ambition and wanted to try some time apart, she had morphed into a silicone and filler-enhanced pant-suit Barbie he could barely recognize.

Shelton's phone rang. It was the ringtone that signaled his ex-wife. His neck stiffened as he answered.

"Hello."

"These pictures are shit, Shelton. The lighting sucks."

"You said you needed them today," he told her. "The light had already passed. I can get you better ones, but not until the morning."

"They'll work for now, but I need them redone by close of business tomorrow, or I'm not gonna Venmo you the money."

Shelton rubbed the bridge of his nose and, through the rear-view mirror, caught a sympathetic look of male solidarity from Igor.

"I told you the light would be challenging if you needed them tonight," he told her, attempting to moderate the frustration in his voice with little success. "You said you didn't care. You just needed them tonight. I got them to you, shitty light and all. You want me to go back, fine, but that's another gig—one that I expect to get paid for. Now, if you'll please

Venmo me the money for these pics, which I dropped everything to go and shoot, I would be grateful."

"Dropped everything?" she asked, sarcasm falling from every syllable. "As in dropped a can of shitty beer or your hands from some barfly? Don't forget who's doing who a favor, darling."

This was too much for Shelton to bear, even facing homelessness.

"You know what, Darian, do me a favor, and don't do me any more goddamned favors!" he screamed, hanging up the phone and immediately regretting his words.

Darian wasn't Shelton's only friend, but she was one of a shrinking number of people in his immediate circle inclined to do him even a modest favor, let alone with the means to throw him some work. He felt himself filling with anxiety as he silently prayed that Lars would have something substantial enough for him to refrain from having to call her back anytime soon.

"Forget it, my guy," said Igor in his thick accent as Shelton rubbed his palms on his face. "My wife is the same way, always bustin' my hump. Women, am I right?"

****

Ringo could feel his armpits and crotch moisten with sweat as he tried to adjust the rear-view mirror in a manner subtle enough that the state trooper on the motorcycle behind him might not notice. The trooper was speaking into the microphone attached to the lapel of his shirt, undoubtedly calling in the plates so that dispatch could determine whether the driver he'd pulled over had any outstanding warrants or the car had been reported stolen.

He wore gold-framed aviators with dark green lenses, but Ringo was all but certain the cop was looking right at him and had grown suspicious from his repositioning of the mirror.

Ringo had crossed the Texas state line about an hour earlier, but that only meant he was dealing with Louisiana law enforcement. While that may have been only a shade less daunting than an encounter with the Texas Highway Patrol, he could at least be glad that it was the back end of his trip, and he was carrying only cash. Upon completing a more rigorous mental inventory, however, he reminded himself that it was not entirely true.

The UT Austin students Ringo had sold the Florida medical marijuana products to had given him a small Tupperware container filled with pot brownies they had made with the last of the weed that remained from his previous visit. Ringo had thought it a kind gesture at the time, but now found himself mentally calculating whether they likely contained enough THC to be considered possession with intent to distribute and what the Louisiana penalty for such an infraction might be. He'd already eaten one of the eight squares to mellow him out for the ride and, in his edible-enhanced state, decided that munching as much of the rest as time would allow would be the best strategy to avoid serious jail time.

The Tupperware container was on the passenger seat. Ringo carefully slid it closer to him, removing the lid without making any movements in his torso or neck, so as not to alert the trooper who was still running his plate. Once the lid was off, he grabbed two more of the small squares in one of his giant hands, bringing them up along the center of his chest before shoving them in his mouth and attempting to choke them down with a minimum of chewing.

Ringo glanced in the mirror once more as he slowly repositioned his hand to grab two more squares. The trooper was stepping off his rig and walking toward the car, but in a gingerly fashion that suggested he was none the wiser. Ringo shoved the next two squares into his mouth.

"Hey, what are you doing? Hands on the steering wheel," screamed the trooper as he broke into a gallop, placing a hand on the butt of the large pistol in his holster.

Ringo got the squares down, though he choked a bit as he swallowed, letting out what sounded like a cough. Surely, it would give him watery eyes, he thought, the paranoia blossoming under the weight of the first square he'd eaten just after crossing the state line.

"What did you put in your mouth?" the trooper screamed, hand still on the gun as he arrived at the window, which Shelton had opened as soon as he'd seen the lights in his rear view, lest any lingering smell of bud remained in the car—a white 1987 Pontiac Fiero with bald tires and a primer gray front driver's side quarter panel that the giant man barely fit into.

"Just a brownie," said Ringo, his words thickened by the stickiness of the bits still bound to his tongue and the roof of his mouth.

Ringo, hands still gripping the wheel, nodded toward the open Tupperware container now containing three squares.

"I'm gonna ask you this once, sir, and I suggest you give me a truthful answer," barked the trooper. "Do you have any weapons or illegal drugs on your person or in this vehicle?"

Ringo was something of a firearms enthusiast, but he knew that crossing state lines with both guns and drugs meant all kinds of possible repercussions. He hadn't anticipated any trouble with the wanna-be hippy college kids he would be dealing with for the third time, so there were no weapons in the car presently, aside from a blackjack under his seat and a Bowie knife in the frunk, which couldn't be searched without a warrant and didn't count as a concealed weapon since it was not within arm's reach. Fortunately, it was the return trip, so there were no drugs aside from the pot brownies … except for the LSD.

Just then, it hit him like a ton of bricks. Five tabs of sunshine acid were tucked inside a worn open seam in the brown leather correspondent's satchel that held his registration and insurance information. The cop's discovery of it would be next to impossible, but in his THC-induced anxiety, Ringo began sweating more furiously, his brow immediately leaking down his face.

"No, of course not, officer," said Ringo nervously.

"Have you ingested drugs to prevent me from discovering them, son?"

Did this guy have ESP?

"Drugs? Officer, I'm on my way back from Texas," said Ringo. "I was visiting my grandmother in Abilene. She's got the cancer and isn't long for this world. She made me a batch of my favorite homemade brownies, thought it might be the last time she would be able to …"

Ringo put his hands to his eyes and conjured a few tears, helped along by his already watery eyes. The officer softened his stance and let down his guard.

"They're delicious. Would you like one?" Ringo asked, immediately wondering what in the good lord's name he could have been thinking to say something so stupid.

"Thanks, but, uh, we're not supposed to, you know, in case, you know..."

For some reason, Ringo simply couldn't help himself.

"In case they're laced? Dear lord, what kind of idiot would give drugs to a police officer?"

The officer seemed uncertain, but Ringo detected unmistakable salivation from his mouth, and the somewhat rotund man looked like he had not missed many meals.

"They do smell rather tempting," the beefy cop giggled.

Ringo offered the container forward, and the officer took one square, immediately sinking his teeth into the delicious baked good and inhaling it in just two bites.

"Damn, son, your grandmother sure can bake," the officer said, mouth still half full as he continued chewing. "Bless her heart."

"Wow, you scarfed that right down, officer," said Ringo. "I told you they were legit. Here, have another."

****

The Reverend Billy Sunday was enjoying a solitary laugh when he exited the Bearded Clam, a decidedly low-end "gentlemen's club" on a blighted portion of the Tamiami Trail in unincorporated Mullet County. Affixing his Stetson cowboy hat, he was caught off guard by the sound of a familiar voice.

"Well, howdy there, Reverend."

Scotty Bellwether, a twenty-something-year-old member of the reverend's congregation, was carting a dolly stacked with cases of Miller Lite and Mich Ultra that he was to deliver to the club on behalf of Whitehead Distributing. The reverend had sternly warned his congregation about patronizing such establishments, so he'd never worried about running into one of them on his weekly visit, but he had not accounted for such chance encounters.

"Scotty, thank god you're here on business, young man. This den of iniquity is no place for a proper Christian," the reverend told him. "In fact, I ought to talk to Mr. Whitehead about dropping the accounts of such establishments. I'm all for capitalism, as you well know, but there might be less call for such debauchery if there were no booze to tame the shame associated with such putrid sin."

"I don't know, Rev, they got an awfully big account," said the young man.

"I bet they do," said Sunday, spitting on the ground in disgust.

"Mind if I ask what you're doing here, Reverend?" the young man inquired.

"Me?" Sunday asked indignantly. "I'm saving souls, my son. This is a house of sin, a temple to the flesh trade. Poor, young, vulnerable women are being exploited within these walls, getting trafficked for the pleasure of vile sinners. Neither Sodom nor Gomorrah ever knew filth like this, I assure you. It's wretched work, but the bible tells us that godly men must meet the devil where he is."

Sunday pressed his hands together in prayer, raised them high, and closed his eyes for effect.

Scotty wasn't sure what to do, so he bowed his head and gave Sunday an "amen" once the reverend seemed to be finished.

Just then, a young dancer, still wearing only heels, her thong, and sparkly pasties, poked her head out the door.

"Reverend Sunday, you forgot this," she said, handing him a bolo tie with a bright smile.

The Reverend blushed and accepted the tie.

"Uh, thanks, Candy. Now, you remember what we talked about, and I hope to see you at church this Sunday," he stammered.

The woman looked confused but smiled, waved goodbye, and ducked back inside.

Reverend Sunday looked to Scotty.

"Now, you be careful in there, young man," he told the boy while shaking the bolo tie in the air and looking toward the heavens. "The lord sees all. Eyes down until you get to the cooler, lest he turn you to sand like he did Lot's wife or even strike you blind for peeking."

"Yes, sir," said Scotty, making a silent vow that he'd only risk one of his eyes via the peripheral view.

Sunday blessed himself as he trotted off toward his white Lincoln Navigator, which had vanity plates that read, RISEN.

****

It was 3 p.m. when Lars pulled into what had been the "Ramblewood Motel" in his pale red 1976 Jeep CJ-5. The motel, which sat on a bay-access canal near the causeway, had been condemned when Lars found it for sale by a bank shortly after moving to Mullet County. It had been vacant for years and needed a new roof and serious mold remediation, but Lars negotiated a price that wasn't much more than the land itself was worth at the time.

Banks weren't crazy about making a mortgage on such a property, but Lars had enough savings from his Navy career to put 20 percent down. The county was still recovering from the Great Recession at the time, and prices remained depressed as few properties moved. With Micky agreeing to co-sign, it was enough to secure a loan from one of the local banks.

There were originally eight motel rooms, but the mold was so pervasive on the far-end unit, where the roof had essentially collapsed, that it had to be effectively cut off from the structure. Of the seven rooms that remained, Lars converted the first three into a decent-sized one-bedroom apartment for himself, leaving four small studio units for him to rent out.

The Kelly green sign in front of the modest building still stood, though he had painted over the white letters of the word "motel." He liked the sound of *Ramblewood* and would regularly refer to it as such: *I gotta drop by Ramblewood and grab some papers, and then I'll meet you at the office.*

As he pulled into the gravel lot, Lars noticed a late-model white Camaro with black wheels and racing stripes parked in one of the spots. He recognized the car as belonging to Pauly Miguel, whom he'd arranged to meet up with.

As was often the case, Jerry, one of Lars' tenants, was standing sentry in the parking lot. Jerry was in his late fifties. Standing about 5'9, he tipped the scales at just north of 400 pounds. A plethora of obesity-related health problems had shifted him from the workforce to a Social Security disability income decades earlier. Exactly how Jerry managed to stay alive genuinely baffled Lars, who, on three separate occasions, had either phoned 911 or driven him to the ER himself during a cardiac event.

"Hey, partner, how are you doing?" Jerry asked with his unwavering Midwest congeniality as Lars climbed out of the Jeep.

"Hanging in there, buddy, how about you?"

"Just another beautiful day in paradise is what I always say," answered Jerry. "I just got done with my laps around the lot. I'm on doctor's orders to get a little cardio each day. I can't do much, but I add a few steps every time. I'm up to three laps now."

"Good job, pal. Keep it up," said Lars, moving quickly to his door before getting entangled in a conversation.

Lars felt bad for his tenants. It was obvious that they were all terribly lonely, but each suffered from the sort of personality defects that prevented them from getting along with each other, even for the sake of company, which each of them desperately needed. As a result, they were always eager to engage their landlord.

Once Lars had finished the work of fashioning his own apartment, he made modest modifications to the other four units. Drawing on his construction experience with the Seabees, he was able to do nearly all the work himself. He added a little kitchenette to each unit, consisting of a small, upright refrigerator and a two-burner oven about half the size of a standard version, with a microwave mounted above. Lars converted the motel-style sinks to the deep-basin industrial kind, since there wasn't room for a dishwasher, and added heavy-duty garbage disposals.

The rooms were turnkey furnished, outfitted with love seats and recliners he'd found at Salvation Army and Goodwill stores. They came with a dorm-sized extra-long single bed meant to discourage overnight guests, which the leases prohibited. Once they were complete, he deliberately set the rents well below market as he felt renters would be more likely to accept the somewhat strict rules if they knew they were getting a deal that wasn't available elsewhere. Micky, whose passion for affordable housing had seen him acquire an extensive portfolio of modest 3/2 mid-century block home rentals, gave him three pieces of advice regarding tenants.

Rule 1: Don't rent to couples, especially young ones. Domestic disputes are the number one cause of calls for service to the sheriff's department. Once a property was deemed a pain in their ass, it often—and not coincidentally—led to chronic visits from code enforcement. Because the Mullet County codes were so vague and scattershot and were written long after these older properties had been built, a code enforcement officer could easily find half a dozen violations to fine you for on every visit, especially if it gets them in the good graces of a few deputies, considering that code enforcement was something of a waiting room for entering actual law enforcement.

Rule 2: Don't rent to young men … or women. Single men and women in their 20s and 30s like to party and have guests over late. They like to have the opposite sex spend the night, all of which can easily lead to calls to the sheriff's department. And while the leases specified "single occupant only," that wasn't technically enforceable under Florida law, which runs into Rule 1. Call it a "55-plus community" and save the headaches.

Rule 3: No long-term leases. Florida has pretty good landlord protections, and if a tenant is on a month-to-month lease, you only need to give them 14 days' notice to vacate unless the lease specifies otherwise. Hope they stick around, pay their rent on time, and stay out of your hair, but make it easy to cut bait if they don't. Expect them to owe you rent and steal everything that isn't nailed down before they depart, so only furnish the units with cheap wares that can be recovered via the security deposit.

After mere months, Lars devised his own rule number four: no women of *any* age. One of his early renters had been an elderly woman named Shirley. Lars felt bad for her because she had been a housewife for most of her life and hence had only a very small survivor's benefit from Social Security after her husband died, with only $20,000 in life insurance against $10,000 in debt. Lars even knocked $50 off her monthly rent.

However, he quickly learned that the expectations and hence complaints of one female tenant vastly outnumbered those of the three males combined. A faucet was dripping (three to four drops after it was shut off), and the toilet didn't *sound* like it was flushing correctly. She'd seen a cockroach (in Florida!) and all other manner of pains in his ass that cost him far more in time than her meager rent was worth.

Unwilling to kick an elderly woman to the curb, he finally caught his break when her senility took hold. She'd been complaining about the cable being fuzzy, but wouldn't let him into the unit to take a look. Before calling the cable company, he insisted on seeing it for himself, and she finally relented. When he discovered that it was only one Christian broadcast channel high up in the stream that had a bad signal and was coming in the same way on every television, including his own, he tried to explain that it was the signal the station was transmitting to the cable company and couldn't be fixed on this end.

Unconvinced, "Squirrely Shirley," as the other tenants referred to her, began calling Lars at all hours of the night, accusing him of climbing up on the roof (she could hear him) and jostling the cables just to mess with her sanity. Never mind that the cables ran underground. When it became too much to bear, he dug up her lease to find the emergency contact, a niece in South Carolina. It turned out the family had been attempting to put her in a retirement home, and she ran off to Florida in protest, breaking contact with all of them. They eventually got her Baker Acted, and whether she went to a home or to live with relatives, Lars couldn't say. However, he did know he wasn't going to rent to another female.

As a result, Lars wound up with a revolving cast of male tenants who were in their sixties or seventies and had a certain distinct personality common to those who find themselves estranged from ex-wives, kids, other family and friends, living alone in a furnished 450-square-foot efficiency apartment at that stage of life. A personality disorder would probably be a more accurate description. In their estimation, they had all been wronged by a world filled with lesser people than themselves conspiring to do them wrong. *Fuck it*, they told the world. I don't need anyone.

Except they *did*. The hermit construct was a myth in Lars' experience. Humans are social animals, and each one of them craves human interaction. The problem was that the only way these poor souls knew how to interact was through conflict, so Lars spent too much of his time mediating childish disputes between lonely old men. But they paid their rent on time, and a firm "knock it off or your 14-day notice will be tacked to your door," would always settle them down, especially since the recent Mullet County real estate boom meant they could expect to pay more than twice as much in rent for something similar.

Presently, in addition to Jerry, there was Bryce, a 60-year-old conspiracy theorist/born-again Christian who'd done hard time in his youth and found God (along with the Illuminati) while in prison. Bryce was an arch-conservative, owing to two experiences. First, being a man of very slight stature, prison had been brutal, leaving him with a deep disdain for homosexuality of any sort. He was further radicalized when his wife, whom he'd met post-prison, left him after a "tree-hugging liberal," who was "probably a dike" in his estimation, "put all kinds of leftist ideas in her head." Bryce, too, was living on SSDI, though for what disability Lars could not discern.

There was also Larry, a functional alcoholic, who, while amicable enough, was the first tenant in some time to be chronically late on rent. Larry wasn't quite old enough to collect his Social Security, nor had he managed to find another way to get on the government dole. He'd lost his license permanently after his fifth DUI and would ride his bicycle to various nearby jobs he would manage to get, if not keep. Larry had been a cashier at a nearby Circle K, a "sandwich artist" for Subway, and even peddled himself 11 miles away to a wicker furniture factory in one of the county's industrial corridors. However, an impressive ability to sleep through alarms had seen each gig end in short fashion. Lars knew he would soon have to evict Larry.

Old Joe, who'd occupied the final unit, had recently expired in his apartment. No one could say precisely when, as Joe, 94, often went days without being seen or heard from. Lars discovered his corpse after Bryce, who had the unit next to Joe, began complaining about an acrid smell. Lars hoped it was just a possum that had died in the crawlspace, but even as he was low-crawling under the building, he somehow knew it was old Joe, who was bluer than the Gulf waters when Lars discovered his body.

As Lars passed through the front of his unit, he grabbed two bottles of Yuengling Lager from the fridge. Skilled at all matters of carpentry, his 1,300-square-foot apartment was rather impressive in a rustic way, and he always took a moment to admire it upon entering. He'd laid floors made of ancient cherry wood salvaged from a Tampa bowling alley that had closed around the time he bought the property.

Lars had used broad planks of salvaged wood to create plank-board ceilings and shiplap walls. Half of the unit made for a large bathroom, bedroom, and walk-in closet. The other half contained a small kitchen and a rather large living area, where his 75-inch TV and considerable barbecuing skills created a popular spot for Super Bowl gatherings.

The halves were connected by recycled barn-style sliding doors, and there were large, glass, sliding pocket doors he'd installed on the back wall of both sides that faced a bay-access canal at the rear of the property, where he docked his small fishing boat, a kayak, and a canoe. To discourage visits from his tenants to his tranquil little respite, the backside of the other units remained free of exits.

Ramblewoods' colors were white and shades of blue and green sea foam pastels. Everything about the place suggested you were near water, down to the decorative life preserver, starfish, and nautical maps decorating the walls of the units.

Lars opened his back sliders to find Pauly Miguel sitting in one of the navy blue Adirondack chairs facing the canal, talking on his cell phone. When Pauly heard the doors, he told the person on the other end he had to go and hung up.

"Hey, old man," said Pauly. "I hope one of those is for me."

"Sorry I'm late," said Lars.

"Nah, I was early," said Pauly, flashing a big, bright smile. "I'd had a lunch meeting on the island and had some time to kill."

He stood, and the men shook hands before taking seats.

Pauly Miguel was a short, muscular Hispanic man. A former Mullet County Sheriff's deputy, he'd gone to work as a private investigator, primarily working for insurance companies, bail bondsmen, and attorneys. Pauly had been a state-champion wrestler at Mullet High and then an All-American for the University of Florida. After college, he learned Brazilian Jujitsu and some Muay Thai, and even had a brief career in the UFC. Pauly was only 5'8 and weighed no more than 160 pounds, which was still 20 above his fighting weight. However, barely into his 30s, he could take down most men twice his size with little to no effort.

"I'm sorry to hear about Micky," said Pauly, raising his green bottle. "He was a good man."

"He sure was," said Lars as they clinked bottles.

"Any thoughts on who was behind it?" asked Pauly.

"I got thoughts, probably the same as everyone else's, but if I had more than that, I wouldn't have asked you to drop by."

"I figured as much," said Pauly. "How can I help?"

"Amber Pesch wants to know who killed her husband, Pauly," said Lars. "She's cracked open her checkbook and given me a mandate to use all of the paper's investigative resources to turn up whatever we can, maybe even pique the Fed's interest."

"You got Ally," he said. "Between the two of you …"

Lars gave him a grin.

"We need more than that, and you know it," said Lars. "I was hoping I could hire you to help us out."

Pauly sighed.

"I'd love to help you, brother. I really would, Micky was a friend. I mean that. But I have so much on my plate right now, with the second kid and all, I've been looking for someone to help out my damned self."

Lars shrugged and let out a sigh.

"What if we were able to help each other out?" Lars finally said.

"How so?" asked Pauly

"Ally is taking a leave of absence, at least publicly," explained Lars. "She's freaked out and is rightfully worried about the safety of her family. You know she's the best investigative journalist around. What if she could help you out part-time—skip tracing and that sort of stuff? She can take all the tedious stuff off the table, freeing you up for at least a little work for us."

Pauly turned it over in his head for a few moments.

"If she can give me ten hours a week on your dime, I can give you five hours a week on mine, totally dedicated. Money needn't change hands. Would that work?"

Lars smiled and extended his hand.

"It'll have to."

Pauly took a long pull from his beer, admiring the serene view.

"What did you pay for this place back when you bought it?" he asked.

"Just over 300k," said Lars.

"Mind if I ask what you owe?"

"Nothing," said Lars. "I've put every dime of rent into the principal from day one. Finally paid off the note a few months back."

Pauly whistled.

"Damn, thing's gotta be worth over a million with what land is going for these days."

Lars shrugged.

"More or less. I get offers almost every week. But what am I gonna do with a million bucks? Buy a condo on the island or one of Ignacio's McMansions out in east county? No place to put my boat. Besides, where would my derelict tenants go?"

"Touché," said Pauly, toasting the last sip of his beer toward the dock.

****

"You ever just feel like you were meant for something different?" the motorcycle cop asked Ringo as they shared a bag of Cool Ranch Doritos that had been stuffed into the tiny space behind the Fiero's passenger seat.

"Not for one moment," Ringo said with confidence as he clicked off close-up shots of the officer with a vintage Canon 35mm camera. "I was born to be a photojournalist."

"Man, I envy you, Ringo," said the cop, staring at his hand intently as he waved it slowly in front of his face. "You got it all figured out."

"Most of it," agreed Ringo. "There are still a few parts of the metaphysical I'm working on, but, for the most part, I've been closing in on all of the universal truths as of late."

"Did I tell you how I became a motorcycle cop?" asked the officer, who had told Ringo his name was Fred right after the brownies took hold. With a sudden urgency, the cop had asked if Ringo would mind if he sat down in the passenger seat for a few moments to collect himself because he was feeling "sort of funny."

"No, Fred, you haven't, but I'd love to hear the story," answered Ringo as he switched out camera lenses and put in a new roll of film.

"I started out wanting to be a stuntman or even one of those circus bikers who do those tricks inside the chain link sphere on those tiny dirt bikes."

"An honorable trade, either way," said Ringo, still snapping shots furiously.

"But I couldn't break into either business. After a while, my folks started pestering me to do something other than ride my dirt bike all day, practicing tricks for a career that seemed hopelessly out of reach."

Ringo grew excited as he saw the bleakness of the man's plight manifest in the viewfinder. He was getting terrific shots.

"So, here I am," the officer said wistfully. "Some days, I just want to take off my uniform and cut a path on that rig straight to Mexico. I know a little Espanol from high school. I don't imagine their film industry is as highfalutin' as Hollywood. I could be a stunt driver, or I might even get a chance to do some regular acting, you know, Gringo parts. I don't imagine they got a lot of Anglo actors down there."

"I can't speak for Mexico, but I've got some connections in Bollywood," said Ringo. "How's your Hindi?"

"My what?"

"Never mind," said Ringo. "Mexico it is."

Ringo peeled off five twenties from his wad of weed cash.

"Here, it's not much, but it'll pay for enough gas to get you south of the border and probably a few nights in a motel. It shouldn't take you long to get noticed."

Fred looked at Ringo with pure platonic love in his eyes. "You'd really do that for me?" he asked.

I probably shouldn't have given him the acid, thought Ringo. *The brownies alone would have been more than enough.*

Before he could contemplate the matter more deeply, Fred had exited the car, removed his patrol uniform, and mounted the Harley, dressed only in a *wife-beater* undershirt, plaid boxers, motorcycle boots, his helmet, and the aviators.

"I love you, brother," Fred said as he started the big rig, revving it a few times for effect.

"I know you do, Fred," said Ringo. "Godspeed."

The cop began by doing an impressive array of figure eights around the Fiero, which was still pulled over on the shoulder of the interstate. He didn't even seem to be looking as he weaved in and out of the near lane, where cars honked and swerved. Fred was *feeling it*. He was *in the zone*. They couldn't have hit him if they tried.

Meanwhile, Ringo captured the events for posterity with furious clicks of his camera. *I could get a residency with this collection, a Pulitzer even,* he thought to himself.

Chapter 5: Another bite at the apple

When Shelton arrived at the Rusty Rudder, Lars was already waiting at the thatch-covered outdoor bar, watching CNN on a flat screen above his seat.

"There's our guy," said Lars, standing to shake Shelton's hand and give him a bro hug as he approached. "It's good to see you, brother."

Lars had a bucket of Yuengling Lagers on the table and offered one to Shelton, who complied.

"You look well," said Shelton.

"All this clean living," said Lars with a laugh, as he tipped his bottle. "I took the liberty of ordering some hush puppies to start. I'm sure you know the grouper and mullet are both top-notch fare."

"I was thinking about a pound of the steamed shrimp," said Shelton.

"Well, you can't go wrong there," said Lars, toasting his bottle toward Shelton.

"On the phone, it sounded like you were on the skids," said Lars. "Things okay?"

Shelton's anxiety was running up his back, settling at the top of his spine in the form of a thumping pain. Surely, Lars knew about the incident at the Ringling Museum. *Everyone* in the local media ecosphere was aware of it. Was this some sort of sick mind game, a humiliation ritual?

For the fifth consecutive year, Shelton had been assigned to cover the Gulf Coast Wine Festival, which had evolved into one of the top oenophile events in the industry. Each January, the very best wineries in the world send representatives to the gorgeous grounds of the John and Mable Ringling Museum of Art on Sarasota Bay to make inroads in a state with one of the fastest-growing economies in the world.

The museum features Ca'd'Zan, the couple's opulent Mediterranean Revival mansion, an 18th-century jewel-box theater deconstructed and shipped over from a Renaissance-era Italian palace, and the official state art museum of Florida. The latter sits in a large building Ringling had constructed to house his massive cache of fine art—the most valuable private collection in the U.S. at the time of his death in 1936.

The museum building features two side wings that frame a lush courtyard, the centerpiece of which is one of four bronze casts made from Michelangelo's *David*. The 17-foot-tall, dark bronze replica of the famed marble original is framed by palm trees, with the bay's waters serving as a backdrop. The rest of the grounds are littered with rare statuaries Ringling had collected or had been acquired by the museum after his death. This serene, picturesque setting, combined with Sarasota's comfortable winter climate and its impressive wealth, made for the perfect location. Tickets to the festival regularly sold out in mere minutes.

Shelton had started getting into wine when he was still married to Darien, mostly because of its prevalence at the sort of venues and events that were part and parcel of the luxury real estate industry. He knew nothing when he began picking up grocery store Cabs or Merlots instead of six packs of craft beer, but took a studious approach and eventually discovered a taste for Pinot Noirs from Burgundy and the Pacific Northwest, fine whites and reds from Bordeaux, and—particularly on a hot Florida afternoon—Chenin Blanc from South Africa, French Sancerre, Champagne, and Chablis, as well as Spanish Cavas.

Shelton was woefully underqualified in his first year covering the event. However, not unlike his experience covering theater and reviewing restaurants, he quickly learned that the "experts" in the field almost always lacked the storytelling skills to create entertaining critiques. Most readers were themselves novices seeking to learn more about the subject matter and wanted to go on a journey with the author, not be talked down to with condescending snobbery. Shelton may not have had the technical expertise or command of industry lingo, but he put poetry to the experience, adding context, humor, and personal anecdotes that made the reader feel like they were his companion, coming along for the wild ride.

Winemakers are generally hopelessly romantic souls and showed deep appreciation for Shelton's creative descriptions of their wine and, even more importantly, their stories. He would describe their passion and motivations in such a personal and colorful manner. It was as if the reviews became their postcard biography, told even more accurately than they themselves were capable of communicating.

With the publication of his feature for his first year covering the event, Shelton began receiving boxes of small-batch estate wines in the mail, sent from distributors eager to have him train his prose on their creations. The following year, he was invited to several of the private wine dinners held during the run-up to the big event and was seen as more of a celebrated guest than a rank-and-file member of the media.

By his fifth year covering the festival, Shelton had become something of a minor celebrity, and the entire week of the event provided him with the opportunity to live as a true *bon vivant*. Ringo had been pestering him to use his pull to secure an extra set of credentials, since the festival was the one time each year when members of the press were offered a tour of the museum's roof, which is lined with beautiful statuary.

"Think of the collection I could curate," Ringo pleaded. "I could secure an exposition downtown for sure. Come on, it'll be fun, and you won't have to snap a single photo all day!"

Shelton hated carrying a camera during the festival and usually settled for whatever shots he could get with his iPhone, so he figured it would be nice to have a real photographer at his side to capture quality art for his feature. His ego also told him that he would look like even more of a big shot with a dedicated photographer in his employ.

Ringo got the gig, but that was only the start of Shelton's problems. The event was always held on a Sunday afternoon. The night before, he'd attended one of the event's pre-festival wine-pairing dinners at the Longboat Key Club, with Ringo joining as his plus-one. During the dinner, they had been invited by a wealthy financier to come to his island residence afterward for a private tasting from his extensive collection of rare vintages.

With their Uber fares expensed to the Planet, the two men put away an *unthinkable* amount of wine, Ringo's obliviousness to all matters of vino or its associated customs and faux pas notwithstanding. As a result, Sunday morning had brought the mother of all wine hangovers. While the "Grand Tasting" did not begin until 1 p.m., Shelton had been eagerly anticipating the Champagne De Sousa brunch at the Ritz Carlton he'd been invited to attend at 10:30 that morning.

Ringo, who seemed somehow immune to hangovers, was already awake when Shelton came to. He suggested stopping at Memories Lounge, a dive bar on the Tamiami Trail, for a bloody Mary that might get Shelton's head right. They smoked a joint on the way and had a couple of drinks before hitting the champagne brunch, which proved worth the anticipation.

The only problem was that they were already three sheets to the wind by the time they actually arrived at the festival. It was also an unseasonably hot day for mid-January, and Shelton, who religiously eschewed the practice of using tasting spittoons unless it was to jettison a lackluster offering, found himself properly shitfaced by the fourth and final hour of the event. When even matters of simple conversation with inconsequential people became too much to navigate with his thick tongue and booze-slowed brain, Ringo agreed they should get an Uber back to Memories, where being inebriated to such a degree was not so much as frowned upon.

Walking from the museum entrance to the gates, they encountered a 16th-century bronze statue titled "Zeus

Abducting Europa." It depicted the Greek god Zeus, who'd taken the form of a bull for the occasion, with his new consort tied naked to his back, so that she might be transported to the island of Crete, where he would reveal his true self, consummate the union, and make her the island's first queen.

Shelton thought a shot of him riding the bull would be the perfect author photo to accompany his novel, should he ever actually complete it. Finding the proposition all but impossible, he was not serious when he suggested it. However, Ringo immediately swung into action, calculating both the proper angle and likely response time of the voluminous yet ill-equipped security staff. Before he could get a firm grip on what was happening, Shelton found himself atop the bull while Ringo clicked off dozens of shots. Meanwhile, the security team converged much more impressively than their physical manifestation would have suggested.

"Sir, dismount the statue immediately," a muscular senior citizen riding shotgun on a six-passenger golf cart bellowed into a megaphone as the vehicle approached at max speed. At least a dozen other security guards converged from various angles, some of whom seemed to communicate via microphones at their wrists, as if they were Secret Service agents.

Shelton and Ringo had at least a 50-yard head start, and the gates were only 25 yards ahead of them. Still, the geriatric security team—comprised chiefly of retired law enforcement officers—was closing ranks at an impressive rate. Ultimately, they were able to exit the museum grounds with about 10 yards to spare, and the white Tesla 3 Uber they'd engaged was waiting at the curb.

"An extra 20 if you step on it," Shelton told the Middle Eastern driver.

"You haven't committed a crime, have you?" asked the man sheepishly.

"No!" shouted Shelton. "Not a crime against humanity anyway, more like a crime against art. Not even a misdemeanor, to be exact. Now go, and I'll make it $30—plus you get five stars!"

The driver launched the electric vehicle as the golf cart faded into the distance. Twenty minutes later, they were sitting in Memories Lounge, toasting Maduro Brown Ales, looking at the shots Ringo had captured on the digital display of his camera, and thinking they'd gotten away with a story for the ages.

Within the local art community, however, the escapade immediately became a *cause célèbre*. The next day, Shelton was summoned into the editor's office, where he was unceremoniously fired from the Weekly Planet after the briefest of parting lectures.

"Do you know what the term *priceless* actually means, Shelton?" his editor asked. "I don't mean colloquially, like, the look on his face was *priceless*. I mean, where does the word come from?" he asked with an exaggerated shrug.

They sat in silence for more than ten seconds until he was certain Shelton was not going to offer a response.

"Well, it's pretty simple, actually, although I'd never had reason to give it much thought," he finally continued. "It means that some one-of-a-kind item's value is so *fucking* great, and because there is *absolutely no* supply to compete with, it is worth the most considerable fortune the owner is willing to accept *if* he's willing to accept any sum at all. You can't even estimate its worth. Hence, it's... priceless. That statue *you* desecrated is, in fact, *priceless*.

The editor's face was suddenly sweaty and red. A stroke did not seem out of the question.

"Do you know how many of our advertisers are personal benefactors to the Ringling?" he continued. "Do you *know* how many of our media partners have essential relationships with its foundation? Did you know that *we*, in fact, are the beneficiary of a grant from said foundation?"

"No, and I'm not sure I *desecrated* anything, but I think I can infer that all told, it's enough to make your star columnist expendable," said Shelton.

"*More* than enough," said the editor, clasping his hands as he leaned forward. "Pack your shit, Hamner. You're finished here."

Shelton hadn't realized that he'd drifted off enough to create an awkward silence between himself and Lars, who was still staring at him like he was waiting for a reply.

"Lars, let's not play games," Shelton finally said. "I'm a pariah among the SRQ press, a leper even. I need whatever work you can give me."

"Fair enough, my friend," said Lars. "We don't need to get into the whole thing at the Ringling. I've been the victim of a few self-inflicted wounds over the years myself. Look, here's what I can do for you. I'll give you a thousand dollars a week. You said you're about to lose your place?"

"Yep," said Shelton. "The landlord is cashing out. We're exactly two weeks away from being homeless."

"We?" asked Lars.

"Me and Ringo, my roommate," said Shelton. "He's a first-rate photojournalist and usually helps me with research in the field. Does decent A&E work, too. Any chance you can use him?"

"He's the one who shot the, you know, *bull rider* pic?" asked Lars.

"The one and only."

"Well, I can only hire him part-time," said Lars, "but I'll tell you what. I've got a couple of turnkey-furnished efficiency units at Ramblewood that are about to become available. They usually rent for $700 a month, which is already well below market rate. I'll rent two of them to you guys for $500 each, nothing up front, and give you the first month free so you can get ahead a bit. I'll pay your friend $500 a week. Reporters do their own photography at present, so he can handle the art and do whatever else is needed for your pieces. Sound good?"

Shelton stroked his chin in careful consideration.

"How about this: Ringo gets 'free rent' and $300 a week," said Shelton. "Otherwise, he'll get himself in arrears. Neither math nor long-term planning are among his strong suits."

"That's less total money," said Lars, clearly confused by the suggestion.

"I know," said Shelton. "He's gonna bum a C-note a week off of me either way, so kick me an extra hundred, and I won't have to feel bad when he doesn't pay me back. If he does, I can just be more generous picking up drink tabs, and score some goodwill with the maniac. What do you say?"

"I say this Ringo character doesn't sound very reliable," said Lars. "What kind of guy are we talking about?"

"Think of him as sort of an idiot savant," said Shelton. "Or better yet, an evil genius, which is something we'll likely find ourselves in need of before this thing is through."

Lars stared at him for a moment, clearly having at least some second thoughts.

"I'll have the rooms ready on the day you get bounced," he finally said. "Don't make me regret this, Shelton."

"Never," said Shelton, noticing that Lars had suddenly become engrossed in the flat screen above the bar that was broadcasting CNN.

"A motorcycle patrolman with the Louisiana Highway Patrol experienced what is being called a mental break this afternoon," said a female field correspondent reporting from the site of the incident. "The patrolman stripped down to his underwear and T-shirt, got on his motorcycle, and began performing dangerous stunts amid oncoming traffic in the eastbound lane of Interstate 10 just west of Baton Rouge."

The screen cut to B-roll footage showing a stocky man in white skivvies executing impressive figure eights among a thick onslaught of oncoming traffic. He nearly laid the enormous rig on its side with every weave, but somehow managed to recover and slope in the opposite direction with the grace of a swan each time. As the shot panned out, Shelton noticed what at first looked like a Sasquatch hunched on the shoulder of the highway, only it seemed to be snapping photos of the patrolman. As the shot widened, he saw a gray quarter panel enter frame.

"What do you make of this shit?" asked Lars, fully absorbed by the spectacle.

Shelton panicked.

"Forget that tawdry tabloid nonsense," he bellowed. "Let's get down to brass tacks. Who do you think off'ed Micky Fish?"

Lars' attention quickly shifted back to Shelton.

"Easy, brother. You're not even on the clock yet."

"I'm a pro, Lars. We're always on the clock."

"Well, I admire your style, Shelton, that's for sure," said Lars, toasting his bottle again. "Here, have another beer, and I'll flag down a waitress so we can order. We've got all night to talk about that."

Chapter 6: Debate me, bro

Mullet County Sheriff Ray Brock, better known as Rusty, was serving his sixth and what he had vowed would be his final four-year term in the elected office. His father, Clinton Brock, had been the county's very first sheriff. After a long and somewhat illustrious career, Clint retired strategically, allowing the governor to appoint Rusty, who'd been biding his time as a D.A.R.E officer in local schools, to fulfill the final 17 months of his father's term—one month short of triggering a special election. Seventeen months as a Florida sheriff is enough to collect a lot of favors, which meant Rusty had been a shoo-in for his first election, along with each one since.

The old man, now in his late seventies, was living out his days on a rather impressive 600-acre spread in the far east corner of Mullet County. Despite having been employed only in law enforcement since the age of 18, Clint managed to become a millionaire many times over. He achieved this feat primarily by way of early knowledge as to which parcels of land were destined to increase drastically in value when the interstate highways were being built. He then went to great lengths to purchase them, occasionally using the powers of his badge to strong-arm reluctant sellers. He also made a pretty penny on kickbacks for renting out prison labor.

Rusty had always been in awe of his father's ambitious ascent from the son of a commercial fisherman to a wealthy land baron and had begun devising ways he might amass an even greater fortune even before taking the reins as sheriff.

Clint had built Florida's very first work farm, a model that had since been copied by every county in the state. Short of funding in the county's early agricultural days, the elder Brock devised a plan to save money at the county jail by having the inmates man a working farm on some adjacent land he was able to acquire on the cheap, primarily because of its proximity to hundreds of convicts. This drastically reduced the cost of feeding the inmates, and he soon added primitive factories where guests of the county could produce the jail's mattresses and uniforms.

Rusty took it one step further by starting his own personal cattle farming operation soon after taking office. He placed it on his father's land and under an LLC with which he was not directly affiliated, creating some distance between himself and the enterprise. Despite no previous experience in animal husbandry, Rusty proved to be a natural. His cows miraculously gave birth at about three times the rate of those owned by the jail's work farm. Before long, he had built one of the most profitable cattle concerns in all of Florida.

Every once in a while, one might hear a rumor about a calf being transported east from the direction of the jail toward the Brock's ranch in a white F-250 that looked suspiciously like those deputies assigned to the jail drove and even seemed to sport the same yellow county plates, but no one dared make hay. The sheriff of a large Florida county essentially had a militia at hand, along with a lot of friendly faces on the bench. They could make life truly miserable for the less powerful.

Once the development boom took hold, Rusty also thought it wise that his wife, Sherry, get her Realtor's license and open up shop. When Ignacio first came to Manatee County from Miami, Rusty let him know that he had enough juice with the county commission to get him any rezone or comp plan amendment he required, provided Sherry was given a contract to be the Realtor of record for the development, representing the builder on all sales.

After a while, Ignacio found it more efficient to cut out the middleman and just buy the commissioners outright. However, he was smart enough to still throw Sherry, whose real estate agency had grown into a legitimate enterprise, a generous amount of business while remaining the number one donor to Rusty's re-election campaigns, for which he routinely raised hundreds of thousands of dollars, despite either facing nominal opposition or none at all.

When he retired at the end of this term, Rusty planned to do a lot of fishing while he waited for his father to either die or fall infirm so that he could develop the cattle ranch into an upscale housing development before retiring to some land he'd purchased in Costa Rica.

"Alright, Sosnowski," said Sheriff Brock as he entered the small office with a fresh cup of coffee in tow, "where are we on the Pesch homicide? I've gotta give a press conference in an hour."

Chief Detective Al Sosnowski, who'd had his feet on his desk as he read a file, quickly straightened himself up.

"Morning, Sheriff," said the detective. "I was just reviewing my notes on that case. Everything we recovered inside the file cabinets that washed up was FUBAR, soaked beyond recognition. So far, we've got no prints from the boat other than Micky's, and it didn't look like it had been cleaned in a while, so odds are he had entertained few, if any, guests."

"Any shells?" asked the Sheriff.

"No," said the detective. "We had boats trolling the nearby waters for a full day, but the shooter either recovered them or they've floated out to sea, which seems more likely given the ballistics report's indication of where the shot had been fired. We left word at the marinas and with local fishermen that if anyone encounters floating shotgun shells, they should turn them in."

"That's not much, Soz," said the sheriff. "What's your gut say?"

The detective sighed and gave a shrug.

"Guy had a lot of enemies. The development community, for one, but he was mostly just a pain in their asses. They still got what they wanted nearly every time. Gotta imagine the folks at Montage Phosphate weren't big fans, with that documentary and all the editorials. Still, same thing. They always got their way in the end. I don't see a Fortune 500 company, or a billionaire developer for that matter, taking that kind of risk with nothing but a hassle at stake."

"What about those investors trying to get an Indian casino resort permitted on the island?" asked Brock. "They were rumored to have some ties to organized crime."

Sosnowski shrugged again and made a belabored face.

"Eh, coming at it from that angle might be the best guess, Sheriff, but they're not even off the ground in terms of the application process. Too much would have to happen for them to even get within striking distance, and any whiff of scandal would endanger their chances of getting a gaming license. Maybe if Pesch was somehow the last thing standing between them and an approval, but why kick up that kind of sand at this stage? Besides, nothing about it suggests it was a professional hit. Too sloppy. I mean, a double barrel shotgun blast from several feet away? That's not a mob hit."

"I guess," said the sheriff. "But, in terms of not leaving much behind to get you caught, I'd say whoever it was has been pretty damn effective so far, no?"

"So far," said Sosnowski. "We still got some rocks to turn over, though. How well do you know the wife?"

The sheriff shrugged and gave it some consideration as he sipped his coffee.

"Not well," said Brock. "Ran into her with Micky a few times, fundraisers, galas, that sort of thing. I don't see her as the type that could pull something like this off."

"Maybe she wasn't acting alone?" said Sosnowski. "Weren't they ... *estranged*?"

Sheriff Brock shrugged.

"I mean, he'd been living on the boat, but I've been told they were still very much together," said the sheriff. "They still attended social benefits, and they'd been seen all over town having lunch together regularly right up until the murder."

"He had a lot of money," said Sosnowski.

"Yeah, but he gave her anything she wanted," said Sheriff Brock. "What was your impression when you interviewed her?"

"I mean, she seemed genuinely distraught," said the detective. "I didn't like her for it, but you never know. If there was another man, and we know she had plenty of opportunity with him living on the boat, it could've been they planned it together, and he pulled the trigger."

"There's been nothing suspicious with his bank activity," said the sheriff, "but let's put a tail on her for the next three days and see if she meets up with any suspicious characters."

"Will do," said Sosnowski.

****

After a long night of drinking beer with Lars at the Rusty Rudder, Shelton managed to sleep in until nearly 11 a.m. As was his habit, he rolled from the bed onto the floor, knocked out 100 push-ups, and rolled over for 250 crunches. From there, he quickly donned a pair of running shoes and shorts, affixed Bluetooth earbuds, and cued up a podcast to listen to during his five-mile run.

Shelton had turned 37 that February and found that so long as he performed this routine each morning, drank a gallon of water throughout the day, and stayed away from late-night munchies, it wasn't difficult for someone with his body type to stay at his college weight of 175 pounds, regardless of how much wine and beer he tended to consume, which would be considered by most to be, if not yet problematic, knocking on its door.

He had run cross-country in high school and kept in practice while in the Coast Guard and college. When he fell out of the habit in his late twenties, a paunchy gut that was unflattering on his otherwise lean, 5'11 frame inspired him to implement the daily regimen, and he'd come to feel as though he couldn't quite function at an optimal level without it. A

lapsed Catholic, he was still prone to a bit of guilt over any sort
of good time, so he found the penance of running off a
hangover rewarding on two fronts.

This morning's run had been marred by constant podcast
interruptions, courtesy of the buzz of his text message alerts,
which he was sure were from Darien, regarding the photos she
wanted re-shot. When he finished his run, however, he was
surprised to learn that only the first was from his ex-wife, who
cordially told him not to worry about getting new shots, as the
buyer had already accepted an all-cash offer for above the
asking price. The rest of the texts were from Ringo, who was
day drinking at Memories Lounge and imploring him to drop
by so that he could recount his recent adventure.

At least he's not in jail, thought Shelton.

Shelton had already begun gathering, if not packing, his
belongings even before he knew where he would next reside.
He was relieved that the furnished studios would mean they
could discard the thoroughly spent furniture in the bungalow.
He rummaged through the kitchen gear, found the electric
kettle and French press, and began his morning coffee routine
before jumping in the shower. Ten minutes later, he threw on a
rumpled button-down and cargo shorts, put his coffee in a to-go
cup, told an overexcited Rufus he couldn't tag along, and was
out the door.

It was a gorgeous day, and with the top down on the Mini
Cooper, Shelton took in the tranquil view of the palm tree-lined
streets he'd soon be leaving behind, though he reminded
himself that his new neighborhood would not be without its
charms.

When he arrived at Memories, Ringo was one of three
customers who constituted the early afternoon crowd. He was
joined by an old Mexican man who looked to be sleeping at
one of the tables and a thirty-something barfly sitting next to
his roommate at the bar, barefoot, wearing daisy dukes, a
scissor-altered t-shirt, and no bra. Deep roots were coming

through her bottle-blonde hair, and she lit a cigarette with the mostly spent butt she was just about to extinguish.

Angel, a plus-sized barmaid who socialized exclusively with motorcycle club members, was reading the Weekly Planet behind the bar and nodded to Shelton as he entered. He put his index finger in the air, and she brought him a bottle of Yuengling, a Pennsylvania beer brewed in his hometown, notable for being the oldest brewery in America and for its founding family not having sold out to a conglomerate. A decade back, the family bought the empty Stroh's brewery in Tampa to better serve the demand from PA and Jersey snowbirds, making it easy to find at most bars in the Tampa Bay area.

Shelton was speechless as he took a seat, taking a long pull of his beer while holding eye contact with his roommate, or as close as he could given that Ringo was wearing a pair of knock-off Wayfarers that had a snapped arm held in place with electrical tape. He was a beastly man whose size, shape, and surliness all suggested the outcome of crossbreeding a rhinoceros with a hippo.

"Well, hello to you, too," said Ringo, feigning offense. "I'd like to introduce you to Tina. We met yesterday at Gil's, a nice little dive bar in Ocean Springs, Mississippi."

Tina smiled and sipped a well vodka/soda through a cocktail straw.

"I take it that was after your little adventure in western Louisiana?" said Shelton, cocking his head and gritting his teeth.

Ringo was caught off guard.

"How did you know about that?"

"It made national news, you fucking lunatic!" Shelton whisper-screamed. "CNN!"

Ringo waved him off.

"Bah, no one watches them anymore."

"Fake news," said Tina, nodding her head.

"Can we … have this conversation in private?" Shelton asked while jerking his thumb toward Tina.

"She's totally cool, brother. You can say anything."

"It almost cost us our fucking jobs!" shouted Shelton.

"Jobs?" asked Ringo.

"And our new living quarters!"

Ringo looked to Tina and handed her a five.

"Baby, why don't you go play some music on the jukebox?"

"It's Touch Tunes," she told him. "I already got like 20 songs loaded."

Ringo rubbed the bridge of his nose.

"Then why don't you play some pool or maybe some darts?"

"With who? Him?" said Tina, pointing to the napping senior citizen.

"Play with yourself," suggested Ringo.

"Only if you watch," she said in a sultry voice before sticking out her pierced tongue and rushing in to give the big ogre an unpleasantly wet kiss. Shelton averted his gaze.

"Do you want to explain yourself?" Shelton said in a firm but hushed voice once Tina was gone. "What in the hell are you doing bringing a girl from Biloxi all the way to Sarasota?"

"Relax," said Ringo. "She's cool, and I told you, she's from Ocean Springs, totally different vibe. After the whole incident with the highway patrolman, I needed a drink, plus I had the munchies from the pot brownies we had eaten. I pulled off to get some catfish at this lovely little spot under a bridge. After I eat, I go down the street for a few drinks. It's kind of dead; she's working the bar, knocks back a few shots with me, and, you know …"

"No, I don't fucking know!" said Shelton.

"Well, we started talking about Sarasota. She said she'd never been, and I said, Well, this is your chance. She just quit right then—hopped the bar and jumped in the Fiero. She already had a duffel bag because, you know, she'd been couch surfing, so we were off."

"You brought home a homeless barmaid when we ourselves are about to be homeless? Are you daft, man?"

"Relax," said Ringo. "That's the beauty of it. She's a free spirit. She's not encumbered by possessions and obligations. She'll be fine. Besides, you said something about jobs and a new house?"

Shelton drained his bottle and ordered another with a shot of Jim Beam to settle his suddenly frayed nerves. Ringo signaled to Angel to double the order.

"Lars Henson, he's the editor of the DeSoto Gazette, that weekly over in Mullet County?" said Shelton.

"Yeah, the one that hippie activist started," said Ringo. "I dig their work, even though the art's shit."

Angel dropped off their drinks, and, to Shelton's surprise, Ringo paid from a stack of cash he had in front of his spent bottles, winking to Shelton as he did so.

"Well, good news and bad news," said Shelton. "Bad news is, the hippie activist, Micky Fish, is dead. The good news is Lars offered me a job, and I got you on part-time, so the art just may improve some."

Ringo toasted his bourbon shot.

"I gotta give it to, brother. You always land on your feet."

They downed their shots and chased them with a swig of beer.

"What's the pay?" asked Ringo.

"That's the best part," said Shelton. "Lars owns a small studio apartment complex converted from an old motel on a canal over by the causeway. You get free rent in a furnished studio, all utilities included, plus three hundred bucks a week, just for part-time work. You handle whatever photography is needed and help me in the field when necessary."

"Sounds like easy money," said Ringo. "He's cool with Rufus?"

FAWK!, thought Shelton. He hadn't even mentioned the hundred-pound dog with the sensitive bladder to Lars.

"I forgot to mention that part," said Shelton. "But I'm sure it'll be cool."

"Nice," said Ringo. "Let's celebrate."

****

Tampa Bay Environmental Watch—usually referred to as *Tee-Boo*, the phonetic pronunciation of its acronym—was Southwest Florida's premier environmental watchdog group. With formidable funding from a donor base comprised of wealthy, retired liberals from up north and a surprising number of moderate Republican locals, it had a staff of five full-time and eight part-time employees augmented by over 300 volunteers. TBEW didn't by any means have Ignacio Hernandez-level resources. Still, the group employed highly qualified experts, along with a deep bench of retired scientists, engineers, lawyers, and other knowledgeable citizens who dedicated an impressive amount of time to causes the group took on.

As the wetland issue had arguably been the most audacious environmental pillaging since the draining of the Everglades, it immediately evoked an all-hands-on-deck response from TBEW members. In addition to the more than 50 volunteers from Mullet County who had attended the previous county commission meeting, the group also brought a chartered bus full of members from Tampa and St. Petersburg to bolster its presence.

For the emergency meeting that had been called on this evening, nearly 100 people had packed into the Mullet High School auditorium, which they were able to borrow, knowing that the group meeting space at the local library would not be big enough to accommodate the angry members for the group's first gathering since both the infamous vote and the death of Micky Pesch.

"Alright, everyone, if I can have your attention, please, I'd like to get the meeting underway," said Glenn Patterson, the group's founder. When everyone got quiet and found a seat, he continued.

"I'd like to start tonight's meeting with a moment of silence for Micky Pesch," said Patterson. "As you all know, he was a charter member of TBEW, one of our most dedicated activists and generous supporters. He leaves behind a hole that is too big to fill."

Amen, the crowd said in unison.

"For those of you who attended our candlelight vigil two nights ago, I greatly appreciate it. I know the amazing turnout meant a lot to Amber. If any of you have not yet heard, there will be a celebration of life tomorrow evening at the Universal Unitarian Church in downtown DeSoto. It is scheduled to take place from 6-7:30 p.m. with refreshments and time to commune with each other afterward. I'd sure like it if we could turn out another big crowd. At this point, I'd like to turn it over to Dr. Emily Bartleston to give us a policy update."

Dr. Bartleston dabbed her eyes with a tissue as she moved to the lectern.

"Excuse me, everyone, as you know, this has been a rough week," she told the crowd. "I don't really know where to begin. I would like to note that Mrs. Pesch assured us that she intends to fully fund the legal challenge Micky had begun before his … passing—"

"You mean his murder!" a shrimp fisherman named Pope Wallace called from the crowd.

"Okay, Pope," said Glenn, "I know we're all grieving, but let's maintain decorum."

"Fuck decorum," said Pope. "Ignacio and his goons are behind this. We all know it. How long are we gonna let him rape and pillage this community? I say it's time we feed that Cuban bastard to the sharks."

"Now, come on, Pope," said Glenn. "TBEW is a non-violent enterprise. Most of us are pacifists, like Micky was, because, in the end, violence never solved anything."

"To hell you say," said Pope, waving him off as he headed toward the door. "It sure solved Hernandez's Micky Fish problem."

There were murmurs throughout the room.

"I understand that everyone is upset," said Dr. Bartleston. "Believe me, I do. However, we must stay focused. Now, the item will be brought back before the board at Tuesday's meeting for a second hearing. I think it's crucial that we all show up and let them know we're not standing down. It won't change their vote. We all know that. But there are elections next month, and we need to remind them that this community has the power to vote for change. On that note, I'd like to turn the floor over to Greg Osborne, who's challenging Commissioner Connor Welsh for the Ward 2 seat on the Mullet County Commission."

A fit, clean-cut, middle-aged man in a blue sports coat and white Oxford over khakis approached the lectern.

"Thanks, Emily," said Osborne. "And thank you, TBEW, for allowing me this opportunity. As some of you know, I've been a member for almost five years. I grew up in St. Pete but moved to Mullet County more than 20 years ago when my wife and I decided to start a family because it was the best place on the Gulf Coast to do so. I am deeply passionate about preserving our environmental resources. I have a degree in public administration and spent 10 years as a planner with Pinellas County before going into the private sector, where I currently work for an affordable housing trust. I know that smart growth is achievable because I see it every day. People will continue to move to Mullet County because it's a great place to live, but that does not mean we are obligated to build out at a pace that meets demand.

"There's simply no way to do that and adequately support that growth with infrastructure," Osborne continued. "We need higher impact fees on new development, a temporary moratorium on comp plan amendments until infrastructure catches up, and we have to look at the rural areas of east county that are no longer being farmed as ground zero for the planned development of workforce housing. Mullet County will not be successful if our last green spaces continue to be built out as little more than havens for wealthy retirees and bedroom communities for those who work in Tampa or Sarasota. We need vision, and if you vote me onto the county commission, I promise to do my best to deliver it. When my kids are grown and start thinking about starting their own families, I want them to look at their hometown and feel the same way my wife and I did back then."

Margie Holderman, an officer with the local chapter of the League of Women Voters, was the first to raise her hand.

"That sounds good, Greg, it really does, and you know I support you," said Margie. "Hell, I was one of the first to write a check to your campaign. But I've seen the attack ads coming from Ignacio's PAC. They are brutal, and they are *everywhere*. Tell us, how will you compete with that in a grassroots campaign on a shoestring budget?"

Greg Osborne shrugged.

"I'm not gonna outspend him, that's for sure," he told them. "That's why I'm here tonight, and that's why I've spoken at every venue that will have me. I've been to every housing association meeting, every trailer park, every Democratic group, and every Republican one. I'm a moderate independent, but everyone knows you can't get elected without the party vote, and in this county, that means Republicans. They're hammering me on the fact that I was registered as a Democrat 20 years ago when I lived in St. Pete, a place that is just as blue as this one is red, and the only voice you had was in the primary. Ignacio's people are calling me a socialist and a Marxist who will do everything from raise their property taxes to making drag queen story hour mandatory at all preschools."

The crowd let out a collective chuckle.

"But when I'm out talking to people, they're not talking about those things," said Osborne. "They want to know what I'm gonna do about the gridlock and the need for extra lanes on east-west connectors. They want to know what I'm going to do about all of the dead fish washing up on the beach and the mats of green algae clogging the canals behind their homes. My opponent has been on the wrong side of every vote related to any one of these issues. That's why he's refused to debate me. He's counting on people being lazy and disengaged enough that they can be bought off with slick direct mail pieces and angry robocalls about issues that have nothing to do with the work the county commission actually does.

"I really think people are sick of the divisive red meat issues and are finally paying attention to what's important locally. But I need your help. I need everyone here to talk to five friends, neighbors, family members, or coworkers who don't know about this race and get them wise to it. The deadline to switch party affiliations for the primary election is this Friday. There's no Democrat in this race, and there's not a single competitive primary for Democrats on the ballot. They can switch and then still vote for a Democrat in the general election, but do their part to make sure that the Republican on the ballot isn't a developer puppet. If they're a Democrat or Independent, make sure they know that they won't have a voice in any of the three commission races on this year's ballot. But if they switch, we actually have a shot at flipping this board, and there is nothing more important to their overall quality of life than local government."

The crowd was whipped up into a frenzy that would have made a Baptist preacher proud. Margie Holderman smiled at the candidate from her seat, happy he had followed her lead so effectively.

From a couch in the lobby of the DeSoto Gazette offices, Lars watched the debate between Commissioner Candice Hagerty and her opponent in the Republican primary, Mary Porter, on a flat-screen mounted to the wall. Porter, a retired teacher, was a real pistol, just over five feet tall and nearing 70, but brimming with piss and vinegar. Her campaign account had only a thousand dollars that she had loaned herself, which would be drained once she paid the invoice for yard signs. But she'd worn out two pairs of shoes knocking on doors throughout the ward.

Commissioner Hagerty did not believe Mrs. Porter had a snowball's chance in hell of beating her, but nevertheless took great offense at the idea that someone would actually run against her and in the Republican primary, no less. Hagerty saw herself as the embodiment of the modern Republican woman. Aside from having her highlights touched up, getting a bit of Botox, undergoing some laser teeth whitening, doing a slimming body wrap session, and having a mani-pedi, she hadn't actually prepared for the debate. However, she was confident such superficial preparations would be adequate. They were not.

"Commissioner Hagerty, you voted in favor of, um, altering local wetland protections," said the moderator, Art Pyle, Editor in Chief of the Mullet County Monitor. "Some residents voiced their concerns with the new policy. Would you care to defend your vote to the audience?"

Dressed in her most seductive pant suit set, Candice Hagerty flashed a 10,000-gigawatt smile that was so white it was nearly blue.

"I would be happy to, Art," she said, her eyes locked into the camera. "I am a Christian Conservative Republican—in that order. And I do not condone the government taking of private land, which is what we are talking about. There are children in this community who have never learned to swim because there is not enough room on their family's lot to put in a pool due to some additional buffer space that a bunch of RINOs on previous boards voted for. The great State of Florida, under the leadership of my dear friend, Ron DeSantis, has put in place wetland regulations that are more than adequate. I want to give the land back to the people because I truly believe that's what Jesus would do, and whether I'm on that dais or in my pickup truck, God is my copilot."

The commissioner froze in place and flashed an even bigger smile. It was reminiscent of a contestant in the Miss America pageant. She could not have looked more pleased with herself.

"Mrs. Porter, would you like to respond?" asked Art Pyle.

"I sure would," said Mary Porter, who had been a science teacher at Mullet High School. "Everything she just said was pure, grade-A poppycock! My opponent either knows it and is a liar, or doesn't and is too dumb and gullible to be on an elementary school PTA committee, let alone our county commission. The state minimums are just that—the *bare minimum*. That might be fine for inland counties far from the coast, but we live in a unique and complex coastal ecosystem in which wetlands play a vital role in filtering the runoff from development. The state constitution actually encourages local governments to enact wetland policies that best represent their specific environments, and that's what the previous board, which I might add included Ms. Hagerty's own father, voted for. I suppose *he* was a RINO?"

"You keep my daddy's name out of your mouth!" screamed Candice.

"Ladies, please," said Art Pyle.

"All of this nonsense about the taking of property is just that," said Mary Porter. "What about the setbacks we require?

You can't build a swimming pool less than 10 feet from your neighbor's property line either. No one is hollering about that. What about when the county uses eminent domain for right-of-ways and other public uses? This very board is considering the taking of five entire homes and the land they sit on just to widen the lanes on Banyan Avenue heading into Ignacio Hernandez's latest cookie-cutter development. Where's the outrage and indignation from my opponent on that? Is its absence owed to Mr. Hernandez having funneled nearly $100,000 to her campaign and PAC? And as far as kids learning to swim, LeGrotto has been waiting for a public swimming pool for what, 50 years? I haven't seen a bit of concern from my opponent on that issue."

Candice was infuriated.

"This … *woman* isn't even a conservative," said Hagerty.

"I've been a registered Republican for longer than you've been on this Earth, young lady," said Mary Porter.

"She's a liberal plant!" screamed Hagerty as her campaign consultant, Christopher Bacchelli, closed his eyes and rubbed the bridge of his nose backstage. "The Democrats are trying to steal this election just like they did in 2020! They're trying to get their voters to switch their party registration in order to vote in a liberal like her! I went to Mullet High. I remember you, Mrs. Porter. You were always leading the charge on some cause, getting students all riled up about some environmental issue. I ask you, the citizens of Mullet County, does that sound like a conservative?"

"Well, I remember you, as well," said Mary Porter. "Not that you were in any of my classes—I taught AP Science," she said as she turned from her opponent to the camera. "And yes, while my opponent was busy chasing football players and getting busted smoking reefer in the parking lot during prom, some students felt their formative years were better spent contributing to the betterment of our environment. But as for that being *liberal*, as you put it, I'll remind you that Teddy

Roosevelt—who was a Republican, in case you've forgotten your history lessons—had the greatest conservationist record of all presidents. And it was Richard Milhous Nixon who established the Environmental Protection Agency and signed into law the most pivotal environmental regulations in our nation's history, including the Clean Water and Clean Air Acts. Conservation and Conservatism come from the same root word for a reason. Republicans used to believe that conserving our environmental resources was a sound practice both practically and fiscally. As we have all seen, from the Deepwater Horizon to the numerous gypsum stacks left strewn across our state by Montage Phosphate, it costs significantly more to mitigate environmental disasters than to prevent them. It'll be the same thing with our wetlands. We're already spending a small fortune just removing the dead fish from our beaches and the algae mats from our canals. Tourism is the lifeblood of our local economy. If we further disrupt nature's balance, it will be an economic catastrophe, a big, expensive mess, and there will be no tax dollars to pay for it."

"Don't you dare lecture me about conservatism," screamed Hagerty.

Art Pyle was both attracted to and afraid of Candice Hagerty and had given up any notion of maintaining control of the debate.

"This board has nearly doubled the annual budget!" bellowed Mary Porter. "What's conservative about that?"

"Ladies, please!" Art Pyle implored them.

"You're swamp trash!" screamed Hagerty.

Mary Porter looked her opponent up and down with a shit-eating grin, her eyes finally resting on the pink cowgirl boots that matched her ensemble.

"Anyone can wear a pair of cowgirl boots, young lady," said Porter with a wink. "It don't mean that they're ready to do cowgirl shit."

Just then, the front door of the lobby office opened. It was Ally Mason.

"Sorry I'm late," Ally told Lars. "Where are the new guys?"

"Stuck in traffic," said Lars, eyes still glued to the screen. "They should be here soon."

"I started poking around on some of Pauly's cases," Ally told him. "It's kind of fun."

"Don't go getting too fond of it," said Lars, pausing the video. "I expect you back on the front lines when this whole thing is finished."

"From your lips to God's ears," said Ally. "Is this the debate?"

"Yeah," said Lars. "I was watching the replay on YouTube."

"How about Mary Porter?" said Ally. "That little woman doesn't take shit from anyone."

"She doesn't suffer fools, that's for sure," said Lars as he grabbed the remote control and turned off the television.

"You'd think that with all the people who hate the current board and have real money in this town, she'd have been able to raise some," said Ally.

Lars shrugged.

"Half of them don't want to be seen on her campaign finance report—bad for business—and the other half figure it'll be no more useful than wiping their asses with the money."

Just then, the lobby doors opened. It was Shelton, but Rufus shot past him before he could get in and began sniffing Ally, wagging his tail incessantly.

"Oh, look at this handsome boy," she said, in that talk-do-the-dog voice all dog owners seem to produce on cue. "You smell my doggy, don't you? What's your name?"

"That's Rufus," said Ringo, as he entered behind Shelton.

"I'm Lars," said the editor, extending a hand to Ringo.

"Dr. Ringo Khan," he answered as they shook. "No relation."

"Relation to whom?" asked Lars with a look of genuine confusion.

"A.Q. Khan," said Ringo. "I'm Pakistani on my father's side."

Lars shrugged.

"Abdul Qadeer Khan, the nuclear physicist," said Ringo indignantly. "The father of Pakistan's atomic weapons programs?"

"Ah, yes," said Lars. "And allegedly North Korea's as well, if memory serves."

Ringo shrugged.

"Again, no relation."

"Dr. Khan?" asked Lars. "You hold a PhD?"

"I do," said Ringo. "Well, PhD equivalent, to be precise."

"Excuse me?" said Lars.

Shelton rubbed the bridge of his nose and felt a headache coming on.

"A PhD equivalent from Khan Academy," explained Ringo. "Again, though, no relation."

"Is that the online platform where you can watch classes for free?" asked Ally.

"Exactly," said Ringo. "I don't go in for all of that elite academia bullshit. I'm a proletarian despite my penchant for classic automobiles and vintage wristwatches." He flashed his wrist, which sported a calculator watch, circa 1983. "I've done a PhD's worth of credits in World Studies. I even wrote a dissertation on Dr. Strangelove. It's available on my blog, should you care to peruse it."

"Shelton didn't tell me you had a dog," said Lars.

Shelton shrugged apologetically.

"Yeah, he's a rescue," said Ringo. "*Literally.*"

"How do you mean?" asked Ally.

"I was doing a shoot at this abandoned junkyard near Ocala for one of my early exhibitions, just after I'd turned pro," he told her. "I came across Rufus, who was somehow locked behind the fence. At first, I was confused because he barked so loudly that I thought he was an actual guard dog. Like, maybe I'd gotten some bad intel, and the place was still in business. But as I got closer to the fence, I could see how emaciated he was—probably less than half his current weight. He was barking to get out, not keep me from getting in. So, I went back to my car to get some bolt cutters—"

"You keep bolt cutters in your car?" asked Lars suspiciously.

"Sure, like I said, I'm a pro," said Ringo, his tone matter-of-fact. "So, I cut the lock, and he just runs up and starts loving on me. I go back to the car to see if I have anything to give him, you know, a Cliff Bar or something. The windows are down, and he just jumps into the passenger seat. I didn't have the heart to do anything but drive him home. I got a friend to bring me some dog food, and he just ate everything I put in front of him, lapping up water between gulps of kibble. But there's a problem. He starts passing the food, and it's clear straight off that he's in a bad way. I look down, and I see gravel in his stool. The poor guy must have been so hungry he was trying to eat dirt and grass, and there wasn't much of either in that junkyard. Then he was afraid to eat, so I had to give him little pieces of bacon until he'd passed all the rocks."

Ally was teary-eyed.

"Oh my god, that is the saddest thing I've ever heard," said Ally as she resumed her petting. "He's so lucky to have you. I bet you wouldn't give him up for anything in the world."

"You got that right," said Ringo.

Shelton mouthed *sorry* to Lars, who was clearly perturbed at the prospect of a hundred-pound dog in one of his units.

Once everyone was properly introduced, Lars switched the input on the television to HDMI and brought up some notes from his laptop.

"As you probably know, we're a print weekly that publishes daily online. The print edition comes out each Tuesday, with a hard deadline of 10 a.m. Monday for anything that's gonna be in it. Right now, we've got two big things that we're focused on: Micky's murder and the upcoming primaries, in which a majority of the five seats on the Mullet County Commission will be on the ballot. Republicans hold all three seats. Each incumbent is being challenged in the primary with no Democrats running in the general. But because of the write-in loophole, they won't be open primaries. As a result, a lot of Democrats have switched their party affiliation."

Florida primaries are supposed to be open to all voters when they become de facto general elections. However, courts have held that a write-in candidate, who has to do nothing more than fill out paperwork, counts as general election competition. Thus, the candidate who has positioned themselves as the most conservative or liberal in an otherwise open race typically has a friend or associate file as a write-in candidate to close the primary and prevent their opponent from appealing to voters outside the party by positioning themselves as more moderate.

"Do any of the challengers have an actual shot?" asked Shelton.

Lars shrugged and pointed to the screen where the races were laid out.

"That's hard to say. They're all in their first full term—Commissioner Hagerty served out the last year of her father's term on an appointment from the governor after he kicked. Welsh is intensely disliked, more so after the wetland vote, but he's raised the most money, well over a quarter million between his campaign and PAC. He's Ignacio's point guy and, to him, most important in terms of keeping the seat. Hagerty is trading on her daddy's name, and she's got the MAGA vote nailed down and plenty of campaign cash herself. The reverend has the least amount of money, but only because he's got the weakest competition. None of the challengers are competitive financially, but Mary Porter and Greg Osborne are strong candidates. Sunday's opponent, however, Merle Watts, is a little less … exciting.”

“Listening to him is like watching paint dry,” said Ally.

“Why have the wetland vote before the election?” asked Shelton. “Seems counterintuitive.”

“We're really not sure,” said Lars. “Micky genuinely thought Ignacio was nervous about still holding a majority after August. He's got a couple of big developments in the pipeline that represent the bulk of his remaining Mullet County land holdings. Hell, they might represent the bulk of undeveloped land remaining in the county. He's got a solid 5-0 vote right now. We think he might even go for reduced impact fees at Thursday's meeting.”

“Get as much as he can, hope his majority holds, be ready to sue if a new board tries to roll any of it back?” asked Shelton.

“Yeah, something like that,” said Lars.

“How do you want me to divide my time?” asked Shelton.

“Our local government reporter, Ernie Young, covers the breakout stories from the city council, county commission, and school board meetings,” said Lars. “He'd be here, but he's covering a DeSoto City Council meeting today. He's a veteran reporter collecting a pension from the Monitor. He's part-time, attends meetings, and files a nuts-and-bolts article for each. He has a deep well of institutional knowledge, so feel free to lean on him and Ally for background information. Their contact info is in the email I sent you guys this morning.”

Lars returned his attention to Shelton.

“I'm going to let you do a sort of hybrid column like you did for the Planet—a blend of reporting and opining. We'll talk about what you're looking into on Wednesdays and where you're at with it on Fridays, but I'll give you a long leash. It's how I like to operate. Your column will go live online on Saturday after copy editing is complete, then go out in the Sunday email and appear in Tuesday's print edition. Most people read it online, but there are still a lot of older folks who like a physical paper, and it commands more in advertising rates. You've got the meetings, the election, and Micky's murder to work with, so there should be no shortage of subjects. You can also do shorter, blog-like entries if you come across other notable tidbits that don't make that week's columns. We'll put them up as online exclusives and send them out in a breaking news email to subscribers."

He turned to Ringo.

"I'll email you the assignments we need art for each Friday for the following week. Some will be meetings, some will be A&E pieces. Otherwise, you'll be at Shelton's disposal for photography and whatever else. Any questions?" asked Lars, looking at each of them.

Shelton and Ringo shook their heads.

"Alright then. I sent you the details for Micky's celebration of life tonight. It would be a good idea to come by and meet Amber, offer your condolences. Plus, there's no telling who'll show and what might be overheard."

"Roger that," said Shelton.

****

Once everyone had left the Gazette, Lars cued up the debate between the Reverend Billy Sunday and Merle Watts, a rural farmer and sixth-generation Mullet County local. He fast-forwarded through the introductions and opening remarks.

"Mr. Watts," said Art Pyle, "what makes you think you would be a good representative of Mullet County citizens should they elect you to their county commission?"

114

Merle Watts used the first fifteen seconds of his two-minute allotted time stroking his chin in consideration of an answer.

"Well, I done lived here all my life," said Watts in a slow, rural Florida drawl. "My people been farmin' this land since before there was a county or a commission. Used to be she'd give up bumper crops 'bout every dang year. Then all these Yankee carpetbaggers come down and start wantin' to change how we do things. Now, they've got the water all fouled up and done allowed them to develop too much of the permeable land. It's gotta change, so I aim to do just that. If that sounds good, vote me in. I'll sort things out as best I can."

It was the lengthiest statement Merle had issued during the entire campaign, and plenty of time remained on the clock when it became clear he had said all he intended to. Art Pyle asked Reverend Sunday the same question.

"Thank you, Art," said Reverend Sunday. "First, I want to thank my opponent for not only being here tonight but for deciding to mount this challenge, for I believe that a competitive democracy is the most effective kind. In truth, there's much we agree upon. Farmers are the backbone of this ward and the backbone of Mullet County. Merle here is as fine a farmer as they come by all accounts I've heard. I have been a friend to agriculture and a friend to the family farm, so I am interested in hearing his agenda. That said, no one, not myself nor my opponent, is gonna stop the wheels of progress and change here in Mullet County or elsewhere, for that matter. As the price of land continues to soar, some farmers are gonna decide to cash out while they still have enough youth and vigor left to enjoy the retirement they've earned through their labors. Being such a good friend of farmers, I would never begrudge a single one of them the opportunity to do so. It would be un-American to deny the backbone of our way of life their shot at the American dream, would it not? Now, anyone can buy that land when they sell: another farmer, a local business concern, or a developer who wants to build houses so that newly formed families can have their own shot at the American dream, and we all know that home ownership has always been that dream's foundation. We need responsible growth, and with the Lord Almighty as my witness, I will continue fighting for just that."

"Would you like to respond, Mr. Watts?" asked Art Pyle.

Merle stroked his chin.

"No, sir. I believe I done said all I have to say on the matter."

Lars shook his head. Not wanting to endure further disappointment, he turned off the television set and retreated to his office for a glass of scotch.

Chapter 7: Some itches need scratching

The DeSoto Unitarian Universalist Church was located in a relatively small building in downtown DeSoto, just off the main thoroughfare, Hernando Avenue. While both Amber and Micky had been raised Catholic and Amber was still in the habit of attending a few select holiday masses each year, Micky had left the church decades earlier after the onslaught of abuse cases that were brought to light in Boston.

Still, Micky Pesch was as communal as they come, realizing in the early days of his activism that strength lay in numbers. When he began organizing protests and seeking venues to show his documentaries, he quickly discovered that the Unitarian Universalists were among the most welcoming and supportive groups he had encountered.

Unitarian Universalism is a liberal religious movement rooted in early American Christianity and its humanist theology. Its mantra is to build a platform that fosters a free and responsible search for truth and meaning. Unitarian Universalists aren't defined by a creed so much as by covenants, and they are unified by a shared search for spiritual growth. Most attractive to Micky, they eschewed the practice of holding a sacred text, which he felt doomed a religion by making it difficult, if not impossible, to improve over time.

The turnout for Micky's celebration of life was rather impressive, with more than 200 people filling the main hall while dozens more congregated in a nearby rec room. Knowing she would not be able to manage her emotions, Amber chose not to speak, a decision the minister explained in his opening remarks.

While Micky and Amber had been unable to have children, Micky had two siblings: a younger brother, Thomas, who was a surgeon in Toronto, and a younger sister, Mary, who lived locally and had no occupation to speak of. Thomas was three years younger than Micky and moved to Canada after finishing med school. He met his wife, an Iraqi woman named Samira, while they were both doing their residencies in Gainesville.

Samira had Canadian citizenship and an extended family living in Toronto, and Thomas—who'd never been fond of rednecks, mosquitoes, or the Florida humidity—was agreeable to relocating when they married. Like Micky, Thomas had some difficulty getting along with Arturo Pesch and only visited on occasional holidays so his mother could see her grandchildren. He and Micky remained in touch, exchanging occasional letters, but were never terribly close, owing mainly to the distance and infrequent visits.

Mary, on the other hand, was quite a different story. The baby of the three and unable to do any wrong in her father's eyes, she grew up entitled and unmotivated. She transferred colleges twice but never earned a degree. She got pregnant during college, married and divorced the little girl's father, got pregnant again, and stayed married to the father of daughter number two until he keeled over from lung cancer ten years back.

Never one for managing fiscal affairs, Mary, who'd already been a substantial drain on her father's and then her mother's finances, quickly blew through both of her considerable inheritances and had been making regular monetary demands of Micky right up until his death. Clearly, she was worried that Amber, whom she correctly assumed thought of her as a lazy freeloader, might not be as keen when it came to requests for loans that were unlikely to be repaid. So, while Thomas delivered a short but reverent eulogy of his little brother, Mary poured it on so thick that not even strangers bought it.

Not wanting the sibling eulogies to stand as the sole testimony to her husband's life, Amber asked one of Micky's pals, Dutch Wagner, to give the third and final speech. Dutch was a seventy-one-year-old political consultant whom Micky had befriended years back. A Republican power broker during the Jeb Bush wing of the party's decade of dominance, Dutch fell out of favor after backing the old guard rather than the Tea Party in 2010. However, he took his skills north of the river, where Democrats enjoyed their only small stronghold, reinventing himself as a campaign manager for Black candidates in City of LeGrotto races.

It wasn't the kind of money he'd been used to, but it was enough for him to further pad what was about to be a comfortable retirement. As LeGrotto, more often than not, received the short end of the stick on environmental debacles, his candidates were frequently aligned with Micky, whom he genuinely came to like, even back when Micky was being a pain in the ass to his better-paying Republican clients in DeSoto.

"Well, well, well," mused Dutch. "Now, what can I tell you about Micky Fish that you all don't already know? He was smarter than most Mensa folks I've met," he said as the audience mumbled affirmations. "He was quite likely the most generous man in this county, too. I can tell you stories about little kids in LeGrotto with gaping holes in their tennis shoes who found a pair of new Nikes on their porch one morning or youth teams who were wearing plain white t-shirts and drawing numbers on them with magic markers until Micky found out and put a call into DeSoto Sports and told them to outfit those kids with the best uniforms they had at his expense. He had enough money and sailing expertise to buy a 150-footer, set sail, and spend the rest of his days traveling the world, which I suspect would have suited Amber just fine," said Dutch, nodding to Mrs. Pesch, who smiled warmly. "But he couldn't do that, now, could he? There was too much to be done in his hometown.

"More than anything, however, Micky Pesch was a fighter," said Dutch to a crowd that was beginning to be stirred into a frenzy. "And that's likely just the thing that got him killed," he added to more than a few "amens" from LeGrotto Baptists in attendance. "He took on the good old boys, and I believe he was finally just about to lick 'em, too. The Phosphate giants, the developers, them casino boys, he had them all on the ropes in next month's primary. Now, I don't need to tell you that Micky won't be here to see how that turns out, and I'm sure we have a wide variety of ideas on whether there's a life somewhere else after we leave this Earth. I won't claim to be the most religious man, but I will say this. I believe that when the results are announced on August 3, Micky Fish will be looking down on Mullet County, and I aim to ensure that he sees, as his final reward, the victory for which he gave his life. Can I get an amen?"

The mostly agnostic crowd was now showing all the markings of a Pentecostal tent revival. They were on their feet, hooting and hollering with genuine religious fervor by the time Dutch closed out the show.

After the ceremony, the large crowd gathered in the church's ample outdoor space, where multiple food trucks were set up to serve complimentary smoked barbecue, fried mullet, gulf shrimp boils, and other local delicacies. A beer truck from a local craft brewery was also on hand.

"This was a beautiful ceremony," Lars told Amber. "It's exactly what Micky would have wanted."

"You think so?" asked Amber. "I was debating whether or not I should have had it on the water. We're gonna scatter his ashes into the bay this weekend. I'd like it if you were to join us. We were going to do it from the sailboat, but the deputies said the crime scene would need to be preserved during the investigation."

"Sure, I'd be honored," said Lars. "Wanna do it from my boat?"

"Oh, that would be so nice," said Amber.

120

"Perfect, let me know what time and I'll dock at your place to pick everyone up," said Lars, who was wearing his good Stetson and best boots for the occasion.

"Well, if it ain't my favorite editor-in-chief," said Dutch as he approached. "I'm glad to see this old girl is keeping you and that rag of yours in business."

The two men shook hands.

"It's good to see you, Dutch," said Lars. "How are you doing?"

Dutch pulled the Tootsie Pop from his mouth, a device that had kept him off cigarettes for the past five years since the emphysema diagnosis.

"Me? I'm doing *real* good," he said in what had long been his standard response. "I got a slate of good candidates north of the river from the school board to the state house. Ever since LeGrotto got that new interstate interchange and the resort that followed, the money has been pouring into that little city. You mark my words. We won't be Mullet County's red-headed stepchild for much longer."

"From your lips to god's ear," said Lars.

"Lars, can you excuse us for a second?" said Amber. "I've got to, as Micky used to say, take my publisher's hat off and talk business. I wouldn't want to, you know, put you in an awkward position."

"Of course," said Lars with a smile. "Look at her, already got herself a publisher's hat," he said to Dutch affably.

****

"I honestly had no idea Micky was so revered," Shelton said to Ally Mason, who had invited him to sit with her family during the ceremony when it became clear that Ringo would not be meeting him in front of the church as planned.

"Yeah, he was a real man of the people," said Ally. "A lot of folks are indebted to his kindness. All that stuff Dutch was talking about just scratched the surface. That man helped everyone he could."

"Paid for a new transmission on Ally's minivan when it blew out right before Christmas a few years ago," said Ally's husband, Mike. "It really helped us out."

Just then, Ally looked past Shelton and spotted Ringo, who was attempting formal dress in wearing an untucked, sweat-stained, short-sleeved button-down with a loosened tie, jeans, and a pork pie hat. He was dripping in sweat, as was often the case. He was accompanied by Tina, who'd colored her hair an unnatural shade of red and was dressed quite casually in Daisy Dukes and a tank top, again sans brazier. However, given both Micky's association with old-Florida hippies and the Unitarian Universalists' bohemian vibe, several other attendees were similarly attired. Each of them had two drafts of lager in their hands. Ringo gave one to Shelton while Tina remained two-fisted.

"Where on Earth have you been, man?" asked Shelton. "We were supposed to meet out front."

"Tina was having wardrobe issues, and then we got lost," said Ringo. "By the time we arrived, I figured it would be rude to make a scene by entering in the middle of the service. The guy setting up the beer truck looked like he could use some help, so I tried to make myself useful."

"Yeah, I'm sure you lightened the weight of his barrels," said Shelton as he rolled his eyes.

"That's nice ink," said Ally, pointing to a full sleeve of colorful samurai done in vintage pin-up style on Ringo's left arm.

"Thanks," he said. "I got it done in Osaka. It tells the story of an ancient samurai and the lengths he went to be reignited with his one true love."

"What's the story?" asked Ally.

"I said *it* told a story, Ally, not I," Ringo said with a wink, draining half a pint of beer and heading back toward the truck.

122

"You want a beer?" Tina asked Ally.

"Um, no, that's okay," said Ally. "We're gonna go round up our girls. We gotta get home soon."

"Cool," said Tina, downing the rest of her first and sliding the second inside its cup.

"Any luck finding a place?" Shelton asked Tina once Ally and Mike had left.

Tina had been crashing with them since she arrived. Ringo was avoiding any conversation regarding what would become of her when they lost the bungalow and moved into "single-occupancy" residences.

"Nah, but I got a job at Memories Lounge," she told him.

"That's good," said Shelton, swirling a finger in the foam of his beer while suffering through an awkward silence.

"Ringo told you that we're moving out of the bungalow on Wednesday, right?" he finally said. "That's two days."

"Yeah, but he said it would take your landlord two weeks to put me out if I squatted after you all left," she told him nonchalantly. "I'm sure I'll find a place before that, though. Angel's already put some feelers out."

Good, maybe she'll hook her up with a motorcycle club, thought Shelton.

****

"What's on your mind, little lady?" Dutch asked Amber.

"That stuff you said about Micky having them on the ropes next month. Was that true or hyperbole for the occasion?"

Dutch shrugged.

"I mean, it's hard to get accurate data in races of that size, but from what I understand, Ignacio spent a pretty penny on some high-end internal polling right before he plopped down another hundred grand for attack ads," Dutch told her. "You usually don't do that after getting good news."

"How much do you think could be done to influence it our way?" she asked. "What if we created a PAC and flooded the county with just as much dirt? But in our case, all of it would be true. I know Micky didn't believe in money in politics, but he's gone, and I'm in charge now. How much would it cost to get everyone in the county wise to what they've been up to?"

Dutch was shocked, given Micky's strict adherence to never using money to influence an election beyond standard contributions to campaign accounts, which had strict donation limits. He gave the question serious contemplation and shrugged.

"It's hard to say. It's too late in the game to build name recognition for the opposing candidates. Still, if you got enough mud to stick on the incumbents, enough folks might come out and vote for whoever the other candidate is to swing it, assuming it's as close as I think it might be already."

"It's three races," said Amber. "How much do you think it would take to be worth doing at all? I don't want to waste money on a pea shooter if we're going up against a battleship. I want ballistic missiles."

Dutch could see the kind of fire in Amber's eyes that he recognized as the same sort he could spot in a candidate that he knew had a good shot at being a winner, and it gave him a chill.

"Well, Greg Osborne and Mary Porter are the best candidates. Osborne has built a solid grassroots ground game. He'll be outspent five dollars to one, but he's raised enough money that a lot of voters will recognize his name, and he's going up against a candidate the community truly loathes. Anyone who knows Connor Welsh will vote against him. The only problem is that not many people turn out for a primary, and they tend to be dominated by the zealots who are most moved by Hernandez's America First attack ads about illegals, abortion, and the Second Amendment. If we spent a hundred grand on that race and you were willing to go hard in the paint on the ads, I think Osborne wins."

"Go hard on Welsh?" she asked. "That little prick makes my skin crawl. Take the gloves off, so far as I'm concerned. What about Porter?"

"That's a trickier one," said Dutch. "Hagerty has some skeletons in her closet, believe you me. But it's not the kind of stuff that the MAGA crowd gets too lathered up about, and she's got a lot of name recognition with them, as well as with run-of-the-mill Republicans on account of her Daddy's last name, which is why she kept it after getting married, I suspect. Ace Hagerty is fondly remembered in these parts. Porter's a great candidate, and she whipped her in the debate, but she's spent no money, and no one aside from her old students is gonna know her by name. We'd have to spend the same $100,000 going after Hagerty and then probably $50,000 in a blitz to get Porter's name known at least as well as Osborne's."

"That woman is a whore," said Amber. "Money well spent. Okay, a quarter mill so far. What's next?"

Dutch was genuinely surprised by her vigor and found himself wondering exactly how much his recently departed friend had been worth.

"Well, now we get to the tricky part," said Dutch. "You gotta run the table, or it does you no good. I mean, if you don't get all three seats, Ignacio still has the majority for at least another two years, and getting that cotton picker Merle Watts elected will be no easy task. He's got the charisma of a wet dishcloth, and that ward has notoriously low turnout, especially for primaries. Sunday's got his congregation to count on, and that alone might be enough. We'd have to really get the entire ag community out there mobilized, and they're not a particularly political bunch. It'll be like herding cats."

"Would another hundred grand do it?" asked Amber.

Dutch was impressed but didn't want to give her false hope, especially when she was prepared to spend a small fortune.

"I couldn't make a promise, but a hundred grand would go a long way in a small ward like that."

Amber bit her lip as she stared at him intently.

"That's $350,000, Dutch," she told him. "What if I told you I'm prepared to hire you and spend up to half a million dollars to win all three races? I know you don't like to lose. Would you take the job with those sorts of resources?"

Dutch's jaw nearly hit the floor. It had been years since he'd been in such a high-stakes game, and with just over three weeks before the primary, it would be the biggest challenge of his career. He wanted the job, and he wanted it badly. However, he did not want to take it or spend his friend's money unless he was certain he could win.

"Stay right here," he said. "I'll be right back with your answer."

Dutch marched over to the beer truck, where Ringo was still posted up at the window, draining pints of lager.

"Excuse me, big fella," he said, bellying up to the small, makeshift bar. "Give me one of anything, darling," he told the young girl working the beer truck.

She handed him a pilsner, and he drained it in one pull.

"Nice," said Ringo. "Nothing like beer to quell grief. To Micky," he added, toasting his draft.

"You knew Micky?" asked Dutch.

"Not well," said Ringo, which wasn't exactly a lie. "But I work for him, or… his estate, I suppose."

Dutch looked him up and down incredulously.

"Doing what?"

"I'm a photojournalist for the Gazette," said Ringo.

"Since when?" asked Dutch, looking him over more closely this time.

"Since today," said Ringo. "I know they've had some truly poor photography in the past, but the reporting was solid, and I'm about to cure the photographic shortcomings."

Ringo grabbed two more pints, handed one to Dutch, and toasted his glass toward him. They each downed their cups in one pull, though Dutch struggled a bit and lost some out of the sides of the cup on the home stretch. He looked up at Ringo and smiled.

"You and I are gonna get along just fine, young man," he said with a chuckle and a grin. "Now, if you'll excuse me."

Dutch marched right back over to Amber and saluted her.

"I'll take the job," he said.

She smiled.

"I knew you would, Dutch Wagner. Now, let's win this damned thing."

****

"You look like you could use a drink, cowboy," Mary Pesch said to Lars as she approached carrying two drafts.

"I could, at that," said Lars, accepting one of the cups.

"I hear you're not out of a job, at least," said Mary. "I didn't think Amber would keep pissing money away on Micky's passion projects after he kicked, but I suppose she's got plenty to piss these days."

Mary wasn't quite slurring, but she was loud and thick-tongued in a way that suggested she'd had more than a few drinks by that point. Mary Pesch was only three years older than Lars and had been trying to sleep with him since he first met her at a Christmas party Micky and Amber had thrown ten years earlier.

"I'm sure he left you a little something to piss away yourself," said Lars with a wry smile.

"Wouldn't you like to know," said Mary. "He didn't leave me enough to be no sugar momma, I'll tell you that much."

"I'm pretty well set up as a solo act," said Lars with a wink. Lars was something of a catch among the sort of women he enjoyed, which was to say middle-aged divorcees, barmaids, and waitresses. They provided a steady stream of companionship, and he had no intention of risking his now considerable nest egg via nuptial pursuits.

"Darling, you are too old to be my cabana boy," she said while giving him an exaggerated wink in return. "Besides, the fucker went and put it in a trust. Can you believe that shit? Wanted to make sure I didn't spend it all in one place like I'm a child or something."

Lars said nothing, but the expression on his face spoke volumes.

"Oh, fuck you, Lars Swenson," she said in a voice that had definitely deteriorated to a slur. "Always acting like you're so damned highfalutin while livin' in the damned Ramblewood Motel for Christ's sake. You know, we used to rent rooms there for parties when we were in high school? It had roaches the size of mice and mice the size of squirrels. Probably still does!"

"You mentioned that a time or two," said Lars, smiling. "I've got a good pest control service these days. Haven't seen anything other than a gecko or the occasional belly-up Palmetto bug after they spray."

"Is that right? Maybe I'll have to drop by sometime," said Mary in a decidedly more sultry voice as she dipped her finger in his beer. She then stuck it in her mouth and sucked off the suds, while giving him a seductive look.

His phone buzzed, and he looked down to read the text. It was from a rich divorcee on the island, a full-on Christian conservative who liked to hate-read the Gazette. She'd complain about its "liberal bias" every time she would have him over for some wild, no-strings-attached fun.

"Sorry, Mary, I need to make a phone call," he said, walking off.

128

Mary spat on the ground as he turned away.

****

"Holy shit," Ally said to Mike and her daughters as they walked toward their minivan. "Look who showed up. The balls on that one!"

Accompanied by his much younger wife, Ignacio Hernandez strolled across the lawn as if he owned the place. He was dressed in a seersucker suit, a crisp white shirt with the top two buttons open, and a yellow silk pocket square in his jacket. His white hair was pushed back with gel. His wife wore a black cocktail dress that, while the appropriate color for a funeral, was more suited to an evening of clubbing in Miami. He was headed straight toward Amber Pesch.

"Is that—" said her oldest daughter.

"Yup," said Ally.

Mike turned around to see what was happening. His jaw fell.

"Hold up," said Ally. "We ain't going nowhere. I gotta see this shit."

Amber was standing with one of Mary's daughters and her husband. Ignacio was within five feet when she noticed him approaching.

"Mrs. Pesch, my deepest condolences," said Ignacio. "I mean that."

He held out his hand, but she remained frozen, her eyes shooting daggers at the developer whom she didn't necessarily think had Micky killed but knew was anything but *sorry* for her loss.

"Your husband and I were political rivals, yes, but I am genuinely sad to have lost such a worthy adversary," he continued. "We disagreed on much, but I admired his conviction."

Not to be robbed of his dignity by her snubbing of his hand, he sort of curtsied toward her as he finished the sentence.

Amber was holding a glass of Chianti at what was now face level and simply couldn't resist the opportunity. She doused him with it. Mrs. Hernandez gasped.

Ignacio didn't even upright himself before grabbing his pocket square and wiping his face. Red wine stained the lapel of his jacket and the white linen shirt.

"People process grief in many different ways," he said as he turned his face toward his wife. "Come on, darling. We're finished here."

Amber fought the adrenaline-induced urge to stomp off in order to savor the sight. Ignacio took his wife's hand and retraced the path they'd just walked, only at a much less casual pace than when they arrived.

"Fuck me!" said Ally. "That was beautiful."

Her husband and daughters nodded in agreement.

Chapter 8: I need a drink

The commission chambers were already packed when Shelton and Ringo arrived, but Deputy White noticed their credentials and escorted them to the second row, where some seats had been roped off for the press. Two seats remained at the end. Ernie Young was already seated a few spots down the aisle with reporters from the Mullet County Monitor and the Island Telegraph, a DeSoto Beach weekly, seated between them.

Despite being roughly twice Shelton's size and sweating profusely, Ringo opted for the interior seat, enjoying the horror that registered on the face of the Monitor's reporter when he dropped his bag and sat down, spreading his legs as he commandeered the shared armrest. Wearing a loud paisley short-sleeve buttoned halfway and badly wrinkled cargo shorts, his many tattoos on display, he looked like he had spent the night in the drunk tank. Wearing a t-shirt and jeans, Shelton felt downright dapper in his presence. Everyone else wore khakis and dress shirts, but Shelton and Ringo reveled in announcing themselves as the alternative press.

The room buzzed with interest. The board would not only be casting a final vote on the wetland policy, but a last-minute addition to the agenda the evening before proposed cutting impact fees—which were how Florida communities paid for infrastructure necessitated by new growth—by 50 percent.

The item had been caught by the League of Women Voters, who put out email and social media blasts to alert activists who weren't already planning to attend. When Lars received word from the chapter president, he also sent a breaking news email to the Gazette's nearly 50,000 email subscribers and used the paper's website and social media accounts to amplify the article's reach.

Commissioner Dicky Myers called the meeting to order with the Pledge of Allegiance and asked the crowd to bow their heads. Reverend Sunday then said the prayer, asking that the Lord give the board members both courage and wisdom despite having clearly failed to deliver on the same request at just about every previous meeting.

"Now, item number one is regarding the forthcoming changes in the county's wetland policy," said Myers. "I see there is a big crowd again today, so let me reiterate that this is just a re-reading because we are required to have two public hearings before amending our comprehensive land use plan. The vote we took last week was the first, and having received no objections from the state in its review, we simply have to cast a final vote. Because the board remains unified on the matter, we have waived another presentation by our consultant to save taxpayer money. But I would also ask that if you have already spoken on this matter previously and signed up to give public comment again today, you consider that the board remains aware of your position and yield your time so we can get to other items, one of which has already garnered quite a few sign-ups. Would anyone like to yield their time on the wetland policy?"

Crickets. The chairman sighed.

"Alright then, let's get on with it."

One by one, citizens let the board have it, reiterating their deep disdain for the proposed policy, with several referencing Micky's murder. Dr. Emily Bartleston again gave her entire presentation nearly verbatim. Comments had started just a few minutes after 9:00 a.m. and stretched past noon when the board usually broke for lunch. In all, six members of the public were ejected from the meeting.

After the last citizen spoke, none of the commissioners requested a board discussion. Commissioner Welsh moved to approve the policy, and Commissioner Hagerty quickly seconded the motion, which the board approved unanimously. The crowd voiced its disapproval loudly.

"Order in the chambers," barked the chairman. "We will have order!"

"You get your orders from Ignacio, fat man," yelled a retiree who'd been ejected from the prior meeting.

Deputy White approached, but the guy had already stood and waved him off, heading toward the door of his own volition. Commissioner Myers, who had recently started on Ozempic, looked down at his gut as if to assess whether he did, in fact, still look bulbous around the midsection and decided to suck it in a bit.

"Now, we're gonna break for lunch," he told the crowd. "We'll reconvene in one hour." Myers looked at his watch. "I've got 12:17, so let's just say we'll pick it up at 1:20. This meeting is in recess," he added as he banged the gavel.

Emily Bartleston had been seated in the row in front of Shelton and Ringo. When she arose and turned around, Shelton, still seated and packing his laptop into his satchel, grabbed one of his new business cards.

"That was one hell of a presentation," he told her as he handed her the card. "Shelton Hamner," he added.

"Emily Bartleston," she told him, taking the card with her left hand and offering a handshake with the right.

"You work for the Gazette?" she asked. "I'd read that Ally had taken a leave of absence. You're her replacement, I imagine?"

Shelton had noticed Emily was cute when she gave her presentation, but had no idea how genuinely striking the woman was until she turned around and he caught a glimpse of her from straight on.

"Not exactly," said Shelton, a bit disarmed by her beauty. "I'm more of a columnist, although I've done some investigative work in the past. I was supposed to be added to the staff, but then she gave notice, so I'm sort of doing a hybrid gig now, I suppose."

"Shelton Hamner, that sounds familiar," Emily said. "Didn't you used to write for the Weekly Planet in Sarasota?"

Dear god, not this, Shelton thought to himself. She knows the damned story, too?

"I'm a fan of your work," she added.

Yeah, I bet, he thought, sweat forming on his brow.

"I was captivated by that case," she said. "I mean, the girl was so young and seemed so full of life in those photographs. I bawled my eyes out when they found her body."

"Oh, *that* story," said Shelton, clearly relieved. "Yes, it was a genuine shame. Everyone who knew that little girl commented on how sweet and kind she was."

"Hey," she said.

"Yes," he answered.

"They should never have gotten rid of you. I mean, it was one hell of a picture," she said warmly as she flashed a smile.

"That would be my work," said Ringo, leaning over Shelton to shake Emily's hand. "Dr. Ringo Khan, photojournalist," he added as he handed her a card of his own, which read those exact words alone while offering no phone number or even an email address by which to contact the man.

"Nice to meet you guys," said Emily.

"Hey, we were gonna grab some lunch while the meeting is recessed," said Shelton. "Wanna join us?"

"Sure," said Emily. "There's a deli right across the street that I usually go to. The food is pretty good."

"Sounds great," said Shelton, grabbing the rest of his gear.

Downtown DeSoto was small but quite charming. It mainly consisted of enterprises related to Mullet County Government and the City of DeSoto. In addition to the massive county administration building, there was DeSoto City Hall, DeSoto Police Headquarters, and the Mullet County Circuit Courthouse, all within four square blocks. The municipal buildings were surrounded by dozens of law practices, bail bond businesses, and real estate firms. In the middle of it all,

134

Old Main Street was a two-block stretch of nothing but cafes, breakfast/lunch eateries, and pubs that drew brisk breakfast, lunch, and happy hour crowds and then picked up again when the handful of fine-dining restaurants and rowdier bars hosted the somewhat limited nightlife crowd.

Shelton, Ringo, and Emily only had to cross the street to reach Coastal Kitchen, a 7 a.m. to 3 p.m. deli known for making its own fresh bagels and bread. Ringo caught a look at the place, then noticed Durty Nelly's Irish Pub next door.

"Hey, I'm gonna opt for the liquid lunch over there," he told them. "I'll catch you guys after."

"Go easy," warned Shelton.

Ringo gave him a salute that he converted into a middle finger as he walked off on his own.

Once inside, Shelton and Emily were quickly seated at a two-top, the last available seats in the eatery. A waitress brought them two waters and menus.

"Is that some sort of shtick you guys have?" Emily asked with a smile. "Come to lunch with both of us, and one will dip out at the last second."

"Hardly," said Shelton. "He had a late one. If he doesn't get a fix before half past noon, his hands will be shaking too badly to get photos."

"Are you much of a drinker?" she asked.

Shelton was caught off guard.

"Well, I suppose I'm a social drinker, but I'm a pretty social guy in a notoriously social industry, so relatively speaking …" he said, realizing he was babbling. "Having that maniac as a roommate surely doesn't help."

"Relax," she told him. "I'm hardly a teetotaler."

"Oh yeah, what's your poison?"

"I like wine," said Emily.

"Really?" said Shelton, pleasantly surprised. "What kind?"

"Napa cabs, Argentinian Malbecs, and, when it's summertime, I don't mind a good chardonnay or Prosecco."

"So basic suburban white girl grapes?" said Shelton with a smile. "At least you didn't say White Claw."

Emily blushed.

"Hey now, I'm not above a hard seltzer on beach days, but I prefer Long Drink."

"I jest," said Shelton. "I started with BOGO Napa cabs and gas station Merlots. I knew nothing about wine and was too broke for anything good, even if I had."

"How does such a novice become a celebrated critic?" she asked. "They don't let just anyone cover the grand tasting at the Gulf Coast Food & Wine Festival."

"Like most things I've accomplished, I stumbled into it accidentally and faked it until I made it," he told her. "And I'm hardly *celebrated*. I'm persona non grata among that crowd these days. I can't even cover the theater company, as I'm banned from the entire museum premises."

"Well, I had to pay the full $200, and my pictures didn't come out nearly as cool as yours," she said.

"You were there?" he asked. "This year?"

"Yep," Emily said with a chuckle. "My girlfriend and I were waiting for our Uber when your little fiasco played out. We were in hysterics. It was hilarious, epic even."

"At least someone thought so," said Shelton with a chuckle.

A teenage waitress asked if she could take their order.

"Can I get the turkey bacon bagel, hold the onions?" asked Emily.

"Of course," said the waitress. "And to drink?"

"Unsweet tea, please."

"And you, sir?" the waitress asked Shelton.

"Let me get the chicken salad on brioche, and I'll also take the unsweet tea," said Shelton.

"You got it," she said as she hurried off.

"So, are you going to be investigating Micky's death?" asked Emily with an uncomfortable look on her face.

"It's pretty much the only reason I was hired," said Shelton. "Mrs. Pesch has very little confidence that local law enforcement will do much, especially since it occurred in unincorporated Mullet County."

"Her suspicions are justified," said Emily. "Regardless of who shot him, he successfully sued Rusty Brock's department twice. Not that it would matter much if it had happened in DeSoto. The city police department is twice as shady and half as competent."

"You seem rather learned when it comes to Mullet County politics," said Shelton. "You live here?"

"God no," said Emily with a chuckle. "I live in St. Pete, which is a good central location for my job and far more cultured. TBEW covers Tampa to Sarasota, but I might as well live here for all the time I spend on this side of the Skyway. Mullet County is responsible for at least half of the policies we fight, probably more in the last two years, now that Ignacio has full control of the board. Plus, the fish kills from the red tide blooms have been much worse down here, so I've been doing frequent water sampling."

"Where did you grow up?" he asked.

"Gainesville," said Emily. "My father is the chair of the biochemistry and molecular biology department at UF."

"Ah, chip off the old block," said Shelton.

Emily shrugged.

"I think he always viewed environmental science as beneath his only child's potential, but he was a big outdoorsman, so he knows it's kind of his fault. Every weekend, he'd take me fishing, kayaking, or on these little field trips to study mangrove forests or some other ecosystem."

"Here's to only children," said Shelton, toasting his iced tea glass. "What about your mom?"

"She died of Leukemia when I was a young girl," said Emily. "It's been just the two of us for a long time."

"I'm sorry to hear that," said Shelton.

Emily smiled.

"What about you?" she asked. "Where'd you grow up?"

"A little town in the Pennsylvania coal region," he told her. "Pottsville. It's about midway between Philadelphia and the Poconos. The Appalachian Trail runs right through it."

"Good place?" she asked.

Shelton shrugged.

"At times, it's been, I suppose. Less so every year. Typical Rust Belt town. It's loaded with remnants from the Gilded Age, most of which are rotting in place. Mansions built for coal barons diced up into half a dozen Section 8 apartments, rural coal patches with dilapidated tract homes, lots of meth, fentanyl, even bath salts. Black, coal shale hills as far as the eye can see. The two big industries are power plants that burn mountains of waste coal and state and federal prisons. Most of the guys I went to high school with are corrections officers. Most of the gals are nurses or social workers."

"Sounds dystopian," said Emily.

"It's played its part," Shelton said with a wink. "We gave the world Yuengling Beer and Mrs. T's Pierogies, the Dorsey Brothers, and the 1925 NFL World Champion Pottsville Maroons. Plus, I'm pretty sure it's the only county to birth two National Book Award winners."

"Really?" Emily asked. He couldn't tell if she was suspicious or impressed.

"Yep," said Shelton. "Pottsville's own John O'Hara for *Ten North Frederick* in 1956 and Conrad Richter for *Waters of Kronos* in 1961."

She shrugged apologetically. He waved her off.

"No one but English Lit professors remembers either today," he told her. "They were contemporaries of Hemingway and Fitzgerald but weren't as interesting off the page, I suppose. *Appointment in Sammara*, O'Hara's first novel, is still my favorite book, though, and I've read everything Hemingway or Fitzgerald ever wrote."

Emily was now scrolling on her phone and no longer seemed to be paying attention. If Shelton had a nickel for every time he'd bored a woman stiff with his literary interests, he could probably retire.

"I've only read five of them in all," she said while continuing to look at the screen.

"Five of what?" Shelton asked.

"Five of the winners," said Emily, turning her phone to show him the National Book Award recipients list from a Wikipedia page. "T*he Underground Railroad, The Corrections, Cold Mountain, The Color Purple*, and *Sophie's Choice*. Wait, I'm pretty sure that's the Flannery O'Connor short story collection I had to read in college, so maybe six, but I'm not certain."

While Shelton desperately tried not to fall in love, the waitress delivered their orders.

****

Ringo was slouched into the back corner booth, scrolling his phone, when someone plopped down in the seat across from him, having thought the booth empty. To his surprise, it was Mullet County Administrator Wayne Beaufort, who was rubbing the whole of his face with the palms of his hands. He then relinquished a fart that smelled like stale death before he noticed that the booth was occupied.

"Ah, shit," said Beaufort, as he slouched down to eye level. "I didn't see anyone sitting here. My bad."

Ringo remained slouched but pushed away three of the empty pints in front of him to gain a view of his guest, who had what looked like a scotch on the rocks before him.

"No worries," said Ringo. "I won't tell if you don't."

Beaufort noticed the press pass around Ringo's neck and panicked. Then he looked at the three empty Guinness pints and the nearly full one still in the corner closest to the giant ogre across from him. He felt divided. Members of the press were a natural enemy, while fellow day drinkers were a natural ally. Ringo hit his vape pen and offered him a toke. Beaufort shook his head, but the offering was enough for him to relax and take a sip from his tumbler.

"Don't worry," said Ringo, glancing down at the lanyard on his chest. "I'm just a photographer. I've got no skin in the game beyond my artistic scruples."

He drained the rest of his pint in one pull.

"I like you," said Beaufort. "What's your name?"

"Dr. Ringo Khan," he told him. "Yours?"

"Wayne," Beaufort told him. "Good old Wayne."

****

Shelton wasn't surprised to see that Ringo's seat was still empty when the meeting reconvened. It wasn't unusual for his friend to spend the second half of assignment days bellied up to a bar. Ringo could get just the right shot at a moment's notice and would have already had dozens of quality pics for Ernie and Shelton to choose from in what he'd gleaned from the pre-lunch portion of the meeting.

Chairman Myers was about to call the meeting to order when Commissioner Welsh pointed out that Beaufort had not yet taken his seat on the dais.

"He had a minor emergency in the HR department to deal with," said Commissioner Hagerty, who routinely covered for Beaufort, if only to gain leverage over him. "He said to get started without him and that Deputy Administrator Schubert would sit in until if and when he's able to return."

All eyes fell on Schubert, a petite blonde woman who was also used to covering for her boss.

"Yes, of course, how silly of me," said Schubert, gathering her laptop and other belongings to move from a nearby desk to Wayne's seat on the dais.

"Alright, moving right along to item number two on the agenda, the temporary reduction of impact fees by 50 percent to help abate our current housing crisis," said Myers as groans and mumbles filled the chambers.

He banged his gavel.

"We will have order," shouted the chairman. "Mrs. Plavenski, please read the recommendation."

A decidedly frumpy middle-aged woman approached the lectern.

"Rebecca Plavenski, Director of Development Services," she said. "Item number two is a 50 percent reduction in impact fees. This item follows the board's directive to examine the impacts of a fee reduction as a measure to combat the affordable housing crisis in Mullet County. While impact fees are a crucial funding source for roads, parks, libraries, and many other infrastructure needs created by growth, we believe that the critical need for more workforce housing has surpassed these fees in priority and should temporarily supersede other such considerations. The county administrator recommends the approval of this item until such time as the board deems fit to reinstate full impact fees based on economic conditions."

The audience erupted in derogatory comments, so many that Deputy White, confused as to whom he should eject, looked to Myers and shrugged.

"Order in the chambers," screamed Myers as he furiously banged the gavel. "We will have order, or I will have no choice but to recess this meeting and have all of you ejected from it. You'll have the opportunity to weigh in on the proposed policy during our public comment period. Now, Commissioner Welsh, I have you first on the board."

"Thank you, chair," said Welsh. "We are clearly in a housing crisis. The median cost per home in Mullet County is now well over $450,000. And out near the interstate, where new construction provides the only units that cost significantly less than that, prices are being driven up by this baseless—and let's just call it what it is—tax. It ought to be called *the middle-class working-family tax* because that's who it hits the hardest. As a conservative, I am eager to cut taxes any time I can, so I proudly motion to approve this item."

"Second," Hagerty shouted before Welsh had even completed his last syllable.

"I move to call the question," said Welsh.

"Second," shouted Hagerty.

"I have two commissioners still on the board," said Myers, looking at commissioners Sunday and Blanton with a shrug.

"There's a motion on the board," said Welsh.

"Okay," said Myers nervously. "Commissioners, you should have a motion to call the question on your screen if you would kindly cast your vote.

Dicky Myers was also installed by Ignacio, but the developer mostly spoke to him and the others through Welsh, so he understood that he was the chairman in name only. Blanton and Sunday, who hadn't gotten help from Hernandez until after they had built up enough grassroots support in the primaries to convince the developer they were not as useless as he'd first thought, desperately wanted to grandstand on the issue. However, one of Welsh's standing marching orders was to ensure that a controversial vote moved briskly during a meeting and that none of the developer's dimmer stooges said something stupid that could be used against them in their reelection campaigns, as that would cost Hernandez more money to overcome.

"The motion to call the question passes unanimously," said Myers. "I have a motion and a second to approve the item, so, seeing no other commissioners on the board, I'll open it up for public comment. When I call your name, please come to the lectern, and you'll have three minutes to speak. First, I've got … oh, Dr. Emily Bartleston. Good afternoon, doctor," the chairman said, flashing a smile that instantly gave her the creeps.

"Dr. Emily Bartleston and I have been sworn," she said from the lectern. "Commissioners, I believe that you are making a grave mistake today in considering the passage of this ordinance. The state of Florida allows cities and counties to collect impact fees as a way to ensure that growth pays for itself. Every study on the subject, which I've sent to each of you, shows that for every dollar that growth generates, it costs about $1.25 in new services. Look at the gridlock we've got in this county. TBEW has estimated that Mullet County has nearly doubled its automotive carbon emissions in the past decade, not only because we've added so many more cars to our roadways as our population has ballooned, but also because inadequate road improvements require them to be idling at a standstill for more and more minutes and even hours each day. We're not investing in enough parks, which not only serve to ensure that the residents in these rural areas we're developing have adequate amenities but also as a way to preserve green space and the permeable land that can recharge our aquifers as more and more of it is elevated and hardened, causing water runoff and all of its pollutants to end up in our rivers, the bay, and eventually the gulf where we're seeing a massive increase in algal blooms. I was just here last week and again this morning, warning about the similar effects of eliminating the wetland buffer requirements. All of these things are connected, commissioners. The giant sinkholes in the northern corridor, the overflow discharges from sewage treatment plants that lack adequate capacity, the algae mats in the canals, the red tide, and the fish kills on our Gulf beaches. It's time we—"

The alarm beeped. Commissioner Welsh reached over and hit the button he'd installed at the chairman's station to cut the microphone. Myers gave him a mopey look.

"I'm sorry, ma'am, your time has expired, and many people are waiting to speak," said Welsh, looking sharply at Myers.

The crowd in the chambers hissed and booed. Chairman Myers banged his gavel.

"Alright, folks, that's enough," he said. "Dr. Bartleston, I apologize, but we have much to get through today. Again, if you'd like to discuss any of this privately—"

This time, Welsh didn't even try to be discreet when he leaned in and kicked him in the shin.

"Dammit!" Myers yelled, immediately reaching down to rub the point of contact.

Emily was furious. She grabbed her belongings and looked toward Shelton as she moved toward the exit, shaking her head and gritting her teeth. Shelton looked to his right and saw Ernie Young scribbling furiously on his notepad. He decided he'd seen enough to opine on the political theater, grabbed his gear, waited a moment to allow for some distance, and followed her out.

When Shelton opened the door from the lobby to the street, Emily had put her purse and bag on the ground, her head in the air, and her hands outstretched toward the heavens.

"FAAAWWWK!" she screamed into the sky.

"Warning, if you stroke out, I don't know CPR," he told her.

She shook her head and giggled, a bit embarrassed by her outburst.

"I just feel like there's no fucking point sometimes," she said. "It's like I'm living in a damned cartoon."

"Better than a sitcom," said Shelton. "Wanna get a drink?"

"Yes!" said Emily.

She looked at her watch.

"It's not even 2 p.m., but I think my bosses would understand. What's the Gazette's policy on drinking during work hours?"

"It hasn't been mentioned, but given that Lars keeps a bar in his office, I can hardly imagine it's forbidden."

They walked across the street to Durty Nelly's and grabbed two seats at the bar.

"So, are you gonna educate me on proper wines?" she asked, grabbing the menu that was uprighted at the paper towel station.

"In an Irish pub?" said Shelton with a look of horror. "Sure, I'll have them bring us two of their finest cans of chateau de pape."

Emily laughed.

"What can I get you?" asked the bartender, a hulking man of around 60.

"I'll have what he's having," said Emily.

"How about two shots of Black Bush and a couple of Yuenglings," said Shelton.

The bartender grabbed two cold bottles of Yuengling from the cooler.

"No Black Bush," said the bartender. "I got white label, Powers, or Jameson."

Shelton gave him a look that conveyed disappointment in an Irish pub finding itself without Bushmills Black Label in the middle of a weekday.

"Don't look at me like that," the old man said. "Blame those two lads in the back."

They turned their attention to the corner booth where Ringo and Wayne—no longer slouched since the recess crowd had long exited—were sloshing imperial pints of Guinness with nearly as much spilling onto the table as had been making its way into their gullets.

"I really like you, man," Beaufort was telling Ringo. "You understand a guy like me, the pressures I'm under."

"To tell you the truth, I'm surprised you've held up this well, Wayne," replied Ringo. "They ought to give you some sort of civic award for your perseverance."

"I was named Rotarian of the year in 2018," said Beaufort, toasting his pint.

"I'll drink to that," said Ringo, clinking glasses and taking a long pull of the stout.

"Holy shit," said Emily. "Is that—"

"Yep," said Shelton, "and don't be surprised. Ringo has a knack for befriending anyone with a taste for the sauce. It doesn't matter their politics, level of wealth, social rank, you name it. If they possess a derelict drinking streak, he's their man."

"What about you?" she asked, sipping her beer.

"What about me?" said Shelton.

"Are you a troublemaker?"

"The best kind," he told her, toasting the shot glass of Jameson the bartender had placed before them.

"Are you going to make a proper toast?" she asked.

"Sure, what are you in the mood for?" asked Shelton.

"I'd settle for something hopeful," said Emily.

Shelton stood and cleared his throat.

"Ring the bells that still can ring, forget your perfect offering, there is a crack in everything, that is how the light gets in."

Emily's eyes widened.

"For fuck's sake, did you just quote Leonard Cohen to me?"

"You're a fan?" asked Shelton.

"Full on fanatic," she told him.

"You'd have to be to catch a line from *Anthem*," he said with a laugh.

"I saw him on the 2009 tour," she said. "Beacon Theatre in New York. I had chills throughout the whole show."

"I came to him rather late," said Shelton. "I deeply regret never having seen him live. I've got some good vinyl, though. The Live from London album from that same tour is my favorite."

Emily gave him a curious look that made Shelton think she was assessing something about him.

"What?" he asked with a nervous smile.

"I'm trying to figure you out," she said with a smile of her own.

"I can assure you it's all pretty much up there on the surface."

She smirked.

"Don't give me any of that bush league self-deprecation meant to lower my expectations and hence make it easier to impress me later bullshit, Mr. Hamner," she told him with a wink and a wry smile.

Shelton put up his hands defensively, giving her a small, guilty-as-charged smile of his own.

"What about you? What's your story?" he asked.

"My story?" she said with a chuckle. "You wanna do the thing, do you?"

"The thing?" he asked.

"The thing where we try and stretch the first paragraph of a Tinder bio into a casual conversation."

"It was the only way to do it for thousands of years," he told her. "And I'd definitely argue we were better for it."

"Oh, you're not one of those hopelessly nostalgic fellas, are you?" she asked teasingly. "They can be such bummers."

"No, we just came of age in the sweet spot," he told her. "After personal ads and video dating services, but before smartphones or even match.com."

"And here we are, meeting and getting to know each other the old-fashioned way," she said with a slightly bigger smile. "In a bar."

"If you'd like the Reader's Digest version," said Shelton, "I'm 37, married in my mid-twenties, a few years later, no kids. After high school, I did a short stint in the Coast Guard, which brought me to Florida. Then I studied English at Eckerd College, hoping to be the next Great American novelist. I met my ex-wife there. She was a theater major, but after school, we got caught up in the real estate world and slowly drifted apart until we no longer recognized anything we'd ever found attractive in each other. So, we split. I landed a bottom-rung job at the Weekly Planet, she eventually married a partner at the real estate firm she'd been working for, and we were both better off for it."

"I would not have pegged you for an Eckerd guy, but I guess that makes sense," she said.

"Yeah?"

"Great writing program from what I hear," Emily told him with a toast of her glass.

"So?" said Shelton.

"So?" she asked.

"Your turn to do the thing," he told her.

"You want my Reader's Digest bio?" she asked.

"Short-form, long-form, my undivided attention is yours, madame."

She took a sip of her beer.

"Well, I'm 35. I've also been married and divorced. No kids. I did my undergrad in Gainesville, graduate work at Florida Atlantic, and got my PhD at Florida Tech. I met my husband during grad school. He was a TA in the history department, working on his PhD. He was several years older and seemed much more mature than the guys I was used to dating, yada yada. A few years went by, and I sort of caught up to him, you might say. I began to suspect there might not have been as much *there* there as I'd initially thought. He secured a full-time faculty position and wanted to start a family. I had just finished my dissertation and wanted to jump into my career, so we shook hands and parted as friends. Because of our respective educations, half the marriage had been long-distance anyway. It may have been the least devastating divorce on record. I did some teaching on the East Coast, then moved to St. Pete when TBEW hired me five years ago."

"You like St. Pete?" Shelton asked.

"I love it!" she told him. "It's a perfectly sized city. There's so much culture—the art, the music, the theater. And the restaurant scene is fantastic. The beaches are all gorgeous and easy to get to. Traffic is manageable, plus you don't have nearly as many bigoted rednecks as there are down here. I wouldn't live anywhere else in Florida."

"Blue city in a red state," said Shelton.

Emily looked at him inquisitively.

"All my favorite places are blue cities in red states," he explained. "I'm not sure why, but I've noticed it's true: New Orleans, Austin, Asheville, Savannah."

She gave it some thought and shrugged.

"I can't argue against it," she said. "I haven't been to Austin, but NOLA, Asheville, and Savannah are some of the best cities I've ever visited. I guess it gives a certain balance, although I'd hardly use the word balanced to describe Florida these days.'"

"One-party rule is a road to ruin," said Shelton. "From California to Texas to Massachusetts to Florida. Give either side too much slack in the reins, and they'll muck it up."

"Touché," she said with a final tip of the glass before finishing her pint.

"Would you like another?" Shelton asked.

Emily looked at her watch.

"No, I'd better get going before the bridges are gridlocked. Walk me to my car?"

"Sure," said Shelton, reaching for his wallet.

Emily put her hand on his arm.

"No, my treat, I insist. You don't know how much I needed this."

Not having received his first paycheck yet, Shelton was in no position to argue. After settling the tab, they walked across the street toward the parking lot for the administrative building. When they passed his car, Shelton hit the trunk release on his

FOB to toss his satchel into the vehicle in case a kiss seemed in order.

"A rag-top man," she said. "I like it."

"There are few pleasures like crossing the Sunshine Skyway with the wind in your hair and the sun baking your skin," he told her.

"Tell me about it," she said, clicking her own FOB.

Shelton looked toward the sound and noticed the trunk pop on a muscular, blue, late-model Mustang GT convertible. She threw her bag in the trunk, and he hustled ahead to open her door.

"I enjoyed meeting you, Shelton," she said after climbing into the car and buckling her seat belt.

"Yeah, me too," he told her. "Maybe we can do it again sometime?"

Emily reached into her glove compartment and pulled out a business card.

"I'd like that," she said, handing him the card. "Call me."

Shelton smiled and put the card in his pocket. He had been trying to look cool, but when she turned the key, the engine's roar made him jump. She smiled and slowly pulled forward, the purr of the Coyote engine augmenting her sultry grin.

Shelton took a deep breath as he watched her drive off before heading back to the pub to scoop up Ringo.

****

When Lars pulled into Ramblewood, Shelton was sitting at his laptop on a picnic bench in the common area, tossing a tennis ball for Rufus to fetch between fits of typing. Ringo was shirtless, passed out in a chaise lounge with a large sleep mask covering his eyes. His massive girth was spilling everywhere, and it was the first time that Lars realized just how enormous the mountainous man actually was.

150

"Howdy, boss," said Shelton. "Just about finished on a column regarding today's meeting."

"I didn't get a chance to watch, but I heard it was another garden variety shit show," said Lars. "What's wrong with him?" he asked, nodding toward Ringo.

"He's sleeping one off," said Shelton.

Lars looked at his watch.

"It's not even 7 p.m."

He spent the entire afternoon day-drinking with your county administrator," Shelton told him.

"No shit?" said Lars, clearly impressed. "Learn anything useful?"

"I'm sure he did," said Shelton. "We'll know more when he comes to and gets some caffeine in his system."

Just then, a white Camaro pulled into the lot. Pauly was stopping by to give Lars an update.

"Shelton, this is Pauly Miguel," said Lars as Pauly sauntered toward them with a gait specific to men who could kill other men with their hands. "Pauly, this is my new guy, Shelton Hamner."

"Good to meet you," said Pauly, offering Shelton a firm handshake. "What's that?" he asked, nodding toward Ringo as he slapped his thigh to call Rufus over for a belly rub.

"My new photographer," said Lars, shaking his head.

Pauly pulled down his aviators, arching his brows.

"He's better than he looks," Lars told him with a shrug.

"He'd have to be," said Pauly as he began aggressively petting an eager Rufus, who immediately rolled onto his back.

"I'll meet you out back," said Lars, heading into his unit.

"You were a big local wrestling star," said Shelton, "spent some time in the UFC, as I recall."

"Yeah, a short stint a while back," said Pauly in his faint and indiscernible accent. "Fortunately, my knees gave out before I got my brains scrambled. Unfortunately, it was before I made any real money."

"What do you do now?" asked Shelton.

"I'm a P.I.," said Pauly. "Mostly for law firms. I got a side business doing some bounty hunting for local bail bondsmen."

"Sounds like interesting work," said Shelton.

"Yeah, that's what I thought," said Pauly with a laugh. "But most of the time it's boring as fuck."

The men laughed.

"You working on Micky's murder?" Pauly asked.

"Among other things," said Shelton, "but I have the impression that's the brass ring in all of it."

Pauly nodded.

"I'm helping out part-time," he said, handing Shelton a business card as Rufus took off in a sprint. "Unofficially, just gathering intel. I used to be a deputy and still have a lot of contacts within the department. Feel free to reach out."

"Sounds good," said Shelton.

Rufus darted back, tennis ball in hand. Pauly picked it up and gave it a soft lob. It landed on Ringo's chest. Rufus leaped onto the chair, turning it over on its side. Pauly and Shelton laughed as a confused Ringo began to come to.

"Nice meeting you, man. I'll catch you later," said Pauly as he headed toward Lars' back patio.

"What the hell is going on?" said Ringo as he struggled to right himself. "Who the fuck is that?" he asked, nodding to Pauly as he rounded the corner.

"Pauly Miguel," said Shelton. "He was just fucking with you. Tossed the tennis ball your way, and Rufus did the rest."

"Fucking with *me*?" said Ringo, dusting off his dirt and gravel-strewn chest."

"He might be half your size, but he's an NCAA champion with a black belt in jiu-jitsu, so you'd better grab a gun if you mean to have revenge," Shelton told him with a chuckle.

Ringo waved it off.

"So, you learn anything from your new friend Wayne?" asked Shelton.

152

"I sure did," said Ringo.

Shelton shrugged.

"Relax, I've got all the necessary starting points," he told him. "A couple of days, and I'll have a whole bunch of dirt for you."

"Anything that will help find Micky's killer?"

Ringo sneered.

"You think whoever killed Micky told that barfly anything?"

"What kind of dirt are we talking about?" asked Shelton.

"The kind that wins elections," said Ringo. "Micky's old lady is nearly as eager to flip the board as she is in finding out who killed her husband."

"And you know this how?" asked Shelton.

"She hired Dutch Wagner to run a PAC aimed at every incumbent," said Ringo. "Got a six-figure investment in their primary challengers, too."

"Who's Dutch Wagner?" asked Shelton.

"Good god, man, am I the only one doing any work around here?" said Ringo, as he ran his fingers through his hair, picking out debris.

Shelton was speechless.

"He's a political operative, or 'old Irish ward heeler' as he puts it," said Ringo as he pulled a dirty t-shirt over his head. "These days, he mostly handles campaigns in LeGrotto. He's getting up there in years, but he can still run circles around that moron from Sarasota who's handling things for Ignacio."

Ringo lit a fat joint and donned his Jerry-rigged sunglasses. Then he dumped some water from Shelton's bottle onto his hands and ran it back through his wavy hair, the closest he ever came to combing it, tying it in a top knot with a rubber band he'd pulled from his pocket. He looked like some sort of mutant sumo/samurai combo.

"Where are you going?" asked Shelton.

"To meet Dutch at the American Legion," he said as he slipped into a massive pair of extra-wide black Crocs.

"Can I come with?" asked Shelton.

"That depends," said Ringo. "Do they admit puddle pirates at Legion posts or just real soldiers?"

Shelton flipped him the bird.

****

Lars turned over a massive flank of mahi mahi on the grill while sipping his Yuengling.

"I hope you're hungry," he said to Pauly, turning his attention to the hush puppies sizzling on the side burner.

"Another beer should have my belly nice and limber," said Pauly, pulling two more from under the ice in the large cast-iron tub Lars kept on his back patio, which doubled as a cooler and an ice bath—a setup that proved easy once Lars got the motel ice machine working.

"So, anything newsworthy to report?" asked Lars.

"Checked off all the obvious boxes," Pauly told him. "MCSO didn't find shit, has no leads—surprise. Fortunately, Micky didn't have his cell on him when he went over, and despite the boat having been tossed, neither the shooter nor MCSO found it onboard."

"But someone did?" asked Lars.

"Yep," said Pauly. "Amber knew that Micky always kept it in a hidden compartment he built after getting one too many wet, and despite it being a crime scene, the boat is still unsecured in the bay, or was as of Monday morning, anyway."

"So, you got his phone?" asked Lars.

"Unofficially," said Pauly. "I took a kayak out to the boat right before dawn. Amber unlocked it and gave me permission to go through it. I haven't found anything yet, but there are half a dozen recurring phone calls from an incoming number that lasted between 3 and 37 minutes each."

"You don't think…?"

154

"A side chick?" asked Pauly. "Not likely. There are no outgoing calls to that number. I mean, it could have been a burner phone if the woman was married, and maybe he called her on a different line, and she only used that one from home, or the deal was she always had to call, but it doesn't track with his GPS locations. If he were having an affair, he'd be going someplace, probably the same place, after each or most of the calls. He did get a call from that number on the morning of the shooting, however. I mean, it's not right before or anything, but it's something, and right now, it's the most we've got. Micky had a lot of money. Maybe someone was shaking him down."

"So, what's your gut telling you?" asked Lars.

"I mean, it could have been Big Phosphate, the casino boys, or Ignacio's goons, but I cross-checked the calls with meetings, articles, and court hearings, and none of them are on a timeline to suggest they were threats about something Micky was doing at that time. Could be nothing, but I haven't been able to get any info on the other number yet, so I'm guessing it's a clone or a burner. I don't have a strong feeling either way, at the moment, but if I had to guess right now, I'd say either he had some kind of damning evidence of foul play one of those parties wanted to get their hands on, or someone outside of the obvious suspects was trying to shake him down over who knows what. Mickey was into a lot of stuff, Lars."

Lars nodded and realized he'd forgotten to flip the fish. When he turned it onto a large metal cookie sheet, the perfectionist in him was dismayed that it looked mildly overcooked.

****

The Village of Hernando was a slice of old Florida, an unincorporated fishing village between DeSoto City and the Ave Maria Causeway. Its American Legion post was next to a U.S. Coast Guard base where Shelton had been briefly stationed. It was only a three-minute drive from Ramblewood, which Lars liked about the property's location, as he was a frequent visitor to the Legion himself. When Shelton and Ringo walked inside, they saw Dutch seated at a nearby table.

"These fellas are with me, Annie," Dutch said to the old woman behind the bar. "Go ahead and sign in," he told them. "Get them whatever they want, darling, and put it on my tab," he said to the barmaid.

"Two Yuenglings, please," Shelton told the woman.

"You boys from around here?" she asked, drafting a beer into a frozen pint glass.

"Indirectly," Ringo told her.

"We just moved here from Sarasota," Shelton explained, noticing everyone at the bar was looking them over. "We live over at the Ramblewood."

"Y'all are Lars' new tenants? Tell him Annie said hello," the woman said.

"Will do," said Shelton as they grabbed their beers and headed toward the table.

"Have a seat," said Dutch, who looked to be drinking a rum and Coke. "About the only place left in these parts where you can get a beer for under three bucks," he added, nodding to their glasses. "$2.50 for a well cocktail," he said, sipping his. "And let's just say Annie gives a *generous* pour. Either of you boys serve?"

"Uh… not domestically," Ringo said awkwardly.

Puzzled, Dutch let the comment pass.

"What about you?" Dutch asked, looking to Shelton.

"Coast Guard, four years," he said somewhat sheepishly.

"Ain't nothing wrong with the Coast Guard," said Dutch. "Although they were a pain in my ass back in my youth when I used to run grass. It significantly reduced our weed supply when they built the station here in the '80s. Once Miami got too hot from the coke trade, many of those planes started dropping their square grouper into our waters. Became enough

156

of a PR problem that they eventually had to do something about it."

"I've heard that story," said Shelton. "I actually finished my time at the local station. Landed the dream assignment—Key West—and nearly cried a river when they told me I had to leave for some Gulf Coast town I'd never heard of. But it was slow going by comparison, and I liked the area well enough to enroll at Eckerd after I was discharged. What about you?"

"Nope," said Dutch. "I have no shame in admitting I had no interest in serving during Vietnam and was lucky to be young enough that one college deferment kept me undrafted. I'm a member of the Sons. My daddy served in World War II and Korea. Came home crazier than a shit house rat. About my only fond memories were the times he'd take me to the Legion with him, let me sit at the bar and sip Cokes. Still got a soft spot for them, I suppose, but these days I like a splash of rum."

"I gotta hit the head," Ringo said, taking a long pull of his beer as he walked toward the men's room.

"What the hell did he mean, not domestically?" asked Dutch once Ringo was out of earshot.

Shelton let out a whistle.

"The crazy fucker went over to Ukraine right after the Russians invaded to do some photography on the front lines. He learned quickly that every able-bodied man on the front was expected to shoot more than cameras. I can tell you this. He's armed like Fort Knox, shoots like a sniper, and, to use your words, is as crazy as a shit house rat."

"I knew there was something I liked about that son of a bitch," said Dutch. "I can see you boys put 'em away fast. Go grab a pitcher from Annie."

When Shelton returned, Ringo had already sat back down.

"Now, this guy Billy Sunday is a real hoot," Dutch was telling him. "He's notorious for evangelizing the gospel in go-go bars, one of his favorite ways to serve our lord and savior. Rumor has it, he has a revolving door of current and *ex*-dancers staying with him out at this big McMansion in one of Ignacio's developments. It used to be a model home. Sunday supposedly rents it, and while the home's ownership is buried in some convoluted mess of LLCs, I'd bet dollars to donuts it still belongs to Hernandez and that soft-headed son of a bitch ain't paying market rent if he's paying rent at all. He's dumber than a bag of hammers, but has somehow managed to avoid honest work his entire life, best I can tell."

Dutch handed Ringo a folder, then picked up another.

"Now, Candy Pants Hagerty is even more colorful," he said, waiving the file. "I used to manage her daddy's campaigns way back before he rolled over for Ignacio ahead of his final term, and I can tell you he's rolling over in his grave if he can see how much further his daughter has taken it. She actually worked in admin for the Mullet County Sheriff's Office for a spell. Rumor had it that the only thing she liked more than a man in uniform was getting him out of it. One deputy got suspended for doing her in a supply closet while on duty, and another got a divorce after his wife caught her jumping his bones in the squad car in their driveway—wait for it—newborn baby in tow. She's a bona fide homewrecker who supposedly found Jesus before marrying a wealthy personal injury attorney, but I'd be dipped in dog shit before I believed she's reformed her ways."

Dutch handed the file back and picked up another one, grinning.

"This may be the thinnest file, but it's the one that gives me the most pleasure to fill," he said. "That little turd stain Welsh creases me more than any shitheel politician I've ever come across, and believe you me, I've come across more than my share. I don't have anything damning on him yet, but the rumor mill is cranking out some dark and nasty shit. In my experience, where there's smoke, there's fire."

"What kind of rumors are we talking about?" asked Shelton.

158

"The *worst* kind," said Dutch, adding a dramatic pause for effect. "It's all in there," he said, handing him the file.

Shelton perused the first page and gave a look of disgust.

"Dark indeed," said Shelton, as he peeked at the file.

"The rumors don't seem so far-fetched now, do they?" asked Dutch. "Besides, you can tell the man enjoys playing the heel. In my experience, that kind of personality is built on a lifetime of self-loathing. Nothing concrete, but everything going around town is in that file. I don't expect you'll get anything solid, but I figured I'd let you know so that if someone offers you something solid, you'd best take them seriously."

"Will do," said Shelton.

Dutch leaned back on his chair, clasping his hands behind his head.

"Now, it goes without saying that I wouldn't mind a little quid pro quo," he told them. "If I'm gonna be sharing my opposition research with you, I'd like to be prepared to pounce when something runs, especially since we're so close to the big day."

"I've gotta use the head," said Shelton.

Ringo leaned in toward Dutch.

"He's got more, shall we say, ethical scruples than men like you and me," he told him. "He'd never feel comfortable sharing that sort of information with a political consultant. However, he shares everything with his best friend and co-worker, who is decidedly unscrupulous, especially when it comes to sticking it to bastards like Ignacio."

Dutch smiled.

"In other words, that was him asserting plausible deniability?"

Ringo winked, and Dutch took the last pull of his drink.

"I'm going to head out before he gets back. Show him I got the message, so to speak. I'll make sure Annie knows the rest of your lads' drinks are on me."

Ringo gave him a thumbs-up and smiled.

Chapter 9: Who is Miles?

"For god's sake, turn this damned noise off," Chief Washington said to his nephew, Cornell, as he turned the volume knob in the mayor's Cadillac Escalade all the way left to make the rap music go away.

"Man, you need to get with the times, Unc," said Cornell. "I saw that brother at Rollin' Loud down in Miami last year. Bitches be droppin' panties when that song comes on."

Chief Washington gave his nephew a side-eye glance.

"A *woman* will drop panties on an Al Green or Marvin Gaye track, too, but it'll be in a damned bedroom, not a football stadium," said the chief. "Any woman droppin' her skirt while some cat's screamin' about 'bitches ain't shit,' and 'keeping all his shorties and hoes in line' is exactly the kind of girl a young man wants to stay away from."

At this, Cornell rolled his eyes as he pulled into the entrance of the marina.

"I ain't exactly a young man, Unc."

"I ain't talkin' about you, dummy," said the chief. "But you're the mayor, a *Black* mayor, at that, someone young Black men should be able to see as a role model. You bumpin' around town with that shit blastin', it's an endorsement of all that nonsense. It tells them that this is how they get where you are."

"What's wrong with them emulating me?" Cornell asked. "Huh? I'm the youngest mayor in this city's history."

Chief Washington rolled his own eyes and extended a backhand to the side of his nephew's head.

"Damn, you're gonna make me wreck," yelled the mayor as he rubbed the affected temple.

"What's wrong is that you didn't get there acting like no fool, and your momma never let you listen to that street thug bullshit when you were growin' up. She'd be rolling over in her grave if she saw you riding through her hometown with that garbage on. And the only reason you're the youngest mayor this town has had is because of that family name, because you're Bishop Jones' grandson, and Marvette Jones was your momma. And the fact that you could call yourself a reverend with that crap pumping through your speakers is downright blasphemous!"

"You know I'm ordained—" the mayor screamed as he caught another one of his uncle's giant backhands across the side of his head.

"Most of these kids on the street don't have the people looking out for them you had, Cornell," said Chief Washington. "No guard rails to keep them in the right lane. They hear that shit in those songs and think it's an instruction manual for becoming a man. Young women hear it and think all there is to life is grabbin' that bag by getting pregnant from some gangsta or athlete."

"What'chu want me to play then, Unc?" Cornell asked, rolling his eyes but barely hiding the fact that his uncle had sufficiently chastened him.

The chief tuned the stereo to a jazz station out of Tampa.

"There we go," said Chief Washington. "A little Coltrane. Now *that's* talent. A woman hears that, she knows the man playing it's got some culture, sophistication, a little class. She don't take that from it? Move the fuck on."

The mayor chuckled as he pulled the giant, black SUV into a parking space. The Oyster River Marina was part of a new Hilton resort built on what had formerly been a dense mangrove forest and a mosquito-ridden pier locals used to fish from at the very south end of LeGrotto. It was detached from the city proper and had a beautiful view of the downtown DeSoto skyline and the bridge connecting the two cities across the river.

While locals lamented the loss of their Old Florida fishing grounds, it had provided a much-needed shot in the arm to the local economy, and its owners allowed generous concessions to Cornell in the form of comped suites, and tabs at the resort's bars and restaurants that need not be repaid. After all, Mayor Jones had sold it to his reluctant constituency through a series of speeches that were closer to preaching from the pulpit than extolling from the podium. This, of course, followed several maximum donations to his campaign coffers by various interests aligned with the development of the resort.

"Right there," said Cornell.

"That asshole got another boat?" asked the chief.

"It's good to be the sheriff," said Cornell. "Much more juice than a chief and a mayor put together," he added with a laugh.

"Indeed," said the chief.

As they exited the Escalade, they saw Sheriff Rusty Brock aboard a 39-foot yacht that was considerably more grand than the 30-footer the sheriff had previously been known to troll around in.

"Gentleman," said the sheriff with a salute. "Climb aboard."

As they boarded the boat, Chief Washington let out a whistle.

"Damn, I thought your last boat was impressive, sheriff. You've certainly upgraded."

The chief's tone conveyed maximal subtext.

"Well, my wife told me, 'Honey, you can't take it with you,'" said Sheriff Brock. "'So why don't you go ahead and get that 39-footer you always wanted?'"

"New?" asked Cornell.

"Oh, hell no," said Rusty. "2019 Tiara Coupe. Some snowbird from Maine kicked the bucket, and she went up for sale three slips down from mine. It was like it had been fated."

Chief Washington knew the boat still would have cost well over half a million bucks and wondered just how much of a fortune Rusty and his Realtor wife had been able to amass. He himself was looking at no more than a state pension, but he had a feeling his nephew had been more industrious and could tell from the way Cornell was sizing up the boat that it was inspiring unseemly ideas in his nephew's mind.

"I appreciate the professional courtesy, sheriff," said Cornell. "My uncle and Micky were tight. Mrs. Pesch was devastated when he notified her, and he'd like to stay up to speed, if you don't mind."

The sheriff popped the caps off three bottles of imported beer and handed one to each of his guests. The three men raised a silent toast before taking a sip.

"Well, I appreciate you notifying next of kin," said Sheriff Brock, looking at the chief. "I don't imagine it was easy, and she sure as hell wouldn't have taken it any better from me."

Chief Washington nodded and took a long pull from his beer.

"So, I've been getting daily briefings on the investigation, and I assure you we are putting every resource we have into this thing," said the sheriff. "I know that a lot of people think Ignacio is somehow behind it, and, given that he's been … *supportive* of my campaigns and goes back quite a ways with my old man, they figure we'd somehow turn a blind eye. But seriously, Lawrence, the Cuban didn't do this."

"That what he told you?" asked the chief, casting a wry look at Sheriff Brock.

The sheriff frowned.

"The detectives cleared him because he was in front of around a thousand onlookers that night for an art gala down in Sarasota," said Brock. "His wife's on the museum board. They spent the night in a suite at the Ritz. A dozen staff members confirmed seeing them at various hours. He didn't get home until—"

"You know he wouldn't pull the trigger himself," said the chief, no longer tempering his tone.

"Did you see the evidence?" asked Brock. "Did that look like a professional hit to you? The thing was sloppy as hell, and you know Ignacio doesn't operate that way. Hell, if he were

gonna have him bumped, he would have used real pros from
Miami—Haitians or Jamaicans. He would've covered his tracks
so intently that he could get away with bragging about it. I'd
expect he'd even wink and nod toward me just so that he knew
I understood he was untouchable."

"That does sound more like the Ignacio that I know," said
Cornell.

"So, who else are your people looking at?" asked the
chief.

"I'm telling you, Lawrence, for how sloppy this was, we
still haven't been able to turn up anything resembling a solid
lead. Ballistics gave us next to nothing. It looks like somebody
made their way out to the boat, probably on a skiff or even a
canoe, shot Micky in the chest, and made their way back
without leaving anything behind or being seen. He was
anchored in the middle of nowhere. Some people at the DeSoto
marina and that condo complex reported hearing the blast, and
a few said they scanned the horizon, but no one saw or heard
anything else, so they assumed it was fireworks. It was a dark,
moonless night. Next morning, a woman from Sea Grape Cove
discovered the body while walking her dog and called it in.
You know how cases like that go. Lest someone comes forward
with something more, ain't a whole lot of police work that can
be done."

Unfortunately, Chief Washington knew this to be true. The
murder rate in LeGrotto accounted for half of Mullet County's
total homicides, despite representing only around 10 percent of
its population. The cases that got closed usually had witnesses,
maybe a snitch who came forward, or someone who traded the
information when they got into a tight spot themselves. When
none of those things happened, the murder weapon was found
on a suspect, or the department got lucky with ballistics. It
suddenly became painfully clear to the chief that unless some
sort of damning lead fell into their laps, Amber Pesch would
probably never know who killed her husband.

164

"Alright, then," said Chief Washington. "Thanks for the beer."

"You buy his story?" asked Cornell after they'd climbed back into the Escalade.

"I hate to say it," said the chief, "but I do."

****

The housing situation sorted itself out more easily than Shelton or Lars could have imagined. Gary, still deep in arrears, had sneaked away in the middle of the night, so there had been no need for Lars to evict him, making the rooms available a few days earlier than expected. Meanwhile, Angel had found Tina a roommate arrangement with another barmaid from Memories Lounge. As such, no squatting would be required.

Moving into smaller environs meant less room for non-essentials, however. Because neither Shelton nor Ringo was willing to spend money on a storage unit, which were presently going for what an efficiency apartment would have fetched just a few years earlier, they made several trips to a Salvation Army donation center a block from their rental to lighten their travels. Then they squeezed the rest of their belongings into a U-Haul.

From the driver's seat, Shelton took one last look at the home, which he was quite fond of. He had long harbored the dream of buying it himself, but realized in the moment that this was indeed the last goodbye and had to admit he was more saddened by the idea than expected.

"I'm gonna miss this place," he said to Ringo, who was riding shotgun.

"Yeah, she's a beauty," said Ringo wistfully. "Hold on," he said. "There's something I really want to do before we leave."

Shelton was surprised as Ringo had often expressed considerable disdain for nostalgia, which he deemed to be a weakness of the highest order. When he opened the back of the

U-Haul, Shelton assumed he was grabbing a camera to commemorate the farewell. However, what he pulled from the box was a Griffin Armament mk2 he had modified with a forced reset trigger. He walked around to the driver's side of the vehicle.

"What in God's name are you doing, you maniac?" yelled Shelton when he realized what Ringo had in tow.

Ringo reached into the cab and laid on the horn, which blared loudly. After no more than 20 seconds, the big ginger who had terrorized Shelton on the 4th of July emerged.

"Hey, motherfucker, you trying to wake the dead?" Red screamed.

Ringo swung toward him, and at the sight of the menacing assault rifle, the man dove back into the house headfirst.

Ringo trained the weapon on the man's heavily modified Ram 2500 pickup truck, specifically its 22-inch wheels and, more specifically, the $2,000 worth of Fury Country Hunter off-road tires they were outfitted with.

"Someone's calling the cops, man," pleaded Shelton. "You're gonna show up on someone's Ring cam and wind up on one of those YouTube channels you like to watch."

Unfazed by Shelton's warning, Ringo expended the 20-round magazine in one burst, successfully annihilating all four tires. The truck's height was instantly reduced by a foot. Ringo casually walked back to the rear of the U-Haul, swapped magazines, and grabbed what appeared to be a small hand grenade from the same box. He raised his rifle toward the sky and walked around the side of the house.

Shelton desperately wanted to drop the truck into drive and take off, but remained paralyzed in a common-sense-defying fit of loyalty, since he knew Ringo was only acting on behalf of the story he'd recounted to him while they had been drinking at Memories' on his first day back from the Texas weed run.

Once in the home's backyard, Ringo pulled the pin and lobbed the small grenade into the above-ground swimming pool, spraying at least ten rounds at its walls, turning away milliseconds before the grenade detonated, walking casually, cool as a cucumber, in what would have looked like a perfectly choreographed action movie stunt had anyone been watching.

He dropped the rifle back into the box, closed the roll-up door, walked around, and climbed into the passenger seat of the cab. Shelton, still aghast, was frozen.

"Come on, man, before the cops arrive," Ringo said, rolling his index finger in the on-with-it signal.

****

Ally mostly worked from home, but had been coming into Pauly Miguel's office most days since Lars had arranged the labor-sharing agreement. His setup was rather impressive, and he had access to multiple subscription-based skip-tracing databases not available to the general public.

She had used LexisNexis for much of her investigative reporting, but after a brief tutorial from Pauly on the additional tools, a whole new world had opened up to her. Ally had been banging away on the keyboard when Pauly entered the office.

"Hey, rock star, what's going on?" said Pauly. "Come across anything interesting?"

"As a matter of fact, I did come across something curious when I pulled Mickey's credit reports and noticed a couple of surprising associations in an old one," said Ally. "Did you know Micky had a son?"

Pauly gave her a puzzled look.

"I always understood that he and Amber were unable to conceive," he told her.

"Not with Amber," Ally said.

"Like out of wedlock?" Pauly asked suspiciously.

"No," said Ally. "Well … yes, technically speaking, but not while he was married to Amber. Before that."

"I'd always heard they'd been together since they were kids, like high school sweethearts," said Pauly.

"They got married when he was 19, and she was 18," said Ally, opening a file and fishing through its documents. "It seems he fathered a child in 1977 when he was barely 17," she said, looking at the page she had been searching for. "The mother was a Helena Redfeather, 20 at the time, born in unincorporated Mullet County. The child's name was Miles Pesch, but the last name was changed to Redfeather just months later, then Conepatchie when he was three, and the mother looks to have married. There's no social associated with any of these records, unfortunately."

"What became of them?" asked Pauly.

"The mother died of natural causes while living on the Miccosukee Indian Reservation in 1986, when Miles would have been nine. Miles drops completely off the radar after that. I'm guessing he changed his name again or possibly even moved out of the country, because I can't find anything on him, and with no social security number to cross-reference, I hit a dead end. It might also just be that records from Indian reservations don't always hit the public sources. The whole thing might be nothing, but I never knew Micky to have a kid, and when I told Lars, he seemed certain it's a mistake of some sort."

Pauly stroked his chin in contemplation.

"Good work, young lady," Pauly told her.

"I'm older than you are, kiddo," she replied with a wink.

****

The subdivision where the Reverend Billy Sunday and his family lived was called Cobalt Ridge. It was part of a "master-planned community" named Bellwether Harbour. This was just one of many bland, uninspired, homogeneous, suburban hellscapes that Ignacio had developed on what had long been endless acres of farmland in the once-rural northeast corridor of Mullet County.

There were only four models to choose from, and Sunday inhabited the "Berkshire," a four-bedroom "coastal contemporary" design replete with quartz countertops, brushed aluminum appliances, and porcelain tile meant to look like marble.

Sunday was partial to the "Gibraltar," a "neo-Mediterranean" design that was essentially the same home, but with a clay barrel tile roof instead of aluminum, and granite replacing the quartz. Both had the ever-popular barn-style sliding doors made from compressed particle board separating each room, but the Gibraltar used dark woods, while the Berkshire's were white.

Sunday had mentioned this preference to Ignacio on more than one occasion, prompting the developer to once again remind his political charge that he was renting a fully decked-out model home spec-build for what amounted to a Section 8 price. And while this was to rectify the fact that Sunday did not own nor could afford to rent any home in the ward for which he would be running for office, the developer reminded him that he could stick him in a 1,300-square-foot starter home elsewhere in the development should the assigned home prove inadequate.

"Billy, baby, what happened to that air pump?" a young topless woman with an impressively augmented bosom asked from the pool deck as he turned over steaks on the built-in grill of the patio. "The raft is a little low."

"I hardly think you're in danger of sinking, my dear," Sunday said, pausing to admire the more than adequate flotation devices embedded in her chest cavity.

"Flip that steak, baby," said another impressively endowed and equally topless young lady who had saddled up behind him. "I know you like your meat pink."

Sunday felt a twitch in his swimsuit as her bare breasts pressed against the hairy jowls of back meat that drooped from his shoulder blades.

"I need someone to lotion my back," said a third young lady who was sunning her thong-clad buns on a chaise lounge nearby.

The reverend, already sweating from the grill heat and proximity to the woman behind him, jumped when drops of perspiration fell from his brow and hissed as they collided with the grill.

"Ladies, please," he implored them. "One at a time. These are grade A prime ribeyes and require my complete attention at the moment."

The young lady behind him pressed against his backside and dropped her hand over the crotch of his swim trunks.

"What if I want a tube steak instead, Daddy Billy?" she asked with a chuckle.

The reverend tried to flip one of the steaks, but his hand was shaking so badly, he couldn't manage. Just then, an electronic noise signaled that the front doorbell had been rung.

"Dammit, is there not a moment's peace in this life?" Sunday complained, pulling on a terry-cloth robe as he walked through the sliding glass doors toward the front door.

Through the peephole, he saw Mary Ann Gossamer, head of the Cobalt Ridge Homeowners' Association. Sunday's neck stiffened. Under his swimsuit, what had been an ambitious erection deflated so quickly it was as if it had been punctured. He took a deep breath as he opened the door.

"Blessed day, Mrs. Gossamer," he said with the best fake smile he could manage. "What might I do for you?"

"Well, reverend," the middle-aged woman said with unmistakable contempt for the title. "We have received yet another complaint of topless sunbathing at your swimming pool that is in view of neighboring properties. I don't need to remind you that there are children in this cul-de-sac."

170

"Of course, there are children, Mrs. Gossamer," he said. "I've got six of my own, as you well know. Blessed is the fruit."

Mrs. Gossamer bit down on her lower lip.

"Speaking of which, where is your pack of offspring? I haven't seen them since school let out."

"Well, they are in Charleston with their mother, visiting with her parents," said Sunday, his voice dripping with condescension. "Unfortunately, both my church and my position as an elected official have prevented me from joining them at present. As you know, it's an election year. And as I've told you before, there are no limits as to how far some people will go to unduly influence the outcome. Now, I assure you there are no—"

A shriek caught both of them off guard. Then the darkly-tinted sliding glass doors at the back of the home quickly slid open, leaving the Reverend Sunday with a sudden disdain for the Berkshire's open floor plan.

"Billy, baby, there's a peeping Tom out there," shouted a young topless woman sporting a dark bronze tan with nary a tan line in sight.

In the backyard, Ringo shimmied down the queen palm he'd been hanging from, a 35mm Nikon strapped around his neck. The exotic dancers attempted to cover their unnaturally large breasts with their naturally small hands, wondering if it was a man or the fabled Skunk Ape, given the sweaty figure's size, hirsuteness, and adeptness descending the tree.

Billy Sunday frantically waved the topless young lady back toward the pool deck. When he turned back toward Mary Ann Gossamer, her hands were on her hips, and her eyebrows arched.

"That's my niece," he stammered. "She's, well … European?"

The woman began writing in a notebook she'd taken from her side pocket.

"These women were being sex-trafficked!" Sunday shouted. "I rescued them! They're reacclimating to Christian life!"

"And I'm going to have to ask you to have whichever guest owns that eyesore of a car to move it," she added, still writing. "Its wheels are on the Miller's grass."

The reverend looked toward a banged-up white Fiero with a primer gray quarter panel on its driver's side. Then he heard the clicking of a camera and looked to see a giant beast of a man snapping photos, which also seemed to catch Mrs. Gossamer off guard.

Ringo holstered his Nikon in its bag, gave a middle finger in their direction, and got in the car.

"Eyesore, my ass," he mumbled, as the car struggled to achieve ignition. Once its engine knock died down to a hum, he put the pedal to the floor, managing a modest chirp of the bald tires.

Chapter 10: Date night

Shelton hadn't been on anything you would call a proper date in longer than he cared to remember. For the past several years, his love life had consisted of random hookups on dating apps or occasionally going home with either a barmaid or a barfly.

It was just past quitting time on Friday. He'd finished his piece for the Sunday online edition and had stopped by Trader Joe's to pick up a dozen white roses on the cheap, although he did spring for the optional baby's breath and had meticulously arranged the bouquet, carefully peeling the sticker off the cellophane to hide its provenance. He was hoping to make a clean getaway, but Ringo and Bryce were engaged in conversation at one of the shared picnic tables.

"I know, right?" said Bryce. "The tower was hot enough from the burning jet fuel to melt steel beams, but they somehow found one of the terrorists' passports intact, just sitting atop the rubble?"

"Inside job, for sure," said Ringo, who, like Bryce, was a sucker for a good conspiracy theory.

"Yeah, inside Israel," said Bryce, tilting his head and arching his eyebrows for effect.

"Where are you at on the moon landing?" asked Ringo.

"Well, when you consider the amount of fuel those Saturn rockets would require and then—"

Ringo put up his palm when he noticed an inordinately dapper Shelton approaching him in light colored linens and dress shoes, flowers, and a bottle of wine in tow.

"Where you off to, Romeo?" he asked.

"I'm having dinner with Emily," Shelton told him, somewhat sheepishly.

"Nice!" said Ringo. "Where are you taking her?"

"She's making dinner, actually," said Shelton.

"Better still, that's how come you sprung for a Barolo?" he asked, nodding to the wine bottle.

Shelton shrugged.

"It's Costco Barolo, but yeah."

The wheels of Lars' Jeep crunched shells as he pulled into the parking area.

"Where's our boy going all cleaned up?" he asked as he pulled up next to the group.

Shelton, who never really liked being the center of attention, could actually feel his cheeks flush.

"He's got a date with that hottie from TBEW," said Ringo.

"Emily Bartleston?" asked Lars, somewhat incredulously.

"You don't have to sound *that* surprised," said Shelton.

"No, color me impressed," said Lars. "You're breathing rarefied air. Every guy in town that's met that woman has their eyes on her, but none of 'em have ever gotten so much as a smile, let alone a date."

"Well, we're just hanging out," said Shelton.

"Yeah, okay," said Lars, eyeing the wine and roses and smiling wryly as he gave an up-down look to Shelton's much fancier than usual threads.

"Tina is bartending at Memories tonight," said Ringo. "Hit me up there when you're finished."

"That doesn't look like a man who plans on coming home tonight," said Lars, eyebrows arched.

Shelton, in a full-on blush now, defensively issued a middle finger as he climbed into the Mini Cooper and lowered its top.

****

When Shelton arrived at the address Emily had given him, he found a perfectly charming craftsman-style bungalow accented with all manner of lush greenery. He pulled his car into the spot behind her Mustang in the driveway and took a deep breath before approaching the porch.

Shelton wondered why he was so nervous about a first date, but he knew it was because he couldn't remember the last time he'd met someone so genuinely interesting. Physical attraction and shared passions and interests rarely overlapped between prospective partners in his experience, but Emily had checked every block and then some.

"You found it," she said, having stepped out onto the porch when she heard the car.

"Good old Apple Maps," said Shelton, suddenly self-conscious and wondering if it sounded as dumb to her as he feared it might. *Good god, man, pull yourself together*, he thought. *You were perfectly cool when you had drinks after the meeting. Stop acting like it's your first time courting a woman, for Christ's sake.*

"Are those for me?" she asked, nodding toward the roses.

"I hope you like white," he said. "The red ones were a bit past their prime."

"White roses and red wine," she said. "I like the contrast."

Dammit, man, he thought to himself. *You should've gotten a nice Chardonnay and made a theme of it. After all, you're wearing light colored linens. If you spill any ...*

Shelton could feel his armpits moisten and felt what he could only imagine was the onset of a panic attack.

"It's Barolo," he stammered. "Ever had one?"

"I can't say that I have," said Emily, in a much calmer voice and steadier tone than he had managed.

"It's made from the nebbiolo grape," he told her, still speaking too quickly. "One of Italy's very best. Perfect for lamb chops."

"Speaking of which, let's get inside so I can check on them," she said.

As they entered the home, Shelton noticed how meticulously it had been maintained. The original narrow-plank oak floors were varnished to a high sheen, and both the brick fireplace and built-in bookshelves were thick with frequent new coats to keep them a beaming white. Several beautiful paintings and gallery-wrapped photography adorned the walls. The mantle was aglow with tea-light candles, and larger ones illuminated the room from the vintage speakers of her rack system, which was broadcasting *Last Goodbye* by Jeff Buckley on vinyl. A Buddhist-inspired incense box wafted subtle smoke and scent into the air.

"Nice place," said Shelton, "and the food smells amazing."

"Thanks."

Emily poured water into a glass vase at the sink.

"There's a corkscrew in the drawer to my right if you want to decant the wine," she said with her back to him.

"I actually opened it before I left so it could breathe on the drive," he told her.

"Risky, especially with red wine," she said. "Weren't you worried it would spill?"

"As a degenerate wine hound, I've learned a few tricks," he said with a laugh. "An insulated wine chiller, in a box, on the floor of the back seat. Provided you don't get pulled over and slapped with an open container citation, it works perfectly."

"I'm impressed," said Emily, handing him two glasses from a nearby bar cart.

Shelton admired the quality of her stemware.

"Canapé?" she asked as he poured, nodding toward a large cutting board filled with hors d'oeuvres.

Shelton handed her a glass, then picked up a water cracker topped with goat cheese and sliced fig and another with cream cheese, smoked salmon, and cilantro, placing them on a small plate. Emily nibbled a grape and inspected the wine, sniffing its bouquet.

"Smells lovely," she said.

"And the ambiance is perfect," Shelton told her, nodding toward the record player and candles.

"Cheers," she said, offering her glass.

"To gastronomic pleasures," he said.

"And the many adventures that may accompany them," she added.

They clinked glasses and imbibed.

"Oh, this is divine," said Emily, pulling her glass away to admire the wine's color.

Shelton finally felt himself come to ease, wondering only how he had managed to discover such a rare flower out in the wild.

****

Connor Welsh slammed the stack of papers onto the desk.

"How on earth are we spending this much PAC money on attack ads and trending in the wrong direction?" he asked the olive-skinned mustachioed man on the other side of it.

Christopher Bacchelli was a high-priced political operative out of Sarasota who served as a consultant to all of Ignacio's candidates, while also running a near-endless array of dark money political action committees from which the Cuban would fund smear campaigns against his political foes. He hadn't been expecting a visitor this late, especially on a Friday, and had been caught on his heels.

"A small dip in the aftermath of the wetlands and impact fee votes was to be expected," said Bacchelli. "We're dropping robocalls and two direct mail pieces this week to remind voters who the *real* conservative is. It's nothing to worry about."

"A small dip?" yelled Welsh. "I've lost eleven points!"

"And yet you're still up eight," said Bacchelli. "You'll recover three to four points with this ad-buy and be ahead by double digits again. Election Day is too close for him to close that gap, especially given the limited cash he has to burn. Plus, we've already got through all of the politically unpopular votes, and you're still in the lead. So what if it's a bit tighter than last time? That's normal. You're an incumbent. You've got votes to defend. You only need one more vote than your opponent to win."

"I don't want to squeak by, Christopher," yelled Welsh. "It would make me look weak, vulnerable, paint a target on my back. I don't want anyone to dare oppose me in four years, and I don't want any other commissioner on that board to think I've been weakened."

"Let me handle all of that," said Bacchelli, easing back in his chair and clasping his hands on his belly. "I've got a piece on Osborne's divorce from his first marriage going out to evangelical likely voters, and another on two foreclosed rental properties during the recession, and a reckless driving citation following an accident going to Republican super-voters. They portray him as immoral, irresponsible, and reckless. He won't get anywhere near you."

"Call Art Pyle," Welsh told him. "I'm doing the debate."
Bacchelli rolled his eyes.

"Connor, how many times have I told you, when the election is in the bag, don't do anything that can pull it out of that bag," he said slowly but sternly. "You're *way* ahead. You do a debate, go on TV, or a podcast, it doesn't add anything to your lead. But you slip up and give them one inartful soundbite to clip out and run with, and suddenly this thing is a horse race. The risk isn't worth the potential reward."

"I haven't done anything this time around," he huffed. "A few short stump speeches at Republican clubs and fundraising events. It looks like I'm scared of that empty suit."

"You haven't had to," said Bacchelli. "You've got the biggest campaign war chest in this county's history. That's the beauty of all those resources. You just sit back and let me do my thing."

"I'm doing the debate, Christopher!" he boomed. "It's not up for negotiation."

Bacchelli could feel his blood pressure rise, but knew it would be useless to argue. Instead, he'd casually mention it to

Ignacio and hope the man pulling the strings agreed with him and could talk Welsh out of such foolishness.

****

"That was utterly magnificent," said Shelton, sopping up the remains of the mint demi-glace with a piece of the baguette Emily had made from scratch.

"I'm glad you liked it," she said with a smile. "There's key lime pie for dessert if you saved room. Store-bought, but it's from this amazing little bakery downtown, one of the best I've ever had."

"Sure, but I'm going to need some time for this to settle," he laughed, splitting the remaining Barolo between their nearly empty glasses.

"I have a Chardonnay I can open?" said Emily.

"That would pair well with the pie," he told her.

She grabbed a wine key and cut the foil before setting to work on the cork.

"May I?" he asked, signaling toward the record player, which had long since finished the second side of *Grace*.

"Of course," she told him. "I have to admit, as much as I love the warmth and richness of vinyl, I'd forgotten how much of a pain it was to keep flipping records every 20 minutes."

"A well-rewarded labor," he said, while thumbing through a milk crate filled with albums.

Shelton grew excited when he spotted a copy of *Popular Problems*, Leonard Cohen's penultimate studio album, released just two years before his 2016 death. He cued up the first song on side two, a blistering ballad called *My Oh My*.

Shelton met Emily's eyes as the distinct opening chords crackled through the speakers. She smiled in approval.

"May I have this dance?" he asked, extending his hand and offering a curtsy.

"You want to dance with me?" she asked, sporting a coy smile.

"More than anything."

He drew her close, noticing the way the candlelight flickered in her big dark eyes as her head came to rest on his chest, fingers ever so gently stroking the nape of his neck, sending electrified chills straight down his spine. The scent of Moroccan oil wafted up from her hair, mixing with the cocoa butter lotion on her skin to create a bouquet that smelled like all the things a man could ever desire of a woman. She pressed closer to him, and he could feel her warm breath under his chin. In the final notes, she withdrew just enough for their respective gazes to meet, and they fell into a soft and sumptuous kiss that would rank high on the list of the very best he had ever known.

****

Dutch hated dropping in on Amber Pesch at nearly 8:30 p.m., but he also knew from experience that people are far more likely to be talkative during evening hours, especially if you can ply them with a bit of drink. Amber was almost certain to be home alone, and he knew her well enough to suspect that she wouldn't be offended by a knock before at least 9 p.m., especially at a time of year when the sunsets could stretch past eight as it had that evening. In fact, the sky was still in golden hour when she came to answer the door, and he was pleased to see that she was dressed well enough to not feel awkward receiving company.

"Well, hello, young lady, how are you on this beautiful evening?" he asked her, employing a touch more drawl than usual.

"Hey, Dutch, what are you doing out at this hour at your age?" she asked with a smile.

"I had this here bottle of Haitian rum and thought you might be so kind as to have a drink with an old man while his liver remained agreeable to such a proposition."

She held open the door and turned toward the kitchen.

180

"What do we need?" she asked as she opened the fridge.

"A bit of ice, maybe some soda water; lime chunks if you got any."

"I believe we have it all," she said, positioning a stainless steel bucket under the automatic ice maker on the door of her SubZero refrigerator, as she realized there was no longer a *we* in the equation.

"Grab two tumblers off the wet bar, and I'll meet you out on the deck," she said, handing him the bucket. "I was just out there. The sky's beautiful."

Outside, he noticed a nearly empty Chardonnay bottle next to one of the Adirondack chairs, along with a lipstick-stained glass.

"This is my happy place these days," she said, closing the sliding glass door, before placing a tray with two cans of soda water and a lime with a paring knife on the table between the two chairs.

Dutch made quick work of the lime and tossed some ice into each tumbler. He splashed a bit of the Barbancourt into the one with the most ice and filled the rest with soda water. He handed it to Amber and filled the other glass with only rum, tossing in a few lime chunks.

Amber held up her glass in a toast.

"To Micky," she said.

"May he have been in heaven for an hour before the devil knew he was dead," said Dutch as he clinked her glass.

"So is this a campaign call or are you paying a proper visit?" she asked, easing back into her seat and looking out at the very last embers of daylight beginning to fade into a fiery orange horizon.

"Somewhere in between," he said with a bit of unease in his voice.

"I don't like that inflection," she said. "Cut to it, old man."

Dutch took a big gulp of the rum.

"When was the last time you heard from Miles?" he finally asked.

Amber maintained her sights on the horizon, letting out a long, exaggerated exhale.

"Or, more specifically, when was the last time Micky heard from him?" Dutch added.

Amber, clearly a little uneasy with the question, dropped her head back in thought.

"To my knowledge, it had been at least seven years, maybe more," she finally said. "And I don't think he would have failed to tell me if it had been more recent. Why do you ask, Dutch?"

"Well, we gotta look at all angles of this, Amber, and Miles had … you know, some PTSD and mental health challenges and … well, was capable of considerable violence."

"Dutch," she said, her tone suggesting she would prefer he drop the line of questioning.

He put a hand up defensively, but still pressed on.

"There were some untraceable calls from a burner phone, which would sort of fit his … *lifestyle*. I mean, last I heard, he was living out of his car at a tent encampment when Micky pulled some strings to get him into a halfway house."

Amber shook her head.

"Oh, Dutch, I can't believe Miles had anything to do with Micky's death," she said, continuing to shake her head as she lifted her glass for a sip. "Yes, he's got his issues and has not always been his best self when he's not on his meds, but the idea of him hunting down Micky on his boat and blasting him with a shotgun out of the blue? The halfway house thing was the last time I knew of them interacting, and there wasn't much direct contact between them even then. Micky received a courtesy call from a detective in Sarasota he knew. Hobart, I think his name was. Anyway, he informed Micky that Miles had been living on the streets. Micky called in some favors and managed to get him in at a place way out in Arcadia. I don't

182

think he'd heard from him since. To be honest, I had wondered if he was even still alive."

"I can't even be certain he is," said Dutch. "You mind if I ask whether he was in the will?"

"No, Micky left his sister a small trust and cursed me with serving as trustee, left his boat to Lars, and left it to my discretion as to how I wanted to help any other family members with what was left. More than half of the money went into various trusts and donations serving different non-profit organizations he favored. Tampa Bay Environmental Watch alone got a million bucks."

"I can't imagine old Mary was pleased about that arrangement," he said.

"None too much," affirmed Amber. "But I don't know what the hell she thought she was gonna get. She burned through both her inheritances from their folks with impressive speed, and Micky had bailed her and the girls out to the tune of several hundred thousand dollars over the years. I figured he thought giving her more cash in a lump sum wouldn't be any more useful than lighting it on fire in the driveway."

"He'd have surely been right about that," said Dutch.

"Don't I know it," she said with a chuckle. "But she's got a formidable allowance that won't require her to work if she can maintain a modest lifestyle and doesn't do anything stupid."

"Those are two mighty big ifs," said Dutch with a chuckle of his own. "Do me a favor, though. If Miles, for some reason, reaches out to you, let me know right away."

"Sure," she said.

"I mean immediately, and do not make plans to meet him without consulting me first. Can you promise me that?"

Amber looked at him solemnly.

"I promise," she said.

****

Shelton was still thinking about the dizzying kiss goodnight Emily had planted on him as they said their goodbyes on her front porch, when he realized he'd passed Memories Lounge and would have to bang a U-turn at the next light. He had caught a bad case and knew it would take everything he had to keep his head straight. He had never even brushed up against anything quite like her: brains, beauty, independence, and, above all, blazing passion set to worthy objects.

Shelton had always felt like he was on fire for life, and that it was his indefatigable desire to squeeze every drop of adventure out of it that proved so incompatible with the rhythms of most other people. In Ringo, he'd found a kindred spirit, someone even more hellbent on recklessly pushing the envelope than he had ever been; a giant beast of a man who barreled through the world full tilt like an elephant on amphetamines. Everyone else, with their dull jobs and spare time passed with mundane hobbies—yoga meetups, Netflix binges, game nights, karaoke, and adult kickball leagues—they might as well be dead as far as people like them were concerned.

They needed to paint outside the lines. They needed the unknown, the unpredictable, a bit of regularly occurring danger, and even the occasional possibility of mortal wounds. Ringo's women had always been trainwrecks, the sort of people whose own lives were so torn and frayed that having even minimum expectations of someone else would be too absurd to consider. As impossible as it might seem, Ringo had always been the one who had it more together in his romantic relationships, and it gave him the breathing room he required.

Of course, it would still end badly, almost without exception, but Ringo was comforted by the idea that it was always him throwing in the towel. Whereas with Shelton, whose partners tended to be somewhat conventional, at least by comparison, he was more prone to being on the receiving end of the *this just really isn't going to work* conversations. But this woman had a smoldering fire at her core, an intense passion for what was important to her, and she seemed just adventurous enough to come along for the wild ride without pulling him over the edge—or even to be too salty about having to pull him back from it. It had been one dinner, he reminded himself. Time would tell.

As he pulled into the lot, a crowd began hurriedly spilling out of the bar as though there had been a raid, or perhaps even a kitchen fire. It was clear they were running *from* something, not to it. The last person to exit passed through the door with propulsion that seemed to originate from beyond his own body. He was a big man, well over his skis, and after four cartoonishly fast, skidding steps forward as the others peeled off quickly to either side of his impromptu lane, he fell flat to his belly and chest like a baseball player skidding headfirst into home plate.

As he pitched forward, large yet gangly arms whooshed upward behind him, revealing that the man had been tossed forward by an even larger human. Ringo shifted slightly sideways to pass through the doorway and met the man where he lay.

"I didn't tell you to think about it," he told the man who was trying to upright himself by pushing off the ground to his knees. "I told you to run."

Ringo raised a size 14 Doc Marten and kicked the man's buttocks as if it were a football on a tee, instantly rendering him prone once more.

"Fawk!" the large man on the receiving end squealed, instinctively attempting to push up his upper body once more.

This time, Ringo brought the boot down on the man's right hand and ground it into the macadam He howled in pain.

"I'll fucking kill you, you animal," the man screamed.

"Leave him alone," an acquaintance of the man who was among the onlookers screamed.

Lars came running out the door and immediately saw Shelton, who put his hand up to signal that everything was okay.

With his right hand still underfoot, the man on the ground took his left hand and reached into the waistband of his jeans, now worn plumber's style, and removed a small hunting knife. Ringo spotted him before he could effectively grip the weapon and quickly removed a black jack from his own waistline. Pivoting 45 degrees to keep the man's right hand underfoot, he brought the blackjack down sideways on his left hand so that the metal weight would make contact as a hammer might. There was an audible crack, and the man shrieked in pain as the knife fell loose. His friend began to step forward, but Lars, looking menacing in a tight T-shirt and his gas-station cowboy hat, stuck out a hand and shook his head. The man stilled himself.

"Might I ask what this is all about?" said Shelton.

"This asshole likes to put his hands on women's asses without an invitation," said Ringo, finally lifting his foot from what was now the man's *good* hand.

"It was an accident," the man said, rolling to his back and clutching his left hand, which was already changing colors and beginning to balloon. "I'm drunk, my hand slipped, I didn't even realize …"

"Yeah, my hand slipped too," said Ringo.

Lars approached the man's friend, who stepped back in fear. Lars softened his stance and put his hands up defensively.

"I'm not gonna hit you," he said. "This your buddy?" he asked.

The man nodded.

"Get him to a hospital," Lars said, pulling a wad of cash from his cutoffs. "This is for his copay. Tell 'em he was performing drunken carpentry and hit his hand with a hammer, and don't do nothing stupid like call the police or come back here with a gun or something. That lunatic is armed to the teeth and even dumber than you two yokels. Plus, what your friend did constitutes misdemeanor sexual battery, and it was that guy's old lady, so she *will* testify if your buddy wants to press assault charges."

The man shook his head.

"He's on parole," he said. "He's not even supposed to be here."

"Oh, good," said Lars. "Seems it's all gonna work out after all."

The man stuffed the money into his pocket and moved toward his friend, pulling him up and hurrying him toward a large gray Nissan pickup truck.

"Shall we adjourn to the bar and have a drink?" asked Lars.

Shelton looked at Ringo and chuckled as he shook his head.

"Who says chivalry is dead?" asked Ringo.

"Touché," said Shelton, and the three men walked inside.

"I don't see any police lights," said Angel from behind the bar. "Do I need to call an ambulance?"

"No, but there is an ER visit in that fool's future," said Lars. "How about a round of Yuengling and …"

He looked for Tina and finally found her passed out face-first in a booth next to the jukebox.

"I think she's good," said Shelton.

"Never mind her, she started early," said Ringo. "How was your date?"

Shelton smiled.

"That fucking good?" blared Lars, throwing a meaty hand onto the scruff of his neck.

"It was a lovely evening," said Shelton. "She cooked, played good music. She's got a great sense of humor. What else?"

"Oh, you're fucking *ruint*, aren't you?" asked Ringo.

"*Ruint*?" asked Lars.

"Yeah, you know, *ruint*," said Ringo, "like suede in the rain."

"Oh, ruined," he laughed. "Yeah, our boy looks *ruint*, alright."

"I'm fine," Shelton told them. "What have you guys been up to aside from mud-stomping rednecks?"

"Big break in the case," said Ringo. "The boss and I are here sorting it out, while you were out chasing tail."

Shelton looked to Lars.

"He does always seem to be recreating when the rest of us are Scooby-Doing this shit, doesn't he?" Lars said jokingly, looking to Ringo.

"He does it for the paycheck, brother," said Ringo, "while we do it for the love of the game."

"That was my first date in three months, for fuck's sake," said Shelton. "Give me a break. What do we got?"

"Well," said Lars. "It turns out Micky has an estranged son."

"Really?" asked Shelton. "And you had no idea?"

"Yep, and nope," said Lars. "He was just a kid. A year or so before he got with Amber, he apparently knocked up a Seminole girl from north of the river."

"Where'd this little piece of intel come from?" asked Shelton.

"Ally found it," said Lars. "Told you she was good."

"Did anybody know?" asked Shelton.

"I confirmed it with Dutch," Lars told him. "He went over to see Amber tonight, see if she had any idea where this kid—well, he'd be closer to my age at this point—might be found."

"You think he might be a suspect?" asked Shelton.

"I think it's worth taking a look at," said Lars. "Apparently, he was a vet, has some PTSD issues, and might also be bipolar or manic depressive. He's had some anger issues, and a rich dad who wasn't in his life."

"She have any idea where he's at?" asked Shelton.

'Nope," said Lars. "Last she knew of Micky's interactions with him, he'd gotten him into a halfway house out in Arcadia. A friend with the Sarasota Police Department had given him a heads-up that Miles, that's his name, had been living in a homeless camp downtown. The detective's name is Hobart. I figured we'd start there."

"Hobo Hobart?" asked Shelton.

"You know him?" asked Lars.

"Sure, I know him," said Shelton. "Not a bad guy, likes to see his name in the papers. We've helped each other out over the years, shared notes on that abduction case and a few other stories when I was with the Planet."

"You still got his number?" asked Lars.

"Yeah, I'll call him first thing in the morning," said Shelton. "Hell, what time is it? He's likely at the Waffle House on Tamiami this time of night."

Ringo stood up, poured the rest of his bottle into a plastic to-go cup, and filled it with what was left of Shelton's, much to his chagrin.

"You're driving," Ringo told him.

Ringo set the beer on the table where Tina slept, gingerly threw her over his massive left shoulder, and grabbed his cup with the free hand. He took it to his mouth and bit the top of the cup to hold it in place while he pushed the door open and headed back out into the night.

"I guess we're off," said Shelton.

"You need backup?" asked Lars.

"No, and it'll already be a tight squeeze with that lush sleeping in the backseat of the Mini."

"Make sure she knows she has to be here at 11:30 tomorrow morning," said Angel as she wiped the overflow from Ringo's beer consolidation from the bar."

"Right-o," said Shelton, saluting as he headed toward the door.

About a mile and a half before the Waffle House, they hit an inordinate amount of traffic near the marina downtown. As they inched closer, police lights came into view.

"Oh, fuck!" yelled Ringo. "It's a DUI checkpoint."

"No, they don't do those here," said Shelton. "I think it's an accident or something."

"Man, don't fuck around," said Ringo. "We got a young lady who's dead to the world back there. If we get hassled, you're gonna have to blow."

"I'm fine," he said. "You drank most of my beer, and it's been hours since I had wine."

Ringo took a long pull from a vape pen.

"What are you doing?" screamed Shelton.

"Getting my head straight," said Ringo. "You said we were fine."

As they got closer, it was clear something big was happening. In addition to at least six law enforcement vehicles, there were multiple ambulances and two firetrucks. Shelton hooked a left into an alley and parked in the fenced driveway of a municipal building.

"What are you doing?" asked Ringo.

"If Hobo's working, he's at whatever that spectacle is," he told him. "And we're not going to get any closer than this. You wait here with Tina, I'll go check it out."

"She's fine," said Ringo, grabbing a camera from his backpack. "You sure it's okay to park here?"

They looked toward a sign that read, "All unauthorized vehicles will be towed."

"Anybody interested in that is sure to be tied up over there," said Shelton, nodding toward the lights.

When Shelton and Ringo arrived, a massive crowd was assembled behind the crime scene tape. It was the heart of downtown, in front of a gigantic new Four Seasons hotel and condominium tower that featured a trendy restaurant, a cafe,

190

and a boutique-filled retail space in the building's large ground-floor arcade.

A large gaggle of city police officers and county sheriff deputies formed something of a spherical wall around the circular shower-curtain-like drape EMTs sometimes use for particularly gruesome fatalities. What appeared to be concrete and glass debris could be seen nearby.

Some of the credentialed press, mostly television news crews, had successfully jockeyed their way to the front row. For some reason that Shelton never entirely understood, both onlookers and law enforcement were oddly deferential to television press, a courtesy they did not tend to extend to print media.

It was almost as if a local news station's microphone flag and a video camera suggested that they had nearly as much right to access the scene as the first responders themselves. At the same time, print journalists were no more entitled than the average lookie-loo from among the general public. Fearing that Ringo—who had already begun using sharp elbows as he waded forward, clicking off shots—might get himself in trouble, Shelton scanned the scene for a friendly face.

"Hey," he told Ringo, pointing toward a man in a cheap suit standing off to the side of a patrol car while munching on a gas station hot dog. "There's Detective Hobart. Let's see what he knows."

Marty Hobart was the city's lead homicide detective. A salty, veteran cop who loved to find himself quoted in the paper, Shelton had scored points with him by occasionally enhancing a quote in a way that made the detective sound as hard-boiled as he tended to envision himself.

This wasn't considered ethical in the journalism trade, but Shelton learned early that the quickest way to have someone falsely claim you'd misquoted something you hadn't been able to record was to allow them to sound as dumb as their own words seemed to convey. In their mind, it was as bad as when it seemed newspapers deliberately chose the least flattering picture to accompany a story, a petty move that Shelton would himself indulge in when he had particular disdain for the subject.

"Detective Hobart," Shelton shouted with a raised hand.

The detective recognized him and gave a limp salute as he took another bite of the dog.

"What do we got, a jumper?"

"Not exactly," the detective answered, pausing just before he finished to attempt a smile as Ringo clicked off shots.

"A Michigan couple on their honeymoon," said the detective. "The bride went splat."

"She get pushed?" asked Shelton, arching an eyebrow.

"Repeatedly, it would seem," said Hobart.

Shelton arched his eyebrow a bit higher and tilted his chin.

"Couple's on the balcony of a top-floor suite," said Hobart. "As you can see, they got those 48-inch tempered glass barriers instead of rails or concrete. All form, no function. She's facing the ocean while he's giving her the old standing heave-ho from behind when the glass breaks away from the frame, likely on account of the humidity and an epoxy not intended to withstand subtropical weather in late July. She goes plunging toward her death, and naturally, he retreats by way of instinct."

"Holy shit," said Shelton.

The detective nodded.

"If he'd been in a forward thrust rather than retracting his gait when the glass gave way, he likely would've followed her to the ground."

"That's one lucky son of a bitch," said Ringo.

"You're tellin' me," said the detective as he pushed the final piece of the hot dog into his mouth.

"No chance of foul play?" asked Shelton.

"On the record, we'll need to see the ballistics and conduct interviews with family and friends," said Hobart. "Off the

192

record, my gut tells me the guy's being straight with us. He was still naked and crying on the balcony when the first unit arrived. Still seems to be genuinely in shock, and there's no obvious motive. Second go-round for both of them, each is in their mid-40s, work for the same IT firm, made the same money more or less, says they didn't have life insurance on each other yet."

"Ever seen anything so crazy?" asked Ringo, using his finger to identify the location above Detective Hobart's lip where a spot of mustard remained.

"You shittin' me?" asked Hobart as he dabbed the spot with a napkin, getting some of it. "I'm coming up on 30 years. This isn't even the first time I saw a bride fucked to death on her honeymoon."

"Get out!" shouted Shelton while Ringo attempted unsuccessfully once more to alert the detective's attention to the location of the remaining mustard.

"Get this," said Hobart, attempting futilely to dab it. "About twelve years back, I catch a case over on the island, that resort that got knocked down when they built the Grand Hyatt. Newly married husband wakes up, wife's not in the bed. He figures she's in the bathroom or something. It's one of those two-bedroom suites. Last place he looks is the other bedroom. Opens the door, she's cold and starting to turn blue."

"What happened?" asked Shelton.

"It turns out that while he was giving her the high hard one with bridal night enthusiasm and a blue genie enhanced boner the night before, he poked through her vaginal wall," said Hobart. "He says she was having some pain during sex and told him she needed a break. She's not feeling well, but still thinks they just overdid it and complains about some cramps while they're lying in bed. He falls asleep, at some point she apparently decides to lie down in the other room, goes into sepsis, only to croak sometime around dawn."

"Good god, man," said Shelton.

"It's a dog-eat-dog world, gentleman," said the detective as he began to walk back toward the crime scene. "I'd advise you to put on some Milkbone underwear."

"Wait, I need to ask you something?" said Shelton.

"You may have noticed I'm busy," said the detective.

"Micky Pesch," said Shelton.

"He's also dead," said Hobart, "but I don't think he got fucked to death—not in the literal sense, anyways."

"I know, but I'm working for the Gazette and, well, to make a long story short, I was told you helped him out a few years ago. Halfway house in Arcadia?"

Detective Hobart's eyes lit up a bit.

"This about the bastard son? You think he had something to do with the murder?"

Shelton shrugged.

"No idea, to be honest, but Micky had been receiving calls from a burner phone leading up to his death. It's all we got right now, and given none of us knew he had a son, not even Lars, we figure it's worth taking a look at.

The detective nodded.

"You got any idea where we might find this Miles guy?" asked Shelton.

"Haven't seen or heard of him since we got him a bed," said Hobart. "To be honest, it would surprise me to learn he was still alive more than to find out he was dead. Name of the halfway house is My Brother's Keeper. It's the street behind the Dollar General, about two blocks west. I doubt he's there, of course, but if he's still in Arcadia, they'd be most likely to know about it. I'm afraid that's the best lead I can give you."

"It's much appreciated," said Shelton. "I owe you lunch."

"I'll hold you to it," said Detective Hobart. "And before you go checking up on Miles, I should tell you he's a bit of a loose cannon. Spent some time in the military, special forces of some sort, then supposedly the CIA. Plus, there are some organic mental illness issues to speak of. He's a quiet guy, likes to be left alone, but he's formidable. A few of his run-ins with law enforcement were related to, shall we say, enthusiastic self-defense.

Shelton nodded as he processed the advice.

When they arrived back at the car, a tow truck had indeed backed into the alley, its driver intent on adding Shelton's Mini Cooper to that evening's fares. Ringo put two fingers in his mouth and whistled. The driver, a hulking middle-aged man standing at least six foot six with a ponytail sticking out of his trucker hat and a ZZ Top-length beard pulled into a second ponytail hanging from his chin, didn't make eye contact. He simply pointed to the No Parking sign and set about connecting his truck, the classic hook and chain variety, to Shelton's bumper.

Among Shelton's immediate concerns, though admittedly not first on the list, was that Tina might still be in the back seat of his car. The top was down, but she was of slight frame and had been covered by a Navajo blanket that ordinarily functioned as protection for the leatherette (his Mini sported the Premium Package, after all) against the razor-like talons on Rufus' rarely manicured paws.

That concern was erased, however, when he heard her slurring as she yelled from behind.

"There you are, baby," she drunkenly yelled in Ringo's general direction. "This motherfucker woke me up and called me a cunt. Then he said he was towing us."

At this, the tow-truck driver finally offered his attention. His size alone had probably ensured a minimum amount of conflict even within this loathsome profession in which customers, if you could even call them that, offered less enthusiasm for your presence than they did a dentist, a proctologist, or even a door-to-door Jehovah's Witness. Additionally, he gave off the vibe of a man who was handy with a tire iron on multiple fronts.

When he saw Ringo approaching, however, it was clear that the driver was having second thoughts about resorting to violence. At six foot three, with a weight that fluctuated between 240 and 260 pounds depending on how bloated his recent food and alcohol intake had rendered him, Ringo was a formidable man by any standard. His exercise routine consisted of three 30-minute workouts each week, intense bursts of activity that consisted only of wind sprints, the hoisting of kettle balls, and the repeated throwing of a massive truck tire. He saw no point in training for endurance or cleaving extra weight from his frame. He was only interested in doing the least amount of work that would result in maintaining his impressive ability to damage other humans within short, violent bursts.

Everything about his gait suggested as much, and as he hastened his approach, the driver put up both palms defensively.

"I didn't call her a cunt until after she spitted at me, brother, I swear."

"Spat," said Ringo as he withdrew his blackjack from his belt and lowered his center of gravity.

"Huh?" asked the driver.

"You spit, and once you have, you've spat," said Ringo. "Just like you shit, and once you have, you've shat."

The man now wore a look of profound confusion, unsure he'd ever heard the term *shat* to describe the past tense of having vacated one's bowels. But he'd never said that he'd *shitted* either. Racking his brain, he realized that he had always described the enterprise as having *taken* a shit, which he now understood for the first time made no sense at all, given that, if anything, he had, in every instance save the time he'd placed his scat in a paper bag so he could light it ablaze on an ex-wife's porch after, well … a spat, otherwise left his fecal expulsions wherever they had parted ways with his body. He

196

was certain that leaving something was the exact opposite of taking it.

"Unhook it," Ringo said flatly as he began to raise the blackjack, having closed all but about seven yards between the two large mammals.

Normally, this was when Shelton would at least attempt to intervene in his friend's savagery. However, given his own contempt for tow truck drivers and general lack of desire to settle impound lot fees, he found himself to be, at the very least, neutral in this conflict.

"Look, brother, I don't want any trouble," said the man, lifting his uniform shirt—one of those button-down polyester numbers with his name (Earl) stenciled into an oblong circle above the breast pocket—in order to show the butt of a revolver.

"Then unhook the fucking bumper, *Earl*," said Ringo, the blackjack now raised to striking height.

Earl was doing the mental math to calculate whether he would have a chance to deploy the pistol before that black jack came crashing down on wherever this maniac aimed to put it, but math had never been Earl's strong suit. Plus, the two Jack and Cokes he'd had earlier weren't helping. Earl had never read Shakespeare, but nonetheless decided discretion was indeed the better part of valor as he set about unhooking the bumper.

"Look, brother, I'm just doin' my job," he told Ringo as he finished disconnecting from the Mini.

"Is that right, Earl?" said Ringo. "Someone call you and complain?"

The man called Earl lowered his head, a bit of shame creeping onto his bearded face.

"No, but, I mean, there's … you know, a sign," he said, sheepishly.

"Roving tow," Ringo said to the man. "You're cruising for violators this late on a weekend night because you know there are a few poor sots who've tied one on and Ubered home, while not limber-minded enough to address whether their car was parked in the appropriate zone."

Ringo spat on the ground in disgust.

"That's lower than whale shit, Earl, and whale shit sits on the bottom of the ocean."

Earl had never given it any thought but was at that moment wondering why it didn't float, the way human feces generally seemed to.

"And you're looking at a man who lost the front quarter panel of a classic automobile to a parking boot," Ringo added.

Shelton knew this to be true but thought it a bit unfair for Ringo to withhold the crucial part about only losing the quarter panel after deciding to attempt to drive away with the boot still clamped on his wheel after Sarasota Sheriff Deputies realized that the person the car was registered to had an outstanding parking ticket debt so large that, if paid, might actually solve some of the county's budgetary issues.

"We don't have nothing to do with the boot devices," said Earl in his most defensive posture yet.

"Fuck you, you fascist bastard," screamed Tina as she left her feet to deploy another mouthful of saliva toward poor Earl. It landed flush on his left jowl, deep within his prized beard.

"You did call her a cunt," said Ringo sympathetically, patting Earl on the back as he returned the blackjack to his belt.

Fair play, thought Earl, remembering what his father had told him when he was young about deploying the C-U Next Tuesday, which amounted to thinking long and hard, as you generally only get to say it to a woman once. He couldn't think of anything even approaching witty to say in response, which would have been a heavy lift for Earl even if he hadn't been so flustered or imbibed the previously mentioned Jack and Cokes. So, he decided to take it as a learning experience.

Earl was content to know that he had indeed been spat upon. Or was it spatted, he thought silently. And did it further matter that there had been plural offenses, he wondered. At

198

least one of the three people presently backing out of the alley
in the tiny convertible was sure to know, but Earl was mentally
exhausted by this point and decided that the most sensible
course of action was to return to the bar and have another Jack
and Coke.

Chapter 11: Gun meets foot

Art Pyle had been all too relieved to have finished the county commission debates seemingly without upsetting the balance of power between the publishing and editorial wings of the floundering newspaper enterprise from which he was hoping to retire to a modest pension the following year. The media empire that presently owned the Mullet County Monitor had left it to die on the vine, so to speak.

McManus Media Inc. had already farmed out the relatively small amount of printing the Monitor still did to a neighboring publication, laying off dozens of employees in the process. The company then offered structured buyouts to most senior staff and pretty much stopped making new hires as others fell off until the paper had become little more than an ad circular with high school football coverage, arrest reports, and news as to which restaurants had failed their latest health department inspections.

If it were not for the accounts of Emblem Homes, Montage Phosphate, and a locally owned chain of new car dealerships, the paper would not be able to keep the lights on. So when Art got word that Connor Welsh had changed his mind and would be debating Greg Osborne after all, he suddenly needed to double up on his acid reflux meds. Welsh was Ignacio Hernandez's prize pol, and Art would be expected to take extra care to make him look good. But, Welsh being Welsh, he knew that would be a tall order, to say the very least.

"Mr. Welsh," said Art, "Your opponent has accused you of being unduly influenced by development interests who have supported your campaign. How do you answer that accusation?"

"I am a pro-business, Christian conservative," said Welsh. "I believe in hard work and competitive capitalism framed by my Christian values. Of course, the business community of Mullet County has supported my campaign! I'm proud of that fact. Think not only of all the hard-working tradesmen in our community who are employed by developers, but also the real estate agents, the mortgage brokers, and the title companies. I suspect my opponent would rather have them all standing in the unemployment line, drawing benefits, and relying on government dole to feed their families. Other nations have run that experiment. It was called communism, and it failed every damned time! Greg Osborne wants to turn Mullet County into a socialist hellscape, and I say, not on my watch!"

Christopher Bacchelli was pleasantly surprised by his candidate's message discipline, which had not always been his strong suit. He nodded his head and offered a thumbs-up when Commissioner Welsh looked over to him at the end of the answer.

"Mr. Osborne, I'll allow you a quick rebuttal," said Art Pyle.

"I don't even know where to start," said Greg Osborne.

"That's the truest statement he's made all night," bellowed Welsh, "and precisely why the voters of Mullet County must reject this socialist charlatan!"

"Commissioner Welsh, please, it's Mr. Osborne's time," said Pyle.

"Look, this idea that if you're against anything but wild west style development where anything goes, you must be some kind of communist is just ridiculous," said Osborne. "I'm not against development. Hell, I've spent most of my adult life trying to facilitate it. But when you build out a county based solely on what's best for the builder's bottom line without consideration for the community as a whole, you're going to get the sort of mess Mullet County residents have made it clear they're fed up with. We don't have the infrastructure to support the number of homes we're building, especially in the places we're building the most of them, so our roadways are chronically overburdened. We haven't invested in adequate stormwater management. So, the new developments, which have to be built at higher elevations to comply with the current code, cause runoff that floods the older ones nearby.

"We just gave away hundreds of millions of dollars in impact fees, which means we are going to be even less able to address these issues. The residents of these new developments will want things like parks and libraries. Where will the money come from? These developers don't care. They are parasites who will have moved down the road to make some other community their new host by the time the next generation of Mullet County residents are left having to figure it out. I'm a capitalist. Hell, I studied business at Cornell, and I was taught that in a free market, the producer of a good is responsible for bearing the cost of bringing their product to market. But we're not doing that. We're forcing existing residents to essentially subsidize developers who are already drowning in profits. Emblem Homes is a billion-dollar enterprise. Its owner can afford to pay the costs associated with his developments, but it's cheaper to buy a county commissioner's seat and keep the rest for himself. That's why Ignacio Hernandez, his company, and hundreds of LLCs associated with it have poured over a quarter of a million dollars into my opponent's campaign, and that's why he's voted with Emblem projects 100 percent of the time."

"I reject the assertion that I am influenced by those who support my candidacy," screamed Welsh.

Bacchelli rubbed the bridge of his nose as he felt his neck stiffen. It was just this sort of common-sense connecting of the dots that the flashy, expensive negative attack campaigns he specialized in were meant to obscure.

"They support my campaign because we share conservative values, unlike my RINO opponent, who is openly pitching himself to Democrats. He's a Trojan Horse liberal elitist, and the good people of this community will not be fooled by some slick talking Ivy Leaguer who's not even a Mullet County native!"

Art Pyle was caught drinking Maalox straight from the little plastic bottle when the camera panned back toward the moderator.

"Uh, time for the closing statements, gentlemen," he said in a defeatist tone.

****

Commissioner Candice Hagerty had just pulled up to a stop sign on Riverfront Road when police lights began flashing in her rear-view mirror. She bit down on her lower lip and tightened her grip on the wheel. When the deputy arrived at her door, she waited for him to tap on the window with his flashlight before lowering it. Once it was down, she didn't move. Still looking straight ahead, she addressed the officer.

"What seems to be the problem, deputy?"

"Do you know why I pulled you over, ma'am?" asked Deputy White.

"Because I'm a bad girl who needs a spanking?" she asked, before turning toward the deputy and licking her upper lip, which was coated in a glossy pink lipstick.

"Why don't you pull off that little side trail near the dead end, and we'll get this sorted out," said the deputy, running his large hand over his freshly shaved head."

Commissioner Hagerty put her white GMC Denali in gear and headed toward the spot where Riverfront Road came to an end, facing the bridge that connected DeSoto City and LeGrotto. She turned right onto a shell-paved private road, canopied by large oak trees. About a quarter mile in, she put the car in park and climbed into the backseat.

By the time Deputy White opened the rear door of the SUV, she had already hiked her skirt and climbed to all fours, arching her back and presenting him with a splendid view of her ample derriere.

"I've been a bad girl," she said, as he admired the scene.

"Well, we'll have to get that sorted out now, won't we," he said as he delivered a forceful hand across her creamy-white cheeks.

****

Amber Pesch was enjoying a glass of Sancerre when she got an unexpected notification from her Ring camera that someone was approaching the door. She could see from the video on the app that it was her ne'er-do-well sister-in-law, and she let out a deep sigh. She waited until Mary had rung the doorbell twice before getting up.

"It's late, Mary," she said with another sigh when she opened the door.

"Well, nice to see you, too, Amber," Mary said with a slurred voice that sounded like it had been induced by her habit of mixing Valium and vodka. "Are you gonna invite me inside or do I have to stand here like I'm selling solar panels door-to-door?"

Amber turned and walked up the small set of steps to the living room, leaving the door open to signal that Mary was welcome to follow without having to verbally invite her in. When they got to the living room, Mary took the liberty of pouring herself a glass of the white wine.

"Ooh, the good stuff," said Mary. "Must be nice."

"Help yourself," Amber said sarcastically as Mary filled the glass to near capacity.

Mary took a long sip of the wine.

"Mmmmn, you sure do know your wine, I can't deny that."

"Okay, Mary, it's late. To what do I owe this visit?" asked Amber with as much courtesy as she could muster.

"I have a business opportunity, one too good to pass up, but I need a small advance on my *allowance*," she told her.

"A business opportunity?" asked Amber, unable to mask her skepticism.

204

"*Yes*, a business opportunity," said Mary indignantly. "You think you're the only one who wants to live the good life a little before you fuckin' up and die?" she added, waving her arm to signify the beautiful trappings of the home.

"What exactly is this opportunity you speak of?" asked Amber.

"The Driftwood Inn is for sale," said Mary. "Dallas McMasters wants to sell the thing and retire to Key West. Bobby Stokes, who runs the place, is a friend of mine, and Dallas is offering him a *real* good deal on the place before it even goes on the market. No Realtor fees or nothin'. If I can put up forty thousand for the rest of the down payment, we can be partners. Bobby will run it, and I'll be in charge of fixing it up and marketing it better. This could be my ticket, Amber."

The Driftwood Inn was an ancient shack of a dive bar, nestled on a small sliver of land at the east end of the Ave Maria Island Causeway. It was joked that it had literally been built from collected driftwood, but had weathered and deteriorated to such an extent that younger generations of the derelicts who patronized the bar took it as fact. It was also one of the few remaining smoking bars in Mullet County, leading many to wonder how it had not yet burned to cinders.

The building was barely a structure and would never meet the codes required to build even a yard shed today. However, since Mullet County, like much of Florida, did not have building codes when it was erected in the mid-1960s, it was grandfathered in, sort of. The shack had unfinished, uneven wood floors and a scattering of thick pylons holding up a rusted-out tin roof with aluminum patchwork applied to fix various leaks over the years. The walls were made from plywood roofing sheets, with large windows cut into them that rendered the bar "open air," with opaque plastic window tarps that were rolled down whenever it rained.

The bras that had been hung from the ceiling in its more prosperous days were darkened with mold to the point that they were no longer recognizable as women's wear, and many of the dollar bills that had been signed and stapled to the walls over the years had been pulled down when some boozed-brained patron ran out of money for the juke box or pool table. The latter of which was so crooked that only those who'd played it so often that they knew its intricacies could get through a game—with those who knew its tendencies particularly well holding a significant advantage.

Still, it was a cash-only enterprise subject to dirt-cheap property taxes and minimum maintenance to retain its ramshackle personification, so Dallas, an industrious and deceptively intelligent Florida cracker who'd owned it for the last 30 years, had probably squirreled up a small fortune over the decades, as evidenced by his intention to retire to Key West at 60. However, Amber knew good and well that Mary was capable of fucking up the proverbial one-car funeral, so skepticism filled the air.

"The *rest* of the down payment?" asked Amber suspiciously.

"Bobby is coming into some money any day now," said Mary.

"Bobby Stokes is coming into some money?" asked Amber, in the same suspicious tone.

"*Yeah, Amber,*" Mary said with a sigh. "His aunt died and left him some money. He's just waiting for it to clear probate."

"What do you know about running a bar?" Amber asked.

"Seriously?" slurred Mary, taking another long pull from her glass. "You forget that I worked *at* the Driftwood? I know that place inside and out, everything about it. And besides, Bobby's been running it for years, and he'd be my partner. I'd just make it better. Old Dally made a mint off that bar over the years. Probably got millions saved up in coffee cans and buried in his yard."

Amber had, in fact, forgotten that barmaid at the Driftwood Inn was one of many short stints of employment that peppered her wayward sister-in-law's resume. The sum total of what Mary knew about the Driftwood, however, was surely 90 percent owed to her hundreds, if not thousands, of drunken nights as a patron rather than her season of semi-drunken nights behind its bar nearly two decades prior.

"You said, forty grand for half the down payment," said Amber. "The building itself isn't worth half that. What's the sale price?"

Mary sighed.

"It's waterfront property, Amber. Dallas is gonna give it to us for eighty thousand down, and two thousand dollars a month in cash for three years. That's less than $160,000 for a beachfront bar. When was the last time one sold for less than a million, the damned '90s? Bobby says the place clears three to four thousand a week. It's easy money."

If Amber had learned one thing from her husband, it was that there was no such thing as *easy* money, so long as it was earned honestly.

"There's only a category two hurricane standing between that bar and its washing down the river into the bay," said Amber. "You can't get permits to fix it up in any meaningful way without a code enforcement inspection, which would *not* go well, and if it suffers storm damage that FEMA assesses at more than 50 percent of the structural value, you'd have to rebuild the entire thing to current code, which would include elevating it. And if it were demolished, that sliver of land doesn't have enough room for setbacks to build anything larger than an outhouse."

"Oh, now, all of a sudden, *you're* the expert," shouted Mary. "What business did you ever run? You're sitting back, all high on the hog on *my* family's money, which my daddy built up with his bare hands. It's bad enough that I gotta come over here hat in hand to ask for some crumbs of what should be my birthright without you making me beg for it."

Mary took the last sip from her wine glass and looked at it disapprovingly.

"I think this wine has turned!" she said, putting down the glass and marching toward the door.

****

Candice Hagerty was mounted atop Deputy White, bouncing at a furious pace when Ringo approached the vehicle. He momentarily considered opening the door, which he did not hear lock after the deputy entered the backseat, but that wasn't the shot he was looking for. He had something more salacious in mind, but having already passed on the fellatio scene earlier, he couldn't be sure how much opportunity would still present itself, and he would get only one chance if he were lucky.

He had been recording audio as a backup, and Commissioner Hagerty proved herself to be a loud, talkative, and particularly saucy-mouthed lover, but that was only going to be a supplement. He needed a money-shot. Suddenly, the bouncing shocks stilled.

"I want you to get me from the back," she said.

Shifting ensued, and Ringo silently prayed they didn't open the rear passenger door he was standing next to in order to fold down the seat. He quickly grabbed his gear and moved silently to the back of the vehicle. Within seconds of each other, both rear doors opened, and he could see the deputy's leg extend to the ground, but neither exited the SUV.

Once the bench seat had been lowered, both Hagerty and White would be facing the back window, and he was not entirely certain he would not be visible through the darkly-tinted rear window, but the unlit road and a foggy, moonless night played into his favor. He had already unscrewed the bulb in a rear-yard light of the only house near the road, and, absent a faint glow from the last street lamp at the end of Riverfront Road, it was pitch black.

Ringo quietly set up a mounted construction light he'd paid cash for at a pawn shop the day before and adjusted its stand to the proper height. Once his camera was set, he tiptoed toward the hatch of the SUV.

"Oh fuck! Yes, give it to me, baby!" screamed the commissioner.

The SUV was jerking furiously on its struts when he gently pressed the button to open the hatch. Once it started to slowly rise, he hurried to the construction light. With one hand on its switch, he readied his camera, and as the hatch passed its halfway point, he turned on the ridiculously bright light and began clicking off shots as rapidly as he could.

The illuminated scene that played out before him could not have been bawdier. Commissioner Hagerty was on all fours, face looking directly at his camera, courtesy of the fact that Deputy White, wearing only a bulletproof vest, was aggressively pulling on her ponytail, which was wrapped tightly around his fist as he gingerly smacked her bottom—a move Ringo recognized as the "wrap and slap," which he himself was known to employ.

"Respect," he mumbled.

"What the fuck?" screamed Candice, although it took several seconds for the deputy to break stride. "Who the fuck is that?"

Ringo snapped two more quick shots and bolted toward Riverfront Road. He'd had the light just enough in front of his body that he was invisible behind its immense glare, which blinded both Candice and the deputy for long enough for him to get to his car, which was parked at the dead end. He fumbled with the keys, looking back and forth at the start of the canopy road.

"What are you waiting for?" screamed Candice. "Get them!"

Deputy White gave her a look of confusion while shielding his eyes from the blinding light.

"I don't see anyone?" he said.

"Well, that light didn't put itself there!" she screamed.

Ringo turned the ignition, but the Fiero balked, its starter seeming disinterested in anything greater than a token effort.

"Not now, baby, daddy needs to get down the road pronto," he mumbled as he turned back the key and gave it another shot. Finally, he heard the engine knock as it turned over.

Deputy White tossed on his boxer briefs and climbed out through the rear hatch. Still shielding his eyes from the light, he knocked it onto its side and began running, only to jump in pain when a large shard of shell pierced the heel of his bare foot.

"FAWK!" he yelled.

"What are you doing?" screamed Commissioner Hagerty.

Ringo put the car in drive and floored the pedal. The Deputy heard a slight chirp from the Fiero's tires and looked toward Riverfront Road. His eyes, not yet recovered from the light, could only make out the shape of a small car, either white or gray, perhaps both.

****

Seated across a two-top table from Amber Pesch at the Rusty Rudder, Dutch cut open his hush puppies to let them cool. The lunchtime crowd was brisk, but they had managed to score a quiet table on the back patio. The waitress topped off both of their iced teas and told them to let her know if they needed anything else.

"So what's been troubling you, young lady?" Dutch asked once they were alone.

"It's probably nothing, but I had to stop at the Sheriff's office yesterday to pick up Micky's possessions. And, well, the only things they recovered aside from his clothes and wallet were that shark tooth necklace and some of those bead bracelets he wore."

Dutch gave her a curious look.

"His watch," she said. "You know that he almost never took it off, and it wasn't on the boat, either."

"Interesting," said Dutch, as he stroked his chin. "You mention that to the deputy when you signed for them?"

"No, it struck me, but I figured it might have been missed on the boat, or that maybe someone in the department might have, you know, had sticky fingers."

Dutch paused in consideration.

"There is something else, now that I think about it," said Amber.

"Go on," said Dutch.

"Well, the watch was supposed to go to Miles," she said. "It wasn't in the will, but Micky had told me offhandedly a long time ago that I should give it to Miles if he ever passed. I forget how it even came up, but the watch had been his father's. He probably told you that. Well, the only thing he had ever really given Miles was Arturo's car."

"What?" asked Dutch, a rare look of confusion on his face.

"Arturo had an old muscle car, some kind of Chevy with racing stripes and a loud exhaust. He had it since it was new, kept it garaged, and almost never drove it. The only two flashy things the old man ever owned were that car and the Rolex, which was even older. Micky had been cut off from all the money in his dad's will, but Arturo left him the car and the watch. He was never sure whether it was genuine or some kind of fuck you where the old man could get over on him and have a laugh from the grave. Anyway, Micky hated the car, being such an environmentalist and all, so he gave it to Miles. They were still in touch when Arturo died. It was probably because Arturo resented the idea of Micky having a *bastard son*, as he so delicately put it. Giving Miles Arturo's beloved car might have been Micky's way of having the last laugh."

"Sort of like pissing on his grave," laughed Dutch. "But Micky kept the watch?"

"Yeah, I never really understood why, other than I think he might have genuinely liked it," she said. "You know how he appreciated vintage stuff, and apparently, it was just like one that Paul Newman, his favorite actor, had worn. Micky wore that thing every single day. Anyway, I don't even know how the subject came up. I think I asked about getting him a new one, maybe for an anniversary or something, and he said he was kind of set on wearing that one forever. I said something about donating it to a museum after that, being that it was so old, and he sort of chuckled and said, *nah, give it to Miles.*"

"He did?" said Dutch, chewing on that bit of intel.

"I'm not saying it means anything, but you did say to tell you anything that came to me, and you having mentioned Miles, and the connection with the watch, it's all probably nothing, but I just thought it was weird enough to mention."

"You did the right thing, darling," said Dutch. "We gotta pull on every single thread."

"I just don't want to make any sort of unnecessary trouble for Miles," she said, "especially if he's been staying out of trouble. If getting harassed needlessly by the police were to send him into a spiral, I wouldn't forgive myself."

Dutch nodded.

"I don't see any reason to involve the law at this point, but it's good information for us to have on our end in case it matches up with anything else we learn."

"That sounds good," she said.

"Perfect," said Dutch. We'll keep that card close to our vest for now."

****

That evening, Dutch was parked at his normal seat at the Legion post when Lars entered and joined him at the bar.

"Thanks for dropping by," said Dutch. "Annie, get our guy a Yuengling."

"No problem," said Lars. "What's up?"

"Well, we need to talk a bit more about Miles," said Dutch.

Lars nodded.

"Gotta say, that one threw me for a loop."

"Well, it wasn't something Micky often spoke of," said Dutch. "Tender subject, I guess you could say."

"My guys got the name of the halfway house Hobart helped him get set up at," said Lars. "It was a busy day at the office, but they're gonna head out there tomorrow and just do a little recon. See if anyone knows his whereabouts. But I take it you've got something for me?"

"I guess I ought to start by giving you the whole backstory," said Dutch, picking up his drink and motioning for Lars to join him at a table near the back of the hall that was out of earshot from the other patrons.

Once they were seated, Dutch took a sip of his drink and stared at Lars for a moment in what amounted to a dramatic pause inserted at the very beginning of a conversation, an affectation Dutch often employed.

"When Micky was 16, he met an Indian woman—feathers not dots," Dutch finally said. "He hadn't had much experience with women at that point, and this girl was a real looker, and something of a wildflower, to boot. You know how it can be with some gals, they just got this certain thing, and you don't even know what it is, a pheromone or something that just gets your head all twisted up?"

Dutch arched his brow and paused.

"Sure," said Lars. "We've all been there."

"Ain't that the truth," agreed Dutch. "If you're lucky, you get it out of your system and then settle into something sensible, something you treasure but that you can control yourself around, make good decisions, and so forth. Well,

Micky ultimately found that when he met Amber, but whilst he was head over heels for this stunning squaw, they went and made a baby. Arturo was none too pleased, as you can probably imagine. That man was a proper dago who looked down upon anyone further down the ladder in the American hierarchy than Italians were at the time. The fact that he'd married the daughter of Irish immigrants notwithstanding, he didn't look kindly on the union, especially the mixed kid angle. They still called them half-breeds back then. I believe that's where the contention between him and Micky first took root."

"I can't see Micky leaving her just because Arturo didn't approve," said Lars.

"You'd be correct," said Dutch. "In fact, it likely caused him to settle in deeper still. But the woman happened to be crazier than a shit house rat. Probably bipolar or something, but definitely not right up here," he added while tapping his temple.

"So what becomes of the relationship?" asked Lars.

"She left town right after the baby was born," said Dutch. "Micky had only seen Miles a few times before she split. If I had to guess, I'd say old Arturo had a hand in it. Probably gave the girl or her daddy a chunk of money to facilitate her relocation. Family was dirt poor, made cast nets they sold to local fishermen. Lived in a shanty on the north side of the river. No indoor plumbing or running water to speak of. Dirt floors. Wouldn't have took much."

"That was the end of it?" asked Lars. "I mean, did Micky ever see the kid again?"

"Not for quite some time," said Dutch. "Micky harbored a lot of guilt about it and eventually hired a private detective to locate Miles. He wrote him a letter when Miles was about 13, but didn't hear back until the boy had graduated from high school and enlisted in the Army. The mom had passed from cancer. He'd been living on a reservation with an aunt or cousin, and they made plans for him to come up here before he

214

had to report for duty. I believe there was some correspondence while he was enlisted, but he wound up in special ops and then sort of fell off the grid."

"That might explain the trouble Ally and Pauly had digging up more current info," he said.

Dutch nodded.

"Then Micky heard from him years later," he continued. "Miles passed through town when he got back to Florida. He'd apparently been doing some *wet work* for the CIA. Micky was heartbroken, said the kid seemed dead inside, no spark in the eyes. He started getting into trouble—bar fights and such. Developed a little opioid problem, which he later kicked. Whether it was PTSD or he'd inherited some of his mother's mental health issues, no one could say. I do know that Micky felt some shame about being a bit afraid of his own offspring. They had some contact, but Miles continued to go downhill. Micky didn't really like the idea of him being around Amber, since he seemed a bit unstable, so they drifted apart. Last Micky had heard from Miles, as far as Amber knows, is several years back, when he got into a scuffle in a homeless encampment down in Sarasota."

"That's when Micky got him into the halfway house out in Arcadia?" asked Lars.

"Yep," said Dutch. "But Amber told me one more thing that has me thinking a bit."

"Yeah?"

Dutch nodded.

"Micky's Rolex wasn't among the possessions found on the body, or at least among those returned to Amber."

"It has some connection to Miles?" asked Lars.

Dutch's face contorted a bit.

"Well, not *exactly*, but Amber did say she was supposed to give it to Miles if anything ever happened to Micky. I don't know whether Miles knew of this intention, but if he did, and he was involved, it seems likely he might have kept it, some sort of birthright thing, I don't know, I'm not all that familiar with Seminole customs. Only *Injun* blood in my family tree is Cherokee, and I can't even speak much to theirs."

"A CIA assassin using a shotgun to the chest?" Lars asked suspiciously.

"A long-retired assassin who was last known to be destitute," said Dutch. "What's that saying about beggars and choosers?"

Lars nodded and took the last swig of beer from his glass.

"Maybe. Listen, I gotta get back," he told Dutch. "I'm covering at the radio station tonight. Maurice isn't feeling well."

Dutch toasted his glass.

"Hey," he said to Lars as he turned to leave. "It goes without saying to tell your boys that if they do find Miles, be careful. He's not only dangerous but he's known to have a bit of a short fuse, and none of us knows if he's gotten better or worse in the interim, but experience has led me to believe the latter is far more common."

Lars nodded and turned to leave.

"You can tell one of them yourself," he said as he caught a glimpse of Ringo entering the hall and making a beeline for the bar.

****

Ignacio was seated at his normal table on the veranda of the restaurant at the Sarasota Ritz Carlton when Christopher Bacchelli was escorted to it by the maître d'.

"There's my guy," said Ignacio, actually rising to shake hands with the man he hired to make sure the money he dumped into local elections had its intended effect. Because Bacchelli had fewer scruples than a low-rent pimp, he was *very* good at his job.

In truth, Bacchelli was far more useful to the developer than any of his candidates, even Commissioner Welsh. Ignacio

216

could always find another half-bright sociopath with adequate table manners and deference to the boss, but he would be hard-pressed to find a campaign consultant anywhere in the area nearly as good as the young man seated across from him when it came to turning money into political power.

That said, he was stuck with Welsh for this particular election. Furthermore, what made Welsh a terrible candidate was exactly what made him a useful commissioner. He genuinely didn't care what anyone other than those who put him in power and kept him there thought of him or his antics. That was a rare trait in Hernandez's experience, as politics generally attracts people who are prone to seeking public affirmation.

He hated having to remind his charges that it didn't matter how many insults they heard while shopping at Publix or having a meal at the Rusty Rudder. In fact, he encouraged them to seek their entertainment in Sarasota or Tampa, where they would be less likely to encounter ungrateful constituents, and further encouraged them to spend time at mixers and other events held by the chamber of commerce or one of the many conservative clubs in Mullet County, where they were more likely to have their egos stroked than catch a stray insult.

Welsh, however, was wired differently. Sometimes Ignacio even thought the young commissioner actually enjoyed playing the heel. It was almost as if he derived more pleasure from rubbing his enemies' noses in his relative power than in receiving accolades from the people who actually agreed with what he was doing. This is likely what led to the debate fiasco, and it was only because Ignacio himself had relented and allowed him to participate over Bacchelli's objections that the developer was being uncommonly deferential on this occasion.

"I am not a man who cannot admit his mistakes," said Ignacio as the waiter delivered a $500 Grand Cru for his inspection.

"Whoa," said Bacchelli, a wine enthusiast who, while not above dropping a couple of hundred dollars on a bottle from time to time, rarely indulged in offerings that were this high-end, especially at restaurant markup.

"Please, my friend, do the honors, yes?" he said, directing the waiter to offer the tasting pour to his guest.

Bacchelli swirled his glass and inhaled its bouquet before taking a sip. He nodded slowly at the waiter, winking, and the man poured each of them a glass.

"You were right about the debate," said Ignacio once the waiter was gone from sight. "Our boy shit the bed when he shouldn't even have been sleeping in it."

"It was my job to prepare him," said Bacchelli, putting up a hand. He was deeply relieved, given that when it ended, Ignacio had only texted "that was a fucking disaster!!!!," and had not responded to any of his replies until inviting him to dinner that afternoon.

"No, Christopher, your job is to know the best course of action, and mine is to heed the advice of those I hire specifically for their expertise. But let's not cry over spilled milk. Tell me where we are and what we need to do to improve our position."

Bacchelli nodded and sipped his wine.

"The YouTube video only has 600 views as of half an hour ago," he told Ignacio. "It's hard to imagine even that many people watching the public access broadcast. We dropped 10,000 aggressive direct mail pieces today and have been blasting automated texts and robocalls non-stop since, especially to the eastern edge of the ward, where they're much less engaged. We won't be able to get good polling updates this close to the election, so I'm spending down everything we've got. The little fucker would like to have a nice chunk of change left over for his office account again, but I kind of feel like a bit of humbling might do him well."

Ignacio nodded his head, smiled wryly, and tipped his glass.

"Yes, humility is in short supply with that one," said the developer. "We look like we're good in the other races, no? That Watts character has the charisma of a soiled diaper," he said with a laugh.

"He almost made Sunday sound intelligent," said Bacchelli with a chuckle of his own. "And Hagerty didn't exactly kill it up there, but she's so far out in front with the MAGA crowd that they were sharing it far and wide the next day as if she had won it in a walk. That and her old man's last name should make for smooth sailing."

Ignacio nodded in agreement.

"If you get the sense that we need to spend more money to keep Welsh above water, say the word," he told Bacchelli. "You know how I feel about dissent on that board, and without him captaining the ship, things would not go as smoothly. Hagerty could run point if it came to that, but she's nowhere near as ruthless as that little son of a bitch, and that's saying something."

****

Ringo arrived at Dutch's table with a pitcher of Yuengling in tow, Annie having already been instructed to give him whatever he needed. The plastic cup was clenched in his teeth as he held a manila envelope in the other hand, dropping it in front of Dutch before taking his seat.

"Goody goody gum drops," said Dutch. "What do we have here?"

Ringo began to sip off some of the foam before attempting to pour from the pitcher into the cup. In mere seconds, however, at least three glasses worth of beer had been removed, and it was less than half full after he filled his cup for the first time. Dutch watched him, slack-jawed, wondering how that much beer had disappeared so quickly.

"That's two races in the bag is what that is," he told Dutch with a wink.

The old man couldn't believe his eyes. He began spreading the photos out, but once he caught a glimpse of Hagerty on all fours getting railed from behind, he clutched it to his chest and made sure no one was anywhere near close enough to see.

"Goddamn!" Dutch finally said. "I would have bet dollars to donuts I'd have met my maker without seeing the legendary bosom of Candice Hagerty!"

His eyes looked like saucers, but he quickly regained his composure.

"Then again, I suppose I was in a small club," he added with a knowing arch of the brows.

"Well, judging by the way those sweater puppies swung, she wasn't lying about them being natural," said Ringo. "Wait, though, it gets better."

Ringo thumbed through the photos and produced a blown-up shot that revealed a swastika tattoo on the bald deputy's right shoulder.

"Well, I'll be dipped in dog shit," said Dutch. "These ads almost write themselves."

The next photo was panoramic and captured each of the four topless dancers at the Reverend Billy Sunday's poolside barbecue party.

"And check this out," said Ringo.

He pulled out his phone and began playing a well-lit, high-resolution video of the HOA director's interaction with the good reverend.

"You think Lars and your man will have any qualms about reporting on this?" asked Dutch.

"They'll have no choice once it shows up all over social media tomorrow," said Ringo with a wink.

"You're gonna leak it?" asked Dutch.

"I would *never*," said Ringo, "but I'm awfully clumsy with this thing," he said, bouncing the phone in his giant palm. "I get drunk and leave it at bars. There's no passcode on it because I can't risk forgetting it when I'm stoned. Not to mention these fat sausage fingers, which always make me accidentally send things. I doubt it'll take long before someone gets their hands on this stuff. I might even get hacked!"

Dutch smiled, leaned in toward him, and put a hand on his shoulder.

"That's some mighty fine work, my friend," he said with a wink.

****

"Voila," said Shelton, as he removed the cookie sheet from Emily's oven on the morning of his first overnight stay. She had accepted his offer to return the favor and cook dinner for them the night before, with both parties agreeing that her bungalow would be a more appropriate location than his studio at Ramblewood.

"Now, I've got to warn you, the downside to what you are about to experience is that you will be utterly ruined on any other buttermilk biscuits for all of time," he told her as he delicately brushed the warm delicacies with a coating of Irish butter he had been keeping liquefied in a small milk-warming pot on one of the burners.

"They're painted in butter, are you kidding me?" she asked with a giant smile.

"They are indeed," he said. "And now for the final touch."

He took a wooden honey dipper from the canvas grocery bag he'd used to bring the food supplies the previous evening, along with a jar of honey he had picked up at a farmer's market the morning before.

"Oh my god, I'm going to have to run a marathon," she laughed. "Between last night's dinner, all the wine, and now breakfast, I'm gonna be five pounds heavier."

Shelton gave her a sultry look.

"I believe we burned off enough calories to warrant such an indulgence," he said, referring to the two rounds of glorious lovemaking that followed their dinner of beef bourguignon and two bottles of a surprisingly good lower-end Burgundy Pinot he had splurged on, plus the intense round of morning sex that had preceded breakfast.

She bit her lip and playfully slapped his shoulder.

"You must have been quite confident, mister, seeing as how you brought all that stuff to cook breakfast with on a dinner date," she said playfully.

He put up his hands in mock defense.

"I am, by nature, both hopeful and given to preparation for the unknown," he told her. "It's not like you can be sure to find cream of tartar at any old supermarket these days, or even proper buttermilk, for that matter."

"Local honey?" she asked.

"Do you honestly think I would have come to your house of all places with grocery store honey from god knows where?" he said. "I picked it up on my way here from that little roadside produce stand on the north end of the trail. I usually get the wildflower, but when I saw they had mangrove honey, well, it seemed fated."

She giggled. Shelton placed a biscuit on each of their plates and then drizzled a liberal dose of the sweet syrup on each before quickly reaching for the other copper milk warming pot, which had been heating oat milk and was about to foam over. Seconds later, his antique Bialetti Moka espresso pot began to make its tell-tale sound of needing to be pulled from the opposite burner. He poured some espresso into each of two glasses, and, for his final trick, produced a portable milk frother from the bag and whipped the oat milk into a perfect, foamy cream, which he patiently layered onto each cup of espresso with a spoon.

"Breakfast is served," he told her with a wink and a smile.

222

"Is this what is known in the female podcasting space as being love bombed?" she asked with a laugh.

"I don't know what that means, but I'll take it," he told her.

"It's actually a pejorative term," she said, again with that adorable giggle that Shelton found terribly endearing. "But I think I'd take it too, judging by how delicious this all looks!"

She put a bit of the biscuit into her mouth and immediately cooed.

"Oh my god, Shelton! Are you serious? These are amazing."

"That seems to be the consensus. Just don't get mad at me the next time you have one in a restaurant," he said with an exaggerated shrug and sigh.

"*And the latte is to die for!*" she nearly screamed after the first sip.

"Technically, it's a flat white, given the milk-to-espresso ratio, but the compliment is appreciated, nonetheless," he said with a bow.

"Ruined on two fronts," she said, "whatever will this girl do?"

"Only two?" he said with a mock frown.

"*That* was splendid too, love," she said, leaning in to give him a peck.

"I was talking about the beef bourguignon," he said with a smile, "but, once again, I'll take it."

"So was I," she said, mockingly sticking out her tongue before flashing an enormous smile and slapping his leg.

"Play your cards right, and you might find yourself getting spoiled by this stuff regularly," he said with a wink.

"Play *your* cards right, mister, and you might find yourself getting spoiled with the other stuff, well, semi-regularly," she said, flashing a smile.

He leaned in and kissed the crown of her head, inhaling the sweet Moroccan oil smell of her hair.

"What do you got going on today?" he asked her as he unfolded a copy of Creative Loafing, a free alt/weekly similar to the Daily Planet that he'd picked up from a kiosk near her house.

"Water quality testing on the Clam Bayou Aquatic Preserve," she told him. "Not bad work—basically kayaking through gorgeous waterways for four hours, filling jars, and then spending a couple of hours at the lab afterward, after I drive across the Howard Franklin with the top down, soaking up the sun."

"Gonna be a hot one," he told her.

"Yeah, but most of it is canopied by the mangroves," she said. "It's my go-to kayaking spot in the summer months, so it's practically half a day off. If I could somehow manage to do it on my stand-up paddleboard, it would be even better, but I've got to carry too many jars. I use a two-seat kayak and barely have enough room as it is. When it's a larger waterway, I've got to use one of the canoes."

"How's the red tide been up this way?" he asked.

"Not bad at all," she said. "Just background concentrations last week, and no fish kills to report. It almost seems like if we enact sensible baseline regulations, they go a long way."

"Who would have thunk?" said Shelton.

What's your Friday look like?" she asked.

"Ringo and I are taking a field trip to Arcadia," he told her. "See if we can find out anything about Miles' current whereabouts."

"Ooh, I love Arcadia," said Emily. "Ever been?"

"Only once," he said. "I've got an aunt and uncle who started snow-birding at a 55-plus park on the East Coast, and we met up for dinner last year, since it's the only place that's close to halfway where you'd want to eat."

She chuckled.

"Very charming town," he continued. "The antique shops, that train depot, all the quaint little stores on the main drag. Ringo's gonna have a ball. If it turns out to be a dead end, the day will probably turn into a photo shoot, and I'll be writing from a coffee shop while he does his thing."

"I haven't been in years," she said, "but I doubt much has changed."

"We should go sometime?" he said with a shrug.

"You want to take me on a getaway?" she asked playfully.

"Well, I mean, after last evening, an overnight wouldn't seem nearly as awkward of an ask," he said with a coy arch of his brow.

"I do suppose we're cleared for travel, as one might say," she answered, again biting down on her lip while putting her hand on his.

When they finished eating, Shelton grabbed a quick shower. Emily peeked in before she departed and told him to make sure the door was locked when he left, sticking her head into the shower for one last kiss that became two and then three.

"We still good for the beach on Sunday?" she asked.

"You think I'd turn down a chance to see that body in a swimsuit?" he said with a wink.

She gave him one final kiss and flashed a giant smile.

As he dressed, Shelton realized that the bouquet of her scent, her very essence, was still flooding the small home, and he inhaled it greedily, trying unsuccessfully not to wonder how long it would take for this to go sideways, as things involving the fairer sex always seemed to, at least in his experience.

As he drove over the Sunshine Skyway Bridge, an engineering marvel that connected two counties with breathtaking views of Tampa Bay on one side and the Gulf of Mexico on the other, he thought about how perfect the moment seemed. He was high on the dopamine rush that a newly consummated union could sometimes provide, while enjoying what may well have been the most perfect roadside view he had ever encountered, despite having road tripped through every noteworthy spot of the original 48 over the course of his travels.

Then, as he descended the suspension bridge toward land once more, he caught sight of the "fishing pier" that had been salvaged from the original two-lane beam bridge after a freighter collided with a support beam during a squall in 1980, sending 35 likewise southbound travelers to their deaths. He was suddenly reminded that all good things do indeed come to an end.

"Well, if you're gonna go out, might as well do it surrounded by this kind of beauty," he said aloud to himself before remembering that it had been gloomy and dreary on the morning that the Greyhound bus was plunged into the sea after the bridge gave way.

Suddenly, what had been an utterly serene drive began suffering a relentless torrent of text notifications. With his phone mounted on the near side of the glove box, Shelton saw that they were all coming in from Ally and Lars. Sure that this indicated there had been a break in the case, he pulled off at the exit at the bottom of the bridge, which had a rest stop and access to the fishing pier on the south side.

"Holy fucking *shite!*" he said aloud when he saw the content of the texts.

Chapter 12: How the mighty have fallen

That same Friday morning before the election, the Reverend Billy Sunday was sitting in his office with his shoes off and his feet on his desk, perusing the accounts of OnlyFans models, when he was interrupted by his assistant, Mildred. She was a sturdily built, godly woman of 58 whose greatest joys in life were leading the Bible study group at her church and volunteering at the county animal shelter.

When commissioners Welsh, Sunday, and Hagerty were elected to the board together four years earlier, Welsh had taken it upon himself to assign each commissioner their assistant, even though it was technically an administrative responsibility of Wayne's.

Sunday would learn that it had played out that way because there were two assistants who had served commissioners that Ignacio had successfully ousted when they proved less pliable than he thought when first getting them elected, while a third opted for retirement rather than serve any of "the three shitheads Hernandez had bought seats for." Welsh took advantage of Wayne's complete willingness to let anyone take even the simplest tasks off his plate and hired himself some eye candy while giving his closer ally, Hagerty, a considerably younger and less uptight female, whom Sunday would have liked to see more of.

The reverend had been attempting to convince himself that Welsh was not gay while they campaigned together, but it became a fiction even his relatively simple mind could not successfully maintain. Sunday had a particular disdain for "sodomites," as he referred to them, but ultimately proved even more lazy than he was bigoted. He vowed not to rock the boat by making hay over the sexual habits of Ignacio's most-prized charge so long as it netted him a six-figure salary that required no meaningful labor. Of course, Sunday became more than a little irritated when he allowed himself to wonder why Ignacio hadn't made *him* his right-hand man, so he tried not to.

"Commissioner Sunday, we have a bit of a situation," said Mildred, clasping her hands and lowering her head after she spoke.

"What is it, Mildred?" he asked, failing to look up from his phone or even lower his feet.

"I don't know that I can … find the … the words," she stammered, her face flushing bright red.

Annoyed, Sunday lowered his feet and placed his phone on the desk.

"Mildred, my dear, as you well know, I am a *very* busy man," he told her. "I do not have time for riddles."

Mildred did not, in fact, know the reverend to be busy by any sense of the word. In fact, the slovenly manner in which Sunday seemed to approach, well, everything in life, offended her Presbyterian interpretation of scripture, which, along with its location in a strip mall that also hosted a Chuck E. Cheese and a Gamestop, was one of several reasons she had not taken one of his many invitations to join his Evangelical congregation.

Mildred paused and then raised her head as high as she could manage in her present state of anxiety.

"I think you should just open your Facebook application," she finally managed, before turning around and almost seeming to stomp off, a grave departure from her usual deference.

Sunday picked his phone back up and opened the app, alarmed to see the number 67 over the notifications icon. His mouth immediately dried out, which happened whenever he got nervous. He clicked on the first notification that he had been tagged by someone and was utterly horrified to see a post with multiple images, the top panel of which was a video of his encounter with his HOA director in front of his home two days prior.

Beneath were photos of the young ladies on his pool deck with their bare breasts censored by gold dollar sign emojis. The image in the bottom-right corner had a +37 label, indicating the number of additional photos in the album. He did not click to see the rest. Sunday's mouth was so dry by this point that he could barely open it. When he managed, it still took considerable effort to pry his parched tongue from his palate. The room seemed to spin. He grew dizzy and thought he might be sick or even pass out. His phone buzzed and indicated that his wife was calling, and his symptoms quickly worsened as he turned it over on his desk, allowing the call to go to voicemail.

The commissioner checked when the post had been made and was shocked to learn that, even though it had been up for less than an hour, there were already 172 comments, 83 shares, and 438 reactions, most of which were angry or laughing emojis. His office phone began ringing, then his cell again. He once more allowed a call from his wife to go to voicemail. Sunday needed to get some fresh air and think. He put on his shoes and sports coat and made for the door.

The 7th floor housed the offices of commissioners and top administrators along three of its four walls, with an open space filled with cubicles where assistants and key staff worked. You could have heard a pin drop when the reverend opened his door. Everyone stopped and stared slack-jawed, even those in the middle of phone conversations. Sunday made a beeline for the fourth wall, where a two-car elevator bank was located, and hit the down button at least a dozen times, each time with increasing pressure, until he was banging on it with his fist.

It seemed to take forever for one of the cars to arrive, and it was only when the doors opened that it occurred to him that he should have taken the private elevator between two of the offices on the opposite wall that dropped you off behind the chambers where an exit would have allowed him to avoid the lobby. However, there was simply no way he could turn back around and face the dozens of employees, the eyes of whom he was sure were currently burning a hole in the back of his lumpy head.

When the reverend walked into the elevator car, he didn't even turn around until the doors closed. He quickly grew claustrophobic. His pits and crotch moistened, and a metallic scent seemed to emanate from his suddenly sweaty body. His mouth grew even more parched. His stomach churned as the car gave that slight rise before beginning to descend. Gas bubbled in his guts, but he didn't trust his bowels enough to relinquish even the most tightly guarded of farts. He pounded his fist on the door, willing the car to lower more quickly to no avail.

Billy Sunday's anxiety skyrocketed when the car came to a stop on the fourth floor, a horror he hadn't even considered. Two female employees from the permitting department boarded, and he immediately knew they were aware of his personal nightmare. The women gave each other a knowing glance, each forcing themselves to look down toward their shoes, purse their lips to suppress a giggle, before ultimately giving in to the temptation to make eye contact with each other, where just enough reaction escaped to make it undeniable that they had seen the post. The reverend's phone buzzed, and a picture of his wife and six children once again illuminated his screen.

This was more than the reverend's unstable constitution could manage, and despite his best efforts to suppress his body's inclinations, he broke wind wetly, praying as earnestly as he had in his adult life that the doors would open before the smell would disperse enough to be noticed. His prayer, like so many others, went unanswered. As the car finally came to a stop, one of the women gasped audibly while the other pinched her nostrils with her thumb and index finger.

As the doors opened, the large man forcefully walked through the small space between them, bumping each woman on the shoulder hard enough to move them nearly a foot in either direction. As he moved, he could feel something warm lubricating his steps. Sunday tried to beeline it to the front lobby doors, which were closest, but his horror intensified when he realized there were at least a dozen members of the media standing in a gaggle in front of the reception desk. A bright light momentarily blinded him as a cameraman rushed in his direction with a short female field correspondent chasing behind him, her heels clacking on the terrazzo flooring.

"Commissioner Sunday, do you have any comment on the allegations that you are running a sex-trafficking ring through your ministry?" a male print reporter yelled from the back of the group.

His phone buzzed again, this time with Ignacio listed as the caller.

"Will you resign and withdraw from the election in light of this scandal?" asked the TV reporter, while sticking her microphone inches from his face before clamping down her lips and retreating from a foul odor that seemed to be coming from her interview subject.

Another phone buzz, this time from Christopher Bacchelli.

Sunday needed to get out of there, STAT! He looked over his shoulder toward the back exit and noticed several county employees who seemed to be pointing at him. It suddenly dawned on the reverend that he was wearing khakis, and he was instantly horrified at the thought that the violent shart had stained him beneath the portion of his pants covered by his navy blazer.

"Reverend Sunday, is it true that one of the dancers is underage and pregnant?" asked a reporter he did not recognize.

"No!" he screamed with indignation, before immediately racking his brain to contemplate whether either was plausible.

"Look, this was a setup, you see," he yelled, waving his arms broadly before quickly lowering them to a slouch, lest he reveal more of his backside than absolutely necessary.

"It was one of those deep fakes, or something," he blathered, trying desperately to summon some saliva into his increasingly arid and acrid mouth. "It was photo-shopped, maybe even that AI stuff they've been working on. The liberal media might try to make hay with this, but the moral credentials of Billy Sunday are beyond reproach!"

The reverend's sermon adrenaline was kicking in, and for a brief moment, he thought he might just have it in him to give the kind of rousing pulpit speech that might right his world. But the smell was getting too foul for even him to ignore, and his guts were making gurgling sounds again, so he made the snap decision to sprint toward the back door that led straight to the county garage. He had barely made it to the doors when the sprinting, an act he'd rarely indulged in since his youth, coaxed forth the rest of the putrid liquid stewing in his bowels.

The reverend didn't let that stop him. It was a brutally humid afternoon, and sweat began pouring from his body as if it had been turned on by a switch as he closed in on the garage, and soon he couldn't decipher perspiration from diarrhea. Thankfully, his Navigator was parked in his assigned spot just inside the garage's entrance. *Finally, a bit of luck*, he thought to himself when he arrived at the vehicle, grateful that its leather seats would be easier to clean after they had been fouled by his present nastiness, whereas the cloth seats he'd endured before having his station elevated by Ignacio would surely necessitate a trade in, if not setting the vehicle on fire and collecting the insurance. Sunday shoved a hand into each front pocket of his slacks to grab his keys, then patted his sports coat, but they were nowhere to be found.

"FAWK!" he screamed, realizing he'd left them upstairs in his office.

****

Shelton had yet to receive a reply from Ringo to the text he'd sent before heading south from St. Pete, so he was somewhat pleased to hear music blaring from his unit when he pulled into the shelled driveway of Ramblewood. Bryce and Jerry, who were posted up in front of their respective units, appeared decidedly less enthused by the reverberations of hardcore punk that began causing Shelton's molars to vibrate almost violently enough to dislodge a filling as he approached. He breathed a sigh of relief when he saw that Lars' Jeep was nowhere to be found.

"Good luck," said Bryce with a scowl as Shelton approached. "I've knocked on the damned thing at least five times, and he hasn't answered *or* turned it down."

"I don't mind much," said Jerry. "It's not my kind of music, but I was already awake when it started."

"You were just pissing and moaning about it two minutes before he got here," Bryce snarled at his nemesis neighbor. "You're such a kiss ass!"

"I was just worried that my window might break from the rattling, is all," said Jerry.

"Gentlemen," said Shelton, holding up a hand while still looking straight at the door.

He pounded on it with an open palm and then a closed fist. Ringo could sleep through a category five hurricane, but surely not this auditory assault. It could wake the dead, he thought, momentarily considering more morbid possibilities. When a minute of his hardest knocking did not produce a response, even with a break in songs on what sounded like a Doom album, Shelton began fishing through the leather correspondence satchel that was over his shoulder. He located an old motel key card and a bobby pin and set about picking the lock.

It took Shelton about half of the next track to pick it open, the door's vibrations making the work much more difficult. Once he opened the door, his eyes were set upon a scene he would never manage to forget, despite his most intense efforts.

Ringo was sprawled out on his back across the single mattress of the bed, much of his hulking frame spilling off of it. Tina was atop of him in what appeared to be some sort of modified reverse cowgirl position, violently humping away with superhuman speed and crashing intensely while seeming to be in perfect sync with what he now recognized as Doom's seminal track, *War is Big Business*.

Wanting desperately to retreat, Shelton forced himself forward into the unit, shielding his eyes from the bed as he raced toward the stereo and unplugged it. The music abruptly stopped, but the savage screams and moans emitting from Tina, previously muted by the music, instantly filled the void and, while not quite as loud, seemed infinitely more intrusive.

"Hidey-ho, it's time to go," blared Shelton.

Tina seemed deaf to his presence and impressively kept to what appeared to be the same exact cadence of the song without the music, but Ringo shifted his head and gave something close to a shrug in Shelton's direction, as if to ask, *What would you have me do*?

Shelton exited the apartment and closed the door behind him. Bryce stood gobsmacked to his left, while a blushing Jerry stood to his right, the latter having been embarrassed into an extremely rare silence. Moments later, a piercing moan from Tina that was held for as impressively long as an Adele note appeared to indicate a satiating climax.

Shelton retreated to his car and put on some jazz music to soothe his freshly pillaged eardrums and soul, returning to a restaurant review he had been reading in the alt-weekly. Not ten minutes later, Ringo emerged, appearing freshly showered in khaki shorts, an open Acapulco shirt, and knockoff Wayfarers. A pistol was tucked into his waistband. Tina trailed behind him in Daisy Dukes and a self-altered t-shirt, her hair also appearing wet from a shower.

"We need to drop her off at Memories," said Ringo after pulling a long slug from a can of Four Loko, the morning boost he preferred over coffee. "It's on the way," he added as Shelton glared.

By way of invitation, Shelton waved his hand toward the passenger door. Tina lacked any sort of awkwardness in her demeanor, which left him wondering if she was so entranced she hadn't noticed his coital interruption. If she had, she clearly wasn't any more bothered by it than Ringo had been, indicating to Shelton that this woman may indeed be sufficiently Bohemian for his friend's liking.

Shelton adjusted the rearview mirror so that he and Tina could see each other.

"That was a hell of a Facebook post," he said to her.

She wore a look of confusion.

"This morning, 5 a.m. to be precise?" he said. "Salacious photos and a video of a particular Mullet County Commissioner?"

"Oh, that was him," she said, nodding toward Ringo.

Shelton gave him a menacing look.

"Don't," Ringo warned. "I'm a photographer. I take freelance jobs, and this one just happened to align with the interests of the grieving widow who is presently signing our paychecks, not to mention the editor responsible for our new living quarters. I would think a thank you would be in order."

Shelton lowered his sunglasses so that his glaring eyes did not go unnoticed.

"You couldn't use a few more degrees of separation?" Shelton asked, nodding toward the back seat.

"It's fine," Ringo told him. "From what I understand, Ally and Lars are working on a story as we speak. I imagine Dutch's PAC might be drafting some robocalls and a text campaign."

Neither Lars nor Ally had mentioned Tina in their texts, which left Shelton wondering if they had failed to make the connection, each having only met her on one occasion by that point.

"Hey," said Ringo, with a big smile.

Shelton looked at him.

"That pales in comparison to the one that's in the chamber," said Ringo with a devilish giggle.

"My god, what have you done?"

"Aside from single-handedly taking down two scumbag politicians?"

Shelton took a deep breath after realizing how tightly he was gripping the wheel.

****

The Reverend Billy Sunday quickly weighed his options. He did have his cell phone, but who could he call to bring down his keys, and how long would it be before someone from the press made their way to the garage? Surely, no Uber driver would allow him to enter their vehicle in his present personification.

The reverend noticed an indigent man of about 40 loitering near the exit on the other side of the garage.

"Hey," Sunday barked in a hushed yell. "Hey," he repeated more loudly.

The man finally looked toward him suspiciously.

"You wanna make a hundred dollars?" he asked.

The man took a few steps toward him, still seeming uneasy.

"I don't do none of that gay shit since I quit the oxies," he told him, cautiously moving closer to the large man who seemed to be hiding behind a top-of-the-line Lincoln SUV.

Sunday was repulsed by the suggestion that he would solicit sex from any man, let alone a homeless one, but he was not in a position to offend.

"No, no, nothing like that," said Sunday. "I need some clothes, at least a fresh pair of pants."

As the man closed in on the front of the vehicle, he caught wind of the stench.

236

"Oh, you shit your pants," he said, knowingly. "Why didn't you say so? I'd sell you my pants but—" he motioned to his slender body to indicate the profound difference in size between them.

Sunday couldn't believe that he was lamenting the fact that he could not swap pants with a homeless reformed opiate addict who apparently used to perform sexual acts to pay for his habit, and who he now saw was missing his front four upper teeth.

"Here's what we can do," said the man. "The Salvation Army's shelter is five blocks from here. They got a clothing bank. That's where this outfit came from," he said, looking down at the filthy white painter's pants and faded Florida State Fair shirt he was wearing. "And they got the store next to it that sells the better used clothing donations. What are you, about a 42 waist?"

"38!" said Sunday, his voice dripping with indignation.

To be fair, he would likely have been a 44 had he not taken to wearing his pants beneath his bulbous gut as it had expanded, rather than over it.

"Well, I'm sure I can find something big enough at one of the two," the man said. "And if they're too big, you got a belt."

"Well, go on then," said the reverend, quickly forgetting that his higher social station meant little at the present moment.

The man rubbed his thumb against his first two finger tips to indicate he would require the cash.

Billy Sunday sighed and pulled a wad from his inside breast pocket. Cash was always aplenty, given that 20 percent of whatever went into the collection plate at his church each week was skimmed off the top. The man noticed that he appeared to have hundreds of dollars as he peeled off two twenties.

"Here's 40," he told him. "I'll give you the other 60 when I get the pants."

"Well, if it's a part now, part later deal, $100 ain't gonna cut it, Ace," said the man, who had suddenly grown more confident.

Sunday couldn't believe the balls on this guy. Did he know who he was dealing with? He pointed a finger.

"Listen—" he said, but was immediately cut off.

"No, you listen," said the man. "You're in one hell of a pinch, and I'm flat broke and sleeping on these here streets. If you want my help, you're gonna give me a hundred bucks now, walk three blocks down to the river, get in under the overpass where no one will see you, clean yourself up, and wait for me to come to the rescue. And when I do, you ought to throw in a tip on top of it, seeing as how well-resourced you are," he said before giving a knowing look toward the six-figure SUV.

Sunday peeled off three more twenties and put the cash forth. The homeless man held his nose as he approached and snatched the bills, coughing a bit from the stench.

A line from the Old Testament's Book of Samuel entered Sunday's mind.

How the mighty have fallen

****

The drive through east Mullet County was excruciating. The six-lane state road that had remained unpaved until the early 1980s was completely gridlocked with bumper-to-bumper traffic. On three occasions already, it took them two traffic lights to get through the intersection. When it occurred a fourth time, Shelton partially jumped a curb to enter the right-turn lane for a shopping center with a freestanding Starbucks. He'd passed up a much-needed second cup three times already, but the slogging pace was intensifying his caffeine headache.

"You want anything?" he asked Ringo, opting to park and go inside, given the ridiculous length of the drive-thru line.

"Yeah, get me a double espresso," he said, jumping out and heading toward the shopping center. "I'm just gonna hit that Goodwill real quick. Come grab me when you're done."

Shelton thought about protesting but knew he'd lose more time in argument than acquiescence, as Ringo was a notorious thrift store fiend. His friend's entire wardrobe consisted of vintage finds from Goodwill, the Salvation Army, St. Vincent de Paul, and eBay, plus half a dozen sets of hospital scrubs, which were sold at surprisingly low prices at several low-rent strip malls because of the elderly-laden area's volume of poorly paid home health care workers.

Ringo prized OR scrubs for their comfortable fit and breathable fabric, which were well-suited to the area's brutal heat and humidity. The fact that he often introduced himself as "Dr. Ringo Khan" sometimes caused misunderstandings when these quirks overlapped, such as the time he was asked to give aid to an elderly person experiencing cardiac distress in a Sarasota Walmart. The store had a portable defibrillator, and the maniac quickly accepted and employed the device, despite having no idea whether the man required such measures. Fortunately, the EMS declared that the death was inevitable and applauded the good doctor for his quick thinking.

"Don't get lost in there," said Shelton, fighting back an eye roll.

After suffering through the experience of being behind a middle-aged woman placing an obscenely complex, multi-drink order for herself and her coworkers, Shelton got the coffees and quickly made his way to the Goodwill, which was one of the new, larger outlets the organization had been putting in shopping center anchors affected by a rash of grocery store consolidations. He found Ringo thumbing through some vinyl.

"Come on, we gotta roll," he said while handing him the small cup of espresso.

They headed toward the door when something caught his friend's eye.

"Oh, snap," said Ringo, darting toward a rack of sports coats.

He grabbed a plaid jacket from the rack.

"Burberry!" he screamed loudly enough to cause every shopper in the store to look.

A Burberry jacket for $5.99 was something that even a time-pressed Shelton couldn't argue with, even though the odds of it housing this behemoth seemed slim to none. However, as Ringo threw it on, it seemed to fit near perfectly.

Ringo took an almost cursory glance at the price tag, then did a double take—$59.99. That was understandable, he figured. Some rookie had obviously punched one too many nines on the sticker gun.

He headed toward a gentleman with a stupid haircut and handlebar mustache who was behind the counter of some sort of jewelry/collectible display case marked "Treasure Island," which was closer than the main cash registers up front.

"Sir, I assume this is a mistake?" he asked, holding what he presumed to be the incorrectly marked tag forward.

Silently, the man waved Ringo closer with his hand, squinting to see the digits.

"$59.99," he said evenly.

"I know what it *says*," said Ringo, "but jackets are $5.99, so it's a mistake, no?"

The man managed a feat best described as a sympathetic roll of the eyes.

"That's our boutique section," he said, pointing toward the rack where he had grabbed the coat, which Shelton and Ringo then noticed was under a sign that read, *Boutique*, in vertical letters.

Both men remained confused.

"Surely, you can't mean to say that this sticker is correct?" Ringo asked, feeling his blood pressure spike as the conflict sweats began to set in.

240

"That is a Burberry jacket, sir—a wool one, at that. They typically retail for upward of a thousand dollars when new."

Ringo struggled to control his emotions.

"I'm not sure how that is relevant, my good man," he said, giving off subtle cues that Shelton alone recognized as dangerous precursors to violent rage. "This is neither *new* nor *retail*. We're in a god damned GOODWILL! All the jackets are $5.99—always have been!"

The man looked toward the other end of the store.

"Sir, there are plenty of $5.99 jackets over there, in our *regular* men's section. The boutique section consists of special finds that are priced accordingly."

Ringo rubbed the bridge of his nose.

"Oh, so you didn't *find* this in a black garbage bag or cardboard box at one of your drop-off locations?" he asked, his eyebrows arching to an almost uncomfortable height as he raised the question. "It was a *special* find, was it?"

The clerk's ability to remain calm was a bit disarming.

"Sir, Goodwill Boutique is a special section in certain stores where you can find better brands and names for a price comparable to other boutique thrift shops," he said while returning his attention to the items he was price-marking. "As I said, we have plenty of more modestly priced apparel over there. I'm sure there are plenty of sport coats in—"

"In *what*?" shouted Ringo. "*Lesser* brands? This is a Goodwill, my friend, every last damned thing is supposed to be *modestly priced*. The fact that this particular store exists in a repurposed Winn-Dixie that still has a hint of shine on the linoleum does not change that. Neither does the fact that you've mastered the etiquette and lingo of a 1950s haberdashery clerk, despite the fact that you've got prison ink on your forearms! The whole point of Goodwill is the chance for the working man to score some crumbs off the table every now and again! You scour the jacket racks, and, most of the time, you get faded JCPenny trash with a hard-to-hide cigarette hole, but every

once in a great-goddamned-while you score a vintage
Burberry! It's the only reason you suffer the indignity of the
whole process. It's Powerball for the fashion-sensitive poor!"

"Sir, if you'll please calm down—"

"Screaming Jesus on a Ferris wheel, man, this *is* calm,"
Ringo screamed. "*Boutique calm*, if you will. Look, I get that
there's money being left on the table, and I'm sure the rent on
this Shangri-La you guys are operating out of is much steeper
than the broken-down strip malls where your other shops are,
but let's be honest, shall we? It's not like you guys are sending
buyers out to estate sales and scouring eBay for under-priced
vintage that you can mark up in a traditional antique-like
enterprise. At the end of the day, some guy's wife dropped off a
box with some old bowling league trophies, smelly sandals, fad
diet books, a crock pot, and a jacket her husband hasn't worn in
20 fucking years! You deloused it, because you don't know
where it's been or whether it's got some bathroom buckshot
lurking deep in the fabric, and then you threw it up on a rack
no different than the ones in the more pedestrian section on the
other side of the store! Again, this is GOODWILL!"

"They're calling the cops, man," Shelton said, scratching
his neck and looking at the ground as he donned his aviators,
hoping to make himself less identifiable should a felony
transpire.

Ringo zeroed in on the price sticker gun.

"Change it," he said.

"Sir, surely you're not suggesting—"

"That you commit an act of decency?" Ringo interjected.
"Yes! That's exactly what I'm suggesting, you fucking nonce.
Change the fucking price to what we both know it should be!"

The man seemed uncomfortable but remained silent.
Ringo, intending to offer him a ten-dollar bill for his troubles,
stuffed a hand into his front pocket, causing his recently
buttoned Acapulco shirt to rise up his midriff far enough to

make the butt of the Glock 17 that was tucked into his waistband visible. The clerk gasped and raised his hands.

"I don't want any trouble," the man shouted, drawing the attention of several shoppers in the vicinity.

Initially confused, Ringo soon realized his assumption.

"Oh, no," he said calmly, glancing toward the gun and finally pulling out the ten from his pocket. "I was just gonna throw you a ten-spot on top of the $5.99, a little something for the effort."

The man took the ten, rang the jacket up for $5.99, and put it in a bag with a receipt, refusing Ringo's insistence that he keep the change, sweat beginning to drip from his brow.

"You can't pull that shit these days," Shelton said, walk-running across the parking lot while Ringo casually donned the jacket and hiked its sleeves, the blisteringly inconducive weather notwithstanding. "They've got security cameras everywhere. He's phoning the 5-0 as we speak!"

"Hey," said Ringo, extending his arms and casually doing a 360. "This is a damn sweet jacket, though, ain't it?"

Even in his anger, Shelton couldn't deny that to be true.

****

At the end of a very long day that included bathing in a river, changing into a far too tight pair of sweatpants under an overpass only to still be denied entrance into an Uber, and then hitchhiking across half the county—the final leg of the trip consisting of riding in the back of a flatbed pickup truck filled with migrant farm workers for whom he'd endlessly called for the deportation of—the Reverend Billy Sunday finally found himself sitting in his living room, head in his hands, suffering a lecture from Ignacio Hernandez and Christopher Bacchelli.

"Do you have any idea how much money it has cost me to elevate you to a station in life you have been utterly incapable of even approaching on your own merit?" Hernandez screamed. "Hundreds of thousands of dollars in contributions, this house, donations to your church, and your stupid, bullshit non-profit."

"We rescue women who've been sex-trafficked!" bellowed Sunday, finally coming to his own defense.

"A woman shaking her ass at the Bearded Clam isn't being *sex trafficked*, estúpido!" shouted the developer. "She's trailer park trash with daddy issues.

"This isn't even close to survivable," said Bacchelli. "But it's too late to drop out. The best we can do is double down on the ads and hope that you squeak by on a combination of name recognition and low-information voters. But once you do, Ignacio will have to break with you publicly, denounce your character, and call for your resignation. If you win, you'll resign, and we'll have the governor appoint a suitable replacement."

Tears welled in Sunday's eyes.

"What will happen to me?" he asked. "I've got mouths to feed."

Ignacio rose and wagged a finger in the reverend's face.

"What will happen to you, is you'll get a gracious three more months in this house while you figure out where to fuck off to next, and that is only if you cooperate to my satisfaction, you, you, *tonto del culo*."

Sunday's sadness quickly turned bitter.

"I think you forget how much I know," he said, his lip quivering as it reliably did whenever he became enraged.

Ignacio chuckled.

"And I think you have forgotten the length of my reach and what happens to those who go up against me, *pendejo*," said the developer, holding a devious smile before adjusting his lapels, turning his back to him, and sauntering slowly toward the door.

"You shit the bed, Billy. It's a generous deal, all things considered," said Bacchelli, once Ignacio had completed his exit. "You'd be a fool not to take it. Relocate, come up with a story about the *liberal media's campaign of lies*, start a new church, yada yada."

He rose and patted Sunday on the shoulder.

"Thank your lucky stars you happen to be in the one hustle whose marks are even dumber than they are in right-wing politics."

When Bacchelli climbed into the driver's seat of his $200,000 Mercedes G-Wagon AMG 63, Ignacio turned and looked at him quizzically.

"He got the message, but we have much bigger problems, my friend," said the consultant, offering the screen of his phone, which contained the most flagrant picture Ringo had snapped of Commissioner Hagerty and her paramour.

"Dios motherfucking mio," shouted Ignacio, pounding his fist against the passenger window so hard it would have surely shattered had his consultant not opted for the bulletproof windows in fear that some candidate whose life he had ruined might go postal.

****

Candice Hagerty was drinking a glass of Prosecco while enjoying a foot massage from the much older attorney she had married, in the living room of their west county McMansion, watching a YouTube video about a new cosmetic surgery technique that addressed the aesthetic inconveniences of an aging woman's neck. Cozy and relaxed, her bliss was suddenly halted when her phone began to blow up with notifications related to a viral post on the r/DeSotoCity subreddit that was being endlessly shared across every social media platform.

When she clicked the first image, her heart nearly stopped. It would be curious to most people that her anxiety was mixed with disappointment that she would have to suffer such a calamitous event and, because her unmentionables had been obscured to avoid violating the state's recently-enacted revenge porn law, she wouldn't even have the consolation of knowing that those who viewed the photos would at least know that her massive mammaries were indeed both real and spectacular.

"Fuck," she murmured in a low and defeated tone.

"What is it, my dear?" her attentive husband asked.

She turned the phone toward him with the image of her taking it from behind as the hatch opened on the screen.

"Oh my," said Aaron Bennington, Esquire, whose last name she had declined to take. "That's not going to be good for anyone."

Aaron was not surprised by what the photo depicted. Contrary to what one might hear on the right-wing podcast circuit, the so-called "hot-wife" lifestyle is far more popular in conservative circles than the "trad-wife" trend many Christian conservative influencers had gained fame and fortune promoting on TikTok.

In truth, Aaron had a fetish for being cuckolded by more studly men who were far more capable of satiating his younger, oversexed trophy wife and had, on many occasions, watched her dalliances with Deputy White either in person or on videos she'd record for him. But he knew that public knowledge of this would hurt both her political career and his law practice.

As a personal injury attorney in a state for which that particular lobby was quite prolific, Aaron had long ago amassed generational wealth. However, he treasured his sweet Candice and knew that a quiet, comfortable life of self-imposed exile was not on her bingo card.

Candice's phone began ringing with Christopher Bacchelli's name appearing on the caller ID. She let it go to voicemail and reached for a bottle of Valium on the coffee table, took two pills, and washed them down with the wine.

****

Arcadia is a picturesque, postcard town that sprang to life after a rail line was built to connect the central Florida citrus havens to Charlotte Harbor on the southwest coast of the Gulf of Mexico. It was the county seat of a massive swath of agricultural land that would later be split into several counties, so its downtown is notably fancier and more historic than anything for miles in any direction. After a fire decimated the town in 1905, its main street was rebuilt, and the intricately constructed, early 20th-century buildings that line it remain well preserved.

They found a parking spot at the Arcadia Train Depot Museum, and Shelton felt comfortable enough to leave the Mini Cooper's top down. The halfway house was only a few blocks away, and all of the county government buildings that might have records regarding Miles were nearby as well. Ringo immediately began snapping photos of the beautiful train depot, and Shelton took a moment to stretch after the long ride in the hot sun.

"I suppose we'll start with the halfway house," Shelton said, as Ringo continued to snap off shots of the surrounding buildings, while walking backwards in the same direction.

My Brother's Keeper was an oddly constructed multi-family house that seemed to consist of an old, original structure that had been perpetually added on to until it had ceased to resemble anything approaching coherent architectural design. Such dwellings were not uncommon in a state that had only adopted building codes in recent decades. It might have started as a 3/2 or even a 2/1, but there could have been 20 boarding rooms by this point, from the looks of it.

Rehab facilities, halfway houses, and even third-rate adult living facilities regularly make use of such structures in Florida, often profiting handsomely by combining cut-rate overhead with a subsidized enterprise that exploits those without alternatives. As they approached, a man and a woman standing outside the building stopped talking and eyed them suspiciously. The woman threw her mostly smoked cigarette to the ground and stomped it out.

The man was rail-thin and had compressed facial features, not unlike a rodent. His hair was long and stringy. He reminded Shelton of a down-and-out Kid Rock. The man removed a toothpick, revealing a mouthful of meth teeth, while heroin was Shelton's best guess as to the drug of choice of the equally skinny brunette woman standing next to him, with her spindly arms folded, hands scratching at her elbows nervously. Both drugs had made a ferocious comeback once the state finally took steps to curb its pill-mill problem after Micky's documentary. *Plug one hole, and another opens*, thought Shelton.

"Can I help you folks?" asked the man.

"We wanted to go in and talk to someone on staff," said Shelton.

"We're the only staff that's here," said the man, something sinister in his tone.

Good god, thought Shelton. If these were the people facilitating court-ordered transitional housing for freshly released felons, recidivism seemed inevitable.

"You work here?" he asked, immediately regretting it.

"Yeah, we *work* here," barked the woman. "You expected some banker-looking motherfuckers?"

The man withdrew his hands from his pocket and took a step forward.

"What do you need?" he asked Shelton menacingly.

Shelton took out his phone and opened an image of his digital press pass.

"We're with the press," he said, again instantly realizing he'd taken the wrong approach.

"We don't want nothing to do with no press," the woman interjected.

"No, you don't," barked Ringo, "or code enforcement, or the DOC, or the FDLE, or countless other fucking agencies we've got contacts at who love to swap dirt."

248

The man sized up Ringo and clearly didn't like his chances.

"Come on inside," he said and turned toward the entrance.

The inside of the building smelled of mold, the way all old Florida buildings cooled by window AC units do. Mildew-stained wallpaper ran up from the grimy tile toward the water-stained ceiling panels. The woman offered them seats on mismatched chairs that would have been at home in any American business circa 1970, while the man took a seat behind the desk, and she leaned against the wall behind him.

"There was a Native American gentleman who stayed here a few years back by the name of Miles Conepatchie," said Shelton, who'd taken the seat across the desk. "We desperately need to contact him regarding his father, who recently passed. It seems unlikely he's still here, but we were hoping you might have records of a forwarding address, anything. These are his last known whereabouts, and he's a ghost in terms of an online presence or public records we can find."

The man stroked his chin with the toothpick he'd taken from his mouth and sat silently for a moment.

"Well, *guests of the inn*, as we call them, do have to provide an address when they're discharged, but there's three problems with that," he said, now using the pick to scratch the inside of his ear.

"And what would they be?" asked Ringo, folding his massive arms across his barrel chest, while leaning against the back wall.

"Well, the odds that the address is still good six months later, let alone six years, are about zero, for starters. Second, it's against policy to provide them to anyone, but immediate family or law enforcement, and third, old Miles wasn't here on a court order, so he could sign himself out anytime, no proof of suitable residence required."

Shelton sighed.

"But you know him," said Ringo.

The man smirked and gave a shrug.

"You said six years," said Ringo. "You worked here while he was bedding down?"

"Nope, I was bedding down my damn self," the man said. "Just came off a stretch in Raiford. You know about Raiford?"

Raiford Prison, officially known as the Union Correctional Institution and colloquially referred to as the Rock, is a notoriously hellish place to be incarcerated. Located on barren swampland 35 miles northeast of Gainesville, thousands of Florida's worst criminals are packed into overcrowded cells that do not have air conditioning. At Raiford, rape, murder, and violent assaults are as common as summer rain. It's the home of Florida's death row and was the final earthly domain of many notorious criminals, including Ted Bundy.

"I've heard a thing or two," said Shelton.

The man scoffed.

"Well, I did three stints in that Hell on Earth," said the man, withdrawing the toothpick from his mouth (where it had returned after being inside his ear), to spit on the floor. "You know what that says about me?"

"That you can shit like a horse even after eating a block of cheese?" asked Ringo with an evil grin.

"Joke if you want, big boy," the man told him. "Until you've survived that place, you don't know what you can or would do or endure."

The man unwrapped a Dum Dums lollipop, stuck it in his mouth, and swirled it around with his hand.

"They help me stay off the smokes," he said.

"So, you know Miles?" asked Shelton.

"I don't know if I'd go that far," said the man. "He was a creepy fucker, all dead-eyed, and never talked to no one, but he carried himself in a way I recognized from the prison yard, you know, the genuinely bad motherfuckers, not cosplayers," he said, intending to shoot a glare at Ringo, then thinking twice when it occurred to him that the man possessed similar attributes. "I stayed away from him."

"So, you wouldn't have any idea how we might find him?" asked Shelton.

"I never said that," said the man. "In fact, I know exactly where he beds down these days, but, as you can imagine, shifts at My Brother's Keeper don't pay all that much, and I'd like to take Dawn here out to dinner and a movie sometime, if you get what I mean."

Shelton was used to having to pay for tips on occasion and made a habit of keeping his cash spread out among several pockets so as not let whoever was shaking him down know how much was in the kitty should negotiations be required. He pulled a wad that had three twenties and a ten in it from the pocket of his shorts.

"Independent media isn't exactly a booming enterprise either," he said, "but there's … let's see, 70 bucks here. That ought to cover a night on the town."

"I don't know," the man said. "She likes them big buckets of popcorn, and you know how those theaters are when they got you over the barrel like that. Ought to be illegal what they charge."

"She looks like she gets by on two packs of menthols and a bag of Skittles each day," said Ringo. "Don't get me wrong, I'm into the waif thing, got one nearly as slender myself, but 70 spins is gonna have to cut it today, Ace. Not bad for five minutes of work and a chance to recount days gone by at the Rock, eh?"

Shelton tossed the bills onto his desk and nodded sympathetically. The man collected them and tucked them into the front pocket of his Carhartt shirt.

"You come in from the west end, I take it?" he asked.

Shelton nodded.

"You see that old green motel on the left with the detached units, called the Oaks?

"Yeah, about a half mile out," said Shelton.

"That's the one," the man said. "Miles stays there. I don't know which unit is his, but he's got a clean 1970 Chevelle SS, dark blue with white racing stripes. Thing's cherry as fuck. It's usually parked near the west end, so I imagine it's one of 'em on that side."

"Thanks," said Shelton. "We appreciate the help."

They turned to leave.

"Hey," the man said.

Shelton turned around.

"Don't go saying nothin' about it being me who told you where he was staying," the man said sharply. "I mean that, you hear. I don't wanna get sideways with that dead-eyed motherfucker, not for no 70 bucks."

"Scouts honor," said Shelton, holding up three fingers.

"I bet you didn't think it would go that easy," said Ringo when they got to the sidewalk.

"Yeah, seemed too easy," said Shelton. "And that threadbare bastard lost all his moxy once he started talking about Miles. If we find him, no cowboy shit, you hear me? Don't forget who we're dealing with."

"Well, what's your plan, Kemo Sabe?" asked Ringo.

Shelton took nearly a minute before responding, realizing that he didn't really have one aside from finding Miles. He hadn't thought they would even get that far. It seemed more like a box they had to check. But the man at the halfway house clearly knew Miles and even mentioned the Chevelle that Lars had told him Micky had given to his son years earlier. Should they go to the police? Should he call Pauly Miguel for backup? Should he at least check in with Lars? All seemed like wise moves, but they were already out here, and they had a bead on the man they were all looking for, a man they had no idea was even involved in Micky's murder.

"We came out to pay him a visit at the request of Micky's wife to make sure he was aware that his father had passed,"

Shelton finally said. "That's it. We gauge his response and, without making it obvious, see if we notice a vintage silver Rolex with a green canvas band on his wrist."

"Sounds good to me," said Ringo, reclining way back in his seat as they pulled off.

Shelton's heart began to race when he saw the brake lights flicker on a gorgeously preserved Chevy Chevelle that he surely would have noticed had it been there when they first drove past the motel. It was a squalid place that had served as a fishing camp, then housed migrant farm workers before greening disease took out most of the area's citrus and it further dilapidated into the kind of one-step-above-homeless apartments that littered rural Florida.

The man who stepped out of the car was carrying a single bag of what appeared to be groceries. He was tall and thin, but in that wiry way that suggested a lot of fast-twitch muscle fiber packed into his athletic frame. His black hair had gray streaks. It was long and straight, pulled into a half-back ponytail with the rest flowing down his back. He gave a barely noticeable glance over his shoulder when he heard the car enter the lot, unlocked his door, and entered the unit.

"So, we just knock on the door?" asked Ringo.

"That's the plan," Shelton said.

Ringo reached under his seat, grabbed his backup gun, a Beretta M9, and offered it to Shelton.

"Put that damned thing away, you maniac," Shelton said in a hushed shout.

Ringo shrugged and returned it to the floorboard.

When they got to the front door, Shelton's heart raced. He desperately wanted to turn around and go back to Mullet County and report Miles' whereabouts, but they were beyond the point of no return. If he didn't knock, Ringo surely would, and that would make things at least twice as likely to go pear-shaped.

He knocked once, waited nearly a minute, and knocked again. There was no movement inside that he could hear until the sound of a deadbolt being turned. It was followed by ten seconds of silence, then the door opened.

Miles was even taller than he'd estimated, and his thin-looking frame was chiseled, with large veins bulging along both arms, which were decorated with tattoos featuring both military and Native American symbols. He stood straight and stiff, saying not a word. *Dead-eyed* was indeed a perfect description for the look he offered.

"Miles?" Shelton asked. "My name is Shelton, I work for your … family?" he stammered, not knowing whether Miles was even aware of Micky's passing. In less time than it takes for a light to come on after the switch is flipped, Miles exploded forward, bounding in two steps toward Ringo, correctly assuming he was the only threat present, and shoved him to the ground as if he were a defensive end bull rushing an offensive tackle. Ringo was caught off guard and hit the pavement hard. Miles leaped over his body, took a hard left, and headed for the tree line that was right behind the motel.

After regaining his senses, Ringo executed an impressive rising handspring and was on his feet, his Glock drawn from his waist, heading after him.

"No," yelled Shelton, to no avail.

Ringo sprinted down the small drainage embankment to the tree line and could see Miles' back when he stopped on a dime, turned around, and sprayed what sounded like half a dozen rounds from a very small automatic weapon. Ringo instinctively turned sideways to narrow his profile, then dropped to the ground and low-crawled back toward the motel. Miles disappeared into the thickly wooded wetlands.

"What are you doing, you lunatic?" yelled Shelton. "You were nearly killed."

"He attacked me," yelled Ringo.

"And you chase after an assassin?" Shelton said. "What was that goddamn gun he had?"

"Micro Uzi," said Ringo. "The Israelis make it. It's a three-pound, open-bolt, blowback-operated submachine gun that carries nine rounds, and he's got it modified to be fully automatic. Not a common weapon to come across. I surely didn't think I'd ever live to get shot at with one," he added with a shrug that indicated he was not only unfazed by the event, but a bit proud to have survived it.

Shelton heard a loud hissing sound coming from the lot and turned toward his car, where he noticed that one round had taken out a headlight. Judging from the sound, he assumed another had hit the radiator.

"Fuck," yelled Shelton. "Let's see if it'll make it into town. We gotta get some cover in case that crazy bastard comes back."

"Seriously?" said Ringo, giving him a disappointed look.

It took Shelton a moment.

"I meant it as an expression, I wasn't—"

"I'm just busting your balls, Sally," Ringo said with a wink as he dusted grass and twigs off his hairy chest.

****

Shelton and Ringo were sitting in the Wagon Wheel, a double-wide trailer serving as one of three saloons in Arcadia. The Mini had started up but was knocking and sputtering, clearly unfit for what would have been an hour's drive under ideal circumstances. Shelton called Lars and told him what had happened. Lars said to hang tight and that either he or someone he could send would be there as soon as humanly possible. The car coughed and lurched forward at odd intervals but made it back into town. They pulled into the dirt lot of the saloon, where they proceeded to wet their respective whistles.

From the moment they entered, it was clear that it was *not* a place used to receiving anyone but local regulars. But after

Ringo fed the jukebox and curated a playlist that included Johnny Cash, Waylon Jennings, Merle Haggard, and David Allen Coe, the side-eye glances and murmuring from the other four day-drinking patrons dissipated.

They were a shot of tequila and three cold beers in when they heard an unmistakable southern drawl. Dutch was in his usual khaki slacks and dress shirt, but was wearing his cowboy hat and mirrored aviators, making him a much better fit for this crowd than they were. He was having a conversation via a Bluetooth earpiece.

"I don't know why in the hell he backed him for mayor in the first place," Dutch said. "Well, I know Skip Whitman ain't worth a damn, but how does running a drip like Anderson solve the problem? It's like changing your shirt because you shit your pants."

"Shat," Ringo offered softly.

Dutch motioned to give him a second.

"Nah, Patrick's not bad," Dutch continued. "I mean, he's dumber than a bag of hair, but he just needs a handler present to tell him when it's time to stop talking before he says something stupid, which, in his case, is usually around the 90-second mark. Yeah, I know. Well, listen, I just got to a saloon out here in Arcadia where I have to pick up two members of the fourth estate who got themselves in a gunfight with a crazy Indian, but that's a story for another day. I'll holler at you later, Councilman."

He pressed a button on his phone, which was holstered to his belt, then removed his shades.

"DeSoto City business," he whispered, nodding toward his phone. "Well, look at you two sorry sons of bitches," he said, shaking his head and pulling up a seat.

"Rum and Coke," Dutch told the bartender. "Good stuff if you got it, cheap stuff if you don't."

"I got well, Bacardi, and Captain Morgan," the man behind the bar said.

"Make it a Captain, and get these boys another round of those Yuenglings," he said, placing a twenty-dollar bill on the bar.

"So, old Miles was takin' pop shots at you boys," said Dutch, shaking his head. "I see there ain't no holes in either of you, so it's safe to say he meant no harm."

"My car would beg to differ," said Shelton.

"Don't go worrying about that," Dutch assured him. "I already have a tow truck on its way. It'll be returned to you in good working order, and we'll set you up with a rental in the meantime."

Dutch took a sip of his drink and let out a chuckle.

"Life'll kill you, won't it," he said. "You didn't happen to notice if he was wearing the watch, did you?"

Shelton shook his head.

"It all happened so fast. He was gone in the blink of an eye."

"Those boys at Langley sure do know how to train up a killer, now don't they," said Dutch, toasting the drink that had just been put before him.

"He was wearing *a* watch," said Ringo, "but I didn't get a good look at it."

"How did you pick that up?" asked Shelton, genuinely impressed.

"Because your boy is tactical as fuck," said Ringo, draining his beer. "Another shot of Jame-O, governor," he told the bartender, who silently obliged.

"What now?" said Shelton.

"Nothing, for now," said Dutch. "If Miles is our guy, he'll go into the wind, and no one will ever find him. If he sticks around, we can at least get the police to question him now, and they'll have enough for a search warrant either way. Meanwhile, we focus on getting those three puppets off the board. I don't know that I can do much for Amber in terms of solving a murder, but we're damned close to getting the second item on her wish list, which is flipping the commission, the way Micky had wanted. Those stories have gone statewide, every news station, every newspaper, the damned radio, and forget about social media. Hell, the damned Daily Mirror even covered it across the pond. It is a genuine international scandal, gentlemen. And every last registered Republican in those wards is getting bombarded with robocalls and text blasts. I only wish it wasn't too late for direct mail, get them photos out there on a high-quality, glossy four by six."

"What about Welsh's race?" asked Shelton.

"We're gonna have to do that one the old-fashioned way," said Dutch. "He's the most hated, and he has the strongest opponent, whom we've been pumping PAC ads out for nonstop these past two weeks. Now that it's a fair fight in terms of funding, I like our chances with that race, especially after the debate. We press hard enough these last few days, I think Osborne wins it."

"I'll drink to that," said Ringo, slamming his shot and chasing it with a beer.

****

Shelton and Ringo spent the rest of the evening getting proper drunk with Lars and Tina at Memories Lounge, where Ringo recounted his near-death experience to great fanfare. Shelton awoke with an agonizing hangover that required three Naproxen tablets and a long, torturous run in the sweltering August heat to abate. He spent Saturday writing his column for the Sunday online edition— a hilarious account of why neither Sunday nor Hagerty belonged within a thousand feet of either an elementary school or a public office—and doing an interview with WMLT on the matter.

When Sunday came around, he was grateful for the chance to log some beach time and headed across the Skyway to pick up Emily in the Ford Escape rental Dutch had set him up with on Saturday morning. They took the short ride over the causeway to St. Pete Beach, a gorgeous, sugar-cane sand barrier island just 15 minutes from downtown that was littered with seafood shacks and open-air beach bars. They rented a beach cabana with a couple of chaise lounges and lazed in the sun.

"I still can't believe you got shot at!" she said for the third time since he'd recounted the story.

"Well, I didn't *really* get shot at," said Shelton. "Technically, Ringo got shot at. And, well, my car got shot at, successfully so, at least from the shooter's point of view."

"You think he was aiming for the car?" she asked.

"No, to be honest, I think he was laying down some cover," he told her. "I think the car got shot because he didn't really want to hit Ringo. I'm telling you, that guy was one hell of an operator. No way he doesn't hit him from that distance. They were to scare us off, and it worked, at least it did for me. Ringo wanted to chase after the guy."

"Did he have a gun?" she asked incredulously.

"Ringo? Shit, that man is armed to the teeth at all times. Guns, knives, the occasional hand grenade."

"Oh my god, Shelton, what kind of people do you associate with?" she asked with a giggle that was clearly masking some genuine concern.

Shelton took a sip from the straw of his cold brew coffee and turned to her.

"The serious kind," he said, lowering his shades to issue a wink.

She rolled her eyes and gave a sigh, then rose, removed her sarong, and started walking towards the surf, turning back after a few steps.

"Well, come on, tough guy," she said playfully. "There might be sharks in the water for you to keep me safe from."

Shelton put his cup in the cooler, removed his straw hat and Hawaiian shirt, and followed her as she broke into a trot toward the gulf.

Ignacio was at Christopher Bacchelli's office bright and early on Monday morning. The consultant couldn't recall the last time Hernandez had been at his swanky digs in a glass-walled Sarasota skyscraper. The developer preferred to summon him to the Ritz Carlton or the penthouse he maintained on Sarasota Bay, where he often stayed to avoid an inconvenient commute from his east Mullet County compound when he had business in the neighboring city. But today Ignacio was nervous, which was not a look he wore well, or one Bacchelli was used to seeing on his most generous client.

"How are we looking on poll volunteers?" Ignacio asked.

"We're rock solid," Bacchelli told him. "We have at least two dozen scheduled for each precinct in Hagerty and Sunday's wards, and they have been clearly instructed to only tout the negatives of Porter and Watts, while ignoring any comments about the… scandals. Billy and Candice are obviously gonna skip any sort of Election Day campaigning. It would just be a circus. I'm limiting Welsh to our strongest precincts and some sign-waving on Hernando Avenue West with big crowds alongside him. We have to project strength. Everyone will be in red shirts, lots of flags, MAGA crossovers, etc. He won that seat by 17 points last time around and had a 9-point lead in the last poll. He wins, and we keep a majority. With any luck, either Hagerty or Sunday squeak by, and it's not outside the realm of possibilities that they both do."

Ignacio was pacing the room, snapping his fingers with his right hand while biting the fist of his left.

"That 9-point lead was *before* the debate, chico, and he won by 17 points *before* he spent four years pissing off constituents and being generally unlikable at every turn," he said, continuing to pace the floors.

"90 percent of the people who show up will have no idea who he is outside of our campaign material," Bacchelli told him.

Ignacio pulled a direct mail piece from the breast pocket of his seersucker blazer and held it at arm's length. It had a decidedly unflattering picture of Welsh on one half and a checklist on the other that recounted, "killing wetland protections which will make for worse red tide and green algae blooms; giving away impact fees that pay for infrastructure like your parks, roads, and libraries; voting in favor of every development application, rezone, and density increase his developer donors asked for; $550k in campaign donations and PAC money from developers.

On the other side, it read "Connor Welsh doesn't work for the people of Mullet County, he works for the greedy developers who are destroying our paradise. That's not 'conservative values,' that's the complete absence of integrity. Say no to more gridlock and red tide. Say no to Connor Welsh!"

Bacchelli didn't dare say so, but he couldn't help but be impressed by the work. Dutch Wagner had once been a mentor to him when he first came into the business after five years with a commercial advertising firm. He thought the game had long since passed the old man by, but clearly, the "old Irish ward heeler," as he often described himself, still had it. All it took was adequate resources and a decent candidate. Now that he had both, Dutch was once again a force to be reckoned with.

"That PAC hasn't even been registered for long enough to have filed a financial report, so we don't know what they've spent," Bacchelli said. "How much could they have done in a few weeks? So, Amber or some friends of Mickey's put something together after he died, but how much do you think they really spent, Ignacio? The old lady isn't even political. I don't see her parting with a hundred grand over a local election.

Not even close. It's probably a 10k operation. That won't even put a dent in our campaign.”

Ignacio, pacing even more quickly and now with his hands clasped behind his back, shook his head forcefully.

“I think you underestimate how much money Micky Pesch had, my friend,” he told Bacchelli. “He wasn't flashy with it, but he was a man of means, and you didn't see her face when she doused me with wine at his memorial service. She thinks I killed the son of a bitch. Hell hath no fury …”

Chapter 13: Election Day

Election Day in indie print media is a unique affair. Unlike most days, when government events tend to transpire throughout the workday, there's precious little to report on before the polls close at 7 p.m., and the results come in shortly after. Then it's a long night of reporting results and writing analysis pieces. Lars had told Shelton, Ally, and Ernie Young to sleep in and for Ernie to start hitting polls and doing exit interviews around noon, while he stubbed out all of the stories. Ringo was tasked with getting photos from polling precincts and candidates waving to crowds.

Everyone was to meet at the Gazette no later than 5 p.m. to begin putting things in place. Election nights had always been a big deal at the Gazette/WMLT offices. Micky had a tradition of making a giant seafood boil in the parking lot and filling two giant plastic tubs with ice and beer, rituals Lars decided he would assume in his departed friend's absence.

The newspaper/radio station offices were a popular place for Dutch and his clients who weren't up for election, activist friends of Micky's, and other local luminaries, such as former elected officials who were tight with Micky, to hang out before hitting the campaign party circuit, some of which were victory parties, many more of which were tear-in-the-beer affairs. Amber would be there as well.

Emily had been scheduled to collect water samples from Sarasota Bay that day, and because she also wanted to spend election night at the Gazette, she took Shelton up on his offer to spend the night at Ramblewood the evening prior. The single bed notwithstanding, they enjoyed a lovely evening that included a seafood dinner at the Rusty Rudder and drinks at Ramblewood afterward with Lars, Ringo, Tina, and Pauly Miguel, who stopped by to hear about the events in Arcadia firsthand.

While Emily was getting a morning shower, Shelton jogged the mile and a half to a local bagel shop and grabbed two sesame bagels. It was one of those August Florida mornings that made no secret about the onslaught of heat and humidity that was to come. He was drenched in sweat by the time he arrived at the shop. On his way back, he ran into Ringo in the parking lot, struggling to start his car.

"You need to use the rental?" Shelton asked him.

"Yeah, I wanna get a jump on the polling stations," said Ringo, "and she's being a bit temperamental this morning."

Shelton was pleasantly surprised to see Ringo taking such initiative. Typically, and especially after a late, boozy night like the one before, he'd sleep until well past noon and be scrambling to get the photography before the polls closed and then edit them ahead of deadline, many of which had to be extended on this account.

When Emily finished getting dressed, there were perfect *café au laits* and toasted bagels topped with cream cheese, briny capers, and smoked salmon, at the ready.

"Oh my word, Shelton, this is perfect!" she told him at the first bite. "Where did you learn to do all of this?"

"Mostly YouTube," he told her. "I'm just a hobbyist. If I have something I really like at some restaurant or deli, I like to figure out how to recreate the experience."

"*Ruint* on bagels now, too?" she said with a smile. "Is this how you hook a woman?"

"Don't worry, they eventually manage to escape the line," he said with a wink.

"What do you got going on today?" she asked.

"Not much until the polls close," he said. "Then it'll be a late one."

"I'd ask if you wanted to come along, but I imagine a day on the water in this weather is not exactly what you need before a late night at the office," she said.

"Yeah, wouldn't be a good idea," he told her. "You should take Rufus. He loves boats and would be a better bodyguard."

"Seriously?" she asked.

"Yeah, he's been cooped up here more than he's used to."

"Ringo won't mind?" she asked.

"I'm sure he'd be more than grateful," said Shelton. "I'll text him."

"You'll write a column on the results?" she asked.

"Ernie and 'Staff Report' Ally will file the results for each race, and I'll write commentary on the whole spectacle of it, I suppose. Lars will probably do an editorial, as well."

"Can I come back here to shower and change before heading to the office?" she asked.

"Yeah, let me give you a key in case I'm not here," he told her, taking one off his key ring.

Emily gave him an affectionate kiss, and he walked her to her car, this time a Rav-4 hybrid with a TBEW vinyl wrap and a kayak attached to the roof rack. Ringo met them at the car with a ridiculously excited Rufus, and Shelton handed him the keys to the rental.

When he returned, Lars was standing outside his unit drinking some coffee. Within moments, Jerry and Bryce appeared and took seats at the plastic lawn chairs in front of their window.

"I got a fresh pot in case you need a cup," said Lars, tipping his mug toward him. "I woke up with a big head after last night."

"Thanks, we just had some," said Shelton.

"That seems to be progressing nicely," Lars said with a smile.

"Too early to call it," said Shelton, "but I'm optimistic for the short term."

"She's definitely one of the good ones," said Lars.

"No doubt," said Shelton. "That's why I'm less optimistic for the long term."

Lars laughed.

"Pauly take an Uber home?" Shelton asked.

"Yeah," said Lars with a chuckle. "He really tied one on last night. We stayed up for another hour or two after you guys left."

"Yeah, I could still hear music until nearly two in the morning," said Bryce.

"Well, I see that the good news is you weren't deprived of your beauty sleep," said Lars with a wink.

"I can't sleep much anyway with my back," said Bryce, who could ruin a conversation faster than an ambulance siren.

"I sleep like a rock," said Jerry. "I heard a little bit, but I go to bed at midnight every day, and I had no problem. I don't mind a little noise. It's not like this is the Conrad Hilton."

"Jesus, Jerry, your nose is turning brown," said Bryce bitterly.

"I'm gonna grab a shower," said Shelton, heading into his unit.

"How come they get to have overnight guests, and we don't?" asked Bryce, once Shelton had gone.

Lars laughed again, as Bryce had been both single and celibate since his wife had left him nearly three decades prior. To the best of his knowledge, Jerry remained a virgin.

"Well, I make exceptions for certain tenants that I know won't be a problem," said Lars. "I would hope it goes without saying that you two would be included."

"No thanks," said Bryce. "Nothing but problems, especially these days. They're all liberals, half of them are dikes, and the other half are whores."

Lars chuckled and considered pointing out that MAGA Republican women outnumbered the "liberal" ones of any label at least 2-1 in Mullet County, and from his experience, they were the most sexually adventurous on the ideological spectrum. However, he knew that would lead to a political debate filled with references to the Illuminati and living in a *fallen world* that would soon see Bryce alone among those being raptured upward to the Lord, while he, Jerry, and the rest of the people he knew who had failed to heed his warnings burned for eternity.

"Well, I'm glad it won't be an issue, my friend. What about you, Jerry?"

"I don't even have enough money for me," he said with a laugh. "I couldn't even afford to take a woman to Golden Coral when I take the bus down there on the first Sunday each month. It's up to $21 for the dinner these days, and dinner starts at noon! I mean, you can get the breakfast until noon for $14, but they don't have fried chicken or steak or nothing like that. I only do that if I'm short on funds for dinner, or if I have a little extra near the end of the month and can do both."

Lars knew this because, as with most things, Jerry repeated himself endlessly on the matter. Each year on Christmas and his birthday, he'd slip Jerry a Golden Coral gift card.

"That strikes me as a sound strategy," said Lars, patting him on the shoulder as he retreated to his back lanai to finish his coffee in peace, glad they hadn't brought up the issue of Ringo having a dog—also against the rules—though both liked to compete for Rufus' attention, with Bryce surprisingly holding an upper hand, likely owed to his greater willingness to part with food.

****

Everyone from the poll workers to the campaign sign-wavers were a bit nervous when a giant rhinoceros of a man climbed out of the white Ford Escape wearing cut-off sweatpants with a very wrinkled and completely unbuttoned short-sleeved linen shirt. A camera was hanging around his neck. He also appeared to be wearing a shoulder holster—guns are strictly prohibited at polling precincts.

Ringo took notice of their fascination with him, realized he was strapped, and climbed back into the SUV. He reemerged unarmed, but the crowd seemed to take little comfort in that fact as they whispered to each other nervously. A few jumped, and one man even hit the deck when Ringo dropped into a deep squat and began taking rapid-fire shots with the camera.

"Nice," he said aloud, noticing that their terror registered as an almost stoic look once frozen, adequately capturing the ominous nature of this high-stakes affair. Once they seemed to have regained enough composure to receive him, Ringo ambled over to a courtesy tent for Mary Porter's campaign, where they were giving out snacks and campaign fliers.

Ringo had deduced that Hagerty was the commissioner for the area that included Ramblewood even before the previous evening, when he and the other men (and eventually Tina) ritualistically pissed on a few of the yard signs her campaign had the audacity to put along the right of way in front of the property. *Hagerty for Liberty* signs were everywhere in the neighborhood, ranging from small yard signs on wire stands to the much more difficult to desecrate wooden mini-billboards she'd erected at several spots along DeSoto Blvd.

"Vote for Mary Porter," an elderly woman with a campaign t-shirt told him as he loaded a paper plate with chocolate and powdered sugar mini-donuts before pouring a glass of orange juice. The woman considered mentioning that the food was not meant to provide an entire breakfast, but since he had recently been armed, she thought better of it.

"I'm afraid I just moved here, and it was too late to switch my registration," he told her, assuming this was true, but not knowing for sure. "But don't you worry, I did my part to get her elected," he added with a laugh. "Boy, did I ever."

"Were you a door knocker? I don't recall seeing you at any of the volunteer meetings," the woman said suspiciously.

"I was what you might call a *freelance* volunteer," he told her with a wink. "There's a lot you can do to benefit a campaign with a camera, that is, if you've got the stomach for dirty work."

Could this be the guy who snapped the picture of ...

Ringo moved on to another table, this one representing a school board candidate, where they thankfully had coffee. He downed a cup quickly since it was lukewarm and chased it with some OJ, before reaching down with his giant paw and grabbing the last three mini donuts. He effortlessly put them all in his mouth at once, crushed up his plate and cups, dumped them in the trash, and got another dozen shots from his camera.

Back in the Escape, he quickly went through them, deleting anything he deemed to be less than brilliant. Ringo didn't trust editors, even Lars, to pick his best work for the pieces they'd be featured in, so he would delete shots periodically during a shoot and hand over only the best. Some editors would complain that they wanted more to choose from, to which Ringo would always respond by giving them his entire shoot on a cloud file. Given his penchant for rapid-fire photography, that usually meant sifting through hundreds of photos to pick two or three, and they'd instantly ask him to return to the previous method. Being talented enough to be difficult but tolerated was exactly what he aimed for.

Ringo quickly hit two more precincts and grabbed a couple of shots, and then made his way to Hernando Ave, which ran parallel to DeSoto Blvd. Being the main thoroughfare, it would surely have the most sign holders. This was Welsh's ward, and judging by the shirts, Osborne had even more sign-wavers. Not wanting to waste anymore time on simple tasks, he rolled down the passenger window, leaned to extend his right arm out of it, and beeped the horn with his left, balancing the wheel with the rest of his giant hand.

People responded to the beeps, and he clicked away as he drove. When he got to the corner where the Twistee Treat was located, he noticed that Osborne was waving a sign as he stopped at the light. A loud "Get 'em, Greg!" was enough to draw his attention and a big smile. Ringo snapped a perfect shot as he rolled through the intersection when the signal turned green.

God damn, I'm a pro, he thought to himself, before realizing Welsh and his people were posted up on the opposite side of the street. He quickly banged a left, drawing an angry beep from the car behind him, and yelled, "Hey, Welsh, YOU SUCK!" earning a scowl that he caught perfectly in three different shots.

He turned left on U.S. 301, planning to hit two precincts in Billy Sunday's ward, giving him plenty of time for the long drive ahead.

****

Normally, lounging topless at the pool while Deputy White rubbed her shoulders was an ideal morning, so far as Candice Hagerty was concerned. However, the fact that it was Election Day and she was there serving a time-out imposed by Hernandez and Bacchelli when she would have much preferred to be out waving to her adoring fans in the MAGA community soured her mood.

"It's not fair," she pouted. "This is my big day. I busted my ass campaigning, and Election Day is my reward."

"You still have the victory party at the Rudder tonight," the deputy told her in a soothing tone. "Everyone will be there, and you'll be all dolled up in that new red dress. They'll all congratulate you and tell you how amazing you look."

"That's *if* I win!" she barked. "Those mailers won't get the real Republicans to vote for a RINO like Porter, but what if it suppresses turnout. I'm supposed to run for state house in two years, then maybe even governor. Besides, if I squeak by on a razor-thin victory, I won't be able to show my face at the party

270

anyway. It would be humiliating. I need to be out there rallying my troops so we can get a landslide."

Deputy White had his own problems to consider. His wife had kicked him out as soon as she saw the social media posts, and Sheriff Brock placed him on paid administrative leave pending an investigation over the swastika tattoo. He called in sick for his shift the day the news broke and immediately went to a buddy's tattoo shop, where, behind locked doors and drawn blinds, the swastika was converted to a black square. This, he hoped, would give him enough room to claim the picture had been photo-shopped in order to further embarrass a political candidate.

"What are you gonna say it means?" Werner, the tattoo artist, asked once they had finished.

"I don't know, nothing," said Deputy White. "It's covering up an old girlfriend's initials or something, why?"

"Well, they're gonna ask you all sorts of questions about it during the investigation."

Deputy White had always been extremely careful not to let it be seen or photographed in public, even going so far as to wear a surfing shirt on the occasions he hit the public beach. Still, his friend's question had rattled him.

When he got home, the deputy searched the internet for things represented by a black square. He learned that, in mathematics, it serves as the "end of proof" symbol. In art, he discovered, it is associated with Kazimir Malevich's 1915 painting, titled *Black Square*, a foundational work of something called the Suprematism movement and intended to represent the "zero of form," or the absolute beginning of art.

The deputy could not even begin to get his head around either of these concepts, so he settled on its hoodoo relevance, in which it was believed that it could ward off danger. That seemed to make sense, given that he was in law enforcement. The additional fact that hoodoo is a slave tradition would also sort of make it the opposite of a swastika, in his mind. He could even claim to be an "ally," so long as he didn't choke on the word.

Candice reached for her Valium bottle and took her second of the day.

"Lower," she said, moving the deputy's hands to her breasts.

"*Seriously*?" Deputy White said in annoyance as he looked to the sliding glass doors where Aaron Bennington, Esquire, was doing a poor job of hiding behind the vertical blinds, tool in hand.

"Not now, Aaron, you perv!" Candice screamed, pulling herself away and walking to the outdoor bar to refill her Prosecco … again.

****

Ringo wasn't surprised to find that Miles' Chevelle was not in the parking lot of the Oaks Motel when he arrived in Arcadia. He agreed with Dutch's assessment that the former CIA operative would most likely disappear for the foreseeable future. He doubted he would have left behind the watch or anything else for that matter, but there was a chance that he had left in a hurry or perhaps had only retrieved the car without even entering his motel room apartment after the scuffle.

A guy like that, Ringo figured, probably kept a go-bag in the trunk with a satellite phone, some cash, and a fake passport. Ringo himself had a go-bag in the Fiero, should he ever need to go underground. His own go-bag contained a phony driver's license, an ounce of highly potent pot, an SLR camera, and a burner flip phone.

Of course, there was also an arsenal of weaponry in the modified frunk he'd created. Unfortunately, this meant not having a spare tire, as Pontiac did not include a frunk in the mid-engine car, using the space for its master cylinder, windshield washer fluid, A/C components, and the tiny spare. Ringo had thus far required the use of a spare far more often than the weaponry, but being without the latter when it was needed was a far more serious gamble in his estimation.

Ringo had no trouble picking the lock on Miles' motel room door, which he would have expected a pro to have modified. Maybe this guy wasn't all Dutch had talked him up to be, he thought. Inside, the unit was Spartan, to say the least. If he hadn't cleared the place out, he'd been living like a monk. There wasn't even a television set, just an old radio on the desk. Ringo knew all too well how difficult it was to keep a motel room orderly even before he himself had begun living in one, weeks earlier.

However, he noticed a few shirts hanging from the clothing rack and a modest array of other clothing items in the dresser drawers. Everything was perfectly folded with the same meticulous attention that had been given to the bed, which looked like you could have bounced a quarter off of, given its taut sheets and hospital corners. No sign of a watch, however. There was a laptop on the desk, but Ringo did not have any hacking skills to speak of and figured Miles' cybersecurity would be top-notch, his inferior door lock notwithstanding.

He felt a little silly. What had he expected to find? Aside from the Rolex or a shotgun matching the one that had been used to kill Micky, nothing short of a diary with an entry confessing to the crime would be likely to connect Miles to his death. And what kind of assassin would leave behind either of the two things that would tie him to the murder? The rifle would have been dumped, and if he had taken the watch, it would have been hidden until long after the heat had died down. Ringo was allowing this little epiphany to sink in when he heard the unmistakable rumble of Hooker Headers, a high-performance exhaust system favored by gear-heads. It had to be Miles.

Ringo had a split-second decision to make. Run out of the unit, where he was almost certain to be seen by Miles, or find someplace to hide. He had his Glock. He could emerge from the unit, gun drawn, and quickly indicate that he meant him no harm, and see if he could hold him at bay until he escaped in the now ironically named rental. Ringo heard the car door shut. He ran to the peephole. Miles was too close. He'd draw as soon as he heard the door.

He racked his brain. Where could he hide? There was no closet. The two options were behind the shower curtain and under the bed. Because of the hospital corners, there was nothing draping over the mattress and, despite the limited space, Miles had nothing stowed beneath the bed frame save a pair of hiking boots. Ringo would be too exposed and in a position of tremendous vulnerability. The tub it was. He quickly positioned himself behind the shower curtain, withdrawing his pistol.

He heard the motel room door open, then close. There was the sound of talking that he assumed was an ad on what must have been the desktop radio. Ringo began to feel perspiration accumulating on his brow. He worked to completely still himself. Minutes passed, though they felt like hours. Then he heard steps until someone opened the bathroom door. He tried to recall whether it had been closed when he arrived. Had closing it tipped off Miles that someone had been there, he wondered. Was the curtain about to be ripped aside as in a scene from a movie? Would he have any other choice but to shoot?

Ringo began to sweat harder but fought the urge to wipe his brow before it got in his eyes, lest he make a sound. When he finally heard the sound of Miles taking a piss, he felt a modicum of relief, but when he heard the toilet flush and Miles' footsteps heading back toward the jazz music now coming from the radio without closing the bathroom door, his anxiety intensified. As carefully as he could, he holstered his pistol and removed his cell phone from his front pocket.

Ringo sent a text to Shelton that read, MAYDAY - DO NOT CALL - TEXT ONLY.

He received an immediate question mark response.

IN ARCADIA TOSSING MILES ROOM HE RETURNED - HIDING IN SHOWER!!! NEED HELP!

"Hang tight, on my way," was the response from Shelton.

"Mother of god, what has he done?" yelled Shelton, who had just finished his shower and dressed before attempting to meet up with Ringo at one of the polling precincts where he had thought the madman was shooting pictures. He rifled through a drawer and found the spare keys to Ringo's Fiero, which he'd long been the steward of, as Ringo had a habit of locking his keys in his FOB-less vehicle, as well as misplacing them while out and about.

Shelton sprinted to the car. Once inside, he tried to start the engine, but had no more luck than Ringo when he had attempted to fire her up that morning. He persisted, but each effort yielded less response, and it was beginning to sound like the battery was about to give out. Just then, a Hyundai Tucson pulled into Ramblewood. There was a Lyft light on its dashboard. When it came to a stop, Pauly Miguel exited the backseat, having returned to pick up his Camaro.

"Doesn't sound like she's gonna cooperate," said Pauly. "You need a ride?"

"I might need more than a ride, my friend," said Shelton.

****

By the time her fourth Prosecco had fully coalesced with the Valium in her bloodstream, Candice Hagerty was utterly certain that the only logical course of action was to follow her flawless political instincts and go be a champion to her people. She had seen the Facebook posts from supporters waving signs on Hernando Avenue West and could tell it lacked the energy and enthusiasm that only she could deliver. Deputy White tried to talk her out of it, but it was no use.

"Well, at least let me give you a ride," he pleaded. "If you were to get a DUI, on Election Day no less—"

"Are you fucking crazy?" she screamed. "Us being seen together right now would be worse than vehicular manslaughter! I'll have my dip-shit husband drop me off."

She decided at that moment that this romance had run its course. The well-endowed deputy had been a good boy toy, but once she'd secured another term, she'd have to cut ties with him altogether. She hadn't even wanted to let him crash at their bay front mansion when his wife gave him the boot, but Aaron Bennington, Esquire, had insisted. The deputy had assumed he would be staying in the apartment/pool house out back, or maybe a guest room, but was surprised when the attorney insisted the deputy and his wife have the master bedroom, his only condition that he be able to go in and sniff the silk sheets while they were enjoying their morning coffee.

After quickly disabusing her husband of the notion that she might care to hear his advice on the matter, the commissioner instructed him to drop her off in front of Publix, where her largest group was assembled, and find a parking space where he could wait for her as long as was required. The group was noticeably surprised by her appearance, although they whooped and cheered when she emerged from the same white GMC Denali she'd been photographed in only days earlier.

"Alright, bitches, let's win a goddamned election!" she hollered with a bit of a slur.

The response was a blend of cheers and concerned expressions.

****

When Shelton told Pauly about Ringo's present situation, he insisted on coming along for backup, which was an enormous relief to Shelton, as he had absolutely no idea how in the world he might otherwise help his friend escape being trapped in a small space with a bona fide killer.

"So, what's the plan?" asked Pauly.

276

Shelton shrugged uncomfortably.

"No plan?" Pauly said.

"I just got the text, and this is way out of my wheelhouse, man," Shelton confessed.

"Well, we could call the Sheriff's department," said Pauly. "That's across the county line, so it would be DCSO, and I don't have any contacts there. It would be their show. My guess is they would ask Miles to come outside, apprise him of the situation, and then hit your friend with either a felony B&E, or, if he's lucky, a misdemeanor trespassing charge. And that still doesn't guarantee there isn't a bloodbath, given what we've heard about this Miles character."

"Any other options?" Shelton asked.

"I guess, we could try it the same way without the police," he said. "He knows your face, but I could knock on the door, ask him to come outside to talk, explain things the best I can, and hope for a positive outcome."

"I can't ask you to endanger yourself," said Shelton.

Pauly waved off the notion and pushed the pedal down on his Camaro now that they had successfully navigated the gridlock past the last traffic light on the state highway that led toward Arcadia. The 455-horsepower V8 roared, and the car was approaching 100 mph before he'd even gotten out of second gear, which Shelton figured would cut their travel time by as much as 15 minutes.

****

Candice Hagerty's confidence in her decision to defy her handlers' instructions was initially boosted by the onslaught of honks she received from passing cars. It took only seconds, however, before she was forced to reevaluate that appraisal.

"No way, you Nazi-fucking fascist," screamed a young woman, who flipped her the bird while passing by in her Corolla.

"Just another pink-haired, libtard commie," she slurred, while shaking her head and scanning her supporters for affirmation.

Commissioner Hagerty, however, had been unaware that her supporters had been facing similar harassment all day, which was why nearly half of them had already departed. The loyalists who decided to soldier on in the bleating August heat, faced with the hot mess before them, now began to question their decisions *en masse*.

A white Toyota 4-Runner honked its horn, and the commissioner flashed a big smile, waving her sign above her head.

"Go down on any Nazis today, Hagerty?" screamed the man after lowering his window.

"FAWWWWK YOU!" she screamed, slamming her sign to the ground.

Another horn beeped, this time from a gray Volkswagen SUV.

"What?" she screamed, waiting for the insult.

"We're with you, commissioner," the blonde woman driving it said with a thumbs up, as she and a woman in the passenger seat waved.

"See, you still have plenty of support," one of the particularly loyal volunteers standing next to her said sympathetically, as the others gained some distance.

She handed the commissioner a new sign to wave, but she pushed it away.

****

Ringo finally received a text from Shelton, letting him know that he and Pauly were on their way. He was about to breathe a sigh of relief when he once again heard footsteps approaching the bathroom. Please don't tell me he's planning on a hot shower, Ringo thought to himself as the sweat once more began to accumulate on his brow. If he kept sweating, surely this trained agent would smell another human in his midst. After all, he thought, Native Americans are known for their superiority in tracking animals, and Ringo was pretty sure his scent skewed toward the feral side.

His anxiety heightened when he heard the unmistakable sound of a belt and pants being loosened. He had a hand on his Glock when he heard a loud fart followed by a splash of water. The momentary relief was quickly replaced by the putrid odor that followed. *What had this guy been eating*, Ringo wondered as he fought the urge to cough that had been induced by the stench.

Did he know there was an intruder? Ringo wondered. Was he being smoked out, or, as it was, shat out—although that didn't seem quite right, either. Was this some sort of PSYOP tactic taught at Langley? Was he just a mouse that a cat was toying with before he pounced? Time could not have moved more slowly. Ringo could hear what sounded like the pages of a magazine turning.

Damn it, man, please tell me he's not the kind of guy that sits on the toilet reading Guns and Ammo for half an hour, he thought to himself. At one point, the stench, which Ringo thought he recognized as having been induced by Indian cuisine (dots, not feathers), became so putrid that he almost broke his silence to ask for a courtesy flush. He wondered if perhaps the best strategy would be to burst out of the shower and bolt toward the motel room door. Miles would have to give chase without wiping his backside in order to catch him before he escaped in the Escape. Who would choose such a messy proposition when an armed invader was running *away* from them?

But what if Miles was armed? It was difficult to imagine that he'd brought his Uzi to the toilet, but this guy was a pro. For all Ringo knew, that might have been the first thing they taught you at Langley. *When is it most essential to be prepared for battle, recruit?* When you're most vulnerable, of course, and when is one any more vulnerable than while sitting on the proverbial throne?

Ringo heard the sound of Miles unrolling some toilet paper and thought it was a moot issue until it was drowned out by another loud fart and a plopping sound, followed by a hissing squirt that seemed to signal sincere gastronomic distress. This was it, his best and perhaps last chance to flee his current situation. The increasingly malodorous state of the small bathroom had become more than he could stand anyway. Deciding he was willing to risk death to escape the smell alone, Ringo whipped aside the flimsy, plastic curtain and made a run for it.

As he leaped from the tub, however, his left foot caught the curtain. As the foot struck the floor, the cheap shower curtain rod was dislodged and came crashing down, striking Ringo on the shoulder with one end and Miles across his lap with the other. Ringo managed to keep his balance and continue in a sprint toward the door. Miles was momentarily stupefied. He'd recognized the large, sweaty man as the one he'd shoved to the ground days earlier, but couldn't come to terms with what was happening fast enough to process his options. This gave Ringo just enough time to get to the Escape.

By the time he'd started the car and put it in drive, however, Miles was at the door of the motel room with a scoped rifle. Ringo put the pedal to the floor, and the tires chirped as he cut the wheel to exit the parking lot. Miles seemed to be contemplating shooting a tire, but instead darted toward his Chevelle.

"I'm out of the motel, but that maniac is in pursuit," Ringo screamed into the phone, as he sped down the straight, flat state highway, his speed approaching a hundred miles per hour as the Chevelle appeared in his rear view mirror.

"Where are you?" asked Shelton.

"Heading west as fast as this fucking thing will go, but it looks like he's closing the distance," Ringo shouted, having put

the phone on speaker before tossing it onto the passenger seat
to have both hands on the steering wheel, which was beginning
to shake.

Arturo Pesch had opted for the top-of-the-line Chevelle
SS with the 454 LS6 engine option. With only a few upgrades
by Miles, it made over 500 horsepower. Ringo had only a 1.5-
liter turbocharged inline-three cylinder engine. With only 180
horsepower at his disposal, he knew he wouldn't be able to
hold Miles off for long.

"We're only ten miles out from Arcadia, so we've got to be
close to where you're at," said Shelton. "Pauly's doing 130. Just
hang in there."

"Hang in for what?" screamed Ringo.

It occurred to Shelton that he and Pauly hadn't formalized
anything approaching a plan even before it became a car chase.
They were about to face another challenge, however, as sirens
alerted them to a Mullet County Sheriff's Department patrol car
that cut out from between some roadside trees, lights ablaze.
Pauly flicked on the amber and green "security" patrol lights he
had on the front and rear of his vehicle, hoping the deputy
would interpret emergency motives. However, he pushed the
pedal down in order to put more distance between them,
hoping to buy some time to plan what came next.

"What's the play?" asked Shelton.

"Making it up as I go, brother," said Pauly.

The deputy pushed his pedal down, but even though his
cruiser—a Dodge Challenger with a 5.7-liter HEMI pursuit
package—was a formidable vehicle, Pauly's car was powerful
enough to continue to gain ground as the deputy, now at least
half a mile behind them, attempted to build speed.

Suddenly, Ringo heard a pop and felt the car lurch wildly.
The wheel jerked. He began to slow, and the telltale signs of a
tire blowout set in. Miles was right on his ass. Ringo kept the
pedal down and jerked left, but the car had other ideas. Once
he skidded across the right-of-way, the car was helplessly

drawn toward the drainage ditch and lacked the power to pull out of the slide.

Before he knew it, Ringo was in the ditch, and the wheels merely spun when he hit the gas. He heard Miles' car door slam from up on the road, so he exited through the passenger door. Ringo squatted low and looked under the car. When he saw Miles side-stepping down the embankment of the ditch, the grass of which was wet, he leaped up into a sprint, heading straight up it.

This bought him a moment's time, but Miles quickly adjusted and was in pursuit. By the time Ringo, who had stupidly worn Crocs, had made it to the road, he could hear him closing the gap. Once they got to level ground, Miles jumped onto his back and tried to lock an arm under his chin, but Ringo easily threw him over his shoulder onto the paved road.

"Look," shouted Shelton, pointing to the two cars on the side of the road.

He and Pauly then saw the two figures struggling on the highway and sped toward them. Ringo had attempted to run after the throw, but Miles managed to twist his back ankle, causing him to stumble forward and hit the ground. Then he mounted Ringo's back and attempted what looked like a chicken wing maneuver.

Pauly skidded to a stop in the middle of the barren road and ran from the vehicle toward them. Sirens could now be heard from both directions. Rather than draw his weapon, Pauly instinctively jumped Miles, catching him in a near-perfect rear-naked-choke as he rolled to his back like a gator in a death roll. Miles, who was nearly twice Pauly's size, put up impressive resistance and seemed well schooled at attempting to defend against the hold, but Pauly had leverage from that position, and it was locked in. Ringo had just gotten to his feet, and Shelton finally made it to the site of the conflict when the first deputy burst from his vehicle, followed by the DCSO deputy who'd been coming from the opposite direction.

"Hands up, on your knees," the deputies screamed, nearly in unison, their weapons drawn as they squatted in a menacing position and trained their respective pistols on all four men. Pauly released his hold and came to his knees, hands raised, expecting to be told to lie down flat.

"Jesus Christ, Miguel, what the fuck are you doing?" asked Deputy Chad Barkley, whom Pauly knew from their time together in the department. The deputy re-holstered his pistol, signaling to the other officer to do the same.

****

Candice Hagerty had been unable to keep an accurate score of the ratio of insults to supportive comments in her booze and pill-altered state, but she knew it was far from resting in her favor. Her supporters, who could tell she was deeply inebriated, had been imploring her to drink more water and maybe take a break from the sun in her husband's air-conditioned vehicle.

The commissioner would have none of it. Despite all evidence to the contrary, she clung to the hope that she could somehow reverse the tide. After all, she had always gotten what she wanted. Why should this be different? She had been the captain of Mullet High's cheerleading squad and queen of its senior prom. She had been the most popular member of her Florida State sorority. She had married a rich and distinguished husband who built her a big mansion on the water. She drove the best cars, wore the most expensive clothing, and had amassed a collection of shoes and handbags that would make a member of the royal family blush.

Her daddy's county commission seat was her birthright, and the state house that the local party bosses had promised her was only a stepping stone to governor, and then the day she would be elected to represent her hometown in the United

States Congress. More importantly, Candice Hagerty had been screwing whichever boy she chose since losing her virginity to the captain of the varsity football team when she was a freshman. Why should this time be any different?

It was just this sort of logic she was employing to buoy her spirits when a bunch of young male volunteers for a school board race, positioned in front of a Walgreens on the diagonal corner, began a loud chant.

"Hagerty, Hagerty, please take my virginity," rang the chorus of about a dozen teens to the laughs of female students in the group.

"Real nice," slurred the commissioner. "I bet your mommas are real proud of those filthy mouths."

The chant continued, even as adult volunteers could be seen trying to quell it. As they were chanting, a red Ford pickup truck slowly rolled down DeSoto Avenue.

"Hey, Candice, show me your tits," a twenty-something bellowed so loudly it sounded as if it had been amplified.

Something in Candice Hagerty suddenly snapped.

"Here," she screamed, lifting her shirt over her head before pulling her sports bra beneath her massive mammaries, which sprang forth as if they'd been propelled by some unseen force. "Get a good look, you fucking loser! They're probably the first pair you've ever seen that weren't on the screen of your phone!"

Jaws dropped all around her as she twisted her torso, causing her bountiful bosom to swing wildly in an almost cartoonish manner. The teenage boys across the street, each of whom was, in fact, seeing the first pair of breasts not projected by a cell phone screen, whooped and hooted. Their female classmates stared in wide-eyed disbelief. Cell phones emerged from the pockets of onlookers in every direction, and few people even noticed the cameraman and television reporter who had arrived on the scene.

****

Shelton had thought that Pauly's presence at the scene would make the whole situation go more smoothly than proved to be the case. Once additional backup arrived, all four men were handcuffed and placed into the back seats of separate squad cars. Shelton spent the next two hours sitting alone in an interrogation room, unaware of what was happening outside its door.

He had surrendered his phone, and the room had no wall clock. However, he was sure it had to be close to 7 p.m., when the polls would have closed. Finally, he heard a sound at the door. Sheriff Rusty Brock and LeGrotto Police Chief Lawrence Washington, each of whom Shelton recognized, entered the small room and took seats on the opposite side of the desk.

"Well, you and your friend sure did cause me a lot of needless trouble today," said Sheriff Brock. "It's lucky someone wasn't killed, and I'll make no secret of the fact that I don't like it one bit when law enforcement officers are led into high-speed chases. I've lost good deputies to crashes over the years."

"Yes, sir," said Shelton, not knowing what else to say, or why, Washington, the chief of police for an agency nowhere near any of the day's events, was present.

"In the good news department, it seems that Miles Conepatchie does not want to press charges against your maniac friend for breaking and entering," said the sheriff. "All of his weapons are registered, and he has a valid medical marijuana card for the reefer we found, so it looks like he's gonna get off with a few fines and several points on his license for driving like a fucking idiot."

Shelton assumed that was not the official charge, but it was Florida, so he couldn't be certain.

"In his defense, he was being chased by an armed assassin who may have murdered Micky Pesch," said Shelton, immediately wondering if it had been a mistake to offer any excuse at all for Ringo's idiocy.

"He was being chased by a private citizen whose home he'd broken into, where he proceeded to hide, before emerging armed from a fucking shower while that same citizen was trying to take a goddamn shit," the sheriff barked. "He's lucky he didn't get his big, dumb head blown off!"

Shelton successfully fought off the urge to educate the sheriff on the past participle of shit and nodded silently.

"And he didn't murder his father," Chief Washington added.

"What do you mean?" asked Shelton.

"This morning, my nephew Cornell got a call from his brother, Eddie," said the chief. "They're partners in a pawn shop on the north side of LeGrotto. After hearing that Eddie was a wristwatch aficionado and the kind of guy that might be interested in acquiring a high-end antique watch, a man named Bobby Stokes came in trying to unload a vintage Rolex Daytona. Dutch Wagner had already asked me to tell my nephews to put the word out in the pawn community that if anyone came looking to unload such a watch, they were to get word back to them so they could tell me."

"We executed a warrant on him right around the same time you morons were raising hell out in Arcadia," said Sheriff Brock. "He's in a cell down the hall. Says it was just supposed to be a robbery, but he was coked out of his gourd, and when Micky tossed the watch to him unexpectedly, he panicked and accidentally fired. It took him about ten seconds to roll over on his accomplice, Mary Pesch. I got deputies bringing her in as we speak."

"Mary Pesch had her brother killed over a fucking wristwatch?" asked Shelton in disbelief.

"More or less," said Chief Washington. "The thing was worth about fifty grand. She and this Bobby character were gonna use it to buy the Driftwood Inn of all places, if you can imagine that."

"Speaking of watches, can I ask you what time it is?" asked Shelton.

"Almost half past seven," said the sheriff after consulting his own wristwatch, which Shelton noted was a bit upscale for a public servant. "You're free to go."

"Dutch is waiting in the lobby to give you and your pal a ride," added Chief Washington as both men rose.

Shelton breathed a deep sigh of disbelief and followed them out of the small, stale room. In the lobby, Dutch was conversing with someone via his Bluetooth earpiece, while Amber Pesch stood off to his side.

"No news like good news," he said. "Alright, I gotta spring a couple of bad hombres from the clink. Yep, same fellas. I'll holler back at you in a bit."

"Have you heard any of the results?" asked Shelton when he saw Dutch click off the call.

"All the ones that matter," said Dutch with a broad grin. "We ran the table, my friend," he said, while looking to Amber, who stepped forward and nodded a hello to Shelton.

"Candice Hagerty put the final nail in her own political coffin when she had a mental break on DeSoto Blvd and began flashing her big jugs in front of about a thousand people, not to mention a television news crew," said Dutch. "Mary Porter won by 19 points. Good old Merle trounced the Reverend Titty Club by 21 points, and that smarmy little shit Welsh took the worst beating of all, 23 points and without even a last-minute scandal to blame it on. Mullet County has spoken," he said, throwing an arm over Amber's shoulder and giving her a half-hug.

"Thank you for all your help, Shelton," Amber said, extending her hand.

"I'm not sure I *was* much help," he told her as they shook hands, genuinely wondering what credit he could possibly take in either finding Micky's killer or the election results.

"It was a team effort," said Dutch, as Ringo emerged from a nearby hallway.

"You okay?" asked Shelton.

"I might have a problem getting car insurance," Ringo said with a shrug. "I take it we won all three races?" he asked nonchalantly.

"You bet your big ass we did," said Dutch, while giving him a hearty handshake. "And your photography skills were the MVP of this election, my friend."

"I can't thank you enough," said Amber. "There will be an election bonus for all of the hard work everyone put in, and I really hope you guys will stay on. Ignacio won't take this sitting down. Mullet County will need the DeSoto Gazette now more than ever."

Shelton looked at Ringo and shrugged.

"It's not like we have much in the way of other prospects," Ringo said. "Besides, it wouldn't be fair to tease readers with first-rate photography only to suddenly take it away."

"Well then, it's settled," said Dutch, as the group's attention was diverted by a ruckus at the other end of the lobby.

"Call my fucking lawyer," screamed a drunk and unhinged Mary Pesch, who'd just been perp-walked into the station. "I'm gonna sue the fuck out of all y'all."

Seconds later, Mary and Amber Pesch were staring daggers at each other from a mere 10 feet apart.

"Oh, don't look at me like that, you uppity cunt," Mary finally screamed. "None of this would've happened if you and Micky hadn't treated me like a child on an allowance while you were sitting on a fucking fortune you couldn't spend in two lifetimes!"

"Why you ungrateful, self-centered bitch!" screamed Amber. "He was your own brother! How many times did he come to the rescue when you got yourself in trouble? Let's see how many people line up to get your back this time!"

Dutch put his arms around Amber and steered in the opposite direction while the deputies moved Mary out of the lobby. Just after Mary exited, Miles emerged from the same hallway. A nervous tension filled the air as he approached the group's position. Chief Detective Sosnowski, who was escorting him out, quickly realized the parties were now in the same area and put a hand in front of him.

"Maybe we should use another exit," said the detective.

"No, it's okay," said Miles, calmly walking toward the group.

Amber Pesch looked as though she'd seen a ghost.

To cut the tension, Ringo walked toward him and extended a hand. Miles accepted and the two men shook.

"Thanks for not pressing charges," said Ringo.

"I've seen some weird stuff in my lifetime," said Miles, "but you jumping out of that shower while I was sitting on the toilet takes the prize."

"I had no right to break into your home," said Ringo. "I apologize. I mean it."

"I should have heard you out last week," said Miles. "I'm not sure why I panicked. I had no idea Micky was dead, and I suppose I would have had similar suspicions were our positions reversed. You were trying to find my father's killer. You had honorable intentions."

"Sorry about tossing you," said Ringo. "Although that was a nice move you caught me with."

"You're a worthy adversary," said Miles with a subtle bow.

"It's been a long time," said Dutch, extending a hand that Miles shook.

"Shelton Hamner, we, uh, met the other day—briefly," said Shelton as they also shook hands.

"Miles," said Amber softly, tears beginning to well in her eyes.

"Hello, Amber," said Miles, bowing his head again to greet her.

"I'll catch up with you all over at the office," she said to Dutch, who nodded before waving Ringo and Shelton in his direction.

"Would you mind walking an old woman to her car?" she said to Miles.

"I'm deeply sorry for your loss," he told her. "You were always a wonderful wife to Micky, and I know the two of you loved each other deeply. I can't imagine how difficult this has been for you."

She stepped forward and gave him a hug, then took his arm as they exited.

"You need to know that I never suspected you were involved," said Amber as they walked toward her Mercedes. "I never even mentioned you to investigators. Some of the journalists discovered that you were Micky's son, and when the possibility was raised, I said it wasn't even remotely possible."

"You don't have to explain," said Miles. "Everyone was operating with the best intentions, and my reaction last week would have raised suspicions in any reasonable person. It's just that I'm pretty disconnected from the larger world and, honestly, had not been aware of Micky's passing. I'm pretty much a hermit, and when two people showed up, saying they worked for my family, I thought it was a ploy, some old deed coming back to haunt me. I panicked."

They came to a stop in front of her car.

"How have you been, Miles?" she asked.

"Much better," he told her. "I've been on my meds and living at the same place for six years now. I live a quiet life and don't really interact much with the outside world. I do a lot of hunting and fishing. I read a lot of books. Once in a great while, I even go see a movie."

"Micky left you some money," she said, massaging the truth, and hoping Miles would be more likely to accept if he thought it had been directed in Micky's will rather than offered by her after the fact. "We didn't know how to contact you. There's also a watch he wanted you to have. It's currently being held as evidence, but I'd like to get it to you as soon as they release it. It had been passed down to Micky by Arturo, and he wore it every day."

"The old Rolex," Miles said, nodding his head. "I remember it well. In what sense is it evidence in his murder case?"

"It turns out his sister, Mary, had him killed for it," Amber told him. "Her and some sleazebag bartender were gonna sell it and buy a dive bar. That's what my Micky died for."

"Mary is responsible for this?" Miles asked.

"Yep, you probably passed her in the hallway," said Amber. "The bleach-blonde drunk that the two female deputies were trying like hell to restrain?"

Miles nodded in amazement.

"I did not recognize her," he said.

"Well, the years haven't exactly been kind to her," said Amber.

"Indeed," he said.

"Miles?" she asked.

"Yes?" he responded.

"I would like it very much if we could see each other from time to time and maybe work on building a relationship," she told him. "I know we're not blood, and this might seem selfish, but you're the closest thing to Micky that's left. Micky never explained much to me about the two of you and why you were either in or out of his life, but it was the only thing in the world he kept to himself, so I didn't press him on it."

"It would be an honor," said Miles, opening her car door for her after she'd tapped the FOB.

****

The office was abuzz with news of the election and the solving of Micky's murder having hit within an hour of each other. Lars, Ally, and Ernie were hard at work, banging out content on both matters when Dutch, Shelton, and Ringo arrived at the office. In the parking lot, a large crowd was enjoying beers and a seafood boil. Tina sprinted at Ringo and leapt onto him so hard it would have felled most men, but it was like she'd hit a wall. She wrapped her legs tightly around his thick waist and her arms around his giant neck, while peppering his head with kisses.

When Shelton turned from that spectacle, he saw Emily walking toward him with a broad, tight-mouthed smile on her face.

"I am far too clumsy for that kind of greeting," she told him with a laugh. "One of us would end up in the ER for sure."

"I'll settle for a hug," he told her, extending his arms.

She accepted the invitation, and they embraced.

"I'm glad you're okay, and I would appreciate it if you never do anything that stupid again," she said softly in his ear.

"By the grace of god, I hope not to," he told her, before the two engaged in a long kiss.

"Hamner, quit kissing on the clock and get to work on that column," said Lars, who had just emerged from the building with Pauly, who had been released much earlier, due to his connections at the sheriff's department.

"You heard him," Shelton said to Emily, giving her one last peck.

"I'm glad you're alright," said Lars. "Smart move taking this guy for backup," he added, patting Pauly on the back.

"That was a happy accident," said Shelton, extending a hand to Pauly. "Thanks, brother. I owe you one."

"Don't mention it," said Pauly. "I told you this job is usually boring as fuck. Today I met my excitement quota for the whole year in one day."

"I'm gonna get to it," said Shelton, heading toward the office door.

"Looks like miracles really do happen," said Dutch, as he approached Lars and Pauly, while eating a cob of corn from the boil. "Who would have thought we'd have not only swept the election but solved the murder, and all on the same day."

"I don't think I can take credit for having a part in either," said Lars, "but I'll take it all the same."

"Well, I can tell you this," said Dutch, "Amber Pesch is one happy woman, and I don't see her passion for politics or the fourth estate waning anytime soon."

"Does that mean I'll have to postpone early retirement?" asked Lars with a chuckle.

"More likely, you'll have to start advertising for more help," Dutch told him with a wink.

"How did Amber take finding out it was Mary?"

Dutch shrugged.

"Probably worse in the sense that if it had been a stranger or someone Micky's activism had provoked, it might have seemed less preventable. On the other hand, probably better in that she'll get greater satisfaction in watching a woman she has utter contempt for rot away in a jail cell for the rest of her life."

Lars nodded in agreement.

"Can I interest you in a cold beer, old man?" he asked.

"I wouldn't say no to one," said Dutch, and the three men walked off toward the plastic tubs, where a gaggle of election revelers was posted up in joyous celebration.

****

Within minutes of the results being announced, Connor Welsh found himself utterly alone in his campaign headquarters. Each and every volunteer had abandoned an insufferable candidate they had only worked on behalf of to secure political favors that might aid their own ambitions. He didn't even receive the courtesy of a consolation call from Ignacio.

Billy Sunday had not even scheduled a victory party and had just emerged from a marriage counseling session with a still chafed wife when he received a text informing him of his landslide loss. Candice Hagerty, who'd been escorted home by the deputy that had responded to the commotion caused by her sign-waving breakdown and had been expertly fellated on the ride in exchange for not filing indecent exposure charges, was passed out on her chaise lounge when the results were announced. She would not learn the extent of her misfortunes, which included not only her lopsided loss but echoes of her afternoon antics reaching all the way to CNN, until the next morning.

Deputy White, who'd gathered his things and slipped off to Durty Nelly's when he learned of his mistress's meltdown, was in the midst of tying one on when he noticed that County Administrator Wayne Beaufort had sat down at the seat next to him, where he was delivered a vodka tonic without having ordered.

Beaufort, who had hoped to be chauffeured around to three different victory parties that evening, where he would imbibe liberally while congratulating his benefactors, was instead drinking to forget just how dour his prospects were, now that there was a reform-minded board about to be seated. He had been pacing his alcohol intake throughout the day, but began drinking in earnest from his office wet bar as soon as the results were announced. When he noticed who was sitting next to him, Wayne let out a drunken laugh.

"Something funny?" asked Deputy White.

"Yeah, I'm sitting next to one of the few people having a worse go of it than I am," he giggled.

The deputy shrugged.

"I'll be okay. It was a photo-shopped picture," he said, lowering the tight, black V-neck t-shirt he was wearing to show Wayne the black square.

Beaufort pushed up his bifocals from the bridge of his nose and leaned in to inspect the tattoo.

The county administrator slapped his knee and laughed again.

"Christ, kid, I'd wait until it heals before peddling that story to anyone you need to actually believe it. Even I can tell that's fresh ink, and I'm half in the bag with shit for eyes to begin with."

The deputy felt a flash of anger. Who did this old booze-soaked son of a bitch think he was talking to? The anger fell, however, when he looked down at the cover-up work and saw that the old man was correct.

"Sheriff Brock won't throw me under the bus," said Deputy White. "I'm too valuable."

Beaufort laughed yet again.

"What's funny this time?" said the Deputy, feeling himself warm from the anger that quickly returned, aided by the testosterone shots he routinely gave himself.

"You think Rusty Brock can't find another juiced-up meathead who ain't got no qualms about doing his dirty work?" he laughed. "This is Mullet County, boy. You throw a rock, and you're liable to hit three of 'em."

"Well, how are you gonna fare now that the board got flipped?" the deputy asked before downing his beer and ordering another.

Wayne shrugged.

"I'm sure they'll get around to canning my ass in pretty short order," he said with a giggle. "But I'm in DROP already and have just been padding my pension a bit, my *second* pension at that. My future is filled with beach bars and loose women. Hell, I recently got engaged to a woman ten years my junior," he added with a toast of his glass before taking a long pull from his drink.

DROP is Florida's Deferred Retirement Option Program, a feature of the state's public worker pension that allows employees to essentially retire on paper once they're eligible, while continuing to work for up to five years while accruing equivalent contributions in an account that is then paid in a lump-sum at retirement, just as their monthly pension payments—which are based on salary without a ceiling—begin.

Beaufort's lump-sum windfall wouldn't be as big as it would have been had he been able to complete his final three years, but he had previously done 20 years in the Navy and would indeed be flush in retirement. Deputy White, on the other hand, hadn't worked for the sheriff's office even long enough to be vested. His best prospects, should he be fired, would likely be working security at the Bearded Clam or some nightclub up in Ybor City. It occurred to him that the last thing he needed was to make an enemy of someone as well-connected in Mullet County as Wayne Beaufort, so he decided to take a more tactful approach. After all, at the very least, he needed a couch to crash on and a drunk like Beaufort might be sentimental enough to offer one, should they commiserate over drinks for long enough. Perhaps he and this fiancée of his might be into the same sort of kinky things Hagerty and her husband were.

"Yeah, you'll be alright, they probably won't even fire you," the deputy said. "You're too well-liked by the rank and file. They'd revolt. And you're right, I'm all but fucked. On top of the suspension, my wife kicked me out of the house. She won't even let me see my little girl, Ariana. I was just blowing off steam. Let me buy you a drink, make it up to you."

"Nah, I'll pass, partner," said Wayne, placing his empty glass on the bar, before laying down a ten-dollar bill.

"Come on, have a drink with me," the deputy protested.

"I shan't," he slurred, rising from his stool and shaking his head. "You see, in my line of work, young man, I gotta raise glasses with shit heel politicians, corrupt bankers, crooked developers, greedy attorneys, and any other number of miscreant classes on a fairly regular basis. And I like my job and knocking back the booze enough that I rarely mind suffering through it. But even *I* don't have the stomach to drink with a Nazi, my friend."

Beaufort patted the deputy on the shoulder and said, "Good luck, pal," as he made for the door.

****

The next morning, tens of thousands of Mullet County citizens who had been activated by the events of the primary election awoke to a feeling of hard-earned victory and newfound optimism. And while the viral coverage of the many scandals leading up to that outcome had focused a previously inconceivable amount of attention on their otherwise sleepy coastal community, it was a column by a new journalist at their late friend Micky Fish's little publication that seemed to best capture the spirit of the events that was most broadly shared and commented on by those who had worked hardest to bring the results to fruition.

Oh, Micky, what a pity, you weren't here to raise a glass
by Shelton Hamner

Yesterday, a close-knit cadre of passionate community activists achieved something previously considered beyond the realm of possibility. They proved, for the first time since the Supreme Court of the United States ruled that money is speech and corporations are people, that the grassroots can, in fact, beat special interests, even when the deck is infinitely stacked against them by way of an endless flow of dark money.

Despite the best efforts of some of the shittiest people to ever draw breath, this community came together as one and fought tooth and nail to wrest power from their evil developer overlords. As a result, the good people of Mullet County can count on the principled, well-intentioned, rank and file members of their community now elected to its county commission to restore good government in our little slice of sub-tropical paradise.

To be honest, I had my doubts right up until the results came in, if only because a template for such success did not exist. In truth, I missed the initial reporting of the results, as I was being held in a ten foot by ten foot interrogation room of the Mullet County Sheriff's Department, because on the very day the murder of this paper's founder and publisher was discovered, his dream of defeating the cabal of development interests that were fouling our waterways, overburdening our crumbling infrastructure, and making any drive further than three blocks from our homes an exercise in agony, was also realized.

There is a symmetry and poetic justice to the chronology that I believe a wry, dry-humored, old sot like Micky Pesch would have appreciated almost as much as besting a scumbag as brazen in his corruption as Ignacio Hernandez—never mind sending depraved goldbrickers like Connor Welsh, Billy Sunday, and Candice Hagerty to the unemployment line.

In addition to spending an afternoon in police custody, this past week has seen me engaged in a five-way high-speed chase—all parties armed to the teeth, and—on a different occasion, no less —shot at with a machine gun that thankfully killed nothing but my car. To top it off, I'm apparently one of the few people in the City of DeSoto who failed to glimpse Commissioner Hagerty's now infinitely more infamous endowment when she flashed her cans all over DeSoto Boulevard during what is now

298

being called an "accidental over-medication." Toodle-oo to the dais ta-ta show, I suppose.

What should excite us most, however, is the notion that the aforementioned template has now been etched in stone. Prior to May 6, 1954, the notion that a human being could run a mile in less than four minutes was thought to be a physical impossibility. On that day, Roger Bannister, a British medical student and middle-distance runner, was clocked running a mile in just three minutes and fifty-nine point four seconds. However, his world record would hold for just 46 days. Bannister's accomplishment had a profound psychological impact on other world-class runners. The mental barrier had been shattered. Today, more than 1,500 elite runners have accomplished sub-four-minute miles.

One year earlier, the first climbers had scaled Mount Everest, another feat once thought impossible. Today, thousands of climbers have summited the awesome mountain's peak. The same can be said for women completing a marathon, humans breaking the sound barrier, and many other feats that needed a template before they became all but common.

Money in politics only works when voters do not pay attention. You simply cannot convince someone who is watchdogging their elected officials not to believe their lying eyes. A glossy mailer, slick television ad, or deceptive social media campaign doesn't work on an informed voter. What this community proved in this election is that so long as lazy, low-information voters, easily moved by partisan rhetoric, are outnumbered by thoughtful voters who do their homework, the good candidates can and will be victorious.

Congratulations, Mullet County. You've written a template for how voters everywhere can come together and save this once-great republic from the festering rot of recent years. And if there is a heaven, and I believe there is, Micky Fish is smiling down on you from up high this morning, just as happy that you executed the mission as he would have been were he here to celebrate this historic victory alongside you.

So, join me today in raising a glass to one of Mullet County's favorite sons. Godspeed, Micky. May you rest in power, assured that your many friends will continue to fight the good fight in order to protect the place you so proudly called home.

In loving memory of Carol Ann Felts, a rare elected official who understood who her real constituents were and always did her best to serve them honorably.

If you enjoyed this book, please consider helping it reach more readers by leaving a review at goodreads.com, barnesandnoble.com, or amazon.com. To inquire about author participation in book club events, please email marketing@punkrockpublishing.com.

Yes, I got in trouble for this. Photo by the late, great Brian David Braun.